A HISTORY *of* LONELINESS

Also by John Boyne

NOVELS

The Thief of Time

The Congress of Rough Riders

Crippen

Next of Kin

Mutiny on the Bounty

The House of Special Purpose

The Absolutist

This House Is Haunted

NOVELS FOR YOUNGER READERS

The Boy in the Striped Pajamas

Noah Barleywater Runs Away

The Terrible Thing That Happened to Barnaby Brocket

Stay Where You Are and Then Leave

A HISTORY *of* LONELINESS

JOHN BOYNE

Doubleday Canada

Library and Archives Canada Cataloguing in Publication

Boyne, John, 1971–, author
A history of loneliness / John Boyne.

Issued in print and electronic formats.
ISBN 978-0-385-68330-2 (deluxe trade pbk.).—ISBN 978-0-385-68331-9 (epub)

I. Title.

PR6102.O96H57 2015 823'.92 C2014-907335-6
C2014-907336-4

Cover image: (front) adele spencer/Getty Images;
(flaps/spine) Irur/Dreamstime.com
Cover design: Terri Nimmo

Printed and bound in the USA

Published in Canada by Doubleday Canada,
a division of Random House of Canada Limited,
a Penguin Random House Company

www.penguinrandomhouse.ca

10 9 8 7 6 5 4 3 2 1

Life is easy to chronicle, but bewildering to practise.

E. M. Forster

CHAPTER ONE

2001

I DID NOT BECOME ashamed of being Irish until I was well into the middle years of my life.

I might start with the evening that I showed up at my sister's home for dinner and she had no recollection of issuing the invitation; I believe that was the night that she first showed signs of losing her mind.

Earlier that day, George W. Bush had been inaugurated as President of the United States for the first time, and when I arrived at Hannah's house on the Grange Road in Rathfarnham she was glued to the television, watching highlights of the ceremony which had taken place in Washington around lunchtime.

It had been almost a year since I had last been there and it shamed me to think that after an initial flurry of visits in the wake of Kristian's death, I had settled into my old ways of making only an occasional phone call or organizing an even more occasional lunch in Bewley's Café on Grafton Street, a place that reminded us both of childhood, for it was here that Mam would take us for a treat when we came into town to see the Christmas window at Switzer's all those years ago. And it was here that we ate lunches of sausages, beans and chips when we were brought in to Clerys to be fitted for our First Communion clothes: exhilarating afternoons when she would let us order the biggest cream cake we could find and a Fanta orange to wash it down. We would take the 48A bus from outside Dundrum church into the city centre and Hannah and I would run upstairs to the front seats, holding on to the bar in front of us as the bus made its way through Milltown and Ranelagh, over the hump of the Charlemont Bridge in the direction of the old Metropole cinema behind Tara Street station, where once we had been brought to see *Mutiny on the Bounty* with Marlon Brando and Trevor Howard and been dragged out again when the bare-breasted women of Otaheite made their way in kayaks towards the lusty sailors, garlands of flowers around their necks the only protection for their modesty. Mam had written a letter to *The Evening Press* later that night, demanding that the film be banned. Is this a Catholic country, she asked, or is it not?

Bewley's has not changed very much in the thirty-five years since then and I have always felt a great affection for it. I am a man for nostalgia; it is a curse on me sometimes. The comfort of my childhood returns to me when I see the high-backed booths that still cater for all types of Dubliner. The retired gentlemen, white haired and clean shaven, Old Spiced, shrouded in their unnecessary suits and ties as they read the business section of *The Irish Times* even though it no longer has any relevance to their lives. The married women enjoying the indulgence of a mid-morning cup of coffee with no one but wonderful Maeve for company. The students from Trinity College, lounging around over big mugs of coffee and sausage rolls, noisy and tactile, blooming with the excitement of being young and in each other's company. A few unfortunates down on their luck, willing to trade the price of a cup of tea for an hour or two of warmth. The city has always drawn the benefit of Bewley's indiscriminate hospitality and occasionally Hannah and I would partake of it, a middle-aged man and his widowed sister, neatly attired, careful of conversation, still with a taste for a cream cake but no stomach for the Fanta any more.

Hannah had phoned to invite me over a few days earlier and I had immediately said yes. Was she lonely, I wondered. Her eldest son, my nephew Aidan, was away on the sites in London and almost never came home. His phone calls, I knew, were even less regular than my own. But then he was a difficult man. One day, without warning, he had turned from being a cheerful and extrovert boy, something of a precocious entertainer, to a distant and angry presence in Hannah and Kristian's house, and that fury, which seemed to arrive without warning to poison the blood of his veins, never diminished through his teenage years, only building and swelling and destroying everything it came in contact with. Tall and well-built, his Nordic ancestry providing him with clear skin and blond hair, he could charm the ladies with barely a flicker of an eyebrow and he had a taste for them that seemed impossible to satisfy. It is true that he got one poor girl into trouble when the pair of them were not even old enough to drive and there was war over it for a time; in the end the child was given up for adoption after a terrible row between Kristian and the girl's father which led to the police being called out. I never heard from Aidan now. He had a tendency to look at me with contempt in his eyes. Once, when he had drink on him, he stood beside me at a family gathering, placing one hand against the wall while he leaned too close, the stink of cigarettes and alcohol forcing me to turn my head away, and bulged his tongue into his cheek as he said in a perfectly friendly tone, 'Listen to me, you. Do you never think you wasted your life, no? Do you never wish you could go back and live it all over again? Do everything differently? Be a normal man instead of what you are?' And I shook my head and told him that at the centre of my life was a feeling of great contentment, that although I had made my choices at a young age, I stood by them still. I stood by them,

I insisted, and while he might not have been able to see the sense of my decisions, they had given my days clarity and meaning, qualities that his own life sadly appeared to lack. 'You're not wrong there, Odran,' he said, stepping away, freeing me from the prison of his torso and arms. 'But still, I couldn't be what you are. I'd rather shoot myself.'

No, Aidan could never have made the choices that I made and I feel grateful for that now. The truth is that he did not share my innocence or my inability to confront. Even as a boy, he was more of a man than I would ever be. The talk now was that he was living in London with a girl a few years older than himself, a girl with two children of her own, which struck me as a curious thing since he'd wanted no part of the child that might have been his.

The only other person in Hannah's house now was the young lad, Jonas, who had always been introverted and seemed incapable of holding a proper conversation without staring at his shoes or drumming his fingers in the air, like some restless pianist. He blushed when you looked at him and preferred to be away in his room reading books, but whenever I asked him who his favourite authors were he appeared reluctant to tell me or would name someone I had never heard of – a foreign name generally, Japanese, Italian, Portuguese, in an almost deliberate act of defiance. At his father's wake the previous March, I had tried to lighten the mood by asking is it reading that you're doing behind that closed door, Jonas, or something else? I didn't mean anything by it, of course – it was intended as a joke – but the moment the words were out of my mouth I heard how vulgar they sounded and the poor lad – I think there were three or four other people present to witness the scene, including his mother – went scarlet and choked on his 7-Up. I wanted to tell him how sorry I was for embarrassing him, I wanted it badly, but that would only have made matters worse and so I left it, and I left him, and I sometimes felt that we might never recover from that moment, for surely he thought that I had set out to humiliate him, a thing I would never have done nor dreamed of doing.

At this time, the time of which I speak, Jonas was sixteen years old and studying for his Intermediate Certificate, an exam which was not expected to present him with any great difficulties. He had been bright from the start, learning to speak and to read well before other children of his age. Kristian, when Kristian was alive, liked to say that with brains like his Jonas could become a surgeon or a barrister, Prime Minister of Norway or President of Ireland, but whenever I heard those words uttered, I would think no, that's not this boy's destiny. I didn't know what his destiny might be, but no, that wasn't it.

I thought at times that Jonas was a lost boy. He never spoke of friends. He had no girlfriend, had taken no one, not even himself, to his school's Christmas dance. He didn't join clubs or play sports. He went into school, he came home from school. He went to films alone on Sunday afternoons, foreign films usually. He helped out around the house. Was he a lonely boy, I wondered. I knew something of what it was to be a lonely boy.

So there was only Hannah and Jonas in the house, a husband and father dead, a son and brother away on the sites, and from what little I knew of family life I knew this much: that a woman in her mid-forties and an anxious teenage boy would have precious little to talk to each other about, and so perhaps this was a house of silence, which had led her to pick up the phone and call her older brother and say will you not come over for dinner some night, Odran? Sure we never see you at all.

I had the new car with me that night. Or the new used car, I should say, a 1992 Ford Fiesta. I'd only picked it up a week or so before and I was pleased as Punch for it was a smart little thing that fairly whizzed around the city. I parked on the road outside Hannah's house, stepped out and opened the gate, which was hanging slightly off its hinges, and ran my finger along the chipped black paint which scarred the surface. Would Jonas not do something about that, I wondered. With Kristian gone and Aidan away, wasn't he the man of the house now even if he was little more than a boy? The garden looked well though. The cold months hadn't destroyed the plants and a well-tended bed looked as if it had a hundred secrets buried beneath the soil that would spring to life and spill their consequences once the winter had given way to the spring, which couldn't come soon enough for my liking, for I have always been a lover of the sun, even if, through spending a lifetime in Ireland, I have had little personal connection with it.

When did Hannah become a gardener, I wondered as I stood there. This is a new thing, is it?

I rang the doorbell and stepped back, glancing up towards the second-floor window where a light was on, and as I did so a shadow made its way quickly across. Jonas must have heard the car pulling up and looked outside as I made my way up the short path to their door. I hoped that he'd noticed the Fiesta. What harm if I wanted him to think that his uncle had a bit of something to him? I thought for a moment that I should make more of an effort with the boy, for, after all, with his father gone and his older brother away he might need a man in his life.

The door opened and as Hannah peered out she reminded me of our late grandmother, the way she stood and stared, bent over slightly, trying to understand why a person might be standing in her porch at this time of night. In her face, I could see the woman she might be in another fifteen years.

'Well,' she said, nodding her head, satisfied now that she recognized me. 'The dead arose.'

'Ah now,' I replied, smiling at her and leaning forward to give her a peck on the cheek. She smelled of those lotions and creams that women of her age wear. I recognize them whenever the women come close to shake my hand and ask me how my week has been and would I like to come for my dinner some evening and how are their sons doing, they're no trouble to me now, are they? I don't know what those lotions are called. Lotions probably isn't even the right word. The television advertisements would say something else. There'll be a modern word for them. But look, what I don't know about women and their ways would fill enough books to stock the Ancient Library of Alexandria.

'It's good to see you, Hannah,' I said as I stepped inside and removed my overcoat, hanging it up on one of the empty hooks in the hallway, next to her well-worn navy Penneys coat and a brown suede jacket, which could only belong to Jonas. I glanced up the stairs, suddenly eager to see him.

'Come in, come in,' said Hannah, leading the way into the living room, which was welcoming and warm. She had a fire lit in the grate and the place itself had an air about it that made me think it would be very comfortable to sit here of an evening, watching the television programmes, listening to Anne Doyle describe what Bertie was doing, and whether Bruton would make a comeback, and what poor Al Gore would do now that he was on the scrapheap.

There was a framed photograph on top of the telly of little Cathal, laughing his head off as if he had his whole life in front of him, poor lad. One I'd never seen before. I stared at it: he was standing on a beach in a pair of short trousers, his hair unkempt, a smile on his face that would break your heart. I felt a moment's dizziness overwhelm me. There was only one beach that Cathal had ever stood on in his life and why would Hannah display a memory from that terrible week? Where had she even found it?

'How was the traffic anyway?' she asked me from across the room and I turned and stared at her for a moment before replying.

'Not a bother,' I said. 'I've a new car outside. It goes like the wind.'

'A new car? That's very posh of you. Is that allowed?'

'I don't mean brand-new,' I said, telling myself that I should stop thinking of it in those terms. 'I mean new to me. It's secondhand.'

'And *that*'s allowed, is it?' she asked.

'It is,' I said, laughing a little, uncertain exactly what she meant. 'Sure I have to get around, don't I?'

'I suppose so. What time is it anyway?' She glanced at her watch, then back at me. 'Will you sit down? You're making me nervous standing there.'

'I will,' I said, taking a seat, and as I did so she clapped a hand to her mouth and stared at me as if she'd just had a great shock.

'Jesus, Mary and Joseph,' she said. 'I invited you to dinner, didn't I?'

'You did,' I admitted, aware now of how the smell of food in the air seemed to be more the memory of dinner than the promise of a new meal being prepared. 'Had you forgotten?'

She turned away and looked confused for a moment, scrunching up her eyes so her face took on a most unusual aspect, before shaking her head. 'Of course I didn't forget,' she said. 'Only, well, yes, I suppose I did. I thought it was – did we not say Thursday?'

'No,' I replied, certain that we had said Saturday. 'Ah look, maybe I got it wrong,' I added, not wanting to blame her for the mistake.

'You didn't get it wrong,' she said, shaking her head and looking more upset than I thought necessary. 'I don't know where I am these days, Odran. I'm all over the place. I can't begin to tell you all the mistakes I've made recently. Mrs Byrne already gave me a warning and told me I had to buck up my ideas. But sure she's always giving out, that one. I can't do right for doing wrong as far as she's concerned. Look, I don't know what to tell you.

The dinner's over. Jonas and I ate a half-hour ago and I was settled down to the telly. Can I make you a sausage sandwich? Would that be all right?'

I thought about it and nodded. 'That would be smashing,' I said, and then, remembering how my stomach had been rumbling in the car, I said I'd take two if it wasn't any trouble and she said sure how would it be any trouble, didn't she spend half her life making sausage sandwiches for those two lads upstairs anyway?

'Two lads?' I asked, wondering whether I had mistaken the shadow in the window for Jonas when it might have been his older brother. 'Aidan's not home, is he?'

'Aidan?' she asked, turning around in surprise, the frying pan already in her hand. 'Ah no, sure he's away in London on the sites. You know that.'

'But you said two lads.'

'I meant Jonas,' she replied and I left her in peace and focused my attention on the television set.

'Were you watching this earlier?' I called out. 'Don't they make a terrible fuss all the same, the Yanks?'

'They'd give you a pain in the head,' she said over the sound of the oil spitting in the pan as she laid three or four sausages out to fry. 'But yes, I sat before it half the day. Do you think he'll be any good at all?'

'He hasn't even started yet and everyone hates him,' I said, for I had watched a little of the coverage myself earlier in the afternoon and been surprised by the crowds protesting on the streets of the capital. Everyone said that he hadn't won at all, and maybe he hadn't, but it was all so tight that I found it hard to believe that a Gore inauguration would have been any more legitimate.

'Do you know who I loved?' asked Hannah in a faraway voice, as if she was a girl again.

'Who?' I asked. 'Who did you love?'

'Ronald Reagan,' she said. 'Do you remember him in the films? They show them on a Saturday afternoon sometimes on BBC2. There was one on a few weeks ago and there was Ronald Reagan working on a railroad and he had an accident and the next thing he knew he was waking up in bed with both his legs amputated. *Where's the rest of me?* he shouted. *Where's the rest of me?*'

'Ah yes,' I said, even though I had never seen a Ronald Reagan picture in my life and was always surprised when people talked about how he used to be in films. They said his wife was an awful creature.

'He always looked like he was in charge,' said Hannah. 'And I like that in a man. Kristian had that quality.'

'He did,' I agreed, for it was true, he did.

'Did you know that he was in love with Mrs Thatcher?'

'Kristian?' I asked, frowning. I couldn't imagine it.

'Not Kristian, no,' she said irritably. 'Ronald Reagan. Well that's what they say anyway. That the two of them were in love with each other.'

'I don't know,' I said with a shrug. 'I doubt it. I'd say she's a tough woman to love.'

'I'll be glad to see the back of that Clinton fella,' she said. 'He was a dirty so-and-so, wasn't he?'

I nodded, saying nothing. I was sick of Bill Clinton myself. I liked his politics well enough but he had become so hard to trust, so concerned with saving his own skin, that he had lost me long ago. All those wagging fingers and stone-faced denials. And not a word of truth in any of it.

'Him and his oral sex,' continued Hannah and I turned to stare at her in surprise. I'd never heard such words come out of her mouth and wasn't entirely sure that I'd heard her correctly now either but I wasn't going to ask any questions. She was turning the sausages over in the pan and humming to herself. 'Odran, are you a ketchup man or do you prefer the brown sauce?' she called out.

'Ketchup,' I said.

'I'm out of ketchup.'

'Then brown sauce will do me fine,' I said. 'I can't remember the last time I had a bit of brown sauce. Do you remember how Dad used to put it on everything? Even salmon?'

'Salmon?' she asked, handing me a plate with two fine-looking sausage sandwiches on it. 'Sure when did we ever have salmon growing up?'

'Ah there was a bit of it from time to time.'

'Not that I can recall,' she said, sitting down in the armchair and staring at me. 'How's that sandwich?'

'Spot on,' I said.

'I should have made you a dinner.'

'It doesn't matter.'

'I don't know where my head is at the moment.'

'Don't be worrying, Hannah,' I said, wanting to move the conversation on. 'What did you have for dinner yourselves anyway?'

'A bit of chicken,' she said. 'And mash rather than boiled. Kristian always prefers the mash.'

'Jonas,' I said.

'Jonas what?'

'You said Kristian.'

She looked a little confused and shook her head, as if uncertain what I was getting at. I was going to explain, but at that moment I heard a door open upstairs and the slow, heavy descent of feet coming down the staircase. A moment later, Jonas himself came in and nodded at me, a shy smile, pleasant though. His hair was longer than the last time I had seen him and I wondered why he didn't cut it short for he had a pair of cheekbones on him, that boy, and had they belonged to me I would have had them on display in the front window.

'How are you, Uncle Odran?' he asked.

'I'm very well, Jonas,' I said. 'Have you got taller since the last time I saw you?'

'He never stops growing, this one,' said Hannah.

'Maybe a bit,' said Jonas.

'And what's with the hair?' I asked, trying to sound friendly. 'Is that the latest fashion now?'

'I don't know,' he said with a shrug.

'He needs a haircut is what he needs,' said Hannah. 'Would you not get yourself a haircut, son?' she asked, twisting around to look at him.

'I will if you give me three-fifty,' he said. 'I haven't a spare penny at the moment.'

'Well don't be looking at me,' said Hannah, turning away. 'I'm in enough trouble as it is. Odran, wait till I tell you. Mrs Byrne at work, she told me I had to buck my ideas up or else. I wouldn't mind, but I've been in that job eight years longer than her.'

'Yes, you said,' I replied, finishing off one sandwich and starting in on the other. 'Will you not sit down, Jonas?' I asked and he shook his head.

'I just wanted a drink,' he said, heading for the kitchen.

'How are your studies going?' I asked.

'Fine,' he said as he opened the fridge and looked inside, his face betraying both disappointment and resignation at what he found within.

'That boy always has his head in a book,' said Hannah. 'But sure doesn't he have brains to burn?'

'Do you know what you'd like to be yet, Jonas?' I asked.

He muttered something, but I couldn't make out what he'd said. It was something smart-alec, I thought.

'He could be anything he wants to be, that one,' said Hannah, her eyes fixed on George W. Bush's face as he delivered his inaugural address.

'I'm not sure,' said Jonas, stepping back into the living room and staring at Bush for a moment. 'An English degree doesn't really prepare you for anything, but that's what I'd like to do.'

'You won't be following me into my line of business, will you?' I asked.

He laughed and shook his head, but not in a nasty way, his face colouring a little as he did so. 'I don't think so, Uncle Odran. Sorry.'

'You could do a lot worse, son,' said Hannah. 'Sure hasn't your uncle made a grand life for himself?'

'I know,' said Jonas. 'I didn't mean—'

'I'm only teasing,' I said, not wanting any apologies. 'You're only sixteen years old. In this day and age, any sixteen-year-old who wanted to do what I do would be asking for trouble from his friends, I'd say.'

'That's not the reason,' said Jonas, staring directly at me.

'Did you hear that he had an article in the paper?' asked Hannah.

'Ah Mam,' said Jonas, edging towards the door now.

'What's that?' I said, looking up.

'An article,' she repeated. 'In the *Sunday Tribune*.'

'An article?' I asked, frowning. 'What kind of an article?'

'It wasn't an article,' said Jonas, blushing furiously now. 'It was a story. And it wasn't anything really.'

'What do you mean, it wasn't anything?' asked Hannah, sitting up and staring at him. 'Sure when did any of us ever get our names in the paper?'

'Do you mean a short story?' I asked, putting my plate down and turning to look at him. 'Like a work of fiction?' He nodded, unable to meet my eye. 'When was this?'

'A few weeks back.'

'Ah Jonas, you should have called to let me know. I would have liked to read it. Fair play to you, all the same. A story, is it? Is that what you want to do then? Write books?'

He shrugged and looked almost as embarrassed as he had the previous year when I'd made that inappropriate comment at the wake. I turned back to the television to spare him any further discomfort. 'Well good luck to you anyway,' I said. 'That's a grand ambition to have.'

I heard him shuffle out of the room then and started to laugh as I shook my head, turning to Hannah, who was busy reading the schedules in the *RTÉ Guide*. 'A writer, is it?' I said.

'It's a long walk from Brow Head to Banba's Crown,' she replied, a response which mystified me slightly. A moment later, she put the magazine down and stared at me as if she didn't know me at all.

'You never told me what happened with Mr Flynn,' she said.

'With who?' I asked. I racked my brain; I could think of no Flynns.

She shook her head, dismissing this, and stood up to walk into the kitchen, leaving me bewildered. 'I'll make some tea,' she said. 'Will you have a cup?'

'I will.'

When she returned to the living room a few minutes later, she had two cups of coffee in her hands, but I didn't say anything. I thought there was something on her mind perhaps; she appeared so distracted.

'Is everything all right, Hannah?' I asked. 'You don't seem like yourself. You're not worrying about anything, are you?'

She thought about it. 'I didn't want to get into it,' she said, leaning forward in a conspiratorial fashion. 'But now that you mention it, and strictly between you and me, I don't think Kristian is very well at all. He's been getting these awful headaches. But will he go to the doctor? You try telling him because he won't listen to me.'

I stared at her. I wasn't sure what to say, what she could possibly mean by this. 'Kristian?' I said finally, the only word I could muster. 'But Kristian is dead.'

She stared at me as if I'd just slapped her across the face. 'Sure don't I know that?' she said. 'Didn't I bury him myself? Why would you say such a thing?'

I was confused. Had I heard her right? I shook my head. I let it go. I drank my coffee. When the clock said nine and the news came on I listened to the headlines, watched Bill and Hillary board a helicopter and wave goodbye to the nation, and then said I better make a move myself.

'Well don't leave it so long next time,' she said, neither standing up nor making any sign that she was going to see me out to the door. 'And next time I'll cook you that dinner I promised.'

I nodded and left it at that, going out into the hallway to retrieve my coat, closing the living-room door behind me. As I stood there putting my coat on, the door opened upstairs and Jonas, barefoot, came to the top of the stairs and looked down at me.

'Are you off, Uncle Odran?' he said.

'I am, Jonas. We should talk more often, you and I.'

He nodded and came downstairs slowly, handing me a piece of folded-up paper. 'You can have this if you want,' he said, unable to look me in the eye. 'It's my story. From the *Trib*.'

'Ah great,' I said, touched that he wanted me to have it. 'I'll read it tonight and get it back to you.'

'No need,' he said. 'I bought ten copies of it.'

I smiled and put the paper in my pocket. 'I'd have bought it myself if I'd known,' I said. He stood there nervously, looking back towards the living-room door, bouncing up and down on his toes. 'Is everything all right, Jonas?' I asked him.

'Yeah.'

'You seem like you've got something on your mind.'

He breathed heavily through his nose, unable to look me in the eye. 'I wanted to ask you something,' he said.

'Well go on so.'

'It's about Mam.'

'What about her?'

He swallowed and finally looked directly at me. 'Do you think she's all right?' he asked me.

'Your mam?'

'Yes.'

'She seemed a bit tired to me,' I said, reaching for the latch on the door. 'Maybe she needs more sleep. We could all do with a bit extra, I suppose.'

'Wait,' he said, putting a hand on the frame to keep me there. 'She's been repeating herself a lot and forgetting things. She forgot that Dad is dead.'

'They call it middle age,' I said, opening the door now before he could stop me. 'It comes to us all. It'll come to you too, but not for a long time yet so don't be worrying. It's cold enough out here now, isn't it?' I added, stepping outside. 'Get yourself back inside before you catch something.'

'Uncle Odran—'

But I didn't let him continue. I walked down the path and he watched me for a few moments before closing the door behind me. I felt the guilt of it but could do nothing; I just wanted to go home. As I stepped over towards the Fiesta there was a tap on the window. I looked around and there was Hannah, parting the net curtains and calling something out to me.

'What's that?' I asked, cupping a hand to my ear, and she beckoned me forward.

'Where's the rest of me?' she cried, before laughing heartily, closing the curtains and turning away.

I knew then that Hannah wasn't right, that here was the start of something that would only bring trouble about all our heads, but in my selfishness I dismissed it for now. I would call her in a week, I decided. Invite her to Bewley's Café on Grafton Street for lunch. Buy her a fry-up and a cream bun to follow and one of those coffees with the frothy white heads. I would make an effort to look in on her more often.

I would be a better brother than perhaps I had been in the past.

Before driving home, I decided to make a late-night visit to Inchicore – a longer route, of course, but I wanted to pull into the church and take a few moments at the shrine there, a replica of the grotto at Lourdes, a town I have never visited nor wanted to see. I have little patience for those places of pilgrimage – Lourdes itself, Fatima, Medjugorje, Knock – which seem always to be the inventions of impressionable children or the delusions of tumbling drunks, but Inchicore was no pilgrim's destination, rather a simple church with a shrine and a statue. I often came here at night if I felt unsettled.

I arrived quickly along empty roads, parked the car and entered through the open gates. The moon was out that night, bright and speckled, lending some illumination to the grounds, but as I turned the corner I was surprised to hear a keening of sorts, a kind of terrible anguished moaning emerging from the direction of the grotto. I hesitated, trying to decipher the sound. If there were young people over there getting up to all sorts, then I didn't want to see it, didn't want to know about it, would rather just get back in my car and go home, but after a moment I realized that these were not cries of passion but the deep-plundered howls of uncontrollable weeping.

I stepped forward carefully, and as my eyes focused I saw what appeared to be a body lying face-down, its arms and legs outstretched, a human crucifix prostrate on the gravel, and my first thought was that a crime had been committed, a murder. Someone had come and killed a man in front of the grotto at Inchicore church. But then the body moved; it lifted itself up into a kneeling position and I saw that this was not an injured man at all, but a praying man. A priest, in fact, for he wore the long-sleeved black cassock of the ordained, the garment blowing in the breeze just above his ankles. As he knelt, he raised his hands to the heavens before twisting them into fists which he used to beat himself rapidly about his head, a pounding of such ferocity and wildness that I prepared myself to intervene even if there was a risk that he might turn on me in his grief or madness and do me an injury. He turned slightly and I saw his face silhouetted in the moonlight. A young man – younger than me anyway by a decade or more, perhaps in his early thirties. A mess of dark hair and a prominent nose with a wide bridge at its summit. He let out a cry and collapsed back into the position in which I had originally found him, but although he quietened now, the moaning continued, this interminable sobbing, and I felt a chill run down my spine when I looked to his left and noticed that he was not alone.

For seated in the corner of the grotto, almost hidden out of sight, was a much older woman, in her late sixties, and she was rocking back and forth with tears streaming down her face, suffering distorting her features. As her face caught the moonlight I saw that she shared something in common with the young priest, that aquiline nose, and I knew immediately that he had inherited it from her, his mother.

And so there they were, the young man lying flat, beseeching the world to bring his torment to an end, the mother shaking in pain and looking for all the world as if she would like the heavens to open and for God to call her home without another wasted moment.

It was a terrifying sight. It unsettled me enormously. And while another in my place might have gone over to the pair and offered whatever comfort they could, I walked away, quickly and nervously, for there was something there, some horror looming over us all, which I felt ill-equipped to cope with.

And I look back at that night, more than a decade ago now, and I remember those two incidents as if they only took place earlier this week. George W. Bush has been and gone. But I recall Hannah sitting in her armchair telling me that her dead husband was suffering from awful headaches and I recall this mother and son, weeping and wailing at the grotto in Inchicore. And as I drove back through the streets towards the comfort of my lonely bed, I knew without question that the world as I had always known it, and the faith that I had put in it, was about to come to an end, and who knew what would take its place?

Chapter Two

2006

It was just over five years later that I was taken away from Terenure College, the school where I had been living and working for twenty-seven years. I had long ago accepted that I was at my happiest when hidden away behind the high walls and closed gates of this private and erudite enclave and the change came as a shock.

I had never intended to stay at Terenure for so long. Returning from Rome to Dublin in the middle of 1979, finally ordained after seven years of study but with a slight whiff of scandal still attached to my name, I was assigned to the school chaplaincy with a view to moving to a parish soon after. But somehow this relocation never took place. Instead, I passed the exams for my H.Dip and ended up teaching English, with a little bit of history thrown in. Outside of teaching hours, I ran the library and celebrated Mass every morning at half past six for the same small group of elderly men and women, retirees all, who had never learned the ability to sleep in or were worried that they might not wake up if they did. I was to be a spiritual counsellor to the boys, a job whose demands decreased dramatically as the eighties gave way to the nineties and these in turn yielded to the twenty-first century, for the life of the spirit was one that seemed less important to the students as the years went on.

Our school was a rugby school, one of those elite establishments on Dublin's Southside populated by boys with wealthy fathers – property developers, bankers, businessmen who thought their good times would never come to a halt – and although I knew next to nothing about the sport I did my best to develop an interest, for there was no way to survive at Terenure if you did not. In general I got on well with the boys, for I neither bullied them nor tried to be their friend – the twin mistakes that many of my colleagues made – and somehow this stood to me and I found myself as popular as it was possible to be among the quicksand of arriving and graduating students. They were often an arrogant lot, and could be hateful and wicked in their attitude towards those who had not been born into similar privilege, but I did my best to humanize them.

The phone call from Archbishop Cordington's secretary came on a Saturday afternoon, and if it made me anxious, it was only because I misunderstood the reason for the summons.

'Is it just me?' I asked Father Lomas, his secretary, on the other end of the line. 'Or is there a gang of us being called over?'

'It's just you,' he replied in the driest tone you could imagine. Some of those lads at the Archbishop's residence could be fierce full of themselves.

'Will it keep, do you think?' I asked.

'His Grace will receive you at two o'clock on Tuesday,' he replied, which I supposed meant *no*, before hanging up the phone. And so I drove out to Drumcondra that day with a heavy heart; what would I say, I wondered, if he asked me whether I had ever had any suspicions about Miles Donlan, and if so why I had never reported them to him? How could I answer him when I had asked myself this very question time and again and been met with only silence?

'Father Yates,' said the Archbishop, looking up and smiling as I entered his private office, trying my best not to betray in my expression how uncomfortable the luxury of his surroundings made me. There were paintings on the walls that wouldn't have been out of place in the National Gallery. Indeed, they had probably been selected *from* the National Gallery; it was one of the perks of the job, after all. The carpet beneath my feet was so thick that I thought I could have lain down on it and got a good night's sleep. Everything about the place screamed prosperity and profligacy, concepts that stood in stark contrast to the vows we had both taken. The opulence of the Episcopal Palace reminded me a little of the Vatican, albeit on a far smaller scale, and my mind turned as it so often did to 1978, when I had served three masters over the course of a single year, filling my mornings and nights with servitude, my days with study, and my evenings with standing beneath an open window on the Vicolo della Campana, racked with longing and confused desire.

How can something still feel so painful after twenty-eight years, I asked myself. Is there no recovery from the traumas of our youth?

'Hello, Your Grace,' I said, kneeling down and allowing my lips briefly to make contact with the heavy gold ring he wore on the fourth finger of his right hand, before he led me towards a pair of armchairs next to the fireplace.

'It's good to see you, Odran,' he said, falling into his chair. Jim Cordington, two years ahead of me at Clonliffe College Seminary and once the best midfielder that the Dublin hurling team had ever lost to the priesthood, had grown fat from indulgence and a lack of exercise. I could remember him sweeping up the fields at Holy Cross with the wind behind him and not one of us could have stopped him in his stride. What had happened to him in the years since then, I wondered. His once sharply defined features were now flabby and scarlet-speckled, his nose thickly veined with blood-red capillaries. When he smiled and tucked his face downwards in that curious manner he had, a series of chins made themselves visible, one atop the other like folds of whipped meringue.

'And you, Your Grace,' I replied.

'Ah here,' he said, waving his hands in the air and dismissing this. 'Would you stop now with the *Your Grace*, Odran. It's Jim, you know that. There's no one else in here. We can leave the formalities for another time. How are you anyway? Are you keeping well?'

'I am,' I said. 'Busy, as always.'

'I haven't seen you this long time.'

'I think it was the conference in Maynooth last year,' I said.

'Yes, probably. But look, that's a grand little school you're in, isn't it?' he asked, scratching his cheeks, his nails making a slight sweeping sound against his early-afternoon stubble. 'Did you know that I went to Terenure myself?'

'I did, Your Grace,' I said. 'Jim.'

'Different now than when I was a lad, I'd say.'

I nodded. Everything was different now, of course it was.

'Did you ever hear of a priest called Richard Camwell?' he asked me, leaning forward. 'He was a terrible man altogether. Used to lift a lad out of his seat by the ear and while he was holding him there he'd give him an almighty clatter across the cheek and send him sprawling across the tables. Once, he held a boy by his ankles out the window of the sixth-floor corridor while the lads in the yard below called up *Father, Father, don't drop him!*' He laughed and shook his head. 'We were afraid of the priests in those days, of course. There were some right terrors among them.' He frowned then and looked directly at me. 'But fierce holy men,' he added, pointing a finger. 'Fierce holy men all the same.'

'If you tried something like that now, sure the boys would fight back,' I said. 'And they'd be right too.'

'Well I don't know about that,' he said, sitting back again and looking away.

'Don't you?'

'Boys are terrible creatures. They need discipline. But who am I telling, aren't you there in their company five days a week during the school year? When I think of some of the beatings I took in that school it's a wonder I ever got out of the place alive. Happy days though. Terrible happy days.'

I nodded, biting my lip. There were many things I wanted to say, but fear stopped me from saying them. There had been a teacher at Terenure only the year before, a layman, not a priest, who had cuffed a fourteen-year-old boy across the ear for a piece of back-chat, and hadn't the lad only leaped up and punched him in the face, breaking the poor man's nose. He was a strong wee pup, that boy, and arrogant with it. His father ran a branch of an international bank and the boy was forever talking about how many air miles he'd racked up. In my day, he would have been expelled, but now, of course, things were different. The teacher, a nice man but completely unsuited to the job, was fired and brought up on assault charges by the boy's parents while the lad himself was given four thousand euros by the school in compensation for 'emotional trauma'.

'My granny lived down the road from Terenure, you see,' continued the Archbishop. 'Near the Dodder Bridge. We were closer in towards Harold's Cross but sure didn't I spend half my life in my granny's? She could cook, that woman. She was never out of the kitchen. She had fourteen children over sixteen years, can you believe that? And never complained about it. Brought them up in a house with two bedrooms. You'd wonder now how that's even possible. Fourteen children, a husband and wife in two rooms. Sardines, what?'

'You must have a fair run of cousins then,' I said.

'More than I can count. I have one cousin who works in the

Formula One,' he said. 'In the pit stops, you know? He changes the tyres when the drivers pull in. He told me once that they have to get the car in and out again in forty seconds flat or they lose their jobs. Can you imagine? I'd still be looking for the monkey wrench. Not that I get to see my family very often. There's so many demands in this job, you wouldn't believe it. You should think yourself lucky, Odran, that you were never elevated.'

There was nothing that I could say to this. At Clonliffe College, I had excelled in my exams and been selected for the Pontifical Irish College in Rome, where I had been offered an unexpected position during 1978 that was both a blessing and a curse. Had I completed the year successfully, I would have been all but assured of a quick rise through the ranks, but of course my job was taken off me before the year was up and a black mark put against my name that was impossible to wipe clean.

Other lads in the seminary were very ambitious about their careers, a word which never sat well with me, and perhaps I was too at first, but I don't recall any great longing, even as a young man, for advancement. It seemed clear from the start who was destined for an Archbishopric or, in one case with a fellow only a year ahead of us, the scarlet zucchetto of a cardinal. All I ever wanted was to be a good priest, to help people somehow. That seemed ambition enough for me.

'Are you happy out there anyway?' the Archbishop asked me and I nodded.

'I am,' I said. 'They're good boys for the most part. I've tried to do my best by them.'

'Oh, I wouldn't doubt it, Odran, I wouldn't doubt it. I hear nothing but good reports of you from everyone.' He glanced up at the clock. 'Is it that time already? Will you have a wee dram with me?'

I shook my head. 'I'm grand,' I said.

'Go on, you will. Sure I'm having a small one myself. You won't see me a lonely drinker.'

'I have the car, Your Grace,' I said. 'It wouldn't do.'

'Ah,' he said, waving his hand to dismiss the concept of sober driving as some sort of new-age fad. He dragged himself up and made his way over to a cabinet which supported a fine bronze statue of John Charles McQuaid, whose funeral at the Pro Cathedral I had attended along with all the other seminarians in 1973. He opened it – I'd seen less alcohol behind the bar of Slattery's on the Rathmines Road – and extracted a bottle from the corner, pouring a healthy glass for himself, topping it up with some water and then re-joining me, crashing down into his seat with another loud groan.

'Gets me through the rest of the afternoon,' he said with a wink as he took his first sip. 'I have a delegation of nuns coming in here after you, for my sins. Something about new bathrooms for their convent. Sure I haven't the money to be spending on them when there's priests calling every day about getting broadband installed in their homes. And that doesn't come cheap.'

'You could always divide the money,' I suggested. 'Half for the priests and half for the nuns.'

He let out a great roar of a laugh at that, and I smiled along to be sociable. 'Very good, Odran, very good,' he said. 'You were always quick with a joke, weren't you? But listen to me now, how would you feel about a bit of a change?'

My heart sank a little inside my chest. I thought I was here for one conversation, but no, it seemed I was here for another. Was I to be moved? After all these years? I liked the walls that surrounded the rugby fields, the long driveway to the main building, the peace of my corridor, the silence of my own small room, the security of the classroom. I had dreaded the conversation that I thought I was here to have, but this was worse. This was far worse.

'I wouldn't be looking for a change,' I said. It was worth trying, after all. Maybe he'd take pity on me. 'I feel I still have work to do. There's a lot of lads who need help.'

'Well, the work never ends,' he replied. 'It just gets picked up by the next man. No, I've got a grand young lad that I want to send over to Terenure, I think it'll do him the world of good. Father Mouki Ngezo. Have you come across him at all?'

I shook my head. I didn't know too many of the younger fellows. Not that there were that many to know.

'Black fella,' said the Archbishop. 'You must have seen him about.'

I stared at him, uncertain whether the description was a purely factual one or whether there was something derogatory in the way he said it. Could you even say *black* these days or did that make you a racist? 'I don't . . .' I began, unsure how to finish my sentence.

'He's a grand lad,' he repeated. 'Came to us from Nigeria a few years back. But look, isn't it a terrible thing all the same, the way we used to send our young lads out to the missions and now the missions are sending their young lads back here to us?'

'Doesn't that make *us* the missions?' I said, and he thought about this for a moment before nodding his head.

'Do you know, I've never thought about it like that,' he said. 'I suppose it does. That's a queer pass, isn't it? Do you know how many applications I've had this year to be a priest from the Dublin diocese?' I shook my head. 'One,' he said. 'One! Can you believe it? And I met up with the lad and he wasn't right for us at all. Something a bit simple about him, I thought. He kept laughing while I was trying to talk to him and biting his nails. It was like holding a conversation with a coyote.'

'A hyena,' I said.

'Yes, a hyena. That's what I said. Anyway I told him that he should go away and reflect on whether or not he had a vocation and then we could talk again, and he started crying and I practically had to carry him back outside. His mammy was out in the waiting room and she was pushing him into it, I could tell that.'

'Sure the mammies pushed us all into it,' I said, the words out of my mouth before I could even think about them.

'Ah now, Odran,' he said, shaking his head. 'I don't think we need to go down that road, do you?'

'I only meant—'

'Don't be worrying, don't be worrying.' He took another drink from his glass, a longer drink this time, and he closed his eyes for a few moments, savouring the taste. 'Miles Donlan,' he said after a moment and I glanced down at the floor. *This* was the conversation I had expected.

'Miles Donlan,' I repeated quietly.

'You've read the papers, I suppose? Seen the news?'

'I have, Your Grace.'

'Six years,' he said, whistling through his teeth. 'Do you think he'll survive it?'

'He's not a young man,' I said. 'And they say that prisoners can be fierce rough on . . .' I had the word, of course, but couldn't say it.

'You never heard any whispers, did you, Odran?'

I swallowed. Of course I had heard whispers. Father Donlan and I had worked side by side in Terenure for years. I'd never liked him, to be honest; he had a bitter air about him and spoke about the boys as if they both fascinated and disgusted him at the same time. But yes, I had heard whispers.

'I didn't know him very well,' I said, avoiding his question.

'You didn't know him very well,' he repeated quietly and he stared at me until I could only look away. 'But if you had heard whispers, Odran, or if you were to hear whispers about someone else, tell me what would you do?'

Nothing was the honest answer. 'I suppose I'd talk to the man.'

'You'd talk to the man. I see. Would you talk to me about it?'

'I might, yes.'

'Would you go to the Gardaí?'

'No,' I said quickly. 'Not at first, anyway.'

'Not at first. When might you?'

I shook my head, trying to decide what he wanted to hear. 'Honestly, Jim,' I said, 'I don't know what I'd do or who I'd tell or when I'd say a word at all. I'd have to judge it at the time.'

'You'd tell me, is what you'd do,' he said in an aggressive tone. 'And you'd tell no one else. The papers are all out to get us, you can see that, can't you? We've lost control. And we must regain it. We must bring the media to heel.' He glanced across at the drinks cabinet and the statue of Archbishop McQuaid. 'Do you think *he* would have put up with any of this nonsense?' he asked me. 'He'd have had the printing presses shut down. He'd have taken over the lease at Montrose and evicted the lot of them.'

'Times are different now,' I said.

'Times are worse, is what they are. But look, I'm getting side-tracked. What was I saying before all of this?'

'The Nigerian priest,' I told him, relieved to change the subject.

'Oh yes, Father Ngezo. Actually he's a grand fella all the same. Black as the ace of spades, but there we are. He's not the only one, of course. We have three lads from Mali, two Kenyans and a fella from Chad across there in Donnybrook. And next month a boy from Burkina Faso is coming over to be a curate in Thurles, I'm told. Did you ever even hear of Burkina Faso? I never did, but apparently it exists.'

'Is it somewhere above Ghana?' I asked, examining a map of the world in my mind.

'I have no idea. And even less interest. It could be one of the moons of Saturn for all I care. But look, we take what we can get these days. And I want to give young Ngezo a try out there in

Terenure. He needs a change and he's a great supporter of the rugby. You were never much interested in that, were you, Odran?'

'I rarely miss a cup match,' I said defensively.

'Is that so? I didn't think it was your thing at all. But he'll be great with the boys and it'll do them the world of good to experience other cultures. Would you mind making room for him?'

'I've been there twenty-seven years, Your Grace.'

'I know.'

'It's home to me.'

He sighed and shrugged his shoulders, half-smiling. 'We have no homes,' he said. 'No homes of our own, that is. You know that.'

Easy for you to say, I thought, glancing around at the crushed-velvet seat covers and the lace curtains.

'I'd miss it,' I said.

'But it might do you good to get out of teaching for a while and back to parish work. Just for a while.'

'You realize that I've never actually done any parish work, Your Grace?' I asked.

'Jim, Jim,' he said in a bored voice.

'I'm not even sure I'd know where to start. Where were you thinking of anyway?'

He smiled and looked down at the carpet, breathing heavily through his nose; he wore a slightly embarrassed expression on his face. 'You can probably guess,' he said. 'It wouldn't be permanent, of course. Only I need someone to take Tom's place.'

'Tom who?' I asked.

'Tom who-do-you-think?'

My eyes opened wide in surprise. 'Tom Cardle?' I asked.

'Actually, it was him who suggested you.'

'This was his idea?'

'It was my idea, Father Yates,' he said sternly. 'But Tom was there when all the options were considered.'

I found this hard to believe. 'I only saw him on Friday afternoon,' I said. 'And he never mentioned a word about any of this.'

'Well I saw him on Saturday morning,' replied the Archbishop. 'He popped in here for a chat. He thought you might fancy a change. I thought it myself.'

I didn't know what to say. I found it hard to understand why Tom would discuss this with Jim Cordington without mentioning it to me first. After all, we had known each other for so long and were such close friends.

Tom Cardle and I had arrived at the seminary on the same day in 1973 and found ourselves sitting next to each other as the Canon explained how our daily lives would be organized over the next few months. Tom was up from the country, a Wexford lad a few months older than me, having turned seventeen the previous week. He was unhappy to be at Clonliffe, I could see that from the start. He gave off an air of utter despair and I was drawn to him immediately, not because I shared that emotion but because I was afraid of loneliness and had resolved to make a friend as quickly as possible. I was already missing Hannah and somehow, even at that young age, I knew that I might need a confidant of sorts and so I chose Tom, or rather we chose each other. We became friends.

'Are you all right?' I asked him as we unpacked our bags in the small cell we were to share – we'd been put in together since we were sitting beside each other in the orientation – trying out a bit of Christian charity to see whether it suited me. The room was not much to look at: two single beds pressed against either wall, a gap wide enough for both of us to stand between them, a single wardrobe to store all our belongings, a bowl and a jug on a side-table and a bucket on the floor. 'You look a bit white about the gills.'

'I'm not feeling the best,' he said in a thick accent that pleased me, for I hadn't wanted to be stuck with another Dub. When he told me that he was from Wexford, however, I felt a wound inside me opening once again, for I could never hear that county's name without an accompanying burst of grief.

'Was it the drive up?' I asked.

'Aye, maybe,' he said. 'Those roads are a killer. And I came up on the daddy's tractor.'

I stared at him. 'You drove all the way from Wexford to Dublin on a tractor?' I asked in disbelief.

'I did.'

I sucked in the air and shook my head. 'Is that even possible?' I asked.

'We went slow,' he said. 'We broke down a lot.'

'Rather you than me, boy,' I said. 'What's your name anyway?'

'Tom Cardle.'

'Odran Yates,' I said, offering my hand, and he shook it, looking directly at me, and for a moment I thought he was going to burst into tears. 'Are you glad to be here?' I asked and he snorted something unintelligible under his breath. 'Sure it'll be grand. There's nothing to worry about. A lad I knew came here a couple of years ago and he said it was great fun altogether. It's not just praying and that. There's games and sports and sing-songs all the time. It'll be mighty, just watch.'

He nodded but didn't seem convinced. He opened his suitcase and there was precious little in there, just a few shirts and pants and a couple of pairs of underwear and socks. Sitting on top of all that was an expensive-looking Bible and I picked it up to examine it.

'My mam and dad gave it to me,' he said. 'When I was leaving, like.'

'Must have cost a few quid,' I said, handing it back to him.

'You can have it if you want. I've no use for it.'

I laughed, wondering whether he was joking, but his expression told me otherwise. 'Ah no, it's yours,' I said and he shrugged, took it from me and threw it on the side-table without much consideration. In the years that followed I would rarely see him open that book.

'Tom's only been in that parish a couple of years,' I told Archbishop Cordington, surprised, for this was a quick transfer and Tom had already been subjected to so many over the last twenty-five years. I used to say that he kept a suitcase on stand-by at all times.

'Eighteen months. It's a fair run.'

'Sure he's only settled in.'

'He needs a change.'

'It's not my place to say, of course,' I ventured, wondering whether I might get myself off the hook with a little debate, 'but hasn't poor Tom been moved around enough as it is? Would it not be fair to leave him alone for a while?'

'What is it that Shakespeare says?' asked the Archbishop with a wide smile. 'Ours is not to question why?'

'Theirs not to reason why, theirs but to do and die,' I said, correcting him. 'Tennyson.'

'Not Shakespeare?'

'No, Your Grace.'

'I could have sworn it was Shakespeare.'

I said nothing.

'But my point stands,' he said coldly. 'Tom Cardle's is not to reason why. And nor is Odran Yates's,' he added, taking another sip from his glass.

'I'm sorry,' I said. 'I only meant—'

'Don't be worrying,' he said, slapping a hand down firmly on the side of his chair and smiling again; the man could turn on a penny. 'It'll take you a bit of getting used to, of course. All those parishioners in your ear every day. And you'll be afloat in tea for the first couple of months as all the old biddies invite you over to size you up.' He paused and glanced at his nails, which were finely manicured. 'And sure you might as well take charge of the altar boys too, while you're at it. You're used to the young lads.'

I groaned. The boys I was accustomed to were fifteen and sixteen years of age and I knew how to handle them. I had little knowledge or experience of lads of seven or eight. If I am honest, I have always found them a little noisy and irritating. They never sit still at Mass and parents nowadays have no control over them.

'Might not one of the other priests look after them?' I asked. 'Those little lads can be terrible boisterous. I don't know if I'd have the patience for them.'

'Then develop it,' he replied, the smile fading quickly again. 'Develop it, Odran. Anyway, Tom has them all tamed, so there'll be nothing for you to worry about.' He started to laugh a little. 'Do you know what I heard they call him, those altar boys of his? Satan! God forgive me, but it's funny all the same, isn't it?'

'It's awful,' I said, appalled.

'Ah sure, boys will be boys. There's no harm in any of them – the ones who don't tell lies anyway. They always have nicknames. Sure didn't we have nicknames ourselves for all the priests back in the seminary?'

'We did, Jim,' I agreed. 'But nothing as bad as Satan.'

A silence fell on us; the Archbishop seemed as if he had something more he wanted to say.

'There's something else,' he said.

'Yes?'

'It's a bit delicate. Not for public consumption.'

'All right.'

He thought about it and shook his head. 'Ah no, it'll keep,' he said. 'I'll tell you another time.' He closed his eyes for a moment and I wondered whether he was going to sleep, but then he opened them suddenly, surprising me. 'I meant to ask you,' he said. 'Am I right in thinking that nephew of yours is the writer fella, yes?'

I nodded, surprised and a little unnerved by the abrupt change of topic.

'Yes, Jonas,' I said.

'Jonas Ramsfjeld,' he said. 'Such a name. Where was his father from? Sweden?'

'Norway.'

'He's never out of the papers at the minute, is he? I saw him on the nine o'clock news the other night talking about his book. It's been made into a film now, they say.'

'It has, yes,' I said.

'The boy knows his stuff all the same, doesn't he? Talks very well. And sure he's only a young fella. How old is he anyway?'

'Twenty-one,' I said.

'That's what they call a prodigy,' he said, nodding.

'I don't know if it's good for him at such a young age.'

'Ah sure, good luck to him. I haven't read any of his books myself, of course.'

'There's only two,' I said.

'Well I haven't read either of them then. I suppose you have?'

'I have, yes.'

'And are they any good at all? I hear they're full of effing and blinding. And all this stuff about young fellas and young ones getting up to all sorts together. What kind of books are they anyway? Are they dirty books?'

I smiled. 'They're not as bad as all that,' I said. 'I suppose he'd say that the way he writes is the way that people speak. And that he's not writing for old men like us.'

'But the young people like that stuff, do they? It's not writing though, is it? It's not literature. I don't recall W. B. Yeats sailing away to fucking Byzantium or Paddy Kavanagh talking about the shitty grey soil of Monaghan.'

I stared at him, taken aback by the coarseness of his words.

'Well,' I said, ready to jump to Jonas's defence, 'like you say, you haven't read either of his books.'

'I don't have to eat a cat to know I wouldn't like the taste of one,' he said. 'Actually, while we're on the subject, you might keep that quiet anyway. I don't think people need to know that you're related to him. It wouldn't look good.'

I felt a hundred responses going through my head, but I held my tongue.

'Look, Odran,' said the Archbishop, leaning forward, reverting to a subject that I thought was closed but seemed to be still preying on his mind, 'I know this is a bit of a bolt out of the blue to you. But I've talked it through with Tom and he feels you're the man for the job. He has every confidence in you. And so do I. Will you trust me on this, Odran?'

'Of course, Your Grace,' I said. 'I'm just surprised that Tom recommended me, that's all. Without talking to me about it first.'

'But sure why wouldn't he?' he asked, sitting back and smiling, extending his hands in a magnanimous gesture. 'Aren't you the best of pals, after all, you and old Satan?'

The idea of Tom Cardle as a man who the boys would either fear or hate was a strange one to me, particularly when I thought back to who he had been at seventeen.

That first night, after we unpacked, we went down to the Wide Hall together and ate our dinner side by side. I can remember it still. A bit of plaice with a leaky batter hanging off it, a plate full of chips and a pot of beans in the centre of the table. Fourteen hungry lads passing that pot around and pouring it all over their food to mask the taste. Everyone got stuck in except Tom, whose colouring had returned to normal but who still looked angry and afraid in equal measure. None of us knew each other from Adam, we were strangers still. Our mammies had sat us all down one day and told us that we had vocations and so there we were, ready to dedicate our lives to God. It was a great thing, that's what we thought anyway. Only Tom looked miserable about it.

We were shy of each other when we got back to our cell later. We turned our backs when we undressed to get into our pyjamas and the lights were off by nine o'clock, the sun still peeping through the thin pale curtains. I lay there, my hands under my head, staring up at the ceiling, thinking that this was the beginning of my new life and was I ready for it, I asked myself. And yes, I replied silently. For there was a faith inside me, one that I found difficult to comprehend at times. But it was there.

'Do you have any brothers and sisters?' I asked across the room when the quiet became too much for me.

'Nine of them,' said Tom.

'That's a lot. Where do you come in the rankings?'

'Last,' he said, and I thought I could hear a choked note in his tone. 'I'm the youngest. So I'm to be the priest. Two of my sisters are nuns already. What about you?'

'There's just me and my sister,' I said. 'I had a brother, but he died.'

'And do you want to be here?' he asked.

'Of course,' I said. 'I have a vocation.'

'Who told you that?'

'Mam.'

'And how does she know?'

'She had an epiphany one night while she was watching *The Late Late Show*.'

I heard a strange sound come from the other side of the room.

It was a sort of snort, a half-laugh. 'Jesus, Odran,' he said and I opened my eyes wide. A lad I knew in school had said *Jesus* once in the middle of a geography class and he'd got the leather for it, ten times on each hand. He'd not said it again. 'You're some langer.'

'You don't have to worry,' I said eventually. 'It'll be all right here. I'm sure it will.'

'You keep saying that. Who are you trying to convince anyway, me or you?'

'I'm only trying to help.'

'You're a great optimist, I'd say, are you?'

'Don't you think you'll be happy here?' I asked.

'No,' he said, a bitter tone to his voice. 'I don't belong here. I have no business being in this place.'

'Then why did you come?'

'Because I'm safer here,' he said quietly after a lengthy pause.

And those were his last words for the night. He rolled over in one direction and I rolled over in the other, and since I lay awake for another hour or more out of excitement and apprehension, I heard him as he started to cry, a low muffled weeping into his pillow, and I thought about going over to him and sitting on the corner of his bed and telling him not to worry, that everything would be all right, but in the end, of course, I did nothing.

'Are we agreed then?' asked Archbishop Cordington. 'You'll give it a go?'

I sighed, resigned to it now. 'If that's what you want,' I said.

'Good man,' he said, bringing a heavy hand down on my knee. 'And look, it won't be for ever, you don't need to worry about that. Just a few years. And then I'll send you back to your school, I promise.'

'Really?' I asked hopefully.

'You have my word of honour,' he said, smiling. 'It might not even take that long. Just until everything gets cleared up.'

'I don't follow,' I said. 'Until what gets cleared up?'

He hesitated. 'The whole problem with the applications,' he said. 'There'll be new lads coming down the line soon enough, as sure as eggs is eggs. And then we'll get you back to Terenure, Odran. You do this for me, you keep an eye on Tom's parish, and before you know it we'll have you back where you belong. Right,' he said, pulling himself to his feet, 'I have to throw you out now unless you want to be here when eight nuns arrive to complain about their facilities.'

I laughed. 'I'm grand, thanks,' I said.

'You can thank Tom Cardle,' he said, turning his back on me as he made his way over to his desk. 'This is all down to him. Oh, by the way,' he added before I could leave. 'How's that sister of yours doing? He told me she wasn't well.'

'She hasn't been well for a few years now,' I said. 'We've done our best for her at home but it looks like she'll have to go into a facility soon. Somewhere they can take care of her.'

'And what's the matter with her, if you don't mind me asking?'

'Early-onset dementia,' I said. 'We have one of those home-helps in there to take care of her, but it's getting beyond that now. She knows me sometimes when I visit. Other times she doesn't.'

'She's probably better off not knowing about that son of hers anyway,' he said gruffly. 'What with all his effing and blinding. He's a queer too, isn't he? Did I read that somewhere?'

I felt rattled by this, as if he had suddenly spat in my face, but he wasn't looking at me and didn't seem to expect an answer; he was already searching through papers on his desk for whatever he needed for his next appointment. I said nothing, simply took my leave, closing the door behind me, and made my way down the corridor as eight nuns came towards me, parting in the centre like the Red Sea and standing still as I passed them, a choir of voices saying, 'Good afternoon, Father,' in perfect harmony.

So that was that. And I heard no more from the Archbishop for a long time; once the decision was made, it was made, and I was supposed to just get on with things, even though more than a quarter-century of my life was being pulled from under my feet.

Chapter Three

1964

We began as three, then became four, then five, and one day without warning we were three again.

I was the eldest, alone in the house with Mam and Dad for three years but too young to appreciate fully the luxury of that position. By all accounts I was not a difficult baby, sleeping when I was told to sleep and eating whatever was put in front of me. There was a problem with my sight in my infancy which provoked fears that I might become blind in later life and I was brought to see a specialist in Holles Street hospital, but whatever the issue was it must have righted itself in time, for I never developed any difficulties as I grew older.

Hannah arrived in 1958, a mewling, shrieking presence, given to explosions of temper that led to arguments between our parents, Mam saying that she couldn't cope and Dad clearing off to the pub. The baby refused to eat and there were visits to a second doctor, who said that she must eat or she would die.

'Sure don't I know that?' said Mam, looking around the surgery with the air of one who had come here for help but realized that there would be little of that on offer. I sat in the corner, watching her frustration grow. 'I'm not a complete imbecile.'

'Have you tried cajoling her, Mrs Yates?' the doctor asked.

'In what way exactly?'

'I know that my own wife often cajoled our children to get them to eat. It worked wonders.'

'Could you explain the meaning of the word *cajole* to me, Doctor? And tell me how it might help?'

'Well, it's from the French, isn't it?' he replied, smiling at her. '*Cajoler*. To persuade a person to do something that they are reluctant to do.'

'Hannah is seven months old,' said Mam. 'I'm not certain that my powers of persuasion will work on her. They haven't so far anyway.'

'Try, Mrs Yates,' replied the doctor, opening his hands wide as if the mysteries of the universe could be contained between those palms. 'Try. A good mother will keep trying until she succeeds.'

A comment which provoked a quiet fury on Mam's part, but she was too intimidated by the three-piece suit, the house on Dartmouth Square, the brass plaque attached to the railings outside and the appointment fee of forty pence to challenge him any further. But perhaps, as with my eyes, Hannah's problems simply corrected themselves in time, or perhaps she just grew too hungry to put up any more resistance to her food, for eventually she settled down into a regular pattern of eating and peace was restored.

I loved Hannah from the start, unaware of how much I wanted a younger sibling until one was thrust upon me. She would stop crying when I entered the room, staring up at me with her large wet blue eyes, and her head would turn slowly as I carried on about my business, taking note of my every move, convinced that if she looked away she would miss something important. She would cry out when I left her alone and clap her hands when I reappeared.

Mam didn't have a job, of course; she wouldn't have been allowed. Before marrying my father she had been a stewardess for Aer Lingus, a position that in those days was tantamount to being a film-star, and indeed in later life she loved to tell stories about the glamour she had witnessed as a young woman. Once, she had served lunch to Rita Hayworth on a flight from Brussels to Dublin; another time she had assisted David Niven with a faulty seatbelt as he came in from London to attend a film premiere.

'Miss Hayworth was a beauty,' she told me. 'Such long, red hair. And very polite. She sat in her seat with a black cigarette holder between her fingers and was happy to sign autographs for anyone who approached her. She read the entire way, moving between a copy of *Look* magazine and a script for a feature film. There was a choice of beef or chicken and she took the chicken. Mr Niven was dressed better than any man I had ever laid eyes on, as dapper as could be, and he spoke Awfully Awfully, like they do. He was terrible fidgety though and couldn't sit straight in his seat. And he drank like a fish.'

She had to give up the job once she got married, of course, because in those days Aer Lingus wouldn't employ a married woman. Her own mother, who I never knew, said that she was mad to give up the high life for a semi-detached house in Churchtown, but she said that was what she wanted, and after all, that is what women did in those days: they went to school, they got a job, they found a husband, they left the job and retired to the home to look after the family.

'The most exciting moment of all,' she told me once, 'was the day I was coming through Heathrow Airport and saw Princess Margaret. She was flapping her hands in front of her, as if she could make the crowds disperse simply by waving them away. I could tell just by looking at her that she was the rudest woman on the face of the planet, without an ounce of class. But it was Princess Margaret, all the same, and I thought I'd died and gone to heaven. I only wished I had my Box Brownie.'

She met my father at a dancehall near Parnell Square. He was there with a couple of his pals, wearing his best suit, a black and white striped tweed, his thick dark hair Brylcreemed back with the comb trails still running through it like a freshly tilled field. A cigarette was hanging out of the side of his mouth, and when he spoke, it stayed attached to his lower lip, the ash growing longer and longer but never falling until he tipped it into the ashtray. He spotted her at the same moment that she spotted him and he walked straight over, ending the conversation with his friends in mid-sentence.

'Are you dancing?' he asked her.

'Are you asking?' she replied, the standard answer.

'I am.'

'Might as well so.'

He led her on to the floor and within half a minute she knew she'd hit the jackpot, for here was a man who had both a right foot and a left. No shuffling, no awkwardness, no embarrassment about where to place his arms or hands. He moved with confidence, and as she wasn't a bad little mover herself they put on a good show and the rest of the gathering watched appreciatively. The men muttered that this was a fine little piece that Billy Yates had his arms around, and the women said you'd think he'd take the fag out of his mouth before dancing, sure did he have no manners at all?

'Do you have a name?'

'I've had one for years. Gloria Cooper. What's yours?'

'William Yates.'

'Like the poet?'

'Different spelling.'

Mam told me afterwards that the first thought that came into her mind was this: *Gloria Yates*. She said it had a ring to it.

'Have I seen you here before, Gloria Cooper?'

'Do you mean to say that you'd have forgotten me if you had?'

'That's me told. What do you do then when you're not out dancing?'

'I'm a stewardess for Aer Lingus.'

He paused for a moment, then gave her a spin. 'A stewardess, is it?' he asked, impressed. Most of the girls he'd danced with before worked in cake shops or were in training to be teachers. One girl had said she was going to be a nun and the cigarette had fair fallen out of his mouth then. Another had said it was patriarchal to ask such a question and he'd said, 'Ah, tonight,' and walked away in the middle of Frankie Laine crooning his way through 'Answer Me'. 'How did you get a job like that anyway?'

'I applied,' said Mam.

'Smart enough, I suppose.'

'And you? What do you do?'

'I'm an actor.'

'Have I seen you in anything?'

'Did you ever see *From Here to Eternity*?'

'The film?'

'Yes.'

'Of course I did. I saw it in the Adelphi.'

'Well, I wasn't in that.'

She laughed. 'So what were you in then?'

'Nothing yet. But I will be one day.'

'And what are you doing in the meantime, Burt Lancaster?'

'Stock man for John Player's on Merchants Quay.'

'Do you get the cigarettes for free then?'

'I get them at a discount.'

'You're quick on your feet.'

'You have to be these days.'

That is as much as Mam told me about their first encounter, other than to say that when he asked whether he might call on her the following Tuesday she felt a certain pride in replying that she wouldn't be home until after seven for the flight from Ciampino only got in at five, a remark that made him smile, then laugh, then shake his head as if he wasn't sure whether he knew what he was taking on at all.

They were engaged to be married within six months and soon after exchanged their vows in the Blessed Sacrament Chapel on Bachelor's Walk, before making their way to the Central Hotel on Exchequer Street for a buffet dinner and afterwards taking a taxi to the airport for a flight to Paris. She knew two of the stewardesses on board, but the third was a new girl and seeing her being shown the ropes, she said, filled her with an overwhelming sadness, as if she realized that she might have made a terrible mistake.

'Did you miss flying?' I asked her once, for she only left Ireland on one occasion during the rest of her life, when she and Hannah came to visit me in Rome during 1978.

'Of course I did,' she said with a regretful shrug. 'But then I didn't know what I was giving up until it was already gone. No one ever does, do they?'

Little Cathal arrived only eighteen months after Hannah, when I was already four, and I know now from the way that Mam and Dad behaved at the time that he was a surprise to them and not an entirely welcome one. There was a mortgage to pay, and a cigarette factory was not the first choice for those who wished to become rich. And yet we carried on, the five of us, for a couple of years until Dad made the decision to leave Player's in order to pursue his acting ambitions.

Where these came from is anyone's guess. I never knew my father's parents any more than I knew my mother's, for they were all dead before I turned five, but I have it on good authority that my paternal grandmother was a great woman for the Feis Ceoil and perhaps this is where he got his yearning for the spotlight. As a boy, he somehow found himself in the chorus lines of a couple of Christmas pantomimes at the Gaiety Theatre, and, older again, he joined an amateur dramatics society out in Rathmines, and the bug only got worse from there. Without telling my mother, he handed in his notice to Mr Benjamin at Player's – 'It gave me great pleasure,' Dad said, 'for I never liked working for a Jewman' – and threw himself into going out on professional auditions, taking a part-time job in the meantime at a pub in Dundrum, which Mam saw as a terrible come-down. Packing small boxes of cigarettes into bigger boxes and then loading them on to pallets for distribution to the newsagents and tobacconists of Ireland was apparently a superior task to pulling pints of Harp and Guinness down at the Eagle House three nights a week.

'It's only until I get a decent part,' said Dad, who brushed off all her complaints about the lack of housekeeping money with a dismissive wave worthy of Princess Margaret herself. 'Once I do, we'll all be set for life.'

And then something remarkable happened. He was put up for the part of the Young Covey in a production of *The Plough and the Stars* at the Abbey Theatre, which, at the time, had been relocated to the Queen's on Pearse Street after a fire destroyed the original building. He auditioned in front of Proinnsias Mac Diarmada and Seán O'Casey himself and must have given a decent performance for he was asked if he would understudy for Uinsionn O'Dubhláinn, who was a great favourite with the public at the time. My father suffered mixed emotions at this offer; he was proud to have his talents recognized but saw himself as second fiddle to no man. But then as luck would have it, didn't O'Dubhláinn get offered Laertes at the Old Vic in London and skip off across the water without so much as a backwards glance, and MacDiarmada had no choice but to promote my father from understudy to cast member. O'Casey had his reservations, apparently, but there was no one else who could take on the role at such short notice.

'This is it now,' he said when he told us the news, rubbing his hands together in glee. 'This is only the start of it. The Young Covey is a great part, it's one that gets you noticed. Sure I might end up on the West End yet. Or even Broadway.'

'Listen to Laurence Olivier,' said Mam, putting plates of fish and potatoes in front of us, for now that there was less money coming in, meat was becoming a rare treat.

'Ah, would you go 'way,' said Dad, whose enthusiasm was not to be diminished. 'You won't be making jokes when you're the wife of the most famous actor in Ireland.'

Eoin O'Súilleabháin and Caitlín Ní Bhearáin were playing the lead parts of Jack and Nora Clitheroe, and for weeks all we heard was Eoin-this and Caitlín-that as he came home stinking of drink and telling stories of what was going on backstage to an audience that was growing less appreciative by the day.

'What has drink to do with learning your part?' Mam asked.

'You wouldn't understand, Gloria,' he told her. 'We have to go to the pub after rehearsals to release some of the pent-up energy that comes from being on stage. It's what actors do.'

'It's what drunks do,' she countered. 'And you with a family.'

'Ah, would you whisht, woman.'

'I will not whisht. Do I have to go back to Aer Lingus, is it?'

'Sure they wouldn't have you,' he laughed.

'They would if I told them I was a single woman. I could say that you left me.'

Which put the frighteners on him, sure enough, and he threatened to phone the parish priest, and when she called his bluff he called hers directly back and before the night was out there was Father Haughton, an awful stern man with a face like one of those Easter Island statues, sitting in our front room while Hannah, Cathal and I listened at the door and imagined

Mam and Dad sitting side by side, each more embarrassed than the other by this turn of events.

'Gloria, do you not recognize your husband's needs?' asked Father Haughton in a silky tone. 'This is a big change for him. Sure how many of us even get the chance to visit the National Theatre, let alone perform on its stage?'

'It's not the acting I mind so much as the drinking, Father,' said Mam. 'We have precious little money coming in as it is, and to spend it on pints when I have five bellies to fill in this house—'

'Lower your voice, please, Gloria,' said Father Haughton. 'I'm a patient man, but I have a low tolerance for screeching women.'

My mother did not speak for several minutes afterwards and when she did it was in chastised tones.

'William, you'll try to get home to your family a little earlier in the evening, won't you?' asked the priest.

'I will, Father. I'll do my best. I can promise nothing, but I'll do my best.'

'And I wouldn't ask you to, but as long as you're willing to make an effort, that's what counts. And you, Gloria, you'll be less insistent with your husband, yes?'

'I'll try.'

'Promise me you will, Gloria.'

'I will, Father.'

'There's a good girl. No man wants to come home to a nagging wife. Keep your disposition cheerful and the dinner warm and there'll be no more problems in this house, may God bless all who live here.'

And that was that for the time being. Dad was given leave to do exactly as he pleased and Mam had no choice but to put up with it. In fairness to my father, he made more of an effort for a while to help out when he was at home, but the pints still flowed a few nights a week and the name-dropping became shameless.

I was probably too young to appreciate the play – I was only nine years old at the time – but Mam took me with her to see *The Plough and the Stars* on opening night, leaving Hannah and Cathal in the care of Mrs Rathley next door, and despite my youth I could tell without fear of contradiction that my father was the worst actor on the stage. He shouted when he should have spoken, came upstage when he clearly should have been down, facing the person he was addressing. He grew confused over his lines at the beginning of the third act when he and Uncle Peter bring news of the Rising to Bessie Burgess and she predicts the defeat of the rebels at the GPO. And I remain convinced that in the middle of his argument with Fluther, he caught sight of me in the fourth row and threw me a wink, an unexpected turn that caused Philib O'Floinn to repeat a line and flounder through the rest of the scene.

When the play was finally over and the cast appeared on stage one by one to take their curtain calls, the applause he received was muted, to say the least, and one group to the rear of the auditorium even let out a hiss. O'Casey shunned him at the cast party afterwards, apparently, leaving my father to say that the playwright had no more manners than a pig in a field. The following morning, however, the critic from the *Evening Press* made mincemeat of him in his review, saying that he'd set fire to the Queen's too if he ever saw such a performance on the stage of the National Theatre again. A few days later, MacDiarmada had my father replaced, and if things were bad then, they were about to get much worse, for my father spent the first half of the next night's performance in exile in The Stag's Head, alternating between pints of Guinness and glasses of whiskey, before making his way back to Pearse Street and in through the stage entrance before marching out, drunk and in his street clothes, on to the stage in the middle of the third act, where he threw a punch at the understudy who had replaced him, leading to the farcical situation of a pair of Young Coveys tussling onstage and having to be pulled apart by Mrs Gogan and Mollser, while the audience scratched their heads and wondered whether this was some new scene that had been added to the play for comic effect.

What was it Yeats said at the riots that greeted the first production of that play more than thirty years before? *You have disgraced yourselves again!* Something along those lines. Spoken to the audience, though, not the cast. Sure he never would have imagined that he would have to speak that way to the actors. I have no idea what O'Casey was thinking, but I imagine it wasn't pretty.

My father never set foot on a stage again after that. Sober, he tried to apologize to MacDiarmada, who refused to see him. He showed up at O'Casey's house on the North Circular Road and was given short shrift. He wrote a *mea culpa* to the *Evening Press*, who said he was nothing more than a figure of fun and they wouldn't drag their pages into the debacle by publishing it. A week later, he received a letter informing him that he was banned for life from the Abbey Theatre, and when he tried to put the whole business behind him and started attending open auditions for other plays in Dublin he was met at the door by producers who said it would be a cold day in hell before they risked their investment on a man with his reputation.

'It's not that you made a holy show of yourself, brawling on stage when you were in your cups,' one pointed out to him in the killer blow. 'That I could live with. It's the fact that you're the worst actor who ever had the unlikely opportunity to set foot in a theatre. You've no talent, do you not recognize that?'

'Would you not go back to Player's?' Mam asked him eventually, for we were running out of money fast. 'We have First Communion clothes for Odran to buy, Hannah needs new shoes and Cathal is growing out of everything I try to put on him.'

'This is all your fault,' he grunted, sitting in his chair, drinking, and this was a new thing, for he had always kept his drinking to the pubs before.

'How is it my fault, William Yates?' she asked, her nerves pushed to the brink now.

'You never gave me a bit of support.'

'Sure that's all I've done.'

'What kind of a wife are you anyway? I made a bad choice.'

'For shame, in front of the children,' she said, taken aback by the depth of his anger.

'Are they even mine?' he asked. 'Is it a hoor I'm married to, do you think?'

Which led to her running up the stairs in tears while the rest of us sat crying on the sofa.

He wouldn't allow a television in the house, even though the neighbours all had sets, because he said the actors in the shows were all fellas who couldn't get jobs on the stage or in the films. He said he'd rather be on the dole than work in television, but I knew that wasn't true, for he'd written to RTÉ for a part in *Tolka Row* and never received so much as a reply.

In the end, he was left with no choice, for the man needed money for his own food and drink, and he went crawling back to Mr Benjamin, cap in hand, who agreed to give him a job but on a lesser wage, as if he was just a young apprentice starting out. The other men took great pleasure in his downfall, of course, for he had taken equal delight in saying goodbye to them. Dad never fought back, but he went into himself; he went into himself something terrible.

Five became three later that year, in the closing days of the summer of 1964.

He was still drinking a fierce amount and he and Mam fought all the time about money, about what was the point of earning it if it was just going to end up in the tills at Davy Byrne's or pissed up against a porcelain wall in Mulligan's on Poolbeg Street? Mam was rough on him, there's no denying it, and he stopped trying to defend himself. Perhaps the fight just went out of him.

It was Mam, then, who organized the Big Surprise, a week's holiday in Blackwater village in the county of Wexford, paid for with money she'd been setting aside for just such a moment. We rented a chalet from a widow woman named Mrs Hardy who lived in a bungalow next door with her son, a strange boy who spoke in riddles and who I realize now was probably touched in the head, and three spaniels, each one yappier than the last.

Hannah, Cathal and I could not believe our luck when we got to ride in a train all the way from Connolly station through Bray and Glendalough, onwards to Arklow, Gorey and Enniscorthy, until we arrived at Wexford itself, where we took a horse and trap, all five of us and our suitcases, to that mythological place, our holiday home. It was fairly basic accommodation, as I recall, but we were beside ourselves with excitement, especially at the fact that there were fields to run in, dogs to chase and chickens to feed every morning outside Mrs Hardy's back door.

'Do the dogs not take an interest in the chickens?' I asked Mrs Hardy one afternoon and she shook her head.

'They know what would happen to them if they did,' she told me, and I didn't doubt it for she was a woman with a temper.

There were two bedrooms in the chalet; Mam and Dad took the smaller one with the double bed, while we three children took the larger one with two singles standing parallel to each other on either side of the room, Hannah in one and Cathal and I bunking together in the second, unconcerned by the squash, giggling at the fun of it, kicking each other with our bare feet. At the time, I thought I had never been happier to be alive.

During the day we would entertain ourselves in the fields or take a village taxi to Courtown for an afternoon at the two carnivals, riding on the dodgem cars, sliding down the helter-skelter and throwing our ha'pennies away in the one-armed bandits. I had developed a passion for comics and it was a difficult choice between the summer specials of *The Beano*, featuring Dennis the Menace and the Bash Street Kids, and *The Beezer*, with its Banana Bunch and Colonel Blink. We would eat candy floss and buy inflatable toys. Dad took me to see *Dracula* one afternoon at a local cinema and I upended a carton of popcorn over both of us when I started screaming at the vampire and had to be carried out of the cinema and into the brightness of the afternoon before I would calm down again. Some days we would all make a trip down to Curracloe beach, Dad carrying a picnic box in his hands, and run in and out of the sea, building castles and moats, and afterwards sitting with sand-crunchy Calvita cheese sandwiches, bags of Tayto cheese and onion and warm cans of Fanta and Cidona, feeling for all the world like gods descended from the heavens.

Did I see Tom Cardle on the beach one of those days, I wonder. There were families everywhere and Tom's farm was not far from the place where we climbed over the dunes to catch our first sight of the blue water sparkling like an earth-bound rainbow ahead of us. Was he out there, that tenth child, whose destiny was written down for him on the back of a Bible at birth and who would never know what it was to love another human being? Did I share a joke with him when I joined a group of local lads as they kicked a ball around the beach? Is it possible that we have a shared innocence somewhere in the past? It is; of course it is. But what does any of that matter now? It's all washed away with the tides.

The argument that destroyed my family's life took place on our fifth night in Wexford. Hannah and I were trying to teach Cathal to play Ludo, while all he wanted to do was chase one of

Mrs Hardy's spaniels who had wandered in to see was there any news with us, when Mam made the innocuous comment that a holiday like this was just what she'd needed. 'We should do this every year,' she added.

'Holidays cost money,' said Dad.

'And so does drink.'

'Ah, would you ever go fuck yourself, you oul' bitch.'

We three children looked up in surprise. For all of the anger that was bottled up inside himself, Dad had somehow stopped expressing it aloud, and even when he did, he almost never used language like this. It wasn't that he had allowed himself to become walked upon, it was just that whenever Mam had a go at him he seemed to sink inside himself instead, sometimes for days at a time. He was a victim of depression, I can see that now as I look back. His life was not the one he had hoped for.

Words were exchanged between my mother and father, words that are difficult to recount and even harder to forget. Mam had the heartlessness to quote verbatim the words of the newspaper critic who had threatened arson if there was a chance of William Yates appearing on the stage again. Dad asked her what she knew of the acting world anyway, sure wasn't she nothing but a jumped-up little nobody who'd seen her chance and taken it.

'My chance?' she roared. 'Sure didn't I already have my chance and I was too blind to see it? I might have been a transatlantic stewardess by now. I might have been *running* Aer Lingus! Instead of a doormat to you.'

'It was all I wanted,' he cried, bending over in his chair, his fury and venom turning to bitter self-pity and recrimination; he buried his face in his hands, the snot running down from his nose, and little Cathal and I started to cry to see how much pain he was in while Hannah simply grew pale and stared, her tongue sticking out of her mouth in shock. 'And you took it from me,' he added, looking around at us. 'You all took it from me.'

'We took nothing,' shouted my mother, who had had enough of this by now. She picked up a heavy saucepan and banged its base time and again against the wooden table in a fury, and it made a horrible sound that left Cathal with his hands over his ears and Hannah running from the room in fright. 'We took nothing off you, you miserable man. You miserable, good-for-nothing sad pathetic excuse for a man and a husband and a father. We took nothing from you!' she screamed.

'You took what I loved,' he cried, rocking back and forth. 'You took the only thing I loved. What if I took something from you that you loved? How would you like that?'

'Take it!' she roared, throwing the saucepan away from her now; it clattered across the floor as she stormed off to the bedroom. 'Take it all, William Yates. I don't care a jot for another bit of it!'

Little Cathal was sent in to sleep with Mam that night while Dad took the other side of the bed to me, and there was no giggling then and no kicking each other with our bare feet. Instead, I lay there, anxious and alert as I heard a sound that terrified and appalled me in equal parts: the sound of my father, a grown man, muttering incoherently like a madman into his pillow. Years later, I would hear something similar come from Tom Cardle's bed on our first night in Clonliffe College.

I don't know what time I woke the next morning, but it was bright when I stepped into the living room and, to my surprise, my father was standing there in fine fettle, overflowing with good cheer, pouring my Alpen out for me into the red see-through bowls that I loved – Alpen was kept as a special treat for the holidays and never permitted at home – as Mam sat in a deckchair in the garden with her book, completely separated from him. She was reading *The Country Girls*, just for devilment, because she knew that the sight of that beautiful woman on the back jacket drove my poor father to distraction. He said she had a mouth on her and that she should have been brought to heel long ago.

'There you are, son,' he said, grinning at me as if none of the events of the night before had ever taken place. 'Did you sleep well?'

'Not really.'

'Oh no? Is it a guilty conscience you have?'

I stared at him. I had no answer to this.

'I'm going for a swim in a few minutes,' he told me then. 'Will you come down to the beach with me?'

I didn't fancy it and said so.

'Ah, of course you'll come,' said Dad. 'We'll have a great time, just the two of us.'

But I shook my head and said that I was too tired. The truth was that after all the trauma of the night before, the thought of dragging myself down to Curracloe beach and into the cold waves was, for once, an unappealing one. I could still see him rocking back and forth, blaming all of us for his own failures; I could still hear the sound of Mam banging that saucepan against the table. I wanted nothing to do with any of them.

'Are you sure?' he asked, standing before me now, a hand on both my shoulders. 'I won't ask you again.'

'I'm sure,' I said and he seemed to sigh a little in disappointment as he turned away from me and looked over towards the four-year-old boy playing in the corner. 'It'll have to be you then, Cathal,' he said. 'Go along there now and get your togs.'

And like a dog who never refuses a walk, my younger brother jumped up from whatever he was doing and ran to the bedroom to get changed for the beach, scampering back out with his bucket and spade in hand.

'You won't need them,' said Dad, taking them off him and laying them down on the floor. 'We're swimming, that's all. Just the two of us. No playing of games.'

Off the pair of them went a few minutes later, before Hannah had even risen from her bed, and I watched them as they wandered down the path and turned left, disappearing behind the trees in the direction of Curracloe, and thought not another thing about it, but wondered instead whether the donkey in the next field along might be out for his morning amble, and if he was, wouldn't he think me the best lad alive if I brought him a few cubes of sugar and maybe an apple, if I could find one, for his breakfast?

It was a Garda with a Mayo accent, I remember, who arrived at the house a couple of hours later with the news. He must have been stationed in Wexford in the way that they always send them to a county that isn't their own, where they don't know the people they have to arrest or to whom they have to break bad news. I was out in the front garden, running around; Mam was in the kitchen preparing a late lunch, but she stepped out on to the porch when she saw the Garda car pulling in and coming to a halt.

'Odran, go inside,' she said as she came out, the dish towel still in her hands, and I stared at her but didn't move and she didn't ask me twice. 'Are you lost, Garda?' she asked, smiling brightly as if this was a great joke.

'Ah no,' he said, shrugging his shoulders and looking around with an expression on his face that said he would rather be anywhere else in the world than standing there. I remember thinking that he had the look of John Wayne. 'Fine day, all the same.'

'It is,' agreed Mam. 'Will it rain later, do you think?'

'It can be changeable,' said the Garda, looking at me for a moment, frowning, his forehead crinkling up something terrible.

'Where's that accent of yours from?' asked Mam, and even in

my childishness I thought that this was a strange conversation for the pair of them to be having. Gardaí didn't show up at the house to make small talk. They surely had better things to be doing with their time than that.

'Westport,' he replied.

'I knew a girl from Westport once,' said Mam. 'She worked with me in Aer Lingus. She had a fear of heights, so never looked out the windows of the planes. I wondered why she'd bothered getting a job there at all.'

The Garda laughed, then seemed to think better of it and turned it into a cough. 'It's Mrs Yates, isn't it?' he said.

'It is.'

'Sure we'll go inside, will we? And sit down for a minute?'

I looked at Mam and saw her close her eyes for what felt like a very long time, and to this day I think it was the guts of half a minute before she opened them again and nodded, turning away and opening the door to lead him in, and even in those thirty seconds I would swear that she aged a decade.

Now here is what is known: a family on the Curracloe beach, a mother and father with twin boys, were setting up a wind protector when they saw William Yates and Cathal out there in the waves, apparently having a great time altogether, splashing away to their hearts' content. The mother said she thought that the boy was very young to be out so far and the father took a notion that they were in difficulties and so threw himself out into the water to help. But he was not a strong swimmer and it wasn't long before he began to struggle in the waves, and afterwards he said that it looked to him as if the man was trying to drown the boy, for he was pushing down on his head and every time the little lad came up for air the man pushed him down again and held him there until he rose to the surface no more. He swam further on then, away from the beach, out into the ocean, further than any sensible person would ever swim, and the boy floated back towards the shore, his face down, his arms outstretched. The father from the beach dragged him back in but there was nothing that could be done to save him, for little Cathal was drowned, and by the time Dad's body was washed back in with the tide a couple of hours later, half the local Gardaí were on the scene, and an ambulance from Wexford town, and what could be done but bring them to Courtown hospital, where the candy floss was still on sale in the streets outside, where the dodgems still bumped up against each other in the afternoon sunshine, and write up the death certificates and call the funeral parlour?

And here is what is unknown: what was it that happened out there? Was it a suicide on my father's part? Depressed, rejected by the world, packing cigarettes at the Player's factory on Merchants Quay when he wanted to be Alas-poor-Yoricking on the stage of the Abbey or tutoring Eliza Doolittle in her elocution lessons in the Theatre Royal, Drury Lane. Was it a suicide, I'm asking. It was, I am sure of it now. And was it a murder? Yes, to that question too. But why did he choose to take one of his own children with him? First me, who turned down the offer, then little Cathal. Why did he want to take one of us with him? What was the sense of that? What good did it serve? Would it take away the words of the critic from *The Evening Press* or give him access to Seán O'Casey's house on the North Circular Road? Would it put him in front of Caitlín Ní Bhearáin or Elizabeth Taylor as they looked into his eyes and said their lines?

I have thought of this a hundred times, a thousand times, ten thousand times over the years between then and now and have resolved it in my mind by saying that this man, my father, was not in his right head at the time, that he was ill, that he did something that he would never have dreamed of doing if the world had treated him with a little more kindness. *What if I took something from you that you loved?* he had asked my mother the night before, and only a man who was suffering and not in his proper senses could ever have considered such a plan. I tell myself this because to think otherwise would open up a sea of pain that would swallow me as easily as the Irish Sea swallowed my younger brother.

What a world it is that we live in and what injuries we do to children.

I think of little Cathal struggling in the sea, feeling the sandy base disappearing from beneath his feet, crying out as his father's hands pushed him down, wondering was this a new game of some sort. Terrified but obedient, trusting that whatever was happening was supposed to be happening, but then realizing that no, this was something peculiar, this was something he would not survive, this was the moment of his death and he would never get to play with Mrs Hardy's spaniels again. And I imagine the water filling his lungs and the dizziness he would have felt as he gasped for air. And they say that drowning is a painless way to go, but why should I believe this, for who has ever succumbed to such an ending and returned to tell the tale? And I have an idea that my father came to his senses when he saw his youngest child giving up his struggle, his body going limp, and realized the terrible thing that he had done, and sure what could he do then but make wide-angled strides off in the direction of the horizon, knowing that it was only a matter of time before his arms gave out and his breath closed down and his legs stopped kicking and he sank beneath the water where he might find some peace at last.

That's what I believe anyway. I have no way of knowing.

And so we began as three, then became four, then five, and one day without warning we were three again.

We came home to Dublin and Mam was no longer a married woman, she was a widow instead, and the loss of her youngest child changed her in ways that I never would have imagined. She turned to God, and in Him she hoped to find her relief and her comfort. She began taking Hannah and me to Mass in the Good Shepherd church early every morning before school, where previously we had only sat on those pews for the ten o'clock Mass on a Sunday, which was a notoriously short one, and made us say our prayers for little Cathal, although never for our father, for once the funerals were over she never spoke his name again in her entire life. And in the evenings, when the Angelus came on the television, she would order Hannah and me to sink to our knees to say all five decades of the rosary and the Hail Holy Queen, which we tried to do without laughing, but, may God forgive us, that was a struggle at times. She brought me across to see Father Haughton and said that I had expressed an interest in being an altar boy, which I had never done in my life, and before I knew it I was being measured up for my surplice and soutane. Statues of Our Lady were placed around the house. Pictures of the Sacred Heart, which I used to call the Scared Heart until she clipped me round the ear for my insolence, were pinned to the walls. Mrs Rathley from next door went to Lourdes to take the cure and brought us back a clear plastic bottle in the shape of Jesus on the cross, filled with holy water, and we were made to bless ourselves with it every morning and every night as we rose from or went to our beds, and we would ask God to take care of little Cathal and keep him safe and warm until we were able to join him in our reward. Our house, which until then had been peculiarly secular for the times, became a house of religion, and it was on my next birthday, as I turned ten, that she ran into my bedroom in the middle of the night, switched on the light, rousing me from my fanciful dreams, and looked at me with an expression of wonder on her face, before declaring that she had just had a great epiphany, one for which we should all be grateful. It had come to her while she was watching *The Late Late*

Show, she said, and she had leaped from her chair and run up the stairs to rouse me and look into my eyes, and now that she did, she knew that she was right. She could see it in my face. She could tell it from the way I held myself in her arms.

'You have a vocation, Odran,' she informed me. 'You have a vocation to be a priest.'

And I thought if she said so then she must be right. For wasn't that the way that I'd been brought up, after all? To believe everything that my mother told me?

Chapter Four

1980

At first glance, the train appeared to be completely full and my heart sank at the idea that I might have to stand for two and a half hours as it wound its way south to Kildare, then back north as far as Athlone before making its way towards Galway station.

I was tired, having only returned from Norway the previous afternoon, following an exhausting week attending Hannah's wedding to Kristian Ramsfjeld. Of course, I should have cancelled my cross-country trip, but it seemed as if the act of picking up the phone and making my excuses would command even more effort than simply going, and so I had unpacked one set of clothes from my suitcase the night before and then packed another, before enduring an unsettled night's sleep and making my way to Heuston station for the westbound train.

I had travelled alone to Norway, Mam refusing to have anything to do with any of this due to the fact that Kristian was not a Catholic but, like most of his countrymen, a Lutheran, a denomination which was akin to Satanism as far as she was concerned. But this was not her only issue, as she had also hoped that her daughter would join the nuns at the Loreto Abbey in Rathfarnham, insisting that she, like I, had a vocation. Hannah had refused, laughing at the very idea, leading to ructions at home, and when the name of our lost Cathal was invoked it seemed as if our mother would stop at nothing to make her fall in line.

'Didn't you get your way with poor Odran?' Hannah roared when I came over one evening to try to broker a peace between the pair of them. 'Isn't he after throwing his life away because he was too afraid to stand up to you?'

'Ah now,' I said, wounded by this, for what Hannah refused to acknowledge then, and never grew to accept fully, was that Mam might have pointed me towards a path that she had laid out for me, but it was one that I was eminently suited to walk along.

'A little harlot is all you are,' shouted Mam, who was able to give as good as she got with the decibels. 'Spreading it about for all the lads.'

'And sure why wouldn't I?' asked Hannah, hands on her hips. 'If you have it, flaunt it. And I have it in spades.'

'Odran, will you not make her see sense?' asked Mam, appealing to me, but what could I do, for my sister had already admitted to me that not only would she rather die than become a nun, but that she never even went to Mass any more, leaving the house on a Sunday morning and taking the bus into town to see a film instead.

Hannah and Kristian met at the Bank of Ireland on College Green, where she was in training as a cashier on the foreign exchange desk, spending half her day converting Irish punts into dollars or sterling for those young men who were cashing in their meagre savings to try their luck abroad, where, rumour had it, there was work to be found, for God knows there was precious little of it in Ireland at the time. Kristian was studying philosophy across the way in Trinity College and would wander in every day during his lunch hour with a couple of hundred Norwegian kroner to exchange.

'You don't want to swap all of this in one go, do you not?'

Hannah asked him on his fourth appearance in as many days. 'You realize you're paying a commission every time?'

'But then I would not get the opportunity to see you each day,' he replied, smiling at her, and she told me afterwards that she felt the room spin a little when she realized that here was a boy who liked her, a good-looking, confident boy with bright blond hair, clear skin and a way of wearing clothes that put the Irish lads to shame.

'And he doesn't just want to take me to the Bad Ass Café all the time either,' she added. 'We go to plays and concerts and last week he brought me to the National Gallery to see an exhibition of Nordic paintings that was on display. And he wasn't faking, Odran, he knew all about them.'

They courted for a year and then there was an evening when Mam bit the bullet and invited the pair of them for dinner, but an argument broke out somewhere between the melon slice, toothpick-pierced with a glacé cherry, and the roast of lamb; Kristian refused to engage for he was a placid and even-tempered boy, but that only made my mother more aggressive, and after that he was no longer welcome in the house, a fact which bothered him not a bit. I wasn't present – I was still in Rome at the time – but I assume that religion was at the heart of the quarrel, as it so often is in Ireland.

The marriage took place in the town of Lillehammer, a couple of hours north of Oslo, where Kristian had grown up, and was attended by his extended family, dozens of hearty, cheerful Ramsfjelds, each one with a name more difficult to spell or pronounce than the last. Minuscules and angstroms ran through or sat above their vowels, dividing their 'o's in two and crowning their 'a's. The juxtaposition of 'j's and 'k's in their names made it difficult for me to pronounce them without making Kristian's cousins laugh and try to correct me, even though what they said and what I said appeared, to my ears, to be exactly the same. His father, like Hannah's and mine, was dead. By a cruel coincidence he had also drowned, in Lake Mjøsa, although he had taken no one with him and it had been an accident, nothing more. He and Kristian's mother had actually divorced some four years before that and Beate Ramsfjeld had married again, to a man who apparently had a good chance of a Nobel Prize in Chemistry, a fact which, when revealed to my mother, led her to claim that Kristian's mother was therefore living in sin, for God had not dissolved the union with her husband and she had not taken the new sacrament after that man's death. It was a complicated business, certainly, and not one that I had any desire to debate with her.

Hannah didn't care that our mother would not be taking the plane from Dublin to Oslo, but I felt sorry for her when I understood what a wonderful experience she was missing out on: the laughter-filled journey northwards with Kristian's uncle and two young cousins, the beautiful church at the heart of Søndre Park that resembled something out of a Walt Disney cartoon, the visit to the Maihaugen and the walks in the countryside around the town itself. If anything, my sister seemed relieved by our mother's absence, but I wished I was not travelling alone to this strange and fascinating country, but that she was there to enjoy six happy days eating pinnekjøtt, fårikål and brunost – all of which tasted better than they sounded – washed down with litres of aquavit and glasses of mjød, which left my head aching in the mornings and thoughts of my new life as an ordained priest in Dublin far behind.

I liked Kristian from the start. He was a thoughtful, intelligent man with a passion for the mountains that surrounded his childhood home. And although he went on to live the rest of his days in Dublin, he and Hannah had long planned to retire finally to Norway, an ambition that would be achieved by neither of them, for he was felled by an unexpected brain tumour only a few days after his forty-second birthday, and of course Hannah's mind began to go only a year after that. But back then, in 1980, they were a glorious young couple, full of life and beauty, enraptured by each other, as deeply in love as any two people I have ever known; that they only shared another twenty years together seems a cruel and inexplicable brutality on the part of whoever decides our fates for us, that entity that I call God but that acts on a whim to destroy our happiness and yet still somehow commands the loyalty of a faithful flock.

But here I was home again, far from the Rondane Peaks and the Peer Gynt Trail, deciding not to visit Mam until the following week as I had no patience for her bitterness when I was still filled by such exultation, but to go westward instead.

I made my way slowly through the six carriages, but it was a Friday afternoon and every student in the city seemed to be heading out of the capital for the weekend. Only when I got to the very last one did I give up hope and allow my shoulders to sink a little in resignation, throwing my case on the luggage rack above the seats and making my way back towards the standing area by the doors. Leaning into the corner, I opened the novel I had started at Oslo airport the previous afternoon, a book about a young man who plans to release all the bears from Vienna zoo, and began to read. It had made the flight pass in what felt like a few minutes; perhaps it would do the same for the train journey.

'Anthony,' said a middle-aged woman with an old-fashioned beehive hair-do seated in a four-seater berth as she beckoned a little boy sitting across the aisle from her. 'Anthony, come over here and sit on my lap and let Father sit down.'

'Don't want to,' said the boy, placing his little finger inside his left nostril. I glanced in their direction, praying that he would be left in peace.

'It's fine,' I said. 'Sure it won't do me any harm to stand for a while. The train will probably clear out a bit after Kildare or Tullamore anyway.'

'Father, come here and take this seat,' called a man old enough to be my grandfather, seated three more rows along, as he stood up and started gathering his possessions: the peeled skin of a banana and a copy of that day's *Irish Independent*, Charlie Haughey's terrible crooked head grinning out from the front page with an expression that said that while he had not quite emptied the pockets of the Irish people just yet, he soon would.

'No, no,' I said quickly, waving my hands at him. 'Not at all. Stay where you are, there's a good man. I'm grand here.'

'Father, will you not take the weight off?' This time a heavily pregnant woman seated near the doors.

'I offered the seat to Father first,' insisted the first woman, raising her voice now so everyone could hear, as if her initial question had given her a proprietary interest over me. 'Anthony, get up right now or you and I are going to have a conversation.' And this time the boy leaped to attention as the heads of the passengers turned to see what kind of terrible child would refuse to let a priest sit down, let alone what sort of mother would permit such disrespect. 'Anthony can sit on my lap. We're only going as far as Athlone, Father,' she said, her tone changing in an instant from fury to obsequiousness. 'He'll be perfectly comfortable until there.'

'Really, there's no need,' I protested, but the child had moved now, dragging himself across the aisle and leaving me with no choice but to take his vacant seat, blushing furiously, embarrassed by this attention, wanting nothing more than to retrieve my case from the rack and run back through the carriages to the far end of the train.

I was on my way to Galway to visit Tom Cardle. I had not laid eyes on him since leaving for Rome at the end of 1977. Throughout my time there, I had written long letters to Tom with news of my life and asking for all the gossip from Clonliffe, where he was now in his final year. *How are you getting on with the language?* he asked me in one reply and I fired off a quick postcard – *Grand, Tom, I've taken to it like an anatra to acqua*. His letters seemed sorrowful and bored; he regretted the fact that we wouldn't get to spend our last days at the seminary together, but said that the Dublin lads always got the best treats as it was still Dubs who ran all the dioceses and everyone knew that they looked after their own. His bitterness surprised and hurt me, for he had seemed pleased for me when I learned of my selection for this great honour. He told me that he had been forced to share a cell with Barry Shand, whose flatulence was legendary, since Barry's cell-mate, a cheerful Kerry boy by the name of O'Heigh, had run off with a girl in his fifth year, providing us with the best bit of scandal we'd had for a long time.

Shortly before his ordination, Tom wrote to tell me that he'd been assigned to the same parish where he had done a final-year placement – 'some godforsaken hole in the arsehole of Leitrim' was the way he put it – and I could almost hear that county's name come spitting from his mouth in disgust, even at a distance of some twelve hundred miles.

I was cheered up enormously, however, when he finally arrived as the new curate in that parish and, after only a gap of a few short months, wrote to say that things were not as bad as he'd expected, that there was a great deal of difference between being a seminarian and an ordained priest, and that there were advantages to his position that he hadn't even imagined before he took it on. Leitrim, he insisted, was a godless backwater and the sheep were more interesting than the people, but he'd developed some new hobbies – he didn't explain what they were – and was starting to realize how this life might not be such a bad one after all. *And the respect we get, Odran,* he added. *It's like we're gods now! Nothing like the way we've been treated for the last seven years.*

His tone was so positive that it came as a great surprise to me when, within a year, he was abruptly moved from Leitrim and relocated to a parish in the Galway diocese. Typically, a new priest would be given three or four years at his first appointment to find his feet. But not Tom; he was moved almost immediately.

Throughout my busy year, throughout 1978, we sent letters back and forth between Ireland and Rome. I confided in him the honour that had been conferred upon me and he wanted to know details, details I could not provide, for a veil of secrecy was drawn over my daily routines. And then came September and he must have written every day, wanting to know what the papers couldn't or wouldn't say, whether the conspiracy theories were true, little knowing that I was in disgrace and as far from the news as he was. This went on through October and November and even until Christmas when things finally began to settle down again in the Vatican. *Tom,* I told him time and again, *Tom, I can tell you nothing. My lips are sealed.*

Playing the big shot, for the truth was that I knew nothing at all, for hadn't I abandoned my post on the fateful night that was the subject of so much global conversation? Hadn't I given in to my baser instincts? Hadn't I shamed myself, allowed myself to be utterly humiliated by a woman whose name I would never even know, and left a good man to die alone?

But back in Ireland, my Roman days behind me, it was time to renew our acquaintance in person and so this weekend had been planned and I had looked forward to it enormously. I'd been working at Terenure College for a couple of months by now and had settled in well. I was getting along with the lads, tried coaching a little rugby, failed miserably and the boys said, *Father, will you not stick to what you know best?* But they were kindly about it and meant no harm and I traded in the tracksuit for the library, where those boys who had the guts to say that they had no interest in sports sat, and this suited me better. The accountancy teacher, Father Miles Donlan, took my place with the rugby team and of course, as things turned out, that was a terrible mistake and one for which the college, and a handful of innocent boys, continues to pay.

Although I almost never talked about Rome and the position that I had been given, the word leaked out somehow and the teachers began to ask questions, but I kept my counsel despite their interest, refusing to pander to their desire for gossip. And when young Harry Mulligan, a bright lad who brought the house down with his tomfoolery playing Bottom in the Christmas production of *A Midsummer Night's Dream*, put his hand up once in the middle of a lesson and said, 'Father, is it true that you were there the night the Pope died?' I was quick off my feet with an answer that made even me smile, despite the solemnity of the question.

'Which pope?'

'Are you a priest?' said a voice to my right and I turned to the little boy seated next to me, well dressed but looking terribly tired.

'I am,' I told him. 'Are you?'

The boy shook his head and I glanced across at the woman by the window with a little girl seated next to her and she smiled; she was the mother, of course, and the children were twins. They all looked alike.

'Ezra,' she said. 'Shush.'

'Don't be worrying,' I said. 'He's curious about this, I expect.' I raised my index finger to my collar, which was feeling a little tight that day, and tapped it, the sound ringing out like a hushed knock against a wooden door.

'He's curious about everything, this one,' she replied, placing her book face-down on the table between us.

'He's young,' I said. 'How old is he, seven?'

'We're both seven,' said the little girl quickly.

'Are you indeed!'

'Our birthdays are December the twenty-fifth.'

'What a day to be born,' I said, smiling at her. 'Do you get double presents?'

She frowned, apparently uncertain what I meant by this, and turned to look at her mother with a quizzical expression on her face.

'We won't disturb you,' said the woman. 'You were reading.'

'So were you,' I said, lifting her book now and examining the cover before tearing a corner from a newspaper on the table and using it as a bookmark, replacing the book the right way up. Her mouth opened as if she wanted to say something and I realized that this had been an arrogant move on my part. Who was I, after all, to tell her how to keep her place? 'Sorry,' I said, embarrassed, but she dismissed my apology just as the boy, Ezra, let out an extravagant yawn.

'He's tired,' I said.

'We've had a long flight. We just want to get home now.'

'Where were you coming from?'

'A visit to my mother and her husband.'

'Your mother and her . . . ?' The phrase struck me as odd, but then I made sense of it. A widow, or divorced. Remarried, just like Beate Ramsfjeld. 'Your mother and her husband,' I repeated, nodding. 'A pleasant trip?'

'A long trip. Six weeks. Too long.'

'Might I ask where they live?'

'Jerusalem,' she said, smiling a little.

'A beautiful place.'

'You've been there?' she asked and there was something in her voice, a foreign twist that I could not easily identify.

'I haven't,' I admitted.

'Then how can you know?'

'I meant it in the sense that I've heard it's very beautiful. I know people who have spent time in the city. I'd like to go myself, one day.' She nodded and stared at me, and for some reason I found myself beginning to babble. 'I haven't been anywhere much, to be honest,' I told her. 'Only Italy. And Norway. I just got back from there, as it happens. Tell me what Jerusalem is like. Is it how I imagine it to be?'

'I don't know what goes on in your imagination,' she said and I laughed, then stopped myself, for perhaps she hadn't meant it as a joke.

'I think of it as being very warm,' I said.

'Ah. The weather,' she replied, nodding. 'Yes. It can be warm. And sometimes it can be wet.'

'Shall I leave you to your book?' I asked, for I had the sense that, unlike her carriage companions, she wanted nothing much to do with me.

'I'm sorry,' she said, relenting a little as she shook her head. 'I'm tired too, that's all. I don't mean to be rude. It was a long flight back. Seven hours.'

'It's a long journey for this pair,' I said, nodding at the children.

'They didn't mind. It was only their second time on a plane so they were excited.'

'Where did they go the first time?' I asked and her expression relaxed, revealing pure white teeth and a smile that might have made a good dog break his chain.

'*To* Jerusalem, of course,' she said.

'I'm not usually this dim,' I told her, embarrassed by my own stupidity. 'I promise.'

I tapped my fingers against the table and she looked out of the window at the passing scenery. I felt awkward, uncertain whether I should pick up my book again.

A hand, tapping my shoulder from behind. The old man from

a few seats back with the *Indo* and the peeled banana. 'I'm going down to the buffet car, Father,' he told me. 'Can I bring you back a sandwich?'

'No thanks,' I told him. 'I'm grand as I am.'

'Ah, sure you'll have a sandwich, Father,' he insisted. 'What do you like, ham or turkey? Or maybe a bit of raspberry jam on a slice of toast?'

'Honestly, I ate lunch before I came on board. You're very kind though.'

He nodded, winking at me, and continued on his way. The woman across the aisle had been watching this exchange and looked, I thought, a little put out that I had been speaking to the mother of the twins instead of her. 'Anthony has a packet of Tayto in his bag,' she told me now. 'You'll have them if you're hungry, won't you?'

'No!' roared the boy in horror and the woman leaned across and slapped him across the arm, hard.

'Be quiet, you,' she said.

'Ah now, there's no need,' I said, upset by this. 'I don't even like crisps,' I added, turning to Anthony, who was looking at me with fury in his eyes as he decided whether or not to cry.

'Well if you change your mind, Father,' said the woman, 'you only have to ask.'

'I won't. But thank you. You're very kind. As are you, Anthony.'

'Does that happen often?' asked the woman opposite me after a few silent minutes had passed, keeping her voice low so as not to be overheard. 'Do people try to feed you wherever you go?'

'Unfortunately, yes,' I said. 'Sure I'd never have to step inside a grocery store if I didn't want to.'

Years later, I would think of this moment whenever I heard the story about Jack Charlton paying for everything he bought in Ireland with a cheque. Sure who would ever cash it? They'd frame it and hang it on the wall. The man never had to put his hand in his pocket once. Now, however, the woman shook her head, an expression on her face that suggested she didn't know why people would behave in such a fashion. I was unaccustomed to such disinterest, intrigued by it, even. This was not the respect that Tom Cardle had spoken of in his letters; if anything, she seemed distrusting of me.

And who, in 1980, ever had cause to distrust a priest?

'Do you call it the homeland?' I asked her, anxious for some reason to lower whatever barrier seemed to exist between us.

'I'm sorry?'

'Israel,' I explained. 'Do you call it the homeland?'

She thought about it for a moment. 'My mother does,' she said. 'And my stepfather. I don't though, no. I've only been there twice. It would seem ridiculous to call it home.'

'You don't like to go?'

'The air fares are very expensive,' she told me. 'I can't afford it.'

'Of course.'

'I saved a long time for this trip. I wanted Ezra and Bina to meet their grandmother.'

'Bina,' I said, smiling at the little girl, who, like her brother, had now fallen asleep. The boy's head, in fact, had slipped on to my shoulder and I had to rotate a little to get him to move away. 'That's a pretty name.'

'It means understanding,' explained the woman. 'And wisdom.'

'And your name?' I asked.

'Leah. Which, appropriately, means to be tired.'

'Odran,' I told her, pointing a finger at myself. 'And I have no idea what that means, to be honest with you. I've always wanted to visit Israel,' I added, which wasn't entirely true as I'd never given much thought to the matter. 'And Sydney. I'd like to see Australia. Someday, maybe.'

She laughed aloud, making the woman on the other side look

over in disgust as if she suspected her of flirting with me. 'Two very different places,' said Leah.

'They are,' I admitted. 'But there's something about the idea of Australia that's always appealed to me.'

'The idea of a place is sometimes better than the reality,' she said, before waving her hand in the air as if to dismiss the idea. 'But this is an argument I have been having with my mother during our visit. The idea over the reality.'

'You can't win an argument with a mother,' I said. 'Trust me, I know all about that.'

'No.'

'You don't like it then?' I asked, leaning forward, for the subject interested me. 'The idea of a Jewish homeland?'

'I have a homeland,' she said. 'Here. Ireland. I wasn't born here, of course, but this is where we came after the war, my mother and I.'

'And your father?' I asked, uncertain why I was asking things that were no business of mine. 'Did your mother meet your father here? Oh no, of course not, how could he have if you came too.'

'She survived,' said Leah simply, looking me directly in the eye. 'He did not.'

'Father, I got you a ham and cheese roll in the end,' said the old man, returning to the carriage at that moment and placing a clear wrapped package before me. I looked up in surprise, the meaning of the woman's words hitting home. 'And a bottle of 7-Up. Do you like the 7-Up? It gives me gas but I can't stop drinking it. And a packet of King. They had no Tayto. The Tayto are better, but they only had the King.'

'I told you Anthony had a packet of Tayto crisps for Father,' said the woman across the aisle.

'Sure what harm if he has two?'

'Anthony, give the Father your Tayto.'

'No!' shouted Anthony.

'Anthony, are we to have a conversation?'

'They're mine!' insisted Anthony.

'Eat up that roll there, Father,' said the old man. 'Can I get you a Kit-Kat for afterwards at all?'

To my astonishment, I found my hand banging down hard on the table before me to shut the pair of them up. It sounded loud and aggressive against the Formica, as startling as Mam banging the saucepan against the table in Wexford had been, sixteen years before. 'I told you I didn't want any food,' I shouted. 'I said I'd eaten before I came on board, didn't I? Were you not listening to me, no?'

The old man reared back in shock; he couldn't have looked more upset if I'd stood up and struck him. Anthony's mother glared at the old man as if this was all his fault. Leah simply watched, quietly. The children next to me woke, startled. I closed my eyes and breathed for a moment.

'I'm sorry,' I said, when I opened them again. 'I apologize. Truly, I'm very sorry.'

'It's all right, Father,' replied the old man, looking down at the floor, unwilling to catch the eyes of the other passengers. 'Don't be worrying about it.'

'How much do I owe you?'

'You don't owe me a thing.'

I decided not to pursue it. 'I'm sorry,' I repeated and he smiled and shook his head and returned to his seat.

'God love him, sure isn't he only trying to be friendly,' said the woman across the aisle, who had obviously decided to turn on me now for refusing her son's Tayto crisps.

If they'd just leave me alone, I thought. All of them. If I could just get a bit of peace.

'You don't like the attention,' said Leah and I shook my head.

'I don't,' I admitted. 'It was easier to remain anonymous in

Rome. Every second person on the street was a priest there. Here, though . . . ah it's a bit much sometimes.'

'They respect you, that's all.'

'But why? They don't know me.'

She tapped a finger to her throat and I nodded, wondering how a small twist of white plastic could inspire so much devotion. I glanced towards the twins: Ezra was asleep against the window now, Bina against her mother's shoulder.

'Can I ask—' I began and she shook her head.

'I'd rather you didn't,' she said.

'All right.'

'It's thirty-five years ago,' she added with a shrug. 'I try not to think of it.'

'Do you succeed?'

'Of course not.'

'And your mother? Your stepfather?'

She leaned forward and shocked me by the sudden abrupt change in the tone of her voice. 'Why do you think you can ask me these questions?' she asked. 'What gives you the right?'

'I'm sorry,' I said, feeling a wave of shame through my stomach. 'I didn't mean—'

'I know what you meant. You want to tell me that there was a reason behind it all. That it was all part of God's plan.'

I shook my head. 'I am as ignorant of God's plan as you are,' I said.

'He doesn't exist, you know.'

'Who?' I asked, frowning.

'God.'

'Ah now,' I said, unsettled by the suggestion, and she smiled a little at my discomfort.

'Don't get me wrong,' she continued. 'The rules you've all made up, the idea of living with kindness and generosity and charity, these are good ideas. And if it makes you happy to dress in black and wear a collar and put your robes on every Sunday, then what harm does it do anyone? But he doesn't exist. How could he? You're fooling yourself.'

She said all this in a perfectly calm tone, as if explaining to a child the rudiments of basic arithmetic or the letters of the alphabet. And I did not know how to respond to her. She who had experienced more of life than I ever would. The train pulled into the next station and she gathered her children up and their belongings.

'I'm sorry if I upset you,' I said.

'You didn't,' she said. 'You couldn't. You should eat your sandwich,' she added as she walked away. 'The old man bought it for you out of respect. And one day that might change. And then there will be no more food for you and your friends. And you will all go hungry.'

I didn't reach Galway until late. Tom had told me that the parochial house could be a little difficult to find so we had arranged to meet at O'Connell's pub on Eyre Square. When I entered, heads turned to stare at me, half-smiles on the faces of the men as I looked around for my double, my twin, the other black-suited man in his mid-twenties, but I could see no priest in the room.

'Odran,' came a call from the side of the bar and there he was, seated in a corner with a pint in front of him and a copy of that day's *Sun*. I was pleased and relieved to see him and tried not to make it obvious that I was surprised to find him wearing jeans and a chequered shirt like any other man might wear. 'What are you like?' he asked, grinning as I approached him. 'Would you take the collar off at least?'

'I won't,' I said, shaking his hand. 'How are you anyway, Tom?'

'Surviving. What will you have?'

'A Fanta.'

'Ah come on.'

'I'm thirsty.'

'Then I know the very thing. Sit down there.' He walked over to the bar and raised two fingers in a practised gesture and a moment later I saw two pints of Guinness landing on the counter with a couple of whiskey chasers. I exhaled slowly, irritated now. Why would no one believe that I was capable of deciding what I wanted to eat and drink?

'So how was it?' he asked as he sat down, the drinks before us, and all I could think was that this must be a strange sight for anyone looking over; I had assumed that we'd meet here and be on our way.

'Is this all right, Tom?' I asked nervously. 'We won't get in trouble?'

'In trouble with who?'

'The bishop.'

He laughed and shook his head as he started to drink, a rich creamy moustache forming above his lip that he wiped away with his fingers. 'Sure if he was to come in, he'd probably stand us the next round.'

'Ah no rounds, Tom,' I said. 'One will be enough for me.'

'The night is young. And so are we.'

'It's been a long week. I'm tired.'

'Of course, your sister's wedding. How was it?'

'Very enjoyable.'

'What's himself like?'

'Great. A really nice fella.'

'Must be nice to have a brother again.'

I hesitated, my pint hovering in the air. It was a vulgar sort of remark, although not meant unkindly.

'Sorry,' said Tom. 'Was that the wrong thing to say?'

'No, no. Not at all.'

He smiled and shrugged his shoulders, glancing across at a

couple of young lads throwing darts in the corner. One must have got a bull's-eye, I suppose, for he leaped in the air, grabbing his friend in delight and spinning him round, and I noticed Tom watching, his expression falling a little. 'So how was it?' he repeated after a moment, turning away.

'The journey down?'

'The Vatican.'

'Political.'

'That doesn't surprise me. The dioceses here are like hornets' nests. I can only imagine what it's like in Rome. And what's the new fella like?'

'The new fella?'

'Himself. The boss.'

'Determined,' I said. 'Ambitious. He wants to change everything while still maintaining the status quo.'

'That'd be some trick. Can you have a laugh with him at all?'

'No.'

'Why not?'

'He's not looking for friends,' I said. 'But he's fierce intelligent. And intimidating too. A little scary, at times. He has a different face for the world than he does for the curia. But then, I suppose he has to. It's 1980, after all. It's a new world.'

'You wouldn't have wanted to stay on with him?'

'A year is all we get, I told you that.'

'But what a year, Odran! You couldn't have picked a better one.'

'I suppose that depends on your point of view,' I said. Perhaps there was a part of me that enjoyed the idea of others thinking that I had been part of the drama. Even the cause of some of it. That I had insights I could not share.

'Do you know what I was doing the night the Pope died?' asked Tom, skulling back his pint like one of those old men who practically lived inside these country pubs.

'Which pope?' I asked, echoing my words to Harry Mulligan in the school.

'The middle one,' he said.

'Go on,' I said. 'What were you doing?'

'I was having an argument with a couple in Leitrim. Parishioners of mine there. They'd come to see me for the marriage class—'

'I have a dread of running one of those,' I said. 'Sure what do either of us know of marriage?'

'The pair of them were the same age as me,' he continued, ignoring my question. 'He was a farmer's son who wanted to be a painter—'

'A house painter?'

'No, a real painter. You know, an artist. Like Van Gogh or Picasso.'

'Ah right.'

'I asked him had he ever shown his work to anyone and he said that he'd had an exhibition in the parish hall a few years before and taken a train to Dublin afterwards to show some of his work to a man who runs some galleries there, only they said he wasn't ready, that his style needed more development. And the girl chimed in then, saying that the Dubs look after themselves and they don't care about the rest of us. You should have seen the cut of her, Odran. All made up as if she was going to a disco, not a parochial house. And the little short skirt on her too.' He gave a little whistle and shook his head. 'Legs that went all the way down to the floor.'

'Sure where else would they go?' I asked and he shook his head, laughing.

'It's a saying, Odran. Did you never hear it? Anyway, she had a bit of a reputation, that one. She was known for being a bit of a goer, but himself mustn't have minded since he was marrying her regardless. So they're sitting there, the two of them, smirking away, and I can tell that they'd rather be anywhere else in the world, and they gave me the usual guff about how they don't see why they can't get married without having to go through all of this palaver and I told them that many couples found it a great benefit to talk through some of the issues of marriage before they walk down the aisle. Household finances, keeping a clean home, the importance of the . . . well, you know, the other business.'

'Sex,' I said, for I could see no harm in using clear words to define what we meant; we were not children, after all.

'Yes, that,' he said, looking awkward, shifting a little in his chair.

'I don't think I'd feel qualified for any of that,' I told him. 'I hope I never have to give those classes.'

'Sure why wouldn't you be qualified?' he asked, surprised. 'Weren't we trained for long enough?'

'Our knowledge is a theoretical one,' I said. 'We don't keep our own finances, the Church does that. We don't clean our homes, we have housekeepers. And sure what do we know of sex?'

'We're not all as innocent as you, Odran,' he said irritably and I frowned, wondering why he was saying such a thing when I had known him since he was seventeen and he had confided in me before that he had never so much as kissed a girl. 'But look, the point is that I could see they were just going through the motions since they had no choice. Father Trelawney, he was my parish priest, he made it clear to them that there'd be no wedding in his church until they took the course and so what could they do but fall in line? Anyway, the whole thing was going dreadful and I wanted to finish up as quickly as possible. But then I tried to lighten the mood a little by saying that one thing this girl didn't have to worry about was changing her name after the wedding.'

'And why was that?' I asked, two more pints being placed on the table before us; he must have ordered them with a wave of his hand without my even noticing.

'Well here's the thing,' said Tom, leaning forward, drinking his whiskey in two swallows before starting in on the second pint. 'Sláinte,' he said, raising his glass. 'The lad's name was Philip O'Neill, all right? And the girl's name, by pure chance, was Rose O'Neill. They were both O'Neills, do you see? No relation of each other, thank God, even if it was the middle of Leitrim where you can marry a hen if the spirit takes you. But an O'Neill was marrying an O'Neill. It happens, I suppose. Especially with a common name like that.'

'Ah right,' I said, nodding and giggling a little, as if this was a great joke. The drink might have been getting to me. I had an empty stomach. I hadn't even been able to look at the ham and cheese roll on the train.

'So I made this joke and the girl pipes up, good as you like, saying it wouldn't matter anyway because she would never change her name after getting married. *What's that?* says I. *Sure you have to take your husband's name, it's the law.* And she laughed at me! She laughed in my face, Odran. She said it wasn't the law at all and that if I wanted she'd bring me in a copy of Bunreacht na hÉireann and challenge me to find where it said such a thing.'

'Well she's right,' I said. 'There's no law. But it's the natural order of things.'

'That's what I told her,' he insisted. 'A woman takes her husband's name. And don't be telling me what they do in Dublin, I told her, I don't want to hear about any of that rubbish. But again she just laughed and said that it didn't matter because she was sticking with her own name after the wedding and that was the end of that. *But your name is O'Neill,* I told her. *Yes,* she said. *What's your point? My point is that you will be O'Neill after you're married so you'll be taking your husband's name regardless.*'

'She must have loved that,' I said.

'Oh she looked furious, the dirty little tart.'

My eyes opened wide in surprise. Had he said what I thought he'd just said? He didn't seem to notice if he had.

'Anyway,' he continued, 'at this point, the boy joins in and says that Rose is perfectly right, that neither of them have any time for this patriarchal society and that they've already discussed it and agreed that once they are married, he will remain Philip O'Neill and she will remain Rose O'Neill. She won't change to Rose O'Neill, those were his exact words. Now can you see the difference there, Odran?'

'Well, not in the names, no,' I said. 'Of course not. But what he means is—'

'Sure I know what he means,' he snapped, raising his voice. 'And then he said, *I will be my O'Neill and Rose will remain her O'Neill. And if we have children they will take both our names.*'

'So the children will be O'Neill-O'Neill?' I asked.

'That's what he told me.'

'What if they have a son named Neil?'

'What?'

I started to laugh and before I knew it the tears were rolling down my face. I'd never heard anything so ridiculous in all my life.

'What are you laughing at, Odran?' asked Tom, but it was difficult to recover, faced with the serious expression on his face. 'Do you think this is a joke? A girl like that making a laugh of me? Making a laugh of a priest?'

'Sure they're young, Tom,' I said, for the drink had surely affected me now and my spirits were high. 'They're just challenging your authority, that's all. It's what young people do.'

'*I*'m a young person, Odran.'

'Ah would you go away, you're not.'

'I'm twenty-five!'

'It's different for us though. We don't get to live as they do. They'll always be younger than us.'

He sat there, furious now. 'I don't know why they even bother to get married if they're going to be modern like that,' he said finally. 'They're just making a farce of the sacrament.'

'Did you tell them that, Tom?'

'I did, but it went in one ear and out the other. They're married now. And I know for a fact that they're using johnnies because the pharmacist told me when I went in to ask about them.'

'You went in to—'

'They should be locked up, the pair of them,' he said, his face turning red with anger. 'I should call the police on them. The pharmacist should be locked up too. They should all be locked up,' he roared now, and I put my hand on the table to settle him.

'Would you calm down?' I said. 'People are staring.'

'Ah,' he said, turning away, practically trembling with anger.

'Why did you tell me that story?' I asked, after a long silence between us.

'Because I wanted you to know that while you were running around Rome having a great time for yourself, I was dealing with the likes of them and it wasn't fair, because I would have liked to have gone to Rome too. I'm not blaming you, Odran, but that Rose O'Neill bitch was right about one thing anyway, that the Dubs have it all sewn up between them and they don't give the rest of us a look-in.'

'Well at least you're in a bigger parish now,' I said, hoping that this might soothe his rage, for I had no desire to spend a week-end listening to Tom Cardle complain. 'You're glad to be out of Leitrim, I'd say?'

And it was now that his face clouded over. 'Don't talk to me about Leitrim,' he said. 'Bloody place.'

And so we didn't. We didn't talk about Leitrim. In fact, it was more than twenty-five years before we ever did talk about Leitrim, and sure by then it was too late.

Chapter Five

1972

I WAS SIXTEEN YEARS old when a family from England moved in two doors down from us, turning half the Braemor Road upside-down with curiosity and disapproval. Newcomers were always the focus of gossip, of course. A German man in his sixties who arrived a couple of years earlier had inspired fevered speculation about where he had been and what he had done during the war. Some claimed that he had served as a guard in a concentration camp, others that he had hatched a plot against Hitler and escaped to Switzerland when his plans had been discovered. Particular disapproval, however, was reserved for the English. Where one family came, after all, others might follow, and this might in turn lead to an invasion, and the feeling was that we'd spent long enough driving the Brits out of Ireland without welcoming them back in with open arms.

Word spread that our new neighbours were a pair from across the sea with two children between them. Mr Grove was a widower with a twelve-year-old son named Colin, who had the guts to tell me one day that he wanted to be a ballet dancer, God love him, while Rebecca Summers, the woman with whom Mr Grove lived, was a divorcée with a seventeen-year-old daughter, Katherine, who wore short skirts and tennis shoes and always seemed to be sucking provocatively on a lollipop. She wasn't especially pretty, if I am to be honest, but she had an air of danger about her, a suggestion that she could be trouble in the right hands at the right time, and I found that an intriguing possibility, more so than Mam did anyway.

'They're living in sin,' declared Mrs Rathley from next door, who had been in tears at the notion of living so close to English people, but who was almost apoplectic to discover that they weren't even married to each other. 'Here in Churchtown! Did you ever think you'd see the day, Mrs Yates?'

'I didn't, Mrs Rathley,' replied Mam, shaking her head sadly.

'This country is going to hell in a hand-basket. You only have to open up *The Evening Press* to see that. There's killings and murders going on everywhere.'

'Killings *and* murders,' agreed Mam. I was in the living room at the front table, being forced to listen to them as I pored over the *Modh Coinníollach*, trying to make sense of it. I would have dearly liked to close the French doors between us for a bit of peace, but Mam wouldn't allow it; she said that solitude would give me ideas and the last thing a boy of my age needed was ideas.

'I thought we'd seen the last of this sort of thing when Sharon Farr moved away,' continued Mrs Rathley. 'But maybe that was just the start of it.'

'Do not mention that girl's name in this house,' said Mam firmly, putting her cup down. 'Little pitchers, Mrs Rathley. Little pitchers.'

I looked up, offended. Was I the little pitcher with the big ears? I was sixteen years old by now and thought that I had progressed past such concerns. But then Hannah was outside playing in the garden – the back door was open too – and I told myself that Mam was referring to her.

'I'm sorry, Mrs Yates,' continued Mrs Rathley. 'But if you ask me, this area started going downhill when the Farrs were allowed to stay. They should have been made to move away.'

I rolled my eyes with the dramatic intensity that only a teenage boy can muster. Sharon Farr was notorious in Churchtown for what she'd done with one of the Spanish students who clogged up the pavements during the summer holidays with their brown skin, beautiful faces and shouty voices, travelling together in packs, screaming twenty to the dozen in their own language, even though they were here to learn English. A lot of families took in a Spanish student as the Church was behind the scheme and I had wanted one badly, a pet of my own, but Mam had refused, perhaps the only time she ever said no to something the priests wanted. 'My home wouldn't be my own,' she said. 'And besides, you don't know what kind of habits they might have.'

The Farrs, however, had taken in two, a brother and sister, and it was said that Sharon Farr had flirted madly with the boy, who was a year her junior but tall and handsome with it, and the boy had flirted right back and the pair of them had been seen one night down by the Dodder river, one atop the other, a story which grew and developed and sprouted wings as it whispered its way from schoolboy to schoolboy. Sharon Farr was a mad thing, we all said. Sharon Farr was up for it, we all said. Sharon Farr would give you everything you asked for and more.

And then the word came that Sharon Farr was pregnant.

Had Mam turned on the six o'clock news and learned that Hannah had made her way to the Phoenix Park and attempted an assassination on President DeValera she could not have been more horrified. 'That girl was trouble, always,' she insisted. 'The way she dallied with all the boys. And I said from the start that it was a bad idea to bring those Spanish students over. I said that, didn't I?'

The drama only grew when Sharon Farr ran off to Spain halfway through her pregnancy – whether she was following the boy or not, no one knew, but we all assumed that she was – and she had neither been seen nor heard from on the Braemor Road ever since. Mrs Farr was now *persona non grata* and walked up and down the road to Super Crazy Prices in Dundrum with her eyes cast to the ground. Father Haughton named Sharon Farr from the pulpit and made sure that her poor parents were there to hear it; I was there myself and can remember the oration he gave, a spiteful, mean bit of belligerence that felt like it came straight out of a Shakespearean play for the depth and purpose of it. I had an image of him rehearsing his lines in the parochial house in front of his housekeeper and her goading him on. The whole thing was a bad business. I look back now and see that there was precious little compassion to be found in the hearts of anyone in those days, particularly when it came to the lives and choices of women, and in that way, if not others, Ireland has hardly changed in forty years.

'Does Father Haughton know what's going on at number eight?' asked Mam, and Mrs Rathley shook her head.

'I mentioned it casually while I was clearing the sacristy after eleven o'clock Mass on Sunday,' she said – Mrs Rathley was one of those women who helped out behind the scenes of the church and whose day was made if she got into a conversation with a priest – 'and he said that he had heard all about it and had spoken to Archbishop Ryan, but there was nothing that could be done.'

'Did he not think of calling the Gardaí?'

'But sure it's not a crime,' said Mrs Rathley. 'Not one that the courts would recognize anyway. More's the pity.'

'And what of our children?' asked Mam. 'Are they to look at this behaviour and come away undamaged? I have Odran and Hannah to think of.'

'Father said he wouldn't give her the sacrament if she came to Mass.'

'Would he give it to him? To Mr Grove?'

'He said he would. He said that the woman had taken advantage of a poor widower's grief.'

'What kind of a person is she anyway?' asked Mam.

'I think we both know what kind, Mrs Yates. There's a word for her sort, isn't there?'

'There is, Mrs Rathley.'

'And we both know that word only too well, don't we, Mrs Yates?'

'We do, Mrs Rathley. Did the priest say anything along those lines?'

'He was very upset by the whole thing, the poor man. He said that women could be terribly predatory when they set their minds to a thing.'

'Or to a man,' said Mam. 'Poor Father Haughton. I'd say he's terrible shook by the whole business.'

'Oh he is. But I don't think threatening to withhold communion from them will do much good. They're not likely to be going to Mass anyway, are they? They're Protestants, the pair of them. So how in God's name will it matter to them?'

'Ah tonight,' said Mam, throwing her hands in the air, for here was the lowest blow of all. 'Is it Paris we're living in now? Or New York?'

I could listen no more. I got up and left.

I was intrigued by Katherine Summers from the start, with her lollipops, her tennis shoes and her short skirts no matter the weather, but barely spoke to her until the afternoon I spied her leaving the Classic cinema in Harold's Cross when I was cycling along towards home. It was a fine day and she was dressed in such a way that she might have taken the eyes out of a blind man, and I glanced up to find out what it was that she had been to see. *The Godfather* was the only film playing. I had never seen it myself but had heard all about it; it had something to do with the Mafia and there was talk in the classroom that there was a scene in Sicily about halfway through that had to be seen to be believed, but at the time it wasn't the type of film that I'd have been allowed to go to see at all. I slowed down my bike as I drew closer, all the better for a look at her legs, and when there was no more slowing down to do without falling off I sped up again and cycled along, satisfied with the negative beginning to develop in my brain that I could develop later and have a good look at.

'Odran Yates, is that you?' came a voice from behind me and I might have gone under a car for the surprise of it.

'It is,' I said, pulling into the pavement and turning to look at her as if I hadn't noticed her at all until that moment, my face flushing red with embarrassment. I wiped a hand across my forehead to pretend it was the heat of the day that was getting to me. 'How's things, Katherine?'

'Things can only get better,' she said, smiling at me and flicking her hair back in a practised gesture. She reached into her bag and extracted one of her ever-present treats, which she held out for me as if I was a puppy dog learning obedience to her. 'Would you like a lollipop?'

I looked at it for a moment, biting my lip. She might have been Eve handing the apple across to Adam in the Garden of Eden for the provocative way she stared at me, a half-smile across her face, her tongue just teasing out between her lips, but there was no question what I would do. The stomach inside me was lurching like I was on a big dipper and I could feel a stirring down below that threatened to make a show of me. I took it off her and popped it in my mouth like Kojak.

'Were you at the pictures?' I asked as we strolled along, me wheeling the bike on my left-hand side so I was walking next to her. I had read somewhere that you should always let a girl walk on the inside so if a car lost control of itself as it came towards you, then you would go under its wheels and not herself.

'I was,' she said. 'It's such a shame there's only one screen. In London most cinemas have at least three.'

'Is it London you're from then?'

'Yes. Have you been there?'

'I've never been anywhere,' I said. 'I went over to the Northside once, but I got in trouble on account of it.'

'The Northside?' she asked, her face crinkling up so that small lines appeared at the top of her nose, her accent reminding me of Anthea Redfern from *The Generation Game*. 'Do you mean across the Liffey?'

'I do,' I said.

'What's it like over there?'

'Not much different to here,' I said. 'Only they're poor and we're rich. And we have the even-number buses and they have the odd.'

'Are we rich?' she asked in surprise. 'I mean, are *you* rich?'

'Compared to them, we are.'

'What does your father do?'

'Nothing,' I said. 'He's dead. He drowned down at Curracloe beach when I was nine.'

'Where's that?'

'Wexford.'

She considered this and I quite admired the fact that she didn't bother to offer condolences. It wasn't as if she had known him, after all; it wasn't as if she really knew me. 'Did he leave you a fortune?' she asked.

'No, but he had the life insurance,' I told her. 'And Mam works in a shop now.'

'What sort of a shop?'

'Clerys on O'Connell Street.'

'Oh yes, I've been there,' she said. 'Wonderful hats. Pricey though. What does she do?'

'I don't know,' I said. 'I've never thought to ask. She used to work for Aer Lingus before she was married, but they said she was too old to go back to them after my dad died.'

We continued along in silence for a while and I tried to think of things to say. I didn't know any girls, except for Hannah, of course, so had no idea what to say to one. I went to De La Salle school and there were no girls let in there. Katherine seemed content with the peace, however, strolling along and occasionally humming to herself, but the quiet still made me feel awkward.

'Was the picture any good?' I asked her eventually.

'Which picture?'

'*The Godfather*.'

'Oh yes,' she said, nodding her head quickly. 'It was awfully good. Terribly violent though. It was all about this Italian-American family who are all gangsters and they're at war with other gangsters and there's enormous amounts of shooting in it, but the men are terribly handsome.'

'Are they?' I asked. 'I wouldn't know.' It seemed important to me, somehow, to make this assertion.

'James Caan is in it,' she said. 'Do you know James Caan?'

'I don't,' I admitted.

'Oh he's just delicious. Bad to the bone, of course, but irresistible. And he has a younger brother who I could just eat with a spoon. I don't know what his name is. But there's someone in it for the boys to look at too. Diane Keaton. Do you know her?'

'I don't know any of the film stars,' I said. 'I don't move in those circles.' I smiled at her, trying to be funny, and she considered this for a moment before throwing her head back and laughing.

'Oh yes, I see,' she said, and for a moment I thought I could have been talking to Princess Anne. 'Oh, that's awfully good. You're a funny little thing, aren't you?'

I frowned, uncertain whether I liked this description of myself.

'Is there a bit in Sicily?' I asked.

'There is,' she said. 'Why do you ask?'

'Someone said something about it to me once.'

'You're thinking about the part where Michael gets married, aren't you? To this sweet little numbskull of a Sicilian girl and she takes her clothes off in front of the camera. She exposes her bosom,' she added in a serious voice before bursting out laughing again. 'I'm surprised the censor over here let it through. Half the audience whooped and hollered, the filthy animals. You'd think they'd never seen a pair of tits before.'

'Ah right,' I said, looking away, sorry I'd brought it up now.

'What was the last film you saw?' she asked me, poking her index finger in my side and making me jump. I had to think about it. It had been that long since I'd been to the pictures.

'*101 Dalmatians*,' I said. 'Mam took my sister and I to the Adelphi to see it before Christmas.'

She laughed again, she seemed to love laughing, and slapped the top of my arm. 'No, seriously,' she said.

'Seriously what?'

'What was the last film you saw?'

'Amn't I after telling you?'

I wondered for a moment whether she was hard of hearing, but then, seeing the expression on my face, she took the lollipop from her mouth and my eyes fixated on the thin sliver of saliva linking her lower lip to the cherry orb and she stopped smiling. 'Oh I'm sorry,' she said. 'I thought you were joking. *101 Dalmatians*. Yes, well. Was it any good?'

'It was great,' I said. 'There's all these dogs, you see, and this awful oul' one who wants to kidnap them and—'

'Yes, I know the story,' she said. 'You must come to the cinema with me some time. We need to broaden your horizons, Odran.

Do you think *Last Tango in Paris* will play in Dublin? They say it'll be banned. It'll be showing at every cinema in the West End. Perhaps we could hop on a ferry and have an adventure.'

I thought my face might explode now. I'd heard all about *Last Tango in Paris*; everyone had. There was not a boy in my school who didn't want to see it. All it took was a mention of butter for the classroom to explode in hysterics.

'Are you blushing, Odran?' she asked, teasing me.

'I am not,' I insisted. 'It's a hot day, that's all.'

'It is, yes,' she agreed. 'Too hot to keep walking. Any chance of a backer?'

'A what?' I asked, looking at her half horrified, half overcome with desire.

'A backer. You know. You cycle, I sit behind you on the saddle. I wrap my arms around your waist so I don't fall off. Come on, it's too far to walk back and I've no money for a bus.'

'All right,' I said, knowing there was nothing I could do. Katherine Summers wanted a backer on my Grifter and I had no choice but to say yes.

It was no easy task to cycle the pair of us along from Harold's Cross to Churchtown and the sweat fairly poured off my back and through my T-shirt as I pushed my feet on the pedals. I hated to think of her having to put up with that, but she didn't seem to mind. Throughout the whole journey Katherine kept her hands firmly attached to my waist, just above my hips, her fingers pressing tighter when we went over bumps, and once, as we soared down the hill on the Rathfarnham Road, I took my feet off the pedals and let my legs stretch out like wings and she leaned forward and wrapped her arms around my stomach, screaming in delight, her fingers connecting before me as her head rested on my left shoulder, the sound of her laughter in my ears. At another, she dug her hands down a little so the fingertips intertwined just beneath my T-shirt, touching my bare skin above my shorts, and I thought I might crash the pair of us into an oncoming number 16. When we turned on to the Braemor Road I saw Stephen Dunne from my own year at school walking along and when he saw the cut of the two of us on the bike the mouth fairly fell open on him and I couldn't resist shouting, 'How are you, Stephen?' and Katherine repeated the same words, mimicking my accent badly, and Stephen, too intent on staring, walked directly into a lamp-post, bouncing back like something out of a Charlie Chaplin film, which made the two of us burst out laughing. As I finally turned into Katherine's front driveway I saw Mrs Rathley coming down the street with her shopping trolley, watching the two of us carefully, but I looked away. Sure none of this had anything to do with her. She could glare all she liked.

'That was fun,' said Katherine, sweeping her hair back and smiling at me as she stepped off. 'Will you take me again?'

'I will,' I said. 'If you want me to.'

She thought about it for a moment and looked me up and down without an ounce of shame. I grew self-conscious of my Penneys shorts and Donald Duck T-shirt. I looked like a child. But something about my innocence must have appealed to her, for she nodded and smiled at me. 'Of course I want you to, Odran,' she said. 'Why wouldn't I?'

Over the days that followed, I noticed that Mam seemed a bit distant with me and I wondered whether Mrs Rathley had told her what she had seen and she was upset about it. She didn't like the new neighbours, I knew that. She didn't like people who lived in sin. She didn't like girls who walked up and down the Braemor Road in short skirts and tennis shoes with lollipops hanging out of their mouths. And she didn't much care for English people who had turned their backs on the Pope, she said, just so a fat old king could marry a strumpet. But what I had on my side, I knew, was her inability to bring the matter up with me in any direct way, for that would be acknowledging that Katherine Summers and I had any acquaintance at all.

'Is everything all right with you, Odran?' she asked me instead and I nodded and said that everything was grand, thanks. 'Are your studies going well?'

'They are.'

'And there's nothing worrying you?'

'Global poverty?' I said. 'World hunger? Nuclear bombs?'

She frowned and shook her head. 'Don't try to be funny, Odran,' she said. 'It's a deeply unattractive trait.'

Which didn't matter to me in the slightest, for it wasn't her that I was trying to attract.

Matters came to a head two weeks later when Mam was supposed to be in Clerys doing a Thursday late shift, which ran from noon until nine o'clock. Katherine was in the back garden with me, stretched out on a deckchair, her legs and feet bare, her toenails painted bright red, her face turned upwards as she appealed to the sun for a bit of brightness, the ever-present lollipop sticking out of her mouth. I was wearing a pair of blue jeans that I'd bought in Michael Guineys on Talbot Street with practically the entire contents of my piggy bank and a Beatles T-shirt because Katherine had already confided in me that by the time she was twenty-one she would be married to George Harrison – 'only the world's most handsome man and terribly spiritual too, not that it matters when you have a face like that' – and I knew that it would appeal to her.

'Don't you ever wish we lived in a sunnier climate?' she asked me. 'I thought London was bad, but Dublin is even worse. We should live in Spain.'

'You need to watch out for those Spanish lads,' I said. 'Just ask Sharon Farr.'

'Who?'

I told her the story. I didn't flinch from the provocative words and I didn't blush either. I'd made an effort over the last couple of weeks to seem more grown up than I felt inside.

'What a filthy little minx,' said Katherine when I was finished. 'I bet he was gorgeous though. They all are.'

'Who?'

'The Spanish boys. Little Miguel or Juan or whatever his name was. Ignacio,' she added after a moment, sounding out the syllables slowly.

'I wouldn't know about that,' I said once again, asserting my rigid heterosexuality. I'd said it about George Harrison too, even though I, who had no feelings in that way at all, had to admit that there was something about his face that was the work of a benevolent God.

'Oh Odran,' she said, shaking her head, 'you do make me laugh. What shall we do? Are we going to sit out here all afternoon or are we going to find some trouble to get into?'

'I don't know,' I said. 'What would you like to do? We could watch telly, but there won't be much on this time of day. *The Sullivans* might be on, I suppose, although that'd make you want to hang yourself from the nearest light fitting. I could make you a jam sandwich if you like.'

'A jam sandwich?' she said, sitting up straight, her elbows on the seat behind her, and taking off her unnecessary sunglasses. 'Odran Yates, you certainly know the way to a girl's heart, don't you? A jam sandwich? Does your mother know you have these impure thoughts?'

I laughed. I couldn't help it. 'Well I don't know what else to suggest,' I said, and the truth was that in my innocence, I didn't.

'I'll tell you what we could do,' she said, looking me directly in the face.

'What's that?'

'You could show me your bedroom. I've never seen it.'

I swallowed nervously, trying to picture what I'd left on the floor up there. My socks? My underpants? My swimming togs that I'd only used the day before and hung out to dry? They had an 'S' on the left buttock which was something to do with the designer but all the lads said it meant *small*. I'd already planned on throwing them away. 'I don't know,' I said. 'It's a bit of a mess up there.'

'Let's make it messier.' She stood up and went through to the kitchen before looking back at me. 'Well, are you coming or do you want me to look around your room all on my own? I dread to think what I might find.'

I jumped up and followed, my heart beating so hard through my chest that I thought it might leap right out and bounce along the kitchen floor, tripping her up and sending her sprawling. I ran up the stairs just as she chose the right door – it wasn't difficult, it said 'Odran's Room' outside, underneath a wooden picture of the Bash Street Kids – and marched inside.

'Well,' she said, looking around slowly. 'So this is your lair. This is where it . . .' – she lowered her voice – 'All . . . goes . . . on.'

'It is,' I said, sweeping a few things from the floor, desk and bed and throwing them mercilessly inside the wardrobe.

'You have a lot of books,' she said.

'I like books.'

'And a violin, I see. How come I didn't know about that?'

'Mam says when I play it, it sounds like a bunch of cats being drowned.'

'Will you play it for me?'

'No.'

'All right, I won't force you. Who's that?'

I looked at the poster on the wall, a big orange dog with an oversized red tongue sticking out of his mouth. 'It's Pluto,' I said.

'Yes, I thought it was. You're something of a puzzle, Odran, aren't you?' she asked, approaching me, and I didn't step backwards.

'Am I?' I asked.

'Have you ever kissed a girl?'

I shook my head.

'Would you like to?'

I nodded my head.

'Well why don't you then?'

And so I did.

'You're doing it all wrong,' she said a moment later.

'Am I?'

'Try it like this.'

I tried it like that.

'That's better. Shall we lie down?'

She lay on my single bed, stretching out, and I lay beside her, uncertain what was expected of me, nervous and frightened despite my growing excitement.

'What is it with you and Walt Disney?' she asked me between kisses.

'What is it with you and dirty films?' I countered and she smiled, pulling me closer to her.

I don't know how long we lay there together, it might not have been for very long, but at some point I started to get the hang of this whole kissing malarkey, for she seemed to be enjoying it even if I could barely do so myself, so intent was I on not doing anything wrong. One of my hands reached up inside her T-shirt and she let me do a little exploring as hers went downwards and did a little exploring of her own. And as much as I was enjoying it, as turned on as I was by the whole thing, I knew that my mind was confused and that I actually wanted her to leave, even if I couldn't say the words out loud to make that clear. I didn't want this at all, not now, not yet, even though there was many the night I'd lain in this same bed and imagined that I did. I was an innocent boy, of course, and these were innocent times. I had grown up in an innocent house. I was half in love with Katherine Summers, but what was it that made me wish that she would stop kissing me, stop touching me with those long slender fingers, that hoped she would just stand up and say something like *Well that was rather nice, can I take you up on that jam sandwich now?* and we could both go back downstairs and play a game of Monopoly instead. I looked at her and her eyes were closed and there was a faint groaning coming from somewhere deep inside her as she rolled on to her back, making it clear that she wanted me to lie on top of her, and I followed her lead, embarrassed by everything that was going on down below, and it was almost a relief – almost, but not quite – when the door opened without warning and there was Mam, home from Clerys with one of her headaches.

The three of us stayed motionless for perhaps twenty seconds until Katherine stepped lightly off the bed, adjusting her skirt and top before reaching into her pocket and holding a gift out for Mam.

'Hello, Mrs Yates,' she said pleasantly. 'Would you care for a lollipop?'

That, if I am recalling these events correctly, was a Thursday afternoon, and to my surprise it was as late as the following Tuesday before Father Haughton arrived at the house. Mam was barely speaking to me, which was perfectly fine as far as I was concerned for I had no desire to discuss what she had seen. I was embarrassed, of course, but I felt no bravado, no sense of accomplishment that I had kissed a girl over and over, wandered my hands across her breasts and allowed her to touch me in a way that no one ever had before; that she had lain on my bed and rolled me on top of her, feeling the firmness of me, where only the loosening of my belt might have led to calamity.

Instead I felt a terrible confusion, not because I was ashamed but because it seemed as if this degree of physicality, which in my teenage daydreams was something I was certain that I longed for, was not meant for me. I was sure that I wanted sex with a girl, any girl, but given the opportunity it had felt somehow alien to my nature. And it wasn't that I wanted a different girl, or a boy – it was nothing like that. I simply wanted to be left alone. To think. To read. To ask the questions of myself that none of my friends or family ever did. I thought of throwing myself in the Dodder – an over-reaction, of course, but such are the extremes one reaches when one is young and lost in bewilderment.

Father Haughton arrived after our tea on Tuesday evening and for the second time in a week I found myself escorting someone from outside our family into my bedroom. When I heard his voice in the hallway I knew that it was me who he had come to see and I felt no sense of outrage or humiliation. The truth was that I welcomed his visit; in this, I was different to other boys of my age, who would have wanted the floor to open beneath them and swallow them whole. But I had trust in this man, complete trust, and I thought perhaps he could help me.

Yes, I trusted him.

'Where will I sit, Odran?' he asked, looking around the room. 'Will I take the chair here and you take the bed?'

I nodded and he sat down at the desk where I often did my homework and looked out of the window at Mrs Rathley's perfect garden next door. He faced me and smiled and I sat on the bed across from him, ashamed, staring at the floor.

How old was Father Haughton then? At the time I thought he was about sixty-five, but looking back I suppose he was probably forty at most. He was a thin man, painfully thin, with sharp cheekbones and eyes that sunk deep into his face.

'Are you well, Odran?' he asked me.

'I'm grand, Father.'

'You're enjoying school?'

'I am, Father.'

'That's good. What subjects are you best at, do you think?'

I thought about it. 'English, I suppose,' I said. 'The reading and that.'

'The reading, yes. And what are you bad at?'

'Geography. And Irish.'

'It's a difficult language.'

'I was never any good at it, Father.'

'I was never any good at it myself. And what harm did it do me in the end? Did you never think of going to the Gaeltacht over the summer to learn it?'

'No,' I said. 'Mam says that all sorts go on there.'

'They do, they do. Lads from all over the country. And girls, too. Getting up to no good. It's desperate, isn't it?'

'It is, Father.'

He sighed and looked around the room, his eyes falling on the photograph of my father that I kept on my bedside table, a publicity still from when he was the Young Covey in *The Plough and the Stars*. Mam had tried to take it away once but I had refused to give it up; it was the one time, the only time, in my life that I stood my ground with her and won. But it was also the only thing in the room that she never cleaned and every week I had to take a piece of kitchen roll and wipe the dust from the top of the frame.

'You must miss him, do you, Odran?' asked Father Haughton, pointing at the picture. 'A man about the house, I mean. A father. You must miss him.'

I nodded.

'I never knew my father, did you know that, Odran?'

'No, Father.'

'Well you know it now. He died a month before I was born.

Took a heart attack as he stood in a queue at the General Post Office, trying to buy a stamp.'

'I'm sorry, Father.'

'Ah sure.' He looked away and sighed, lost in his own thoughts for a few moments, before turning back to me and offering something like a smile. 'Do you know why I'm here, Odran?' he asked.

I shook my head, even though I knew well.

'Your mam thought we should have a little talk. You don't mind, do you? You're willing to have a talk with me?'

'Of course, Father.'

'I was a boy myself once, you know. Don't laugh' – I wasn't laughing – 'but I know what it is to be a teenage boy. It's not the easiest time of your life. All that schoolwork. You're growing up. And then of course, there's the . . . what shall we call them . . . the distractions.'

I said nothing. I made a resolution with myself that I would not speak, I would not offer anything at all, unless he asked me a direct question. I would let him say whatever needed to be said and I would listen and that would be that.

'Do you find yourself distracted, Odran?' he asked and I remained silent, swallowing audibly and shrugging my shoulders. 'Answer me, boy.'

'Sometimes,' I said.

'In what way do you get distracted?'

'Like I can't concentrate,' I suggested, wondering whether this might be the right answer. I thought suddenly of the minutes I spent waiting outside the confession box every Saturday morning where, rather than actually remembering my sins of the previous week, I would use my imagination to think up what I thought the priest wanted to hear. I'd said a bad word. I'd given cheek to my mam. I'd thrown a stone at a boy down the road for no good reason at all.

'And why is it that you can't concentrate, Odran?' he asked, leaning forward with a look of concern on his face. 'Tell me now. This is all just between the two of us. I won't be talking to your mam about it. Nothing said within these four walls will ever go any further. Why can't you concentrate?'

I knew the answer that he wanted, but I couldn't bring myself to say it; it was too embarrassing. 'The telly,' I said. It seemed like as good an answer as any.

'The telly?'

'Yes.'

He considered this. 'Do you watch a lot of telly, Odran?' he asked.

'I do,' I admitted. 'Mam says I watch too much.'

'And is she right?'

'I don't know.'

'What do you watch on the telly, Odran?'

'Whatever's on.'

'But what? Tell me one of the programmes you like.'

'*Top of the Pops*,' I said.

'Oh yes,' he said. 'That's the music programme, isn't it?'

'It is, Father.'

'Do you like the music?'

'I do, Father.'

'Who do you like? What singers?'

'The Beatles,' I said.

'I heard they broke up.'

'They did,' I said. 'But they'll get back together. Everyone says so.'

'Ah sure that'll be grand. Who else do you like?'

'Elton John,' I said. 'David Bowie.'

'Anyone else?'

'Sandie Shaw.'

'Now I know her, don't I?' he asked, his face lighting up. 'She sings in her bare feet, doesn't she?'

'She does, Father.'

He hesitated for a moment and I noticed how that thin neck of his bulged out as he swallowed. 'Do you like that, Odran, do you? Watching her on the telly in her bare feet?'

I shrugged, looking away. 'I don't know,' I said.

'I think you do know.'

'She has some good songs,' I said.

'Does she now? I saw her on the telly myself once, Odran. At the Eurovision Song Contest. Do you watch the Eurovision Song Contest, Odran?'

'I do, Father.'

'Did you see her on it?'

'I did, Father. It was a few years ago now though.'

'And what did you think of her?'

'I thought she was great.'

'Do you want to know what I thought, Odran?'

'Yes, Father.'

'Will I tell you?'

'Yes, Father.'

He leaned forward. 'I thought she seemed like a dirty girl. Like one of these wans with no sense of decency about her. Showing off her bits and bobs for all the world to see. How will she ever find a man to marry her if she carries on like that, can you tell me that, Odran?'

I shook my head. 'I don't know, Father.' I wanted him to leave.

'There's a lot of them about though, isn't there, Odran? Dirty girls. I see them myself, walking up and down the round without an ounce of shame. Sure this parish has gone to hell altogether. I see them at Mass on a Sunday and the way they dress makes it feel like I went to bed in Churchtown but woke up in Sodom and Gomorrah.'

'Both of them, Father?' I asked, chancing my arm.

'Sodom *or* Gomorrah then. Was that a joke, Odran?'

'No, Father.'

'I hope not. Because this isn't a laughing matter. No, it isn't. We're talking about your soul here. Do you realize that? Your eternal soul. You sit there with your pretty little face, like butter wouldn't melt in your mouth, and all the time you're trying to get away from me so you can go downstairs to watch the dirty girls on the telly. I'm right, Odran, amn't I? Look at me, Odran.'

I looked up at him, slowly, and he moved his chair closer. 'You're an awful man, aren't you, Odran?' he asked quietly. 'That face of yours,' he added with a sigh and his hand lifted for a moment to touch me, his fingers stroking my cheek gently. 'I know that you struggle. We all struggle. But I am here to help you with your struggles, lovely boy.' He took his hand away and placed them both in his lap as he looked directly at me. 'Your mam told me what happened with the English girl,' he said after a long pause.

'Nothing happened, Father,' I cried, but he raised a hand to silence me.

'Don't lie to me. I heard all about it from your poor ashamed mother. Imagine you behaving like that in a house like this, where you've always been given the best of everything. And hasn't your poor mother been through enough with the way your father went? And that poor little lad that he took with him, that innocent poor little boy? So don't sit there and lie to me, Odran. Don't tell me that nothing happened, because I won't stand for it, do you hear me?'

'Yes, Father,' I said, feeling anxious now, for his voice was rising and growing shrill.

'I want you to tell me what happened with the English girl, the dirty English girl. Tell me what you did with her.'

I swallowed and tried to find the words. 'She wanted to see my bedroom,' I said.

'Of course she did. And what did she do when she came in here?'

'She looked at my books. And my violin. And my posters.'

'And did she tempt you?'

'Father?'

'Did she tempt you, Odran? Don't pretend that you don't know what I mean.'

I nodded.

'Did you kiss her, Odran?'

I nodded again.

'Did you like it, Odran?'

'I don't know.'

'You don't know?'

'No.'

'How can you not know?'

'I liked it well enough.'

He breathed heavily through his nostrils and shifted on the chair. His thin face had grown flushed now. 'And what did she do then, Odran? Did she show you anything?'

I looked up, willing him to leave me alone.

'Her little titties,' he said and now I noticed how yellow his teeth were. Did he ever clean them at all? 'Did she show you her little titties, Odran? Did she ask you to touch them?'

I felt my stomach sink inside me. What was he asking? 'No, Father,' I said.

'Did she touch you. Did she touch you down there?' He nodded towards my crotch. 'Tell me what she did, Odran. Did she touch you? Did you touch yourself? Did you show her what you've got? Are you a dirty boy, Odran, are you? I'd say you are. I'd say you get up to all sorts in this room, do you, Odran? Late at night. When you think no one can hear you. Are you a dirty boy, Odran, are you? You can tell me, come on.'

I started to cry. I felt the room spinning, as if I was going to faint. He was saying more, lots more, but I didn't hear very much of it. He moved closer to me, sat on the bed beside me now and put his arm around me, pulling me close to him, and started whispering in my ear and telling me how the dirty girls were out to corrupt all the good boys, the pretty boys, and we had to be strong and we should put our faith in each other and find comfort with the people we knew and the people we trusted and he was my friend and wanted me to know that I could trust him and sure wasn't it all a bit of fun and nothing to worry about and I think I did faint then, for when I opened my eyes again I was lying back on the bed, the room was empty, Father Haughton was gone, and the door was closed.

I sat up and stared across at the poster of Pluto, who was watching me with that great big smirk on his face and that obscene tongue of his lolling out like he wanted to lick me off the bed and swallow me whole; a moment later I was on my feet and ripping it off the wall, tearing that bloody dog into pieces and crumpling the bits into my wastepaper basket. I sat down on the bed and thought about things for a long time. And I moved some things to one part of my mind, and other things to another, where they stayed for many years to come. Then I went into the bathroom, washed myself, and went downstairs, where I found Mam crying at the kitchen table.

'Mam,' I said. 'What's the matter?'

'I'm happy, Odran,' she said, looking up at me, her eyes red-rimmed. 'That's all. I'm happy. Father Haughton says it's true, that you do have a vocation. He says that I'm right and that you should be a priest. Did you tell him that, Odran? Did you tell him that you want to be a priest?'

And I stood there at that kitchen table as my mother cried and there I was, little more than an innocent child. And for all the memories that come flooding back when I think of those days, for all the fine detail of these recollections, for the life of me I can't remember what it is I said to her in reply. But I know that it wasn't long afterwards that I arrived at Clonliffe College on the bus while Tom Cardle made his way up from Wexford on his father's tractor.

And Father Haughton? Well, he died a few weeks later. He was crossing over to St Stephen's Green from Dawson Street and wasn't looking where he was going and didn't he only get hit by a number 11 bus on its way to Drumcondra.

Crowds turned out for his funeral. Crowds.

Chapter Six

2010

It won't be for ever, you don't need to worry about that. Just a few years. And then I'll send you back to your school, I promise.

That's what Archbishop Cordington – by now, of course, Cardinal Cordington – had said to me when I sat in the Apostolic Palace in 2006. Four years had passed since then and I was a curate still, in Tom Cardle's old parish, with no sign of a return to the Eden I had once enjoyed. By now, most of the boys I had taught had completed their Junior Certs, their Leaving Certs, and were sitting in lecture halls in Trinity College, travelling by train from Paris to Berlin with a Eurorail pass secured in their backpacks or working with their daddies in banks or property management companies, wondering whether this was it now, whether this was where they were to stay till their own sons were born and reared to take over from them.

One lad had died, a boy I knew only vaguely, killed when he took his car out along the M50 towards Dún Laoghaire while he had drink on him, taking himself, his girlfriend, her sister and her sister's boyfriend with him. The funeral took place in the church at Terenure and the celebrant, the same Father Ngezo who had replaced me four years earlier, spoke in his deep voice of the boy's commitment to the Leinster Schools Cup, a thought which could not have been much comfort to the three sets of grieving parents whose lives he had shattered. Another had reached the final stages of a television talent show and was all over the papers; it was said that he would earn millions over the coming years with the right management. A third had been arrested for an assault on a young girl at a local disco; he swore he was innocent but I remembered that boy's attitude in the classroom, the swagger of him, the privileged vulgarity he cultivated among his entitled entourage, and somehow doubted that peacock's blamelessness. I followed his trial carefully and was glad not to be called as a character witness; he was found guilty, but of course his daddy pulled a few strings and the boy served not a single day in jail for his crime. The judge declared that the boy had a bright future ahead of him and it would be a shame to deny him a second chance; community service was his punishment. One hundred hours. This was the difference between committing a crime south of the Liffey and north. A picture of the boy smirking on the front page of the *Indo* the next day, while the poor girl he attacked was shown walking out of the courthouse in tears, was enough to make you want to take a can of petrol and a match to all those high-walled schools that would see him and his ilk hailed as heroes for once running down 140 metres of grass to plant a ball on a painted white line.

And yet I missed it, for all that. And I desperately wanted to return.

I dreaded to think about the condition that the library, *my* library, might be in by now. Books out of place, authors shelved in the wrong sections. This modern thing that everyone claims to have, the OCD, when it came to the arrangement of the stacks in my library I always thought that I had a touch of that. But it gave me pleasure in the evenings, when the boys were foot-dragging their way home, to tidy that room, to put everything back where it ought to be. It relaxed me. And in my vanity I assumed that whoever was looking after it now would never appreciate my sense of order.

Instead, I had been forced to settle into parish life, some aspects of which, the pastoral aspects, I came to enjoy and even grew better at as time went on. I felt my relationship with God grow in a way that it never had at the school. Prayer became more important to me than keeping order in the stacks. I had more time to myself and I spent much of it in contemplation, recalling the reasons why I had felt suited to the priesthood in the first place. I spent more time with my Bible, trying to scrape the surface of understanding it. I thought about my Church, the things that made me feel proud of it, the things that bothered me about it. And through it all, I felt like a better man, a more worthwhile man, and yet in my selfishness I still longed to go home.

There were three of us in community together: the parish priest, an elderly man named Father Burton, quiet but hard-working. Committed to his vocation. And his two helpmeets, Father Cunnane and I. Father Burton lived apart from us with only his housekeeper for company, a formidable woman who treated him like a child, washing his clothes and cooking his dinners while acting with the authority of a Swiss Guard when it came to unwanted visitors. Father Cunnane and I had no such luxuries, living next door to each other in two small apartments annexed to the church. We didn't get along, the pair of us, and would you believe me if I said that it was not my fault but his? He was younger than me, of course, only in his early thirties, and all the man wanted to talk about was rugby this and soccer that, boxing this and horse-racing that. I swear he would have been better off as the sports correspondent for *The Irish Times* than living as a curate in a North Dublin parish, and he in turn seemed annoyed to be forced to work alongside a man twenty years his senior, showing his contempt for me whenever I displayed an ignorance about the sporting events that so fascinated him.

'What do you mean you don't know who Rafa Nadal is?' he asked in disbelief when he sought my opinion as to whether Roger Federer's armful of Grand Slam titles would ever be beaten. 'He's famous all over the world.'

'Is he a footballer?' I said, teasing him, for I knew full well who Nadal was but his irritation could be amusing to behold. And anyway, I thought calling him *Rafa* was an awful affectation. Were they friends or something? 'Does he play for Man United?'

'He does on his tits,' said Father Cunnane, who liked to say things that he thought would scandalize me. 'He's a tennis player. Spanish lad.'

'Ah right,' said I.

'Are you telling me you haven't heard of him?'

'I don't know much about the tennis,' I said. 'My nephew Aidan is a great fan of Liverpool Football Club though. Or he was when he was a boy anyway.' Whether or not Aidan was still interested in such things was a mystery to me for I had not laid eyes on him since his father's funeral ten years earlier, when he had sat and brooded, displaying little emotion despite the fact that he had been close to Kristian. He had been contemptuous towards me that day, calling me *Father* over and over again with such disdain in his voice that it had upset me, for I had never shown the boy anything but kindness in his life, but I had put his rudeness down to grief. And despite several attempts in the intervening years to reconnect with him, we had fallen out of touch, and whether or not he was still on the sites in London was a thing I did not know.

'Liverpool?' said Father Cunnane in disbelief, practically spitting on the ground, the word poison on his lips. 'Where are we, 1985? Sure Liverpool are long gone. We'll hear no more of Liverpool, not in our lifetimes.'

Father Cunnane, like Tom Cardle, was a Wexford lad, but for some inexplicable reason he followed West Ham United with a passion that bordered on the religious. Posters of the team's players adorned the walls of his small apartment as if he was still a teenager and he was rarely seen outdoors without a claret and blue scarf wrapped around his neck. He came from the Ferrycarrig area, about ten miles from the beach where my father had taken his own life. Once, with drink in him, he told me of his own childhood and teenage years, of how he was a champion swimmer and took part in something called an Iron Man competition, but had received a calling from God and entered the seminary at the age of twenty-two, dropping out of an engineering course at the University of Limerick to undertake the philosophy course at Maynooth instead.

'And this calling,' I asked him. 'How did it come to you?'

'I was taking a walk up Sinnott's Hill one afternoon,' he told me. 'And what did I see in front of me but a burning bush, and then the clouds parted and the voice of the Lord spoketh unto me and said *Would you ever become a priest like a good lad*.' He waited for a few moments, enjoying the baffled expression on my face, before bursting out laughing. 'I'm only yanking your chain, Odran,' he said then, punching me on the upper arm. 'You don't mind me calling you Odran, do you? Sure we might as well go by first names when there's just the two of us. No, I'll tell you now if you want to know. I had no designs on the priesthood at all, to be honest with you. I wasn't even an altar boy when I was a lad. My parents took us all to Mass, of course – sure they had to or no one in the parish would have come into their shop – but it didn't mean anything to me or to them. And the thing is, I was a terrible man for the women and the gargle, I won't deny it, so it never would have crossed my mind to have a life like this. But wait till I tell you what happened. My brother Mark, older than me by a year to the day, he had a motorcycle accident and ended up in Wexford hospital on a life-support machine. No one knew whether he'd pull out of it or not. The doctors said they couldn't even confirm if there was any brain activity going on. But Mark and I had always been fierce close, fierce close, and when things were looking bad I found myself in the hospital one afternoon, distraught mind, the whole nine yards, and I walked past the chapel and thought, sure what harm could it do? So in I went and got down on my knees and said a prayer to Himself up above, and I asked Him would he ever look after Mark and bring him back to us safely, and if He did, then there was surely nothing that I wouldn't do for Him in return. And I felt something, Odran. I swear to God that I felt something move inside me. Deep down in my guts. I knew at that moment that if I wanted my brother restored to me, then I should devote my life to God, to His service, that I should give the women a swerve for ever more, and when I stepped back out of that chapel into the hospital corridor, it was like I had been reborn.'

'And your brother?' I asked, intrigued by this story, for I had never had such a revelation myself; I had simply been told that I had a vocation and had never thought to question it. 'What about Mark? Did he get better?'

'No, he died,' he said, shaking his head, his face shadowing now with a lingering pain. 'It was a terrible thing. He died, the poor fella. But I couldn't go back on my word. But I didn't blame Him for what had happened. And whatever it was that had stirred me in that chapel wasn't going anywhere, so I paid a call on the Bishop of Ferns shortly after that and asked him whether he thought I should do something about it, and he gave me a number to call and so here I am, ten years later. What do you think of that?'

What *could* I think of it? We all came to the priesthood in different ways. It was not for me to question any of it.

'Now tell me this, Odran,' he added a moment later. 'Who do

you fancy for the World Championship this year, Fernando Alonso or Sebastian Vettel?'

One advantage to parish life, I found, was that my days were often more varied than they had been at Terenure, where a rigid timetable was in place throughout term-time, a college schedule that became only a little more tractable during the holidays for those of us who lived on the grounds.

Some days I had meetings with parishioners, others I might have some parish administrative work to look after. There might be a wedding to prepare for on the weekends and a marriage class, God help me, to give in advance of it. One of the elderly parishioners might be sick and require a home visit; there would be last rites to say or a prayer to be offered over a loved one, struggling for breath or wasting away from a disease. On Friday afternoons there were the altar-boy meetings, where the Masses would be divided up among the lads, and on Tuesday afternoons I kept a little time for myself, for I had a weekly visit that I never missed and that neither of my colleagues knew anything about, for they had never shown any interest in where I disappeared off to that day.

Tuesday meant a trip on the bus – easier than driving – and a short walk from the bus stop to Hannah's nursing home, where I would stay with her for an hour while she reeled in and out of sensibility. One day she might recount events from our shared childhood which she remembered without a single forgotten detail; on another she might tell me a story about a woman she had met while she was serving time in Mountjoy, when my sister has never had so much as a conversation with a Garda in her life. She might ask me whether the Taoiseach was outside in the corridor because she had those papers that he was asking for – *you're sitting on them, Odran, would you get up before you destroy them?* I never met Jonas there – we had an agreement that there was no point in him going to visit his mother when I was already by her side – and he usually went on a Wednesday and a Saturday morning, unless he was out of the country on a book tour or away at a literary festival somewhere, and good God that boy seemed to spend more of his time doing both of these things than I thought could be good for him.

Today, however, was not Tuesday. I would not be seeing my sister nor trying to pull her towards a lucidity that evaded her. It was a Wednesday and I was due to see a parishioner of mine, Ann Sullivan, in the afternoon. I knew Ann a little – she was one of a team of four middle-aged women who looked after the flowers in the church and gave it a hoover every morning after ten o'clock Mass – and she had cornered me a couple of days earlier in Spar to ask whether I might have time to see her during the week, and I had said of course. It was obvious by the expression on her face that she had something on her mind.

'I might bring Evan with me,' she said.

'Evan?'

'My young lad.'

'Oh yes.' I had a vague idea of who she meant. Her son, about sixteen years of age, I thought, dragged to Mass against his will every Sunday morning and whose seat would most likely be empty in another year or two. 'Of course. Please do.'

'And my husband, Seánie.'

'How is Seánie these days? I don't see him at Mass very often.'

'Don't start me on that, Father,' she said. 'I have bigger problems right now.'

'Well if I can help at all, I'll be happy to. Shall we say Wednesday at four?'

She nodded; I could see how much it hurt her to admit that there was a family problem and wished that I had more abilities at my job, for whatever it was that was worrying her, I hoped that I could help.

'Can I bring anything, Father?' she asked.

'Bring anything?'

'A few biscuits, maybe? What do you like, the chocolate digestives?'

It was all I could do not to laugh. 'Ah no, you're grand, Ann,' I said. 'Just bring yourselves. I can dig out a few biscuits myself if we get hungry.'

'Right so,' she said, scurrying away.

Sure enough, the doorbell rang at the appointed time and there was Ann Sullivan outside my door, dressed in her Sunday best and with a fresh haircut, with the boy Evan standing by her side, staring at the ground, and no sign of Seánie at all.

'He had to work,' Ann explained as I made a pot of tea. 'A last-minute thing came up on one of my brother's houses. You know he's an architect, don't you, Father? Seánie does a lot of foreman jobs for him.'

I smiled and didn't enquire any further; I didn't believe a word of it. Seánie was one of those men who had no interest in the church, and good luck to him with that, so I hadn't expected him to show up anyway.

'It's good to see you, Evan,' I said, trying to be friendly with him, for there was no reason for either of them to be here unless it was because of the boy.

'Right,' he said, staring at the ground and sliding his runners around the floor as if he was performing a private dance. I watched him, trying to decipher the expression on his face, expecting to see pain there of some sort, for most of the young lads looked half-traumatized these days, as if they'd spent the last couple of years working down the mines or labouring in a Gulag, but I could see none. If anything, he looked quite placid. And bored. It occurred to me that he didn't resemble his mother in the slightest, who was a plain sort of woman, but then I think someone had mentioned to me once – possibly Ann herself – that he was adopted. He was a good-looking boy, with blond hair divided down his forehead like curtains the way they do in the boy bands on the telly. He reminded me a little of Jonas. A younger Jonas. He had that Norwegian look that defined both my nephews, who had taken after their father rather than my sister. I wondered for a moment whether Evan's natural ancestry might not be Scandinavian as well.

'So how can I help you both?' I asked, opening my hands wide. Ann looked away, embarrassed, perhaps regretting having come here at all now.

'It's Evan,' said Ann.

'Actually,' said Evan, looking up now and smiling at me, all white teeth and dimples, 'it's not me at all. It's Mum.'

'So it's both of you then,' I said, grinning, and in fairness to him, Evan allowed himself a small laugh, a bounce in his shoulders, while Ann shook her head, purse-lipped.

'It's not me,' she insisted. 'It's him.'

'It's not,' replied Evan calmly. 'Sure I'm grand.'

'Lucky you,' said I, and Evan looked across at me and gave me a quizzical look, as if he wasn't entirely sure what to make of me.

'What age are you, Father?' he asked.

'Evan, don't ask Father that,' snapped Ann.

'It's fine, I don't mind,' I replied. 'I'm fifty-five.'

'You must take care of yourself, do you?' he asked. 'I would have said late forties at the most.'

I opened my mouth to answer him but could think of nothing to say. I wasn't sure what to do with that comment.

'My dad's the same age as you,' continued the boy. 'But you'd never think it to look at him. He's a fat bastard.'

'Evan!' said Ann.

'Well he is. I'm not saying it behind his back, Father. I've said it to his face. He never stops eating and he doesn't take any exercise. I'm worried that something will happen to him. But he just laughs when I say it. I love my dad, but the fact is that he's a fat bastard and I don't want him to have a heart attack.'

'Evan, would you stop?' said Ann. 'Honestly, Father, I don't know why he comes out with these things. Seánie's not overweight at all.'

'He is,' said Evan with a shrug.

'He's not.'

'He's a house.'

'Is that what you're here to talk about?' I asked. 'You're worried about your dad?'

'That's not it at all,' said Ann, leaning forward. 'That's just Evan being peculiar.'

'All right,' I said. 'Well look, why don't you tell me what brings you here today? Whatever it is, I'd like to be able to help.'

'I can't, Father,' she said, looking away. 'I just can't.'

I closed my eyes for a moment and exhaled. A vision passed before my eyes: the library at Terenure College, a place where I would have given anything to be at that moment. Chaos in the stacks. Someone shelving William Golding's *Rites of Passage* trilogy in the wrong order. Claire Kilroy's novels mixed up with Claire Keegan's stories. It was at moments like this that I wished I was there to fix things, instead of here, having to dig deep to discover some personal problem that I would probably be unable to solve anyway. Why did they come to me anyway, me who knew nothing of life?

'This is a safe place,' I said finally, sounding like one of those American therapists you see on the television programmes. I'd watched Gabriel Byrne in one of them the night before; he was only mighty. I'd watched six episodes without a break. 'You can say what you like in here, both of you. It will stay within these walls.'

Ann drew in a deep breath and seemed to be building herself

up to something. 'Father,' she said finally, sitting up straight and looking me directly in the eye. 'We need to talk about Evan.'

I was taking a sip of my tea at the time and I came close to embarrassing myself; I don't think she knew why I was laughing, but the boy did because he caught my eye and smirked.

'Are you all right, Father?' she asked.

'Sorry,' I said. 'The tea went down the wrong way.'

'There's something wrong,' continued Ann.

'There's nothing wrong,' said Evan. 'Not with me anyway. On the contrary, everything is pretty good right now.'

'On the contrary,' she said, parroting him and shaking her head.

'What's wrong with that?'

'Oh stop it, Evan, would you? You're not impressing anyone.'

The boy looked at me, baffled. 'All I said was *on the contrary*,' he said.

'Just behave,' said Ann.

'I am behaving,' said Evan. 'Father, does it seem like I'm not behaving to you?'

'Ann,' I said, ignoring his question, 'why don't you tell me what exactly has you so worried?'

'Evan has a . . . he has a friend,' she said after a lengthy pause.

I looked from mother to son in bewilderment. Evan had a friend. Well, good for him. Was this something to be worried about? Did I need to alert the *Six One News*?

'A friend,' I said.

'A good friend,' clarified Ann.

'A very, very, very good friend,' agreed Evan.

'You've lost me,' I said.

'They spend too much time together,' said Ann quickly.

'But isn't that what friends do?' I asked, confused.

'Oh come on, Father,' said Evan, his calm demeanour slipping a little; he looked irritated now. 'Don't play dumb.'

'What if I'm not playing?' I asked. Whatever it was, whatever was going on here, I felt that I was handling it right so far. But then I was used to lads his age, I'd worked with them for years. They didn't scare or intimidate me. I knew the cut of them, I knew the smell of them. There was nothing they could say that could shock or embarrass me, no matter how hard they tried.

'It's not right,' said Ann.

'What isn't?'

'Oh for God's sake,' said Evan with a long theatrical sigh, sweeping the hair off his face in a gesture that I suspected he'd spent hours perfecting in the mirror. 'I have a boyfriend,' he drawled in a bored tone of voice. 'His name is Odran. We're hanging out. And there it is. The world hasn't come to an end or anything.'

'Odran is my name,' I said and he simply stared at me, blinking a little in surprise.

'I'm not sure what to do with that?' he replied in that irritating, American manner, turning a statement into a question.

'This Odran boy is a gay,' said Ann.

'It's an adjective, not a noun,' said Evan.

'It's a what?' she asked, turning to look at him.

'You heard me.'

'He's quite open about it,' said Ann, looking at me again. 'Not an ounce of shame.'

'Right,' I said. 'And is this Odran boy in your class at school?'

'God, no,' said Evan, sneering as if this was a terrible insult. I might as well have asked whether he was a member of the Ku Klux Klan.

'But he does go to school? He's not a grown man?'

'Gross. And yeah, of course he goes to school. He's not a . . . I dunno . . . a delinquent or whatever. He just doesn't go to *my* school. He goes to a proper school. You know, one with girls.'

I tried to process this. I will admit, I was confused.

'You don't like your school?' I asked him.

'Of course I don't. The boys are all Neanderthals. All they talk about is rugby, jerking off and pussy.'

Ann gasped and I closed my eyes for a moment so as not to look at her. I might have known boys his age well, but usually, when they said things like this, their mothers weren't sitting right next to them.

'Evan, come on,' I said.

'Sorry,' he said quickly. He shook his head. 'I shouldn't have said that.'

'No.'

'I only meant that Odran goes to a school where the focus isn't like that, you know? Where they're not afraid all the time.'

'You think the boys in your school are afraid?'

'If you'll excuse me, Father, I think they are collectively shitting themselves.'

'About what?'

'About the fact that they're actually smarter than they let on.'

I thought about it. 'I don't get you,' I said.

'The boys in my school are clever,' he explained. 'You know it, I know it. We're a smart group. We've been well educated. We come from good homes. We're smart enough to know that two years from now we'll all be out of school and those boys who are the kings of the rugby pitches right now will spend the rest of their lives processing people's mortgages or working in the same school they're about to leave. They're shitting themselves that their precious little lives are about to come to an end when everyone else's, the ones who didn't have a life in school, are about to begin.'

I nodded. He was right. It wasn't an original observation. I'd witnessed it many times myself.

'But what has this to do with your friend Odran?' I asked.

'Nothing specifically,' he said, after a pause. 'I mean I was just saying he goes to a good school, that's all. You asked whether he was in my class at school. Well, he isn't. That's the short answer.'

'He's a gay,' insisted Ann.

'Would you stop with the *a gay* thing?' said Evan.

'And you've formed a relationship with this boy?' I asked him, ignoring Ann.

'Well, we're not getting married or anything. But yeah. I have.' He hesitated for a moment, as if he was uncertain about whether he wanted to say what he was thinking out loud. 'He's great,' he added finally.

'And you're upset about this, Ann?' I asked, turning to look at his mother, who was staring at the carpet with an expression on her face that mirrored the pain she was presumably feeling inside.

'Well, wouldn't you be?'

I shrugged. 'If you'd asked me that question ten years ago,' I said, 'I might have had a different answer. You know, I have a nephew who's gay.'

'Ah stop it, Father,' she said, waving a hand in the air dismissively. 'You do not.'

'I do,' I replied.

'You do not.'

I wasn't sure how else to put it. 'I do,' I repeated. 'Really, I do.'

'Ah would you get on with yourself. You don't have to say that to make me feel better.'

I turned to look at Evan, who was watching me with interest. 'I really do,' I told him with a shrug.

Jonas had told me that he was gay a couple of years before and I had been uncertain what response he wanted from me at the time. In retrospect, I don't believe that I acquitted myself well in the conversation. I was embarrassed, and slightly ashamed, not just at the idea of Jonas being homosexual but at the notion of him having any sexuality at all. To me, he was still just a boy; to think of him racked with desire for another person, or being desired in turn, hurt a little when these emotions were alien to me and I found myself unwilling to engage with him on the subject. I had tried, of course. I asked him how he knew and he said that he had known since he was nine years old, that the video of a song called 'Pray' by Take That had set off the alarm bells. *You can blame Mark Owen*, he said; I didn't know what he meant by that and didn't want to. I did, however, ask how long he'd been sure about it and he said that two years before, he'd fallen in love for the first time with a boy he knew from college, a visiting student from Seattle to whom he was very close. They had spent all their time together and eventually he had revealed his feelings to this boy in a conversation in the other fella's flat; it hadn't gone well. The boy who he thought was his friend was very cruel when the truth came out, Jonas told me. So cruel, in fact, that it had set my nephew back a considerable amount. I could tell when he told the story that it still hurt and I felt an anger towards a boy who would hurt a young lad, coming to terms with his own sexuality, for no other reason than because Jonas liked him too much. I couldn't imagine what it would be like to have someone tell me that they were in love with me. But if they did, I hoped that I would show kindness towards them, regardless of who they were. I could scarcely imagine a more wonderful thing to hear.

'He's never even had a girlfriend,' said Ann, glaring across at her son.

'How do you know I've never had a girlfriend?'

'Well, I know that you've never brought anyone home for their tea.'

He laughed. 'Mum, boys my age don't bring girls home for their tea any more. Father, did you ever have a girlfriend? When you were my age, I mean.'

I thought about it. There was Katherine Summers, of course. Did she count? 'Sort of,' I said. 'Nothing serious.'

'And did you ever bring her home for her tea?'

'She wasn't really that sort of girl,' I said, trying to imagine Katherine and my mother sitting around a table together, struggling to make conversation with each other over the pork chops, Mam discussing the parish trip to Lourdes, Katherine talking about all the things she'd like to do to Al Pacino if she could get her hands on him.

'Well then,' said Evan.

'I just don't see what you have against girls,' said Ann.

'I don't have anything against girls,' said Evan. 'I have plenty of friends who are girls.'

'Then you should go out with one of them.'

'*You* go out with one of them if it's that important to you,' he replied. 'I'm already going out with someone. I can't go out with two people at the same time. I'm not that sort of boy.'

'Do you see, Father?' asked Ann, appealing to me now. 'Do you see what I have to put up with? He has an answer for everything.'

I nodded and none of us said anything for a few moments. I looked at Evan, whose eyes were roaming around the room, taking in the names of the books on the shelves.

'How's school going anyway?' I asked him. 'Do you know what you want to be when you grow up?'

His lip curled in disdain as he brushed his hair away again. I could tell that he valued any opportunity to do that. 'When I grow up?' he said sarcastically.

'Cut the shit, Evan,' I said, surprising myself, and I could see Ann's eyes open wide and Evan himself looking at me in astonishment. 'Or don't you know? It's fine if you don't. You're young yet.'

'I have ideas,' he said.

'What kind of ideas?'

'Plenty of ideas.'

'Like what? Seriously, I'm interested.'

'I'd like to be a theatre director,' he said. 'It's probably crazy, but that's something I'd like to do.'

'When was the last time you went to the theatre?' I asked.

'Last night.'

I smiled. Good for him. He had me there. 'And what did you see?'

'*God of Carnage* at the Gate. They've decided to take a break from their regular rotation of *The Plough and the Stars, The Shadow of a Gunman* and *The Field*.'

'My father was in *The Plough and the Stars* once,' I told him. 'In the Abbey.'

'Really?' His eyes opened wide; I could see that he was impressed, and in my vanity this pleased me.

'He played the Young Covey. He got great reviews. How was it anyway? This play that you saw?'

'Ah Father,' he said, grinning at me. 'You have to go see it. It had your one from *ER* in it and your man out of *Father Ted*. Dougal. These two awful couples. And their lives were just *empty*. All they cared about was *stuff* and trying to impress each other by how liberal they were. It can't be summed up by *how was it?* It's, like, a work of art, you know?'

'It wasn't a trick question, Evan,' I said. 'I only meant did you enjoy it?'

He shrugged. 'I did.'

'He took this Odran fella,' said Ann.

'And did he enjoy it?'

'He doesn't get theatre,' said Evan, frowning as if he was trying to figure this out for himself. 'He says he feels self-conscious in the silence. He prefers movies. Big action stuff, you know? Bruce Willis. Tom Cruise. All that shit.'

'But did he enjoy it?'

'I think he did.'

'Ann,' I said – time to cut to the chase – 'You're upset about this friendship? Between Evan and Odran?'

'I am, Father. I'm beside myself.'

'Please don't define it as a friendship,' said Evan, irritated now. 'It's not a friendship.'

'You're not friends?'

'Yes, of course we're friends. But that's not what it is. It's a relationship. It probably won't last, we're too young, but we're not like . . . you know, mates or something.'

'Can you put a stop to it, Father?' asked Ann.

'I can't,' I said. 'And if I could, I wouldn't.'

She looked at me in surprise.

'Ann,' I said, smiling at her. 'I don't know what you want from me. Evan is sixteen years old. You are sixteen, aren't you, Evan?' I asked, looking at him for clarification.

'Yes.'

'So he's friends with this boy. They went to the theatre together. They didn't hold up the Bank of Ireland in Dundrum.'

'Father, I *caught* them together,' she cried, her eyes starting to fill with tears. And there she was, Mam walking into my bedroom, Katherine Summers climbing out from beneath me. The offer of the lollipop. Father Haughton being called to see me.

Father Haughton. I felt my stomach turn at the memory of it. He was not someone I ever thought about. I had made a point of trying to forget.

'Ah stop it, Ann,' I said, my voice rising so that I was almost shouting at her. 'Stop it now.'

'Father!'

'Evan, you're a smart lad, I can see it in you. Have you thought about letting your mother meet this Odran lad one day? Going for a coffee together or something?'

He barked out a laugh. 'I'm not sure they'd get along.'

'Well, they won't if you don't introduce them properly, that's for sure. Listen to me, Evan, do you want to speak openly? Do you want to speak honestly? Do you want to, yes or no?'

He hesitated, perhaps surprised by the rise in my temper, but finally nodded. 'I have been speaking honestly,' he said.

'You like boys, am I right? That's where your interests lie?'

He looked away. He turned his face to the wall and stared at a photograph that was hanging there, taken the day before my father died. And there was Mam and Dad smiling at the camera outside Mrs Hardy's rented chalet, while Hannah, little Cathal and I stood in front of them, big cheesy smiles on our faces.

'Yes,' he said finally. 'I do, I suppose.'

'Well then, Ann,' I said. 'You must make your peace with it.'

A long silence ensued. I watched Ann. Her face contorted in a hundred thousand different ways. She looked at me; she turned to look at her son. It crossed my mind to wonder what hardships she and her husband had gone through in an attempt to have a child of their own, and how long it had taken them to find a child to adopt, how arduous a journey that must have been. It was instinctive to her, like it was with all these women, to fight against difference, to seek conformity, because they were terrified, terrified out of their skins what it might mean to be different, but there it was, he had said the words out loud, he could not have been clearer, and fair play to her, she responded in kind.

'All right then,' she said, surrendering, tears forming in her eyes. 'It's a new world, Father, isn't it?'

'It is, Ann,' I said, reaching across to take her hand. 'It is indeed.'

'Can I ask you something, Father?' said Evan as the pair of them left a little later.

'You can.'

'Is it right what I heard? Is Jonas Ramsfjeld your nephew?'

I smiled in my vanity; how I loved the association! 'He is,' I said.

'Wow,' said Evan, shaking his head, suitably impressed. 'What's he like?'

'Smart,' I said. 'Quiet.'

'Is he the only family you have?'

'I have another nephew,' I told him. 'Aidan.'

'And what's he like?'

'Angry.'

He nodded and considered this.

'Jonas Ramsfjeld is a really good writer,' he said, casting weight on every word as if he wanted me to understand how deeply he meant it.

'He is,' I agreed.

'Will you tell him I said so?'

'I will.'

'*Spiegeltent* is my favourite novel ever.'

'Well, that might be pushing it a bit,' I said. 'But it is good though.'

'It's my favourite novel *ever*,' he insisted. 'Does he ever come to visit you?'

'Here?' I shook my head. 'Not often, no. I think the presence of the church next door puts him off. But I see him a fair bit. Why do you ask?'

'No reason,' said Evan. 'Will you tell him I said that he's a really good writer?'

I laughed and said that I would. So why didn't I?

Friday came and with it the meeting of the altar boys. Tom Cardle had been in charge of them for the two years he'd spent in this parish. In fact, he'd looked after the altar boys in all eleven parishes he'd worked in over twenty-eight years as a priest. Eleven parishes! It was unbelievable, really, when you look back. And of course when I took over from him the job landed on my shoulders.

'I can't be doing with those bloody boys,' said Father Burton, who saw altar boys as a necessary evil of the Church, tolerating their presence on the altar but almost never speaking to any of them. 'They're always picking their noses or forgetting what Mass they're supposed to be on.' And Father Cunnane just wasn't interested. He said he had enough to be doing without looking after a bunch of whingeing brats. So that only left me. And anyway, Archbishop Cordington had insisted that I take on the job.

In truth, it wasn't an onerous task. The boys – there were about twenty of them – met at the parish hall every Friday afternoon at four o'clock. They were aged between seven and twelve and were very conscious of the seniority within the group. At the start of every meeting, I would take my place at the top of the hall and they would sit in two rows on either side of me. To my left, the most senior boy, Stephen, would sit, followed by his closest contemporary, Kevin. Between them, they would cast an eye over the younger lads, telling them to be quiet if they started chatting to each other. Both boys had recently turned twelve and I was awaiting their resignations any day now; I could see that they were growing embarrassed by their roles but were loath to let this part of their childhood go. They might have been young, but they had the sense to see that this would be the first of many instances of change in their lives. The boys sat not in order of age but in order of who had joined first. Those seated closest to me at the top of the right-hand row were the youngest, the most junior of all, the most frightened.

There were twenty-three Masses to be organized: three a day, Monday to Saturday, and five on a Sunday. Some Masses – my early-morning ones, for example, could survive on one altar boy; Father Cunnane preferred to have two at ten o'clock so he wouldn't have to clean up the altar after himself; every Mass on a Sunday required three. Don't even get me started on the dramatics of Easter Week or the Christmas celebrations. I'd work my way along the line, each boy would choose the Masses he wanted, and that would be that, we'd say a prayer and go home. Job done.

When I arrived on this particular Friday, most of the boys were already gathered outside the parish hall, huddled together under the awning to keep dry for it was fairly pouring down out of the heavens, one of the most torrential downpours that we'd had in Dublin in a long time and God knows we have a city here not renowned for its sunshine. I ran from my car, my bag held over my head to keep me dry, and took shelter with them, pulling the hall keys out of my pocket and looking around me, feeling a spring of irritation begin to bubble inside that I was to be kept waiting.

'Father Yates,' said one of the boys, Daragh, a middle-ranking lad who sat at the head of the junior row and was all ready to take his promotion to the seniors once Stephen and Kevin bit the bullet and said their goodbyes, 'can we not go inside out of the rain?'

'Sure a bit of rain never hurt anyone, Daragh,' said I.

'Father, you have the keys in your hand!' said another boy, Carl.

'Ah now,' I replied, looking away from them all as the wind brushed the rain in on top of us.

We waited there, the whole lot of us, getting wetter and wetter by the minute, the boys probably catching enough colds to keep them all off school for the next week, and I standing alongside them, at a slight remove, the keys to the hall pressing into my hands. If I wanted to, I could just unlock the door and we could all go inside and get started. We could get out of this biblical rain. But I couldn't. Not yet.

'Father!' said another boy, who had ridiculously long hair and was wearing a T-shirt with no jacket. 'Please. I'm getting soaked.'

I smiled, shivering through the cold, and shook my head. 'Not yet,' I said. 'Any minute now.'

I watched the road, I watched the cars. *Come on*, I thought. And then finally, at last, I saw the black BMW coming down the road at a fair old pace, barely slowing down as it turned into the parish hall, and then the lights went off and I watched as the driver sat there in the warmth of his car, talking on his mobile phone, the father of one of the altar boys, finishing some deal, leaving us all, man and boys, in the cold and the rain as he made his money.

Finally, he clambered out, pressed a button so the car went bip-bip, and ran through the rain towards us, and now, and only now, could I select the right key, insert it into the lock and open the door. The boys scattered inside quickly, shaking the rain off their bodies like shaggy dogs, everyone pulling their seats out, organizing the rows like they always did, and I took my place at the top of the room, taking out the notebook in which I wrote down who was doing what and when, and the man who had kept us all waiting placed a seat in the corner and started tapping messages on that ever-present phone of his. I was about to get started, but before I could he raised his hand and said, 'Sorry, Father, little boys' room,' and stood up to make his way out into the corridor to where the bathrooms were. I sighed and watched as he stopped in the doorway and turned around to stare at me. 'Father?' he said, a bored expression crossing his face.

'I'll be back in a minute, lads,' I said, standing up and following him out to the corridor, waiting there until he was finished. 'That's grand, thanks,' he said when he emerged again, grinning at me. 'I was bursting.'

And then we could go back inside. To the boys.

We could get started now that we were all there, now that these twenty children were gathered and an adult without a collar was in the hall to ensure that nothing bad happened to any of them, that I didn't try to touch any of them, or bring one into a private room to remove his trousers. Now, supervised, I was allowed to say the words 'Monday, six-thirty am?' and Stephen was allowed to say 'I'll take that, Father,' and we could get on with the quick and boring business of organizing which altar boy was serving which Mass.

And for this level of distrust, I had all my old friends to thank. Was it any wonder that I went home every Friday night overcome with shame?

Chapter Seven

1973

In Cambodia, twelve years of bombing by American soldiers finally came to an end. In Texas, the world's best female tennis player, Billie Jean King, beat Bobby Riggs, who had once been the world's best male, in straight sets. In Sydney Harbour, on Bennelong Point, a queen from England came to open an Australian Opera House while its Danish architect stayed away. And in Dublin that same autumn, as the world was warring, playing and building, eighteen boys marched through the gates of Clonliffe College for the first time, putting their childhoods behind them as they took their first steps towards a life that would prove both rewarding and isolating in equal parts; we were making a commitment and in the hard times ahead we would often need to fall back on that commitment for support.

Eighteen boys; no one knew that this was the peak of it. In Maynooth, that number was probably closer to forty, while around the country – from St Finbarr's in Cork to St Joseph's in Belfast, from St Patrick's in Carlow to St John's in Waterford – scores of boys were taking leave of their families with varying degrees of enthusiasm. And this was excluding those who had decided to join a religious order: the Oblates, after all, ran Cahermoyle in Limerick, with its model farm that made the place self-sufficient and fed the lads with the healthiest, freshest produce imaginable; the Vincentians looked after All Hallows; the Redemptorists had Cluain Mhuire in Galway; the Franciscans ran a seminary in Killarney. How many novitiates might there have been in 1973 alone, spread across the thirty-two counties? Three hundred? Five hundred? A thousand? I try to imagine young Irish men making their way towards the colleges now in such numbers and it's like wondering whether life might be discovered on Mars; you wouldn't want to rule out the possibility of it entirely, but it's not something you'd talk about in public either.

Most of our intake were, of course, from Dublin, but we had a few lads from other counties too. George Dunne, whom we called Kirk Douglas on account of the cleft in his chin, came from Kildare, but his grandparents lived nearby in Drumcondra and this had influenced his application. There was a lad from Kerry, Seamus Wells, whose parents had both died the year before and he'd wanted to get away from Dingle entirely so had written to Archbishop Ryan instead of Bishop Casey; Mick Sirr from Cork City said he'd always fancied life in the Big Smoke, and apparently Bishop Lucey had taken such offence that he'd named him from the pulpit as a renegade and a pup.

One of the Dublin boys, Maurice Macwell from Glasnevin, had a terrible stutter, but no one made fun of him for it and he seemed grateful for such common humanity; he told me once that not a day had gone by in his schooling when a boy hadn't laughed at him. The teachers were the cruellest of all, he said; when he couldn't get an answer out quick enough in class, they would shout at him, which would only exacerbate his condition, and eventually he became so frustrated that he spent half his time out in the corridor or on detention.

And then there was Tom Cardle, of course. From Wexford.

We were friendly, if nervous, of each other. The Dubs all hung around together, sometimes to the exclusion of others. The Cork and Kerry lads sized each other up, historical enmities at work there. There was a set of twins, which I thought terribly strange; it only grew more curious to me when it was revealed that they were actually two of triplets, but that their third brother had shown no inclination towards the priesthood at all and was working for Premier Dairies instead. A lad from Templeogue had all the brains and had written a book about Thomas Aquinas that he hoped to publish one day. But the lad from Dorset Street, Conor Smith – well, Conor didn't make it through the first year. His mother wept when she brought him to Clonliffe and wept even more when she came to collect him again. Which brought us down to seventeen.

Of course, we all had different experiences of adjusting to life in the seminary, but in my case, I did not find the change particularly arduous. Perhaps I have given the impression that I was forced into this life, that Mam pushed me down a road that would offer her some consolation without any consideration for my own feelings – and yes, there would be some validity to that – but this does not negate the fact that I knew from the moment I arrived in the seminary that here was a role to which I was well suited. The fact is that I was a believer. I believed in God, in the Church, in the power of Christianity to promote a better world. I believed that the priesthood was a noble calling, a profession filled by decent men who wanted to propagate kindness and charity. I believed that the Lord had chosen me for a reason. I didn't have to search for this faith, it was simply a part of me. And I thought it would never change.

I felt contented in that quiet community at Clonliffe, with a spirit of learning about us, and I did not lie in my bed at night racked with thoughts of Katherine Summers, Ali MacGraw or anyone else. The truth is that I have never felt my soul stirred too violently in this direction; whether this is some deficiency in my mind or my body I do not know. No, that is a lie: there was one occasion, of course, when such matters threatened to engulf me entirely.

Five years later. In Rome.

We woke early, at six o'clock, Father Merriman – the Wasp – calling down the corridor with something resembling a yodel, and we leaped out of bed. We called him the Wasp because he fairly buzzed around the seminary, his hands constantly tapping against each other, emanating a low humming sound.

Each boy had been assigned a cell-mate on our first day and we were expected to share with each other throughout the years ahead, so it was important that we got along. A curtain could be pulled down the centre of the room for privacy's sake; I never bothered with it myself, but occasionally Tom, who could fall into fierce and bewildering storms of anger, would drag it across and I would hear him crying or raging in his bed and dared not disturb him.

I always rose first and would step across to his bed to shake him to life and he would groan and roll away from me, turning his head to the wall.

'Would you go 'way, Odran?'

Looking out of the window, I would usually see Seamus Wells, the Kerry lad, out in the garden, running his laps around the gravelled circumference, for he had been a great man for the GAA back in Dingle, or so he told us, and would have been up for county colours had he not chosen a different path. He ran around that yard two hundred times every morning, then dropped to the ground and off he went with his push-ups and his sit-ups and all sorts of strange movements and I didn't know where he got the energy from. Mick Sirr sneered at him, of course, but what else would a boy from Cork do to a lad from Kerry?

Opening our cell door, I would find a dozen or more boys making their way in their pyjamas down a cold corridor towards the baths, where we would each take a quick plunge to wash away the perspiration of the night, more curtains pulled between each one of us to preserve our modesty, and I was grateful for that, for I was a thin boy and did not want to display my lack of muscle to the other lads and I had even less interest in being confronted by theirs. There were only four baths and the water was tepid, so first in got the cleanest while last in picked up every other boy's filth and probably would have been cleaner staying out of it altogether. I made it my business to arrive in the first group every morning and always chose the same bath out of habit, for it was nearest the tank and generally the warmest; Tom was always last and always complained.

'Get up earlier then, Tom,' I would say and he'd shake his head in disgust.

'Only the animals are up this early in the morning, Odran.'

'The priests are up.'

'Exactly.'

I didn't care for talk like this. The priests who worked at Clonliffe – there were fifteen on staff; senior and junior lecturers in dogmatic theology, moral doctrine, canon law, scripture and Church history – worked hard as they gave instruction to about eighty boys from the fourth to the seventh years while looking after the spiritual needs and recurring crises of those of us in the first to third years. They were, for the most part, decent men, thoughtful and learned, and had done nothing, as far as I could see, to warrant such abuse.

The Wasp was a great favourite of all, for his quick movements and sudden appearances would provoke laughter. Father Prince – nicknamed Harold Wilson for his unusual similarity to the politician and a firm commitment to his pipe, despite the strictly enforced ban on smoking among the seminarians – held a regular music-appreciation society, and he would lose himself in his records while we tried not to laugh at the expression of ecstasy crossing his face. Father Jarvis – Rudolph, for his bright-red nose – cultivated a small vegetable garden that some of the lads helped out in.

The one who interested me the most, however, was Father Dementyev. Already in his late fifties by the time I arrived at Clonliffe, he was the only priest on the teaching staff who was not Irish, having been born in a small town named Kashin, about a hundred miles north of Moscow. He'd been a soldier in the 322nd Rifle Division of the Red Army that had marched into the concentration camp at Auschwitz in January 1945, liberating the seven and a half thousand inmates left to starve by the fleeing Nazi guards. It was not something he spoke of often, but once, during a walk around the grounds, I found myself in conversation with him and he told me how his faith in humanity had been almost destroyed that day and he had wandered around Europe, soul-destroyed, throughout the remainder of the 1940s, before having an epiphany, which he would not describe, in the cathedral at Chartres, and soon after making his way to Ireland, where he enrolled as a novitiate in St Patrick's College, Maynooth. I knew very little of what Father Dementyev had suffered during his impoverished childhood or during the war, I couldn't even guess what effect seeing those skeletal prisoners in Oświęcim would have had on a young man's psyche, but I knew that for Tom Cardle to call him an animal displayed a stupidity on Tom's part that was difficult to condone.

By half past six all the students would be gathered in the Main Chapel to recite our Morning Office of Prime, after which we would be left to pray in silence before Mass at a quarter past seven. Starving, we would then move quicker than we might all day to the refectory, where porridge was served, and big mugs of tea, great platters of toast seeping beads of condensation on to the china plates, and as much butter and jam as we wanted, for didn't the mothers send preserves to the seminary on a weekly basis – we could have opened a store for ourselves with all that we had. But the priests said that food was not there to be enjoyed but simply to keep us alive. Simplicity of diet was important.

And then, dressed in our black suits and hats, our white shirts and black ties, we first, second and third years would make our way out of the building to the bicycle sheds and travel as a group across the city towards the Earlsfort Terrace campus of University College Dublin to continue our undergraduate degree in Philosophy, the first part of a priest's education and the discipline that we needed to master before we could begin to understand Ascetical and Mystical Theology, the doctrine of the Church or the history of the sacred texts.

What a sight we must have been to those businessmen, housewives, schoolboys and schoolgirls walking along the streets, driving in their cars or waiting at bus-stops: a crowd of about fifty black-suited young men cycling two or three abreast, like a swarm of flies, eyes ahead, seated upright, aware of the power of our collective as we took in the admiring glances of the people whom we passed. How they respected us then! How they longed for their own sons to be among our number.

How they trusted us.

I liked UCD well enough, but for me, the adjustment to life there was more difficult than the adjustment to life in the seminary. We were part of the student body – the BA in Philosophy attracted young men and women from around the country who outnumbered us novitiates by three to one – but we were set apart from them in ways that were often troubling.

We could talk to the other students out of courtesy, if a question was directed towards us, but we could not initiate conversation, and a prefect was assigned, one of the lads from the third year, to ensure that we stuck to these rules.

We could not eat with the others; at the morning break, the UCD students gathered in a big canteen that was always full of noise and laughter and music. Posters of Ziggy Stardust and John Lennon were pinned to the walls; flyers for discos and parties. We had a box-room downstairs where we met with our sandwiches and cups of tea, where we said our Grace before meals and our Grace after meals, before heading back upstairs for the rest of the morning's lectures. The Wasp told us that this apartheid existed so we would not be distracted by the worldly nature of the young people; Rudolph said it was so we would not be contaminated by them.

The UCD lads wore their hair long and their beards heavy; they sported bell-bottomed trousers or flared jeans, brightly coloured shirts and tinted glasses. The girls distracted us with their hot pants and knee-high boots. They talked openly of sex and drugs and continued their discussions in the bars around Dublin after class, going to concerts and all-night parties, while we took to our bikes again and cycled back across the East Wall and down the long road that would take us back to Clonliffe, where we would gather in the chapel to recite the Office of Sext and then all five chapters of the Angelus before dinner was served, throughout which one poor unfortunate boy, usually one from the later years, would be propped up at the pulpit and would read to us from G. K. Chesterton, C. S. Lewis or *The Lives of the Apostles*. We were not allowed to talk, of course. We could eat and we could listen. That was the way of it.

Did I miss out on the experiences that my classmates in UCD were enjoying? I did, of course. And from time to time I would feel a desperate longing to join them as they boarded the buses into town, looking forward to a night in the Long Hall or Mulligan's, where they would talk of how they might change the world over pints and shorts, and cosy up to each other, an arm casually slung across the shoulder of the person next to them, a walk to the bus-stop later, a kiss in the night air, a suggestion of more to come. I did, at times. I missed it terribly. There were a couple of lads and a girl or two whose company I sorely wanted to join, for they seemed so full of energy and youth and life, but I never even exchanged a word with any of them. But then I would arrive back at Clonliffe and think no, I'm home again. This is where I am meant to be.

But I was one of the lucky ones, I think now. For that *was* where I was meant to be. There were others who should have been elsewhere, anywhere else. Far away, and the further the better.

We were back in the seminary after lunch for lectures on spirituality, formation and liturgy, and then after dinner we had an hour to ourselves to do with what we would. A few lads might set up a game of hurley in the yard – we learned early on that to suggest a game of soccer was tantamount to toasting the queen; some might take the cloister walk to be alone with their thoughts; some might go to the music room, where there were two pianos and a violin to be found; some might have a nap; some might play billiards or lawn tennis; some might read.

We were allowed books, of course – our families could send them to us – but they had to be approved by the priests in the mail-room before they could make their way to our cells and modern novels were frowned upon. I read Dickens and Trollope, was denied George Eliot, for there was something disturbing, or so Harold Wilson told me, about a woman presenting herself as a man. 'She must have had a mental disorder,' he said, ripping *The Mill on the Floss* out of my hands and tossing it in the nearest rubbish bin. 'A lot of the women do. It's in their blood.' Virginia Woolf was out too, for hadn't she filled her pockets with stones before taking a stroll into the River Ouse, the biggest mortaller of all.

I read the Narnia sequence, which was well received by the priests, for they said that it was a spiritual work although I struggled to see it myself; I thought it was just about a lion, a witch and a wardrobe. A lad from Howth had a full collection of James Bond novels hidden beneath his bed and these were passed around surreptitiously between us; there would have been murder if they'd been discovered, but they never were. Jack Hannigan from Sheriff Street got into terrible trouble when he was caught with a copy of *Portnoy's Complaint,* which Rudolph said was a filthy book and shouldn't be allowed in a Catholic country. He was sent to the Spiritual Director every day for a month until he saw the error of his ways.

A few boys, gathered together in the half-hour free time before dinner, might occasionally discuss the Church itself, although you were seen as a suck if you brought it up first. It had been almost a decade now since the Second Vatican Council had come to an end and there had been great expectations about modern changes in the Church, discussions about celibacy and marriage, all the things which might have made it more attractive to the young and more in touch with the contemporary world. But John XXIII had died before it could be fully implemented and Paul VI showed no signs of wanting to pursue any path towards secularity, although in retrospect he looks like the Great Modernizer in comparison with the Polish and German popes who were to come in the decades ahead and who would do everything in their power to curtail the implementation of the proposals. How different things might have been if they had.

Towards the end of the day, the Canon would give us a homily and sometimes we would practise our Gregorian chant. The Rosary followed, perhaps a Benediction of the Blessed Sacrament, a light supper, and then shortly before nine we would gather one last time in the chapel for the Office of

Compline, to thank God for the blessings of the day and to pray for His continued benevolence towards us.

After that we were sent to our cells and the Grand Silence began. No one could speak from then until when we woke the following morning and there could be no noise at all; running water was an offence and any boy who had not used the lavatory before arriving in his cell was in serious difficulties for the next nine hours if he had a weak bladder.

In reality, we boys did not always observe the Grand Silence as strictly as we should. Most pairs would whisper to each other before sleep fell upon them, talking about their lives back home, the families and friends we missed, our worries about our futures, the things we liked and didn't like about seminary life. Only Kevin Samuels from Pearse Street, who we had christened 'The Pope' on account of how seriously he took every instruction, fully obeyed the Grand Silence, and his cell-mate, young Michael Trotter from Dundrum, would complain that it was like bunking next to a brick wall and that he'd do anything to get a switch, even if it meant sharing with George Dunne, who might have looked like a movie star but barely washed from one end of the week to the other.

It was hard; of course it was. It was regimented. It was like being in the army at times, or what I imagined being in the army would have been like. Perhaps Father Dementyev would have set me straight on that comparison. But it suited me. It suited me very well indeed. However, it didn't suit Tom Cardle. Poor lad, he hated every minute of it.

The confrontation happened on February the fourteenth. I remember the date well, for not only was it my birthday, but there'd been a bit of scandal earlier in the day when one of the boys two years ahead of us received three Valentine's cards in the post. To receive one was astonishing, to receive two was unheard of, but to receive three? No one could quite believe it. He wasn't even much to look at, and had no life outside the seminary as far as any of us knew. There was talk that his sister had got her friends to send them as a joke, but the poor lad had been mortified by the attention and he got called Casanova for the next few weeks, until the joke wore thin and we found better things to gossip about.

Tom had been in a bad mood since waking. He'd still been in bed when I came back from my bath at a quarter past six and only shifted himself when I told him that he'd be late for Morning Office if he didn't get up and dressed. I could see dark patches under his eyes; he probably hadn't fallen asleep until very late, and he barely acknowledged me as he looked for his trousers and shirt. Although we were friends and had got along well since the first day that we were put together, I knew it was best to stay out of his way when he was in a mood like this. The curtain had been pulled between us the night before and he'd been playing with himself without an ounce of shame; I could hear every turn he made, every groan of pain or ecstasy, the tears that had followed, and he didn't even look at me as he picked up a handful of tissues that had fallen to the floor by his bed before he had finally fallen asleep.

'Are you all right, Tom?' I asked, opening the window, dreading to think what one of the priests would say if he walked in here now and picked up the stale stench in the room.

'Go on up, Odran,' he replied, waving me away. 'I'll follow in a few minutes.'

I didn't see him at Morning Office, although there he was, marching in line with everyone else for communion at the quarter-past-seven Mass. He sat on his own over breakfast, his head bowed low over his porridge, shovelling spoonfuls into his mouth as if he hadn't eaten for a month. We were not due at UCD that day and a retreat of sorts had been planned among the seminarians where our year would gather with one of the priests and discussions on any topic, within reason, could take place. When we walked into the classroom I had a sense from the expression on Tom's face that something unpleasant might be about to happen and my stomach contorted with apprehension. I don't know why exactly, but I felt a sense of obligation to him; we were cell-mates and should never let each other down. That was my belief anyway, even if it wasn't his.

Our instructor that day was a mild-mannered priest from Laois named Father Slevin. A discussion was taking place about the role of women in the Church – as far as I could tell this seemed to be restricted at the time to arranging flowers on the altar, cleaning the sacristy and laundering the priests' robes – and one of the lads, I think it was Michael Trotter, put his hand up and asked Father Slevin whether he thought the day would ever come when a priest might be allowed to marry. A great stirring went around us all and we jeered at Michael. To suggest an interest in the opposite sex was to leave yourself open to ridicule, but he was a tough enough lad and simply grinned at us and told us to behave or he'd put manners on us in the cloister walk later. Father Slevin saw no harm in the question though and began a discussion on theology and the place of women in Church history, how important they had been from the Virgin Mary on down. He made what I think was supposed to be a joke about the fact that there had never been a priest in the history of the Catholic Church who did not have a woman for a mother, but no, he told us, priests would never be allowed to marry, for they were already married to their vocation and sure wasn't that good enough for all of us.

Michael seemed happy enough with the answer – he hadn't been trying to act the guffaw, it had just been a question – but then Tom raised his hand and I looked across in surprise, for there was generally more chance of my cell-mate joining Seamus

Wells for two hundred laps around the yard at five thirty in the morning than there was of him raising his hand in class.

'The honourable gentleman from Wexford,' said Father Slevin, probably pleased to see Tom participate at last. 'You have a question?'

'I do, Father,' said Tom. 'I have a question about St Peter.'

Father Slevin frowned; we hadn't been talking about St Peter. What had St Peter to do with the discussion of the day?

'Was not St Peter married?' asked Tom, and now Father Slevin smiled, as if this was not the first time that this question had been raised to him.

'Ah that old chestnut,' he said. 'Yes, Tom, you're right, St Peter was a married man.'

'And he was the first Pope?'

'Yes, but what you must remember is that St Peter was already married before Jesus chose him as a disciple. And long before our Lord was crucified and declared that Peter was the rock upon which he would build his church. Many of the apostles were married, in fact. They were not told to renounce their wives. Sure that wouldn't have been fair at all.'

'But still and all,' insisted Tom, 'he was married.'

'He was, yes. We read in Luke, chapter 4, how Simon's mother-in-law was affected with a severe fever and they interceded with him – meaning Jesus – about her. He stood over her, rebuked the fever, and it left her. She got up immediately and waited upon them.'

'Of course she did,' said Tom, sneering for all his worth. 'Sure what else would she do but make a few sandwiches and brew a pot of tea, and her only lifted from her deathbed? But there were others too, weren't there?'

'Others?'

'Popes who were married, for example?'

'I don't think so,' said Father Slevin.

'Ah there were now, come on,' insisted Tom. 'I read about it. It's in the *Encyclopaedia Britannica* so it can't be wrong. There was a lad in the sixth century, Hormisdas was his name, and he was married.'

'Pope St Hormisdas was a widower when he took holy orders,' replied Father Slevin warily. 'There are no rules against that. Father Dementyev, as you probably know, was a widower when he entered the seminary.'

I didn't know that at all and I wondered what had happened to his wife; had she been killed during the war?

'And a good job too, since his son became Pope a few years after him,' continued Tom. 'And what of Pope Adrian in the ninth century? I read that he took his wife and kids to live with him in the Vatican.'

'There was no Vatican in the ninth century, Tom,' said Father Slevin patiently. 'It wasn't fully completed until the sixteenth.'

'Aren't you missing the point a little?'

'I don't know much about Pope Adrian,' said Father Slevin. 'And I don't suppose you do either, except for whatever you've dug up out of a provocative book.'

'And there's lots of other examples,' continued Tom. 'A few other wives along the way. Not to mention all the lovers they had.'

'Now Tom—'

'Alexander VI, the Borgia Pope, he was the father of Lucrezia Borgia, wasn't he? And we all know what she was like. Most of the popes in the Middle Ages were having it away with whoever took their fancy. And did I read that Julius III and the Venetian ambassador – a man, mind you – used to share a bed? So if all these popes could get away with it, why not the priests?'

Father Slevin smiled and shook his head. 'It's very easy to pick names out of antiquity, Tom, when times were very different to how they are today, and bandy them around as if they prove your point. But if you were a little better versed in ecclesiastical history and not just mouthing names and stories that you've read somewhere, then you would know that none of the popes you mention were particularly effective in their role. Yes, Pope Innocent was the father of Lucrezia Borgia. But doesn't that rather prove my point? Would we not prefer a celibate pope to one who produces offspring like that? Sure she was a terrible piece, by all accounts.'

Tom sat back and folded his arms. I turned to look at him; he'd made his point well but had been bested.

'Well what about the housekeepers?' he asked after a few moments, when Father Slevin had already turned back to the board and was using the duster to clear a section for something new.

'The what?' he replied, turning around.

'The housekeepers,' repeated Tom. 'Sure they're up and down the length of the country, aren't they? Sharing the houses with the parish priests, cooking their dinners, baking their cakes, picking up their socks and underpants and throwing them in the wash.'

'Ah now, Tom,' said Father Slevin, putting his duster down on the desk, perhaps to spare himself the temptation of flinging it at the boy's head. 'That's enough of that.'

'You don't think there's a little something going on between the parish priests and their housekeepers, do you? The pair of them alone at night, curled up on the sofa with a cup of tea, a slice of Eccles cake and *Coronation Street* on the telly? You don't think that occasionally one thing leads to another and—'

'Tom!' roared Father Slevin, his face puce now with anger. 'You will stop this talk right now!'

'It's a legitimate question.'

'It is not. You're being deliberately provocative and deliberately obscene.'

'Do you have a housekeeper yourself, Father?'

'Of course not. Sure don't I live here with you boys.'

'But you did parish work at some point?'

'I did,' he replied, looking flustered now. 'When I was newly ordained. But that was a long time ago.'

'And did you have a housekeeper then?'

'Yes, Tom,' he said quickly. 'If memory serves, I did. But it is standard practice and—'

'Just one other question then, Father,' said Tom quietly, 'and then I'll let it go.'

Father Slevin closed his eyes for a moment and from my seat I could hear him exhaling carefully. His cheeks were red and his hands were trembling slightly; he wasn't accustomed to this kind of thing and didn't enjoy it. I didn't like it either. I wished Tom would just go back to sleep like he usually did in class.

'All right then, Tom,' said Father Slevin. 'One more question and then we move on. What's your question?'

'Your housekeeper,' replied Tom, a smirk appearing on his face as he looked around the room to make sure that everyone was listening to him. 'Did you ever fuck her?'

After that, he went missing. He simply vanished. He disappeared for a full week. He had been confined to our cell while the Canon decided what to do with him. On the night of the confrontation, I broke the Grand Silence to ask Tom what he had been thinking.

'Just because you're happy here, Odran,' he said after such a long pause that I wondered whether he was asleep, 'doesn't mean that everyone else is.'

'But there are no gates in this college,' I told him, 'either inside or out. Do you not remember the Canon telling us that when we arrived? You don't have to stay if you don't want to.'

He sat up in bed and stared across at me, tilting his head a little to the side as if he was trying to understand how I could be so naive. 'God love you, Odran,' he said. 'You're a pure innocent, aren't you?'

And when I woke up the next day, he was gone. He must have packed a bag without disturbing me, then made an escape from the seminary through the side door off the cloister walk that was often left unlocked, and what happened to him after that I did not know for many years.

The priests were in a distraction when he didn't show up for breakfast the following morning – his absence hadn't been noticed at either Morning Office or Mass – and I think they were at a loss for how to explain it. A confrontation such as the one that had taken place between Tom and Father Slevin the previous day was practically unheard of. We were respectful boys, quiet lads, we didn't argue, we didn't put up a fight. I look back and am not sure why that was the case; after all, we were also teenage boys. Did we have no life or spirit to us at all?

Canon Robson took me into his office and closed the door behind us.

'Did Tom Cardle tell you that he was planning a flit?' he asked me and I shook my head.

'He didn't say a word,' I told him, nervous now, for I had never been inside this room before and didn't like it.

'He never expressed any . . . dissatisfaction?' he asked, opening his hands wide and smiling at me. He had a face that a smile didn't take to easily. I was uncertain how to answer; I didn't want to betray any of Tom's confidences, but then he hadn't presented them to me as such.

'I think he misses his home,' I said. 'I think he misses Wexford.'

'And which of us do not?' he asked. 'Did you know I'm a Wexford man myself?'

'I didn't, Canon,' I said.

'Born and bred. Did you ever get down to that part of the country, Odran?'

I shook my head; I said nothing.

'You've never been to Wexford?' he asked, narrowing his eyes at me and frowning. How much did he know about my past, I wondered. How much had Mam told him?

'I'm not sure,' I said, hedging my bets.

'You're not sure,' he repeated, smiling. 'Right so. But you'll promise me that you have no idea where Tom Cardle has gone?'

'None, Canon.'

'Then I'll take you at your word.' He sat back in his chair, crossing his hands over his substantial stomach. 'It's not easy, sure I know that,' he said after a moment. 'Coming to a place like this, leaving your friends and your family behind. You're all just young lads. Too young, I think sometimes. I often wonder whether it would not be better to join a seminary at twenty-five instead of seventeen. What do you think of that, Odran?'

'I don't know, Canon.'

'You don't know, Canon,' he said with a sigh, as if he'd give anything for a straight answer. 'And he never spoke to his Spiritual Director about his concerns?'

'I don't think so, Canon.'

'You know that's what he's there for, don't you? For any of you that might question your place here?'

'I do, Canon.'

'All right.' He tapped his fingers on the desk and considered this. 'Is it right what I heard about Tom and Father Slevin?' he asked.

'I don't know what you've heard,' I said truthfully.

'You know exactly what I've heard.'

'He gave him a bit of cheek,' I admitted.

'A bit of cheek? Is that what you'd call it?'

'It wasn't right,' I said. 'Father Slevin is a nice man.'

'You don't think he deserved to be spoken to like that?'

I thought about it. The truth was that there were a few of the priests who had a bitter twist to them, a few who could be sharp with us, a few who seemed to like us too little, or too much, but Father Slevin wasn't one of them. He was kind and I liked him.

'No, Canon,' I said finally. 'No, I don't think he did.'

Canon Robson nodded and played with a pen on his desk, one of those fancy white numbers with the red, blue, black and green inks split into four cartridges. 'And what about you, Odran?' he asked. 'Are you happy here?'

'I am, Canon,' I replied. 'I don't think I've ever been so happy.'

He smiled, pleased by my response.

'Good man,' he said. 'Well look, you get on back to whatever it is you do during your recreation hour. What is it anyway? Are you a hurling man?'

'Sometimes,' I said. 'I'm not much good at it. But sometimes.'

'Well take yourself back over there anyway. You have about twenty minutes left before dinner.'

The talk of the yard was all Tom Cardle. Word of his altercation had spread quickly and it was the only thing that anyone could think about. Most of the lads were in shock about it and there was a feeling of discomfort too, for Tom had introduced an adult element into the classroom that was alien to us, a subject that was not going to play a part in our lives. Some of the older lads said it was all for effect, that he was just trying to play the big man, but I knew there was more to it than that. I took Maurice Macwell aside, the lad with the stutter, and confided in him my worries.

'Tom Cardle is a sex maniac,' I said.

'He's not!' replied Maurice, astonished, wide-eyed.

'He is,' I said. 'He thinks about it morning, noon and night.'

'Jesus, Mary and Joseph,' said Maurice. 'What will become of him, do you think?'

'I don't know.'

Maurice thought about this and stroked his chin. 'And what about you, Odran?' he asked.

'What about me?' I asked.

'Do you think about it?'

'I do not,' I said, insulted; I did, of course I did, but I knew that I didn't as much as some of the other boys. 'Why, do you?'

'Well I've kissed a girl,' he said, standing to his full height and puffing his chest out. 'So I know a little bit about the world.'

'Ah right,' said I.

'She was desperate for it,' he told me. 'Mam said she was a trollop. Have you never kissed a girl then, Odran?'

I had, of course. But for whatever reason, I shook my head. 'No,' I said.

'Would you not like to?'

'I don't know.'

'Is there anything you're not telling me, Odran?' he asked.

I frowned. 'What do you mean?' I said.

'Ah, you know.'

'I don't know. What do you mean?'

'Does Tom leave you alone?'

I stared at him. 'Leave me alone?' I asked him. 'I don't know what you're talking about, Maurice.'

He raised an eyebrow. 'You don't, do you?' he said quietly. 'Well, that answers my question so.'

I felt a sense of frustration growing inside me, as if I was being played for a fool. I was ready to raise my voice to him, but Maurice jumped in before I could.

'Listen, Odran,' he said. 'If Tom doesn't come back, do you think I could take his place in your cell?'

'But sure don't you have your own? You share with Snuff Winters, don't you?'

Snuff Winters. A big, burly monster of a boy from Glenageary; so-called because he had a permanent cold.

'I could do with getting away from him,' said Maurice.

'Why? Do you not get along?'

'It's not that,' he said, looking away. I waited for him to continue, but he didn't seem able. We were close to opening up the conversation or shutting it down entirely; we'd have been better off, the two of us, if we'd had the courage to tell each other the truth. 'It doesn't matter,' he said finally. 'But look, if Tom doesn't come back, you'll keep me in mind for the other bed?'

'But sure Maurice, it's not up to me. You'd have to ask the Canon. But I'd have no objections.'

He pursed his lips. I found myself wanting to take a step back in the conversation. 'Who was she anyway?' I asked him. 'The girl you kissed?'

'Sure that's all behind us now,' he said, looking down at the ground.

'I'm happy as I am,' I said finally.

'I am too,' he agreed.

And that was that. We were all happy as we were, it seemed. All except Tom Cardle.

It was a few days after this that he returned to us. During the recreation hour some of the lads had set up stumps in four corners of the yard with our jackets and we were playing a game of rounders. It was a mixed-year game, older lads and younger lads together with Father Dementyev playing umpire, and we were all getting along great guns when a noise from the driveway alerted us to something out of the ordinary and we put down our balls and tennis rackets – we had no cricket bats – and turned to look.

And there was a sight I'd never forget: coming up the driveway on the passenger seat of a tractor was none other than Tom

Cardle, and seated next to him was a man who could only have been his father, dressed in a countryman's day-suit that had seen better days and with a cap pulled low over his forehead, the exhaust of the tractor pumping its black pollution into the air behind them.

'He's not driven that thing all the way up from Wexford?' asked Mick Sirr, a bemused expression on his face.

'That's how he arrived here in the first place,' I said.

'But sure they're not designed for long journeys,' said Mick, astonished and impressed in equal parts. 'Has the lad never heard of a train, no?'

I made my way towards the driveway and when Tom caught my eye he didn't smile or look sad, he simply put two fingers to the side of his head and gave me that tipping-the-hat gesture to say hello. He was back. He'd been brought back. The poor unfortunate tractor stopped with a defeated rattle of its engine, and father and son climbed down and began to make their way towards the Canon's office.

'Tom!' I called out.

'How are you, Odran?' said he.

'Come along, you wee scut,' said his father and then they disappeared. But before they vanished through the doors I had the chance to see my friend's face: the greenish colour around his right eye, the bruises diminishing at last; the nasty-looking cut on his lower lip. And did I mention that one of his arms was in plaster? Here was a boy who had been beaten black and blue. But he had returned all the same, and may God forgive me but I was glad of it, for I had missed him terribly and didn't want to bunk alone or with Maurice Macwell.

Years later, they used to show that film *The Great Escape* on RTÉ around Christmas, and whenever it was on I always tuned in. You could watch that film a thousand times and it would never grow stale. But there's a lad in it, a Scottish lad named Ives, and he's the life and soul at the start of the picture, kicking up great gas, and then he tries to escape one day and he's brought back and from that minute on the smile is wiped off Ives's face and he's only a shadow of the man he was before. He does whatever the soldiers tell him, he goes wherever they order him to go. He gives no further trouble. He tells no more jokes. He has suffered in the period between escape and return. He has been beaten. He has had the Ives beaten out of him. And then, of course, he climbs the fence when the soldiers are watching, for no other reason than he knows that they will shoot him down and he will suffer no more.

And every Christmas when I watched that film and got to that part, I thought of Tom Cardle and how he was when he came back to the seminary from Wexford. He'd run off, he'd had who-knew-what kind of experiences for a few days. He'd made his way back down to Wexford, where his father had taken his belt and his boots and his fists to him, and then he'd been thrown on the side of a tractor and hauled back up the Dublin road, and from then on he was ready to submit.

He never confronted a priest again in the way that he had challenged Father Slevin. He said his prayers, he practised his Gregorian chant, he got up at six and he didn't complain. The Canon had said there were no gates in this college, either inside or out, but he hadn't counted on a man from Wexford who had once been county boxing champion and insisted that his youngest son was to be a priest. Tom Cardle, that spirited boy who knew this was not the life for him, was not Tom Cardle any more.

He'd had the Ives beaten out of him.

CHAPTER EIGHT

2011

I HAD ARRANGED TO meet my nephew Jonas for lunch in a café bar on St Stephen's Green. I didn't often venture into the city centre any more. To be among crowds while wearing my collar could be a demoralizing experience. I would inevitably be on the receiving end of the sneering stares of self-important students or puffed-up businessmen. Mothers would pull their children closer to them and occasionally a stranger would approach me with some provocative or insulting remark. Of course, I could always go about in lay clothes, hidden behind their ubiquitous disguise, but no, I would not do that. I would take the brickbats. I would suffer the indignities. I would be myself.

As the Luas pulled into the station, I saw him standing outside the concave doors of Dandelion next to a young man of about his own age – twenty-six – who was waving his arms in the air dramatically as he talked. It had been a few months since I had last seen Jonas and his appearance surprised me, for he had shaved his shoulder-length blond hair into a tight buzz-cut which accentuated the sharp Nordic definition of his cheek-bones and the deep cerulean of his eyes. As he saw me approach, he glanced at his watch and flicked a half-smoked cigarette on to the street, stamping it out underfoot. He was dressed in a manner that suggested he'd simply thrown on whatever he'd found in his wardrobe that morning, but I suspected he spent a long time planning how he presented himself to the world. His jeans clung tightly to his long, thin legs; his boots were chunky and looked as if they weighed more than a small Protestant; his shirt sleeves were rolled up, and something that resembled a scarf was thrown casually around his neck. He hadn't shaved in a couple of days and I could see girls glancing at him as they passed; he was a good-looking lad, there was no doubting it. He got that from his father's side of the family.

'Odran,' he said as I approached, smiling half-heartedly, extending his hand. He'd long since stopped prefacing my name with the word *Uncle*. His companion, whose stubble was as artfully designed as my nephew's although it didn't suit him anywhere near as well, turned and stared at me as if I was the eighth wonder of the world.

'It's good to see you, Jonas,' I said, shaking his hand and smiling. I thought about reaching forward and giving him a hug, but he held himself so stiffly that it seemed as if he wanted to keep me at a distance.

'It's a bit early in the day for a fancy-dress party, isn't it?' said the boy beside him, grinning like a chipmunk. It wasn't often that I took an immediate dislike to someone, but here was a cheeky wee pup.

'Shut up, Mark,' said Jonas, turning on him, but without any aggression in his voice, more a tone of boredom. 'He's a priest. That's how he dresses.'

'For real?'

We both ignored him.

'Are you hungry, Odran?' asked Jonas.

'I am.'

'Aren't you going to introduce me?' said his companion.

Jonas hesitated, as if he wasn't sure whether he could be

bothered or not, but finally shrugged his shoulders. 'Odran, this is Mark,' he said. 'Mark, Odran. My uncle.'

The boy stifled a laugh. 'You're kidding, right?'

'Why would I be?'

'Oh,' said Mark, looking me up and down. 'You're really a priest?'

'I am, yes.'

'I didn't know you had a priest in the family,' he replied, turning to Jonas. 'That's so 1950s. You kept that quiet.'

'I keep a lot of things quiet,' said Jonas. 'Anyway, when have I ever talked to you about my family?'

'No, I only meant—'

'Look, there's Bono,' I said, pointing towards the Fusiliers' Arch, and sure enough, there was himself – Himself – trotting out in a pair of red wrap-around shades, raising his hand for a taxi as passers-by rooted in their pockets for their cameraphones. The two boys turned and looked across the road, but a moment later Jonas turned away and checked his watch.

'We should go in,' he said. 'Busy day ahead.'

'Of course,' I replied, hoping that Mark wasn't planning on joining us for lunch. I saw my nephew so infrequently that I didn't want to share him.

'Don't you have somewhere to be?' asked Jonas.

'I do, yeah,' said Mark, looking disappointed. 'Can I call you later?'

'You can do anything you want,' he replied. 'My phone might be off this afternoon though. And for much of this evening.'

'Why?'

'Because I'll have it switched off.'

Poor Mark swallowed – he was crestfallen, God love him – and looked down at his shoes. 'All right,' he said. 'Well, I'll try you anyway. And sure if I don't get you I'll leave you a message and maybe we can do something later on?'

'Maybe,' said Jonas, non-committally. 'Not sure what my plans are at the moment.'

'Well I'm fairly free all night.'

He looked at Jonas with the expression a puppy might have when it's hoping its master will dig a hand in his pocket and pull out a treat. There were none to be had here though; Jonas had nothing to offer.

'Well, nice to meet you, Uncle Odran,' said Mark, nodding in my direction.

'I'm not your uncle,' I said, smiling right back at him. Take that, I thought, as he turned reluctantly on his heels and left. 'Will we go inside?'

The venue hadn't been my choice, it had been Jonas's. When I phoned him, he suggested it as it was close to Today FM, where he'd been doing an interview with Ray D'Arcy a half-hour before.

'How are you?' he asked me as we sat down and ordered two salads, a bottle of Heineken and a mineral water; the beer was mine, I felt I needed something to settle me. On the Luas on the way in, two lads had pushed past me deliberately, each boy hitting one of my shoulders with one of their own. As they walked on, unapologetically, one had coughed and muttered '*Paedophile*' under his breath. I had said nothing, simply found a seat and watched as the stops went by. But it had upset me.

'I'm grand,' I said.

'Still doing the parish work?'

'For my sins.'

'No chance you'll get back to your school?'

I shook my head. 'I think that's a lost cause at this point. The man who took over from me, a priest from Nigeria, has shown an aptitude for rugby and just trained the Senior Cup team. And after last week—'

'What happened last week?'

'Well, we won the Senior Cup, did you not read about it in the paper?'

Jonas shrugged, disinterested. I suppose this meant nothing to him.

'The point is, after a win like that, the job's his for life. I'll never get back in.'

'Do you miss it?'

'I do.'

'There are other schools.'

I shook my head. 'I'm a Terenure boy,' I told him. 'And anyway, it's not my choice. I have to go where the Archbishop sends me.'

He looked doubtful. 'I suppose,' he said.

'There's no suppose about it. That's just the way it is.'

'I used to know a boy who went to Terenure College,' he said, looking around the room, catching sight of himself in the mirror and staring at his reflection for a moment before turning back to me. 'Jason Wicks. Did you know him?'

I nodded. 'I knew Jason,' I said.

'Did you know him well?'

I shook my head. 'Not very well, no.'

'And what about the teacher, what was his name again?'

'Donlan,' I said. 'Father Miles Donlan.'

'And did you know *him* well?'

'I knew him well enough. How did you know Jason?'

'We studied English together at Trinity.'

'Are you still in touch with him?'

'No, he's in prison.'

I opened my eyes wide. This was news to me. 'Prison?' I said. 'For what?'

'He held up an off-licence.'

'He did not!'

'He did.'

'But why?'

Jonas shrugged. 'For the money, I expect.'

'But sure didn't his family have lots of money? Wasn't his father something big in the AIB? I remember he used to be at all the rugby matches, screeching like a banshee at his son. He once hit him a slap after we lost a game and Mr Carroll had to pull him off the boy.'

'His father threw him out long ago. He was into drugs and gambling—'

'His father was?'

'No, Jason.'

'I can't believe that.'

'It's true. That Donlan guy really fucked him up. Sorry.' He waved away the word with an apologetic shrug.

'You blame Father Donlan for what Jason did?' I asked after a moment, trying to take this news in.

'Of course I do. I remember Jason from First Year in Trinity. He was filled up with anger. And then after the trial, Donlan's trial, he went off the boil.'

'They're not . . .' I hesitated to ask the question in case it sounded facetious. 'They're not in the same prison, are they?'

Jonas shrugged. 'I don't know,' he said. 'I don't stay in touch with Jason. Why, do you stay in touch with Donlan?'

'No,' I said.

'How long did he get?'

'Six years, if I remember right,' I said and Jonas laughed.

'Jason got twelve,' he said. 'Funny that, isn't it?'

'I suppose it depends on your definition of funny,' I replied, grateful that the food had arrived for I didn't like the tension in this conversation. 'So I saw you on the *Late Late*,' I said, eager to change the subject.

He smiled, pleased. 'Did you?'

Where had that shy, nervous teenage boy of ten years before gone, I wondered. Disappeared off to another place. Now I could sense nothing but superiority in his attitude. Pure arrogance. A need to succeed and to be seen to be succeeding. He wanted people to notice him. Why was that so important to him when it was obvious that he'd already made a good life for himself?

'I did. You've never thought of taking to the stage, have you? You had himself in pieces.'

'No.'

'Where do you get the confidence at all? When you were a young lad you were awful shy.'

'I fake it,' he said. 'To be honest with you, I was drunk.'

'You were what?'

'Well, tipsy. I'd had a couple in the Stag's Head before going over and then there was a lot of booze in the Green Room. I got stuck in.'

'And Peter O'Toole was on after you.'

'He was.'

'Did you get to talk to him?'

'I did. Briefly.'

'What was he like?'

'I don't know. Old? He didn't seem to know what he was doing there. He asked me for the loan of fifty quid.'

'Did you give it to him?'

'I did not. I'd never see it again.'

'How's the book doing anyway?' I asked.

'It's only been out a week,' he said. 'We shall see.'

I'd been walking up Grafton Street only a few days before and saw what looked like twenty posters for it in the window of Dubray Books, just across the way from HMV. Half of them were of the book jacket, half were of Jonas himself. In the poster he looked like one of those lads from the Calvin Klein ads, his shirt unbuttoned halfway down his chest, one hand in his hair, looking at the camera as if he was surprised to see it there. I couldn't help but wonder what it was like for the writers who didn't look like him. Whether the publishers would even let you in the door these days if you looked like a normal person.

'And are you working on something new?'

'I am.'

'What's it about?'

'This and that,' he said, chewing thoughtfully on a piece of broccoli. 'Hard to describe.'

I sighed. Perhaps he didn't like me. Perhaps he was just rude.

'So, your mam,' I said eventually.

'My mam,' he repeated, nodding.

'I saw her the other day.'

'I know. I was there the day after you. One of the nurses said you'd been.'

'She's not getting any better, is she?'

He looked at me and frowned, perhaps a little surprised by my question. 'She's not going to get any better, Odran, you know that.'

'I mean she seems to be going downhill fast. She didn't know me at all for the first twenty minutes, then she came to and was clear as daylight. Then she asked whether Kate Bush was still out in the hallway, and if she was, would I ever get her an autograph.'

Jonas laughed, despite himself. 'Kate Bush?' he asked.

'That's what she said. Maybe she'd heard her on the radio earlier.'

'Probably. I don't think Kate Bush spends much time out in the Chartwell Home, do you?'

I didn't bother to reply to this. I sipped my beer. I picked at my salad.

'Himself outside,' I said. 'Is he a friend of yours?'

'Who?'

'Mark, was it?'

Jonas frowned. 'What about him?'

'Is he your – what do they call it – your partner?'

'Christ, no,' said Jonas, appalled. You'd swear I'd just accused him of dating Dana.

'Well I don't know, do I?'

'He's just a friend, that's all. Not even that. An acquaintance, more than anything else. He's written a novel.'

'Has it done well?'

'It hasn't done anything yet. He's looking for a publisher. He wants me to help him.'

'Is it any good?'

He shrugged. 'I haven't read it.'

'Do you plan on reading it?'

'Not if I can avoid it.'

I nodded and ate some more of my lunch. I was irritated by his arrogance. Finally, this: 'Did no one ever help you when you were starting out, no?'

'Not a single person.'

I turned my head and looked out of the window at the people going by, mostly people Jonas's age, all chatting away and looking happy in their lives. It crossed my mind that my nephew, for all his success and his money, his film and his book after book after book, was far less contented than any of them.

'And is there anyone special in your life?' I asked, knowing full well that a person who spoke like that was struggling to find happiness.

He smiled at me. 'Do you really want to know?' he asked.

'I wouldn't ask if I didn't.'

'No one in particular,' he said. 'I'm happy as I am.'

I asked no more questions on this subject. It wasn't that I was uncomfortable with Jonas's homosexuality, it was just that I had no experience of it, nothing to compare it to. Was I supposed to act as though it was the same as a man and woman, or was that patronizing? And if I acted as if it was something different, was that insulting? The whole thing was a minefield. You couldn't say anything, that was the truth of it. These days, you couldn't leave the house without offending someone. Jonas and I had never spoken of it in any depth, but he spoke of it occasionally in interviews, grudgingly, as if he couldn't quite understand why anyone would care who shared his bed. And in his four novels – I hadn't read the new one yet – he'd only written about it once and that was the book that had made his name. There was a time when it felt like you couldn't move for people reading it.

The novel is called *Spiegeltent* and is set in Australia, of all places, a country that I know Jonas feels a particular affinity to. It's a short book, the shortest of all his books, and takes place over the course of a single weekend when the central character, a young Irishman exiled there in an attempt to find work, sees an advertisement for a concert to be given by a musician he had vaguely known in Dublin some ten years before. The gig is to take place in a spiegeltent – all wood, canvas and mirrors – in Sydney's Hyde Park a week later. He buys a ticket and in the meantime gets a message to the musician, who recalls their brief friendship, and they arrange to go out afterwards for a few drinks. A lot of the action in the book is taken up with the narrator sitting in the second row of the spiegeltent listening to the musician, staring at him, remembering traumatic events that took place in Dublin many years before, events that the musician was, through a mutual friend, distantly connected to. The narrator is gay and so, by coincidence, is the musician. Nothing has ever happened between them, although the narrator had a deep crush on him long ago, and as he sits there he is transfixed by the delicate nature of the young man's music and his almost overwhelming beauty. The singer is rather small in stature and, despite the fact that he's in his late twenties, his face is that of a choirboy. The narrator is lost. He feels as if every moment of his life has led him to this day. He thinks of all the difficulties he has faced since his childhood, all the dark moments that have bookmarked his life, and they appear to be addressed, one after another, by the young man's songs. Afterwards, they find a bar, they drink beer and the narrator hangs on every word the musician says. He wants to tell him that although they barely know each other, he feels a longing for mutual understanding. He is desperate to touch him. He believes that this musician, with his pale-blue trousers that don't quite go to his trainers, his ankles that are visible as he sits on his stool, his undersized guitar in his hands as he plays his songs, is someone he is supposed to know, but he struggles to say anything, for the strength of his feelings is so overwhelming that he believes that to describe them would make him sound either trite or histrionic and would scare the musician away. He simply cannot win; he cannot say anything for fear of saying the wrong thing. Finally, another man comes over to the table with his girlfriend. They have also been at the spiegeltent. They have also heard the young musician and they insist on buying a round of drinks. The twosome becomes a foursome, although neither of the newcomers has any interest at all in the narrator. Finally the musician says that he should leave, that he has to sing again the following evening and should take care of his throat, and that he must go back to his hotel. The narrator is about to suggest that he walk him there, thinking that he might find words along the way to express how he feels, but no, the young couple, tourists both, by a terrible coincidence are staying in the same hotel as the musician and suggest that the three of them take a taxi together. Within a minute they are all gone, vanished with a suddenness that takes the narrator by surprise, and he is left alone. Later that night, the young musician sends him a text; he asks whether the narrator will come to his show the next night, but he says no, that he's too busy, that he has to work. But this is a lie and instead he sits in his apartment and weeps. He can't bear the physical proximity that a second evening would draw him into. But the following evening, as the concert ends, his feet take him to the spiegeltent once again and it's there that the story takes an unexpected twist.

Look, I'm paraphrasing. I'm doing it no justice at all. What Jonas wrote was a lot better.

'Your mam,' I said again.

'My mam,' said Jonas.

'The doctors told me that things might be taking a fast turn from now on.'

'She has the best care.'

'I know.'

'I see her every week, you know. Twice a week, sometimes.'

'I know you do, Jonas,' I told him. 'I'm not criticizing. You're a good son.'

He nodded.

'Have you heard from Aidan at all?'

'Of course.'

'How is he?'

'He's grand.'

'Is he still in London?'

'God, no. It's years since he was there.'

I looked across at him in surprise. 'What's that?' I asked.

'You heard me.'

'But where does he live if not in London?'

Jonas hesitated and took a sip of his water. 'He hasn't told you?' he asked.

'Would I be asking you if he had?'

He looked embarrassed. 'It's not for me to say.'

'To say where he's living?'

'No.'

'Is it a state secret? Is he in the witness-protection programme?'

'Odran—'

'Why won't you tell me?'

'Because if he wanted you to know, then I suppose he would have told you.'

I stared at him in disbelief. 'But why wouldn't he want me to know?' I asked.

'You'd have to ask him that.'

'Well how can I if I don't know where he is?'

He shrugged and looked bored by the turn the conversation was taking.

'What has Aidan got against me? Would you tell me that at least?'

'You'd have to ask him that,' he repeated.

'I can't believe this,' I said, sitting back in my chair. 'Jonas, would you just tell me where your brother lives, for pity's sake?'

'Lillehammer,' he said finally, relenting.

'Lillehammer? In Norway?'

'Yes.'

'Near your grandmother?'

'Yes.'

I shook my head. 'Well that's the first I've heard of this. You talk then, the two of you?'

'Of course we talk. We're brothers.'

'Well I'm his uncle and I never hear from him.'

Jonas swallowed. 'He's so busy,' he said. 'His business has really taken off. And then there's Marthe and the children.'

'I've never even met them,' I said, feeling tears spring unexpectedly to my eyes. 'Has Hannah met them?'

'Sure he doesn't bring them over to Ireland.'

'Why not?'

'He doesn't like coming home.'

'But why not?' I asked, pushing the point.

He shrugged. 'Like I said, he's very busy.'

I shook my head. 'I don't know what I ever did to him,' I said, hearing the sorrow in my own voice. 'I always remembered his birthday, didn't I? I remembered both your birthdays.'

'I wouldn't take it personally, Odran,' he said. 'Aidan's just not that interested in keeping up old acquaintances.'

'I'm not an acquaintance,' I said, leaning forward angrily. 'I'm his uncle, for God's sake.'

'I wouldn't worry about it,' he said.

'I'm not worried about it. I just find it hurtful, that's all.'

'Well you're not the only one suffering.'

I frowned. What did that mean? Was he talking about his mother? Sure didn't I know that Hannah suffered. And that her two sons did too, seeing the state she'd found herself in.

'I could call him, I suppose,' I said eventually.

'You don't have his number.'

'You could give it to me.'

'I'd have to ask him first.'

He looked at me with something approaching contempt on his face before laughing a little. To my surprise he reached forward, picked up my Heineken, took a long drink of it, and then replaced it on the table with neither an explanation nor an apology.

'I'll ask him if you want,' he said. 'Whatever makes you happy.'

At which point a song I had heard many times on the radio during the last year came over the loudspeaker radio, a calm male voice singing with very little effort but a great deal of power, and I saw Jonas's eyes close for a moment as he put a hand to his abdomen, in the way that someone would if they had just been kicked in the stomach. I knew how he felt. I couldn't have been more wounded had he lifted me off the chair and held me by the neck with one hand while punching me in the face with the other. What had I ever done to these two boys to make them despise me so? How had I ever hurt them?

'No, you're all right,' I said, looking away. 'I'll get it off you another time.'

Aidan.

I remember when Hannah and Kristian first started to despair over his behaviour. He was aged around eleven at the time, a couple of years younger than boys usually go off the rails, and was causing them no end of grief with his temper tantrums and his conduct at school. There'd been an incident with another boy, a boy who had been his best friend until a couple of weeks before. They'd had some sort of altercation and Aidan had fought the lad, knocking out one of his teeth, and it had taken all of Hannah and Kristian's efforts to appease the poor boy's parents. And then he'd slashed the tyres on the car of one of his teachers, a priest who had been at the school for thirty years and was due for retirement a few weeks later. Apparently, the poor man had stepped down early on account of it. For this, Aidan had been suspended, and the principal said that if he didn't mend his ways he was for the high jump.

It was Kristian who phoned me and asked whether I might have a word with the boy and my heart had sunk at the idea of it. I liked Aidan and got along with him well enough, but the truth was that I didn't know him very well. One of my great failings in life – and I realize this as I get older – is what a terrible uncle I was to those two boys. Yes, I was always kind to them and yes, as I insisted to Jonas, I had never forgotten a birthday or a Christmas present, but I had not been truly present in their lives, had never given them a reason to care for me. Despite spending seven years in a seminary with young men, despite thirty years in Terenure teaching teenage boys, I always found it difficult to make a connection with Hannah's children, as if the fact that she had a family life when I did not was a hindrance to me somehow. I'm not proud of this; there have been many occasions when I have told myself to work harder at building a relationship with Aidan and Jonas, but then time passed, too much time passed, and the opportunities faded away. So to be asked to have a word with Aidan when he was giving trouble to his parents was something that filled me with apprehension.

'I can't talk to him any more, Odran,' Kristian told me in despair. 'He's in a planet of his own half the time.'

'A world of his own,' I said; one of Kristian's more endearing traits was to get an idiom wrong occasionally, despite all his years living in Dublin.

'Yes, a world of his own. Maybe another man, his uncle, can talk sense into him.'

I promised to try, and sat down with all three of them one afternoon a few days later, Aidan clearly there against his will, and began by asking him whether there was anything worrying him.

'The threat of global thermo-nuclear war,' he replied immediately and I laughed; I had said something similar to Mam years before when she caught me in one of my moods.

'Anything other than that?' I asked. 'Anything on a more personal level?'

'That's not enough?' said he. 'The possibility of mankind's annihilation?'

'Well it's not a cheerful thought,' I admitted. 'But your pal in school isn't responsible for any of that, is he? Or your teacher?'

Aidan shrugged and looked away. He asked Hannah whether he could have a Club Milk and she said no, that it would spoil his dinner.

'Your parents are fierce worried about you,' I said.

He snorted and shook his head.

'They are,' I insisted.

'We are,' repeated Hannah and Kristian in unison and the boy gave a great stretch, yawning in my face.

'Ah come on now,' I said. 'Will you have a bit of manners at least?'

'I'm tired, Odie,' he said. *Odie*. No one in my whole life ever called me that except for Aidan. He'd started it as a baby when he first learned to talk and for some reason couldn't get his mouth around the word *Odran*. And so it had become *Odie* and he'd stuck with it ever since. Had anyone else said it, I would have told them to stop, but out of Aidan's mouth I found it charming. I wondered whether he liked me more than he admitted.

'Do you sleep at night?' I asked.

'He won't go to bed until after midnight,' said Hannah. 'And then he won't get up for school. Is it any wonder that he's tired?'

'How is school?' I asked him, ignoring the interruption. I wondered whether we might not get along better if his parents left us alone to talk, but didn't feel that I had the right to ask them.

'Boring,' said Aidan.

'This is another matter,' said Kristian, throwing his hands up. 'Everything is boring these days. He shows no interest in anything.'

'Why is school boring?' I asked. 'Aren't all your friends in there with you?'

'I don't care about any of them,' he said. 'They're all idiots.'

'Well who do you play with then?'

'*Play with?*' he asked, sneering at me.

'Yes.'

'I don't *play* with anyone.'

'Do you play with Jonas?'

'Jonas is an idiot. And he's boring.'

'You see?' said Kristian, shaking his head. 'I don't know what to do with him. I suggested that he come with me to Lillehammer to visit his grandmother for a couple of weeks over the summer, but he refuses to go.'

'It's boring there,' said Aidan. 'You don't know what it's like, Odie. You've never been.'

'I have, actually,' I said. 'I was there when your parents got married. And I had a great time.'

'Have you ever gone back?'

'No, but—'

'Exactly.'

'Well I don't know what to say to you, Aidan,' I said, already feeling defeated. 'You're just a young lad and you're behaving like some sort of delinquent, and for no reason at all, as far as I can see. When I was your age, I was full of life.'

'I'm not you.'

'No, you're not. But I'm just saying. And I didn't even have all the friends that you have or a happy home to live in. Sure I didn't make a real friend till I was seventeen, when I met Tom Cardle at the seminary.'

'How is Father Tom?' asked Hannah, but I waved away the question; we were here to talk about Aidan.

'I need to go to the bathroom,' said Aidan, jumping up as if he was about to be sick, and I wondered whether this was a ruse on his part to put an end to the conversation.

'Go on so,' I said.

But he didn't go to the bathroom. He went out to the back garden, picked up a handful of stones and one by one broke almost every glass in Kristian's greenhouse, refusing to stop until we ran outside and his father lifted him off the ground and dragged him back in, kicking and screaming. For no reason that I could discern, the boy had suddenly decided to engage in acts of destruction.

And that was a good day. It was downhill for a long time after that, until finally he got out altogether and went off to the sites in London. At which point he seemed to leave my life entirely.

After Jonas and I parted, I made my way down Grafton Street towards Brown Thomas, intending to buy a new pair of gloves. It was the middle of the day and despite everything we heard on the radio about a financial crisis the street was filled with shoppers pushing past each other, impatient to get to where they wanted to go. So much for austerity. Two boys and a girl played guitars and sung an old Luke Kelly number outside Burger King; further along, a string quartet had set up outside a mobile-phone shop and were giving a spirited rendition of Mozart to the considerable crowd that had gathered before them. Outside the entrance to Brown Thomas itself stood one of those gold-painted men on a plinth, completely motionless, staring into oblivion, an upturned trilby placed before him with only a few euros inside. These men confused me. The musicians were at least offering a service; it seemed ungenerous not to reward them for their music. But what did men like this offer? Was I supposed to pay him to stand around stock-still? Why exactly? And where did he get dressed into his gaudy outfit, paint his face, gild his hands? Did he travel home on the bus like this or board the Luas in all his finery? If he rubbed up against someone would they turn gold too?

Another costumed man stood at the entrance to Brown Thomas, but this one opened the door for me with an indifferent 'Good afternoon, sir,' despite the presence of my collar. I have noticed over time how people have become less certain how to address a priest, as if they're embarrassed to say *Father* or are somehow frightened by the word. Inside the store, a few people glanced in my direction and two of the girls behind the make-up counters exchanged a look and a smirk which made me feel self-conscious.

It had been an age since I'd last set foot inside Brown Thomas. It was all glass and white staircases, mirrors everywhere. I could remember when it was Switzer's and Mam would take Hannah and me to see the Christmas window and we would stand in line for the terrifying encounter with Santa Claus in his dark, elf-filled grotto. Now a woman stood provocatively in the centre of an aisle, holding a bottle of perfume in one hand, the other poised over its top as if she was preparing to unleash a grenade, and sure enough, as I watched her, she attacked several unsuspecting shoppers with her spray.

'The men's department?' I asked a passing sales assistant.

'Down the stairs over there,' she said, pointing towards the corner of the floor and marching away without missing a beat. I made my way across and descended the steps only to be confronted by more glass and mirrors, and a floor that was divided into confusing sections, each one wrapped inside others like a Russian doll. The heads of a few young men folding shirts and jeans turned to look at me. I approached one of them cautiously.

'I was looking for a pair of gloves,' I said.

'Whose?' he asked me.

'Come again?' I said.

'Whose gloves?' he repeated.

I stared at him. 'Well, yours at the moment, I suppose,' I said. 'Or the store's. But I want to buy some. So then they'll be mine.'

He sighed as if life was simply too much for him. 'Hugo Boss?' he said. 'Calvin Klein? Tom Ford? Ted—?'

I interrupted; it seemed as if he might go on all day. 'Just a nice pair of black gloves,' I told him. 'No fur on the inside. And nothing too expensive either. I don't mind who made them.'

He turned and led me towards the centre of the floor where a range of gloves, clearly priced, were displayed neatly on a table. I saw the ones I wanted immediately and picked them up. 'These, I think,' I said, trying them on. A perfect fit. I looked at the price tag. Two hundred and twenty euros. 'That can't be right,' I said, pointing at the ticket.

'It is,' he said. 'You're in luck. They're on sale.'

I laughed. 'Are you joking me? You know there's a recession, don't you?'

'Not in Brown Thomas there isn't, sir.'

'Still,' I said, shaking my head at the price. Sure who would pay that for a pair of gloves when you'd most likely forget them on the 14 bus some day?

'They're marked down from three hundred,' he explained. 'They're beautiful, aren't they? Almost too good to wear.'

'Yes, but I want to wear them, do you see,' I told him. 'That's what gloves are for. You don't have anything cheaper, do you?'

'Cheaper?' he asked; it was as if I had just uttered an obscenity in the middle of a funeral. 'We have some of last season's,' he said. 'They range from one hundred and fifty up.'

I laughed and shook my head. 'Would I be better off across the road, do you think?' I asked. 'In Marks & Spencer?'

He smiled; maybe he wasn't trying to make a laugh of me after all. 'They do have a more economical range,' he said. 'But they won't last you as long. It might be a . . . what's the word?'

'A false economy?'

'That's the one.'

'Sure I'll go across and have a look anyway,' I told him. 'And if I don't see anything I like, I'll come back to you.'

He nodded, turning away, disinterested now, and I made my way back up the stairs towards the exit, which is when I saw him. A small boy, no more than about five years of age, standing in the centre of the floor with a frightened expression on his face and no one there to look after him. His lower lip was trembling and I guessed that he was deciding whether or not it was worth his while crying or whether he should give it another minute yet before he gave into his emotions. I looked around, uncertain what to do. I assumed that his mother would appear at any moment, but when she didn't, the tears began to fall and he put his hands to his cheeks to wipe them away.

Now I ask you, what could I do but go over to him?

'Are you all right, son?' I asked, leaning down. 'You're not lost, are you?'

He looked up at me, relieved, but perhaps a little frightened too. He swallowed, then nodded.

'Is your mammy not with you? Or your daddy?'

'I'm with my mum,' he said, almost in a whisper. 'But I can't find her.'

'Is she here in the shop? Will we take a look for her?'

He shook his head and pointed out through the glass door of the side exit, the one that looks on to Weir's the jewellers. 'She went out,' he said. 'She left me here.'

'Ah now she wouldn't have left you on your own,' I said. 'Did she think you were behind her, was that it?'

He shook his head and pointed out on to the street again. I looked around, baffled, certain that his mother would surely appear at any moment, but no one was running around in desperate search of a child. 'What's your name?' I asked him.

'Kyle,' he said.

'And what age are you, Kyle?'

'Five,' he said. Spot on.

'And is it just you and your mammy, or do you have brothers and sisters with you?'

'My sister's in school,' he said.

'All right. Sure we'll take a look around and see if we can find your mam, will we?'

I reached down to take his hand, but he shook his head and

pointed at the door again. 'She went out,' he said. He was insistent. 'She went out on the street.'

And here's where I made my mistake, you see. I should have taken him over to one of the girls by the nail-polish counters and asked whether there was someone who might put an announcement out over the loudspeaker, to ask whether there was a woman in the shop who'd lost a little boy. I should have gone over to one of the security guards who were standing around in all their pomposity. I should have asked to speak to the manager. But I did none of these things. I didn't think as I should have done. I took him at his word, I trusted the word of a confused five-year-old child and decided that perhaps he was right, perhaps his mother really had gone out on to Wicklow Street, believing that the little lad was behind her, and by now she was up along the turn on to Georges Street and looking round in a blind panic, wondering where her son was.

'Well, come on so,' I said, taking him by the hand – my second mistake – and leading him towards the door. My third: I pushed it open and out we went, hit immediately by the cold of the day as the door to the department store swung closed behind us.

'Which way do you think she went?' I asked him. 'Left or right?'

He looked around – perhaps he didn't know which was which – and pointed down past the International Bar in the direction of the Central Hotel.

'Come on so,' I repeated, still keeping a tight hold of his hand as we walked along. 'We'll have a wander and see whether we can find her.'

Up ahead, I could see a Garda standing outside the tea shop and resolved that if I had not found Kyle's mother before I reached him, then I would surrender the boy to the authorities and wait with them until she was located.

And so there we were, wandering along Wicklow Street, a middle-aged priest holding the hand of a five-year-old boy as he was taken away from the place where he'd been discovered. Was I stupid or what? Could I not think? Did I not have a brain inside my head?

'Will you have an ice-cream?' I asked as we passed a newsagent's shop because the boy's tears had started again by now. 'Would that make you feel better?'

But the little lad didn't have a chance to answer, because that was when I heard the shouting and a great commotion behind me, and I turned to see every head on the street looking in my direction as a woman ran like an Olympian towards us, screaming at me to take my filthy fuckin' hands off her son, and before I knew it the boy was snatched from my grip by one man while another pulled me away and punched me in the face, and that was it for the next ten minutes or so – the lights went out.

When I recovered my senses, I found myself seated in the back of a Garda car driving past the front arch of Trinity College towards Pearse Street, where we stopped opposite what used to be the Metropole cinema.

In we went and the officers behind the desk barely looked up as my Garda – I shall call him my Garda for he was the one who had picked me up from the street and summoned a car to take me away from the braying mob who were out for my blood – took me into a cold, white-bricked room and said that he'd be back in a moment and did I have a phone on me, and if I did, would I give it over to him.

'I have this old thing,' I said, handing across a Nokia that I had bought a few years before and which served my purposes well enough, even though Jonas had laughed when he saw it earlier in the day and told me to make sure I left it to the National Museum in my will.

'I'll take care of it for now,' he said, pocketing it and leaving the room, and through my upset I found time to wonder what right he had to do that.

I sat there, alone, and felt a tender swelling beginning to emerge on my cheek where the man had punched me, and considered my situation. Of course I had been foolish. What must it have looked like? And sure didn't everyone think that we were all the same? Out to steal a child and do terrible things to him. I put my face in my hands, aware that this could turn out very badly indeed.

The Garda, my Garda, came back in with a notepad and pen and pressed the red button on a tape recorder.

'Name?' he asked. No introductions. No manners.

'Garda, I need the bathroom,' I said, for the Heineken was working its way through me. 'I'll only be a minute.'

'Name?' he repeated.

'This is a misunderstanding,' I began. 'I was only—'

'Name?' he repeated, staring at me with cold eyes.

'Yates,' I said quietly, looking down at the table top. 'Father Odran Yates.'

'Spell that, would you?'

I spelled it.

'Do you need medical attention, Mr Yates?'

'I don't think so,' I said. 'And it's Father Yates.' I touched my collar. 'Father Yates.'

He made a note of something. 'You know why you're here?' he asked.

'The boy was lost,' I said. 'He said his mother had gone out on to Wicklow Street. I was trying to help him find her.'

'You abducted him from Brown Thomas, is that right?'

I stared at him, unable to find words for a moment; I could feel my stomach twisting a little and feared that I might be sick. 'I didn't abduct him,' I said quietly, trying to remain calm in the face of what I knew was an impossible situation. 'I did no such a thing. I was trying to help him find his mother, that's all. The poor lad was lost.'

'His mother says that she was only a few feet away, looking at handbags.'

'If she was, I didn't see her.'

'And you didn't think to bring the boy to store security?'

'I didn't. I should have. He was upset. He was crying.'

'Are you known to us, Mr Yates?'

He hated me. He despised everything about me. He wanted to hurt me.

'Am I known to you?' I asked. 'What do you mean by that?'

'Do you have any past criminal activity?'

'I do not!' I cried, appalled.

'Any history with minors?'

'I've never done anything wrong,' I said. 'I'm a good man.'

'We have records,' he told me. 'I can go out right now and look it up. If there's something you're not telling me, you're better off just saying it.'

'Go look up anything you want,' I snapped, growing angry now at the injustice of it all. 'I was trying to help the boy, that's all. I didn't mean any harm.'

'Of course you didn't,' he said with a sigh. 'You never do, do you?'

I swallowed. Had something happened to him once and he was taking it out on me?

'Garda, the bathroom, please.'

'Have you been drinking, Mr Yates?'

'I had a Heineken with my lunch. I met my nephew.'

He looked up quickly. 'And where is he? How old is he?'

'How should I know where he is? He's a grown man. He's twenty-six. He went his way after lunch and I went mine.'

'How many drinks did you have?'

'Just the one.'

'We can check, you know.'

'What was she doing looking at handbags?' I asked.

'What do you think she was doing?' said the Garda, my Garda. 'It's a shop. She was shopping.'

'And why wasn't she looking after her boy? Kyle is only five.'

'Kyle?' said the Garda, looking up from his notepad. 'You got his name then?'

'Of course I got his name,' I said, wondering what harm there was to that. 'I asked him his name just as you asked me for mine. The only difference being that I called him by the name he gave me.'

'You told him you would buy him an ice-cream?' he asked me. 'Is that right?'

'He was crying,' I said, feeling that I might start myself at any moment. 'I thought it might cheer him up.'

'Did you offer him the ice-cream to entice him out of the store?'

'No,' I said. 'Sure I only said it to him when we were outside.'

'And where were you taking him?'

'He said his mother had gone up Wicklow Street so I thought we could take a look for her. I saw one of your colleagues up ahead. I was going to leave him with a Garda.'

'But you didn't. You held on to him.'

'We hadn't got there yet! And then I heard his mother coming out of Brown Thomas, running towards us. Please, Garda, I need to use the bathroom. I must be allowed.'

He made a few more notes in his pad and told me to wait where I was, as if there was any possibility of me leaving. He left me sitting there alone for the guts of an hour, writhing in agony, my bladder feeling as if it was going to explode inside me. When he came back in, I was seated in the corner of the cell, my head in my hands, weeping.

'Oh for Christ's sake,' he said angrily before leaning out towards the corridor. 'Joey, get a mop and bucket, will you. The suspect's pissed himself.'

'Are you happy now?' I asked, looking up at him, my humiliation complete. 'Are you satisfied with what you've made me do?'

'Shut the fuck up and sit in that chair there,' he said, pointing at the chair I'd been sat on before moving to the corner. My trousers were soaking and after his colleague came in to dry the puddle on the floor he disappeared again for a moment before returning with a pair of blue tracksuit bottoms with a white stripe running down the side. 'Put them on,' he said.

I took my trousers off, utterly shamed, and did as I was told. It didn't help much as most of the damage was on my underwear. After that, he took down all my personal information and said that he would be in touch with me later, that he needed to interview the mother and the boy. He told me not to even think of leaving Dublin without contacting him and I wondered whether they would be taking my passport off me.

As I left Pearse Street Garda station, the lad behind the counter looked up and hissed something under his breath.

'Paedo.'

'What was that?' I asked, spinning around, furious and upset. This was the second time today that I had been so abused. First the boys on the Luas and now a Garda, who was supposed to be there to protect me, not to call me names when I'd been wrongly arrested and left without any facilities until I'd had no choice but to wet myself. 'What was that you said to me?'

He looked up, all innocent, and shrugged his shoulders. 'I said nothing,' he lied.

Thankfully, I received the call the following morning, shortly after ten o'clock Mass.

'Mr Yates?' said a bored voice on the other end of the phone and I knew immediately who it was.

'Father Yates,' I replied.

'Right, yeah, whatever, I have some news for you.' No stating of his name. Not a word of a greeting. Was this the way that they were trained down there at Templemore? 'We've spoken with the boy and with his mother and we won't be pursuing any charges against you at this time. The boy has confirmed your story and apparently the mother believes him.' He gave a short, rather bitter laugh and I could tell that although Kyle's mother might have had faith in her son, he didn't.

'You said *at this time*,' I replied, trying to keep the relieved tone out of my voice; I didn't want to give him the satisfaction of hearing how difficult this had been for me. 'Does that mean you might return to it at a later date?'

There was a long pause. I wondered whether the Garda was trying to find a way to keep me stewing. Finally he sighed. 'The case is over,' he said. 'We won't be pursuing it any further. You might think twice before you try picking up little boys you find in department stores. OK, *Father*?' he added, spitting out the word like sour milk.

But there was nothing to be gained by looking for further trouble or antagonizing him. He held all the power. And I held none.

'Yes,' I said. 'Thank you.'

I hung up and went into the kitchen, filled the kettle and turned it on for a cup of tea, aware all the time that my hand was shaking badly. A moment later, I turned the kettle off again and poured myself a small brandy, then moved into my study, where I lifted a set of rosary beads, given to me in Rome thirty-three years earlier by the Patriarch of Venice, and held them tightly in my hands. It was early but I needed that drink and the sensation of it flowing down my throat and warming me from the inside was a settling one. I was grateful for it.

I sat down and before I knew what was happening I found myself in tears. Not for myself, I don't think, nor for the horror of the previous twenty-four hours. But for how things had changed. There was a time when a priest was trusted, when you would bring a lost boy to the curate's house, not to the Garda station. Now you couldn't talk to a child without getting strange looks. You couldn't run an altar-boy meeting without a parent present to make sure you didn't start to fiddle with the little lads. And you couldn't help a child who was upset and lost without everyone assuming that you were trying to abduct him and spitting the word *paedophile* in your face.

You bastards, I thought to myself, thinking of those men who had ruined this life for me. The rosary beads in my hands snapped, the beads scattering everywhere, some under my chair, some beneath my desk, others rolling slowly across the floor. I stared at them. I felt no interest in picking them up.

Chapter Nine

1978

I arrived in Italy at the start of 1978. I had never left Ireland nor travelled on a plane before and the excitement of both was intense. The passport had to be ordered – Mam dug out my birth certificate and brought it into Molesworth Street, standing in line for the guts of five hours before her turn came and making sure to tell the girl behind the counter why I needed it – and when it arrived I read every word of it as if it was a great piece of literature.

That I should have been chosen from all the students in my year at Clonliffe College to undertake my final year of studies in Rome came as a surprise to me. Traditionally, one or two boys from each year were selected, but conventional wisdom had it that Kevin Samuels – 'the Pope' – would be offered the place. Or perhaps the Kerry lad, Seamus Wells, who had always been a great favourite of the priests and was a talented athlete as well as an accomplished scholar, which always stood well with the high-ups. But no, it was me. Yes, I had received a First with Distinction in my Philosophy degree at UCD and had performed consistently in my seminary exams – of which there were an extraordinary number – but I hadn't allowed myself to think that I had a chance. I had an aptitude for languages though, having mastered Latin, French, Italian and a little German, and perhaps that was what swung it. Poor Kevin Samuels never got over the shock and didn't even have the good grace to congratulate me. Curiously, the next time I heard from him was fourteen years later, when, to my astonishment, I received a letter from him asking whether I would officiate at his wedding to a girl he had met while hitch-hiking across America. This was a couple of years after he'd renounced his vows, of course. But that's another story.

'God only knows who they'll give me now,' complained Tom on the morning I left as he sat on his bed and watched me pack my belongings in the same suitcase I had unpacked six years earlier. We had stayed as cell-mates through all that time and had got to know each other as well as only those thrust into such close proximity – seminarians, astronauts or prisoners – can. 'Some gobshite, probably.'

'They'll leave you on your own,' I told him. 'Sure there's no one to put in here, is there?'

'I suppose not. I'm going to miss you, Odran.'

'We're nearly finished anyway. Only a year to go.'

'Still and all.'

The truth was that I didn't think I would miss him particularly. I was twenty-three years old by now. I had been living in the seminary since just after my seventeenth birthday and, as contented as I'd been there, an adventure was ahead of me; I had no intention of wasting my time worrying about who was or wasn't going to be sharing a room with Tom Cardle in his final year. He'd changed over the course of our time at Clonliffe. He was no longer the angry, frustrated teenage boy that he had been when we first arrived. He had become resigned to his lot, and if he was not entirely happy about becoming a priest, at least he seemed to have made his peace with it. I'd stopped asking him why, if he was so miserable, he didn't just leave, for he always gave the same answer: that his father would kill him if he did, and the beating that he had received after running away five years previously was proof enough of that.

Looking back, I wonder where his courage was. Why did he not stand up to his father more? And why did the Spiritual Director at Clonliffe not recognize the frustration building inside him and take steps to make peace within the Cardle family while helping to build a different life, a life away from the priesthood, for a boy so patently unsuited to it? That was what the man was there for, after all.

Tom could never talk about his father without becoming angry. His hands would twist into fists and once or twice when I engaged him on the subject he became so incensed that I thought he was going to make himself ill. He had a temper on him and talk of his family would only incite his fury.

We had a physical altercation only once, when I punched him on the nose, sending him toppling back to his bed with blood pouring down his face. It was in our second year and I had just confided in him the story of my summer in Wexford in 1964.

'Lucky you,' he said. 'I wish my father had killed himself.'

Punch.

In fairness to him, he apologized afterwards. It was a thoughtless remark, unworthy of him, but it remained with me. The tone of voice he'd used. The fact that he really meant it.

Another line I remember: Tom remarking to me that the one good thing about Clonliffe was that he could sleep through the night. He said that from the age of nine to the day he left Wexford, he was either woken after midnight by his father or he woke himself, in anticipation of the man coming through the door.

'What was he doing there?' I asked him and he turned away.

'Ah, Odran,' was all he said before going outside and disappearing off to wherever he took himself when he was feeling low.

'Sure we'll see each other again, Tom,' I told him as I left Clonliffe for the last time. 'And just think, when we do we'll be priests at last.'

'Oh happy day,' he said, smiling a little as he shook my hand, the closest we would ever come to any physical display of affection.

Mam and Hannah came to Dublin Airport to see me off and said they'd stay in the viewing lounge to watch the plane depart. I'd been to JWT at the top of Dawson Street a few weeks earlier with the money Canon Robson had given me for my ticket and had even bought myself a pair of sunglasses in Switzer's, for I heard that it was sunny in Rome the whole year round. When they saw me coming in wearing my cassock they rolled the red carpet out and gave me a discount.

'Do you think you'll get to meet the Pope?' Mam asked me and I told her that I doubted it but I would certainly see him when he gave his weekly blessing on a Sunday morning in St Peter's Square or at the regular Wednesday audiences. And I'd surely attend some of his Masses and hear his homilies.

'But he's hardly going to be found wandering down the streets in the evening in search of a bowlful of spaghetti, is he?' I asked.

'Will you have to eat Italian food all the time?' she asked.

'I will, of course.'

'What about your stomach?'

'What about it?'

She pulled a face. 'I'd have more respect for mine,' she said. 'You can't trust foreign food. But look, son, take a photo if you see him.'

'If I see who?'

'The Pope!'

'I couldn't, Mam,' I said. 'Not in a church.'

'No one will know. Send me back the roll of film and I'll get it developed. There's a shop I know on Talbot Street that says they can get them done within two weeks or there's no charge. I'll get a second set and send them on to you.'

I said that I would do my best and kissed them both goodbye. Hannah was twenty by now and had been with the Bank of Ireland on College Green for two years already. It was good enough money, she told me, but she didn't want to end up there for life. Mam said that it didn't matter where she worked, for one day she'd be married and starting a family of her own and her husband would never allow her to have a career if he had anything about him at all.

'You could come visit me,' I told my sister, feeling for the first time a sense of apprehension at what lay ahead, the possibility of loneliness.

'We will,' said Mam. 'On your special day.' One of the great advantages of a final year in Rome was that you were ordained by the Pope himself in St Peter's. 'But write, Odran, son. Write every week. And don't forget the photos.'

I wore the uniform of the seminarian on the plane and because of this, the stewardesses invited me to board first, along with the children and the infirm, and I was given a seat at the front. At Fiumicino, I was met by Monsignor Sorley, who had been head of the Collegio Irlandese, the Pontifical Irish College in Rome, for more than twenty years. The information I had been given was that I was to be taken directly to the college, shown my room and given the timetable for my classes, which would not, Canon Robson had informed me, be all that different from the classes I had studied in Dublin; they would simply be undertaken in Italian. And in a sunnier climate, he added with a smile. And rather than shepherd's pie or chops and potatoes for my dinner, I would be eating pizza, spaghetti bolognese and lasagne.

The plan, however, had changed and Monsignor Sorley told

me that he was taking me to a café instead, for he wanted to sound me out about something before we went to the college. I wondered what was wrong, whether I had already done something to disgrace myself. I had drunk two cans of Harp on the plane, such was my level of excitement; had this something to do with it? Perhaps I was to be sent back to Clonliffe and Kevin Samuels was already on the next plane headed towards the Eternal City.

'We hear great reports of you from Canon Robson,' he said as we sat outside a café on the Via dei Santi Quattro, close to the college itself but with a narrow view of the Colosseum at the end of the street, its tumbling stonework and narrow entryways incredibly close, the noise of gladiators, lions, terrified Christians and bloodthirsty Romans ringing in my ears. I remembered my Robert Graves and wanted to run towards it, charge into the centre of its history, open my arms wide and proclaim that I had arrived here to meet my destiny. 'He tells me you're the cream of the crop. There's high hopes for you, Odran.'

'Thank you,' I said.

'Are you an ambitious lad?'

I thought about it and shook my head. 'No,' I said.

'And yet here you are,' he smiled, opening both hands before me. 'Whose dead body did you have to crawl over to get chosen?'

I sat back, surprised by his choice of words. 'Believe me,' I told him, 'it was as big a surprise to me as it was to everyone else. We all thought it would be the Pope.'

'The Pope?'

'Sorry,' I said quickly, flushing. 'Just a lad in the seminary. He had it all up here.' I tapped my forehead. 'We thought it would be him.'

'Would you be willing to take on a challenge, do you think?' he asked, leaning forward and slurping down an espresso.

'A challenge?'

'Something that requires brains, reliability and a great deal of discretion.'

I hesitated; I felt I was being led down a road that I might regret walking upon. But what else could I say but 'Of course, Monsignor.'

'Good man. But look, before I tell you what it is, you must understand that if you don't feel suited to it, you can always say no. And we'll find someone else. Canon Robson says you're the man for the job, but you might not want it and no one will think less of you if you don't.'

'All right,' I said.

'A position has come up,' he said, leaning forward and lowering his voice. 'A job, of sorts. It shouldn't interfere with your studies, and if it does then it will be taken off you. Every year a seminarian from a different college is assigned to the Vatican to perform certain crucial functions for a twelve-month period. It's a few hours out of your day, nothing more than that. Seven days a week, though. There are no days off. You won't be able to take any holidays either.'

'I'm happy to undertake any work that you assign to me, Monsignor,' I said.

'It's a different nationality every year,' he explained. '1976, there was this awful Icelandic fella in the job. Nose in the air, he had. Last year, there was a lovely little Indian lad. Now it's our turn. It's alphabetical, you see. The only thing is, you'll be sleeping there instead of at our place so you'll miss out on the day-to-day life of the College. They'll give you a room. It's not much of a room, to be honest. More a mattress in an alcove. Can you handle that?'

I stared at him. 'A mattress in an alcove, Monsignor?' I asked.

'It sounds worse than it is.' He shrugged and thought about this for a moment before shaking his head. 'Actually, it doesn't. It sounds exactly like what it is. And you'll have to trek across to us every day on a bus for your classes and then trek back again at night. Which will take a bit of time. Are you up for it, Odran?'

'I am, Monsignor,' I said. 'But what is it? What will be expected of me?'

He smiled. 'Well that's the thing,' he said. 'Don't fall off your seat now.'

I *did* sleep in the Irish College that night. The Monsignor brought me down the road to that great white mansion, where I had a bath and a night's rest, and the following morning drove me across Rome and along the banks of the Tiber, entering Vatican City by the Via della Conciliazione, my first view of St Peter's Square reducing me to silence.

Our appointment was scheduled to last for no more than five minutes, between half past ten and twenty-five to eleven, and as we made our way along the marble corridors my eyes were out on stalks at the lavishness of the wall hangings and the beauty of the painted ceilings. From the windows I could see the tourists gathered in the square below and wanted to lean out, to wave at them and for them to notice me up here, in a place forbidden to others. Such vanity, but I was a young man so perhaps it can be forgiven. Monsignor Sorley rushed me along, however – presumably he had long since grown accustomed to the history and splendour that surrounded us – and we were admitted by the Swiss Guards through a heavy wooden door where we ascended a staircase and found ourselves in a small office, where a secretary – a priest, of course – spoke in Italian to Monsignor Sorley before staring at me warily.

'Your audience will begin shortly,' he said, testing my Italian by speaking very quickly as he glanced at his watch. 'His Holiness is meeting with his Beatitude, the Patriarch of Venice, at the moment but they should not be too much longer.'

We sat down on two well-stuffed velvet armchairs and I could feel my stomach turning in somersaults with anxiety.

'Tell me again what I'm doing here,' I said to the Monsignor, trembling as I sat separated from Pope Paul by nothing but a closed door.

'Your duties are simple,' he replied. 'His Holiness rises every morning at five o'clock. The nuns prepare a pot of tea and bring it to the private parlour which is located just down there.' He indicated a room along the corridor on our left. 'You take the tray and bring it into the papal bedroom. The nuns may not enter until His Holiness has completed his ablutions and is fully dressed. He may make some simple request of you, but that is unlikely; you can just open the curtains and leave the tea on the table when you have woken him. Then you must be here again by eight o'clock at night, in case he decides to retire early. Before he sleeps, His Holiness enjoys a hot milk as he reads; you bring it or whatever else he needs. Again, the nuns will prepare it, but they do not enter the chamber after the Holy Father has prepared himself for bed. Then you sleep on a cot outside in case he needs anything in the night. From what I understand, he never does. It's not a difficult job, Odran. You're little more than a waiter twice a day. It doesn't take more than a couple of minutes of your time. But it's important that you're on hand every morning and every night. You cannot be late and you cannot desert your post.'

'Of course,' I said. 'And my classes?'

'After you have woken His Holiness, you make your way back across the city to the Irish College. There are plenty of buses, but prepare yourself for a crush and the heat. You will study with us during the day until it is time to return to the Vatican. And I hope it goes without saying that you will not speak to the other students of anything that you see or hear in this place?'

'Yes, Monsignor,' I said. I thought about all this. It was a tremendous honour, but I was not thrilled by the notion of travelling back and forth across Rome twice a day for no other reason than to deliver cups of tea or hot milk, even if it was to the Pope. The Irish College had entranced me, with its manicured lawns and proximity to the Colosseum, and I wondered whether I might miss the camaraderie of the other final-year students when I could never spend my evenings in their company.

The door opened and I thought I might be sick as a tall man with greying hair emerged. He smiled when he saw the Monsignor and reached out both hands to him.

'Monsignor Sorley,' he said. 'What a pleasant surprise.'

'Your Beatitude,' replied the Monsignor, smiling too. 'It has been too long. What brings you to Rome?'

'Our beautiful cathedral is falling down about our heads,' he said with a shrug. 'And where else can I turn but to the man who controls the purse strings?'

'Were you successful in your petition?'

He opened his arms wide. 'It is all taken under advisement, my friend. I am to return to Venice and await a decision.' He turned in my direction, still smiling. 'And who do we have here?'

'A final-year seminarian, Your Beatitude. Lately arrived from Dublin. He has been selected to take up the position vacated by young Chatterjee.'

'So you will be first up and last to bed every day in Vatican City for the next twelve months,' he replied. 'You're either very lucky or very unfortunate. Which do you think?'

'Very lucky, Your Beatitude,' I said, dropping to my knees and kissing the golden ring bearing the seal of Venice, a city I had long wanted to visit. I tried to imagine the canals and bridges, the Piazza San Marco, and me wandering alone among the Venetians.

'You might not think that when you have bags under your eyes from so little sleep. The Holy Father is often late to bed and early to rise, they say. There is so much work to be done, of course.'

I nodded, intimidated, uncertain whether I should speak or not. But he looked at me kindly and laughed, placing a hand on my shoulder and looking me directly in the eyes.

'Don't be nervous,' he said. 'This is a place of friendship. What's your name, anyway?'

'Odran Yates,' I said.

'Well, Odran,' he replied, 'you need have no worries. You should relish this experience. 1979 will be here before you know it and then it will be the turn of . . .' He thought about it for a moment. 'Who will come next, do you think? After Ireland?'

I ran through the names of countries in my mind for the correct alphabetical order. 'Israel?' I suggested and his eyebrows raised. He turned to the Monsignor, who covered his mouth to stifle a laugh.

'I don't know about that,' said the cardinal. '*La bella Italia*, of course.'

The sound of a tinkling bell was heard from the next room and the Patriarch turned to Monsignor Sorley. 'It was good to see you, my friend,' he said. 'We will have lunch together when I am next in Rome. And good luck to you, young man.'

He stepped away, the black cassock with scarlet piping, the fascia, the zucchetto on his head all combining to give an air of majesty to this prince of the Church. It had been like this since medieval times and I imagined the Borgias, the Medicis and the Contis all jostling for position in their common apparel. It was an impressive sight, impossible to behold without feeling a sense of one's own insignificance.

The secretary looked up from his desk. 'You may enter,' he said.

'Come on so,' said Monsignor Sorley and I followed him into the next office, where a thin man with deep-set eyes was seated behind a desk, dressed in a white cassock and pellegrina, a gold pectoral cross hanging around his neck, scratching away on a document with a fountain pen. He continued to write as we stood there, ignoring us for perhaps two minutes, before finally standing up; he offered us his hand and we both fell to the floor to kiss it.

'Holy Father,' said Monsignor Sorley. 'This is the boy I spoke to you about. Odran Yates. He'll be taking young Chatterjee's place.'

The Pope turned to look at me, his expression chilly. 'Arise,' he said.

I stood. I dared to look him in the face. His skin was grey and there were dark bags beneath his eyes. He looked exhausted, as if life was ebbing out of him.

'Are you quiet?' he asked me.

'I beg your pardon, Your Holiness?' I said.

'I do not care for noise in the mornings or at nights. It's bad enough with . . .' He waved towards the window, which was ajar to let in some air, and I could hear the sounds of the tourists even from this height. 'Can you promise me that you will be quiet?'

I swallowed nervously and nodded. 'Quiet as a mouse,' I said. 'You'll barely know I'm here.'

He nodded and sat back down. 'Ireland,' he said, considering the word.

'Yes, Holy Father.'

'What will we do with Ireland?'

I didn't answer; I didn't understand the question. He waved me away and that was it; the audience was over. The Monsignor and I took our leave. And over the course of the seven months that followed, these were the only words that Pope Paul VI ever spoke in my presence. I might have been a ghost in the Holy See for all the notice he took of me.

*

I had never experienced profound attraction before. I had read about it in novels; I had seen its victims floundering like drunks or imbeciles on television and in films. But I had not known what it was like to look at someone and feel such intense desire that the rest of the world seemed diminished in comparison. Even during my brief romance with Katherine Summers, I had never felt any great stirrings other than the natural curiosity of a teenager. Unlike Tom Cardle and some of the other boys at the seminary in Dublin, I didn't find myself racked with desire through those lonely nights, tossing and turning as I longed for a woman to do those things to me that other boys of my age dreamed of. Celibacy did not feel like such a terrible burden and occasionally, when I allowed my mind to drift towards these matters, I wondered whether perhaps there was something wrong with me, an element of my personality that had been omitted during my creation.

The subject of women was not one that was discussed often in Clonliffe College. To show too much of an interest in girls was to suggest that your vocation was an unstable one and that you might be one of those who would end up leaving the seminary before ordination or, worse still, resign from the priesthood for a secular life – a wife, children, a job like other men. And so the boys said little to each other on the topic, we carried our secrets and desires tightly within ourselves, furtive and clandestine, just another aspect of the world beyond our walls of which we were afraid to speak.

And then, one afternoon several months after arriving in Rome, I found myself sitting alone at a small café in the Piazza Pasquale Paoli in the late afternoon, the sun descending as I watched the tourists stroll across the Ponte Vittorio Emanuele on their way towards the basilica of St Peter, a copy of E. M. Forster's *A Room with a View* face-down on the table before me. I lifted my coffee to my lips just as a woman emerged from the kitchen to remonstrate with an older man, who I took to be her father. She screamed at him, throwing her arms in the air in a dramatic gesture, but he simply shrugged and dismissed her before flinging his apron off, hurling it to the floor and roaring back with equal gusto. The pair of them were carrying on so much like a caricature of Italian fiery passion that I wondered whether or not it was a show they were putting on for the tourists. Did they do this every afternoon, I asked myself. But the question melted away as I stared at her and that was it. I was lost.

She was not, perhaps, the obvious candidate to turn my head. She was much older than I, perhaps thirty or thirty-one years of age, while I was still a young man of only twenty-three. She was tall, taller than her father – taller than me – with dark hair that was pulled back and wrapped securely into a complicated arrangement at the back of her head that merited further study. Deft fingers, I thought, might unloosen the knots of that package. When she turned away from the man and glanced around at the customers, none of whom were paying any attention to the altercation playing out before them, she caught my eye and raised her hands and shoulders as if to say '*What?*' and I blushed and stared down at the table. When I dared to look up again, she was still there, a half-smile on her face, the third finger of her left hand balanced between her lips as she nibbled at it, and I longed to be a nail upon that hand, an idea that turned my face redder again. I loosened the stiff collar around my neck, its very existence a barrier between us, and tried to return to my book. I couldn't concentrate; the words swam around the page, and when I glanced up once more she had disappeared back inside the kitchen. There was no reason for me to feel such overwhelming desire, but I did. I wanted her to step outside again, to loosen her hair, and to watch as it fell about her shoulders. I wanted her to rage at her father and bring a saucepan down upon his head. I wanted her to come over and lean above me, to reach down and pull the collar from my neck.

I sat there too long; when she eventually re-emerged, she walked slowly towards me, lifted my empty cup and said three words – *'Un altro, Padre?'* – and I shook my head. I could not bring myself to speak. When she turned away, I left, returning to the small cot in the Vatican's papal suite, where I lay on my back and stared at the frescoes on the ceiling above me, considering the extraordinary and turbulent sensations that I was feeling.

This, I realized, is what normal men feel. You're not different at all, Odran, I told myself. You're just like everyone else.

Every day that followed, I found myself back at the Café Bennizi in the Piazza Pasquale Paoli and every afternoon she would emerge to shout at her father, to cry out about the latest injustice, and when her venom was exhausted she would turn to look at me and shake her head, as if I irritated her almost as much as he did. In my imagination, I concocted an elaborate history for the two baristas: he had been widowed at a young age and left to bring up his daughter alone, perhaps with the help of a brash and opinionated mother – in Italian stories, there were always brash and opinionated mothers – and the girl had joined him in his business when she came of age. It was not a criticism of her virtue, but I pictured her with a small child of her own at home, a little boy of three or four perhaps, child and mother abandoned by a worthless priapic Neapolitan who had passed through Rome only long enough to seduce her and leave her with a baby to rear. She wore no wedding ring – I saw that every time she came over to take my cup away and say *'Un altro, Padre?'* – but there was an indentation around the fourth finger of her left hand and I wondered whether she took one off when she was at work; she might hide it in a safe place so that it would not get damaged while she was washing dishes. Or perhaps she left it at home every morning in case it slipped off her hand at the sink. I did not want her to be married, but I did not mind if she had a child. I didn't especially care for children, but I would care for hers. Did she speak English, I wondered. Would she be able to settle in Dublin? Would I, with her by my side? These were the ludicrous thoughts that passed through my head as I sat there each afternoon, drinking coffee after coffee, the only time of day which was mine, where I was neither taking cups in and out of the papal bedroom, partaking of my studies at the Irish College, or saying my distracted prayers in the many churches and chapels around which the streets of the Eternal City were constructed.

I didn't even like coffee all that much.

Occasionally I wondered whether she or her father would challenge me. They must have noticed me staring, thought it odd that I came here at the same time day after day, week after week. The father glared at me sometimes; perhaps he would have told me to leave had I not been in clerical garb. As things were, he could say nothing; there were conventions to uphold. And sometimes when she came over to say '*Un altro, Padre?*' I would catch her looking at me, something in her eye revealing that she knew that the young man at the corner table with the half-finished Forster before him was imagining scenarios, ruthlessly libidinous scenarios, that would have made a dead man blush.

Almost two months into my voyeurism, I was surprised by a hand on my shoulder and looked up to see His Beatitude, the Patriarch of Venice, whom I had not encountered since that first day in the Vatican, standing before me. He smiled down, his expression one of pure happiness and serenity.

'Remind me,' he said. 'You're the Irish boy, aren't you? The one Monsignor Sorley recommended to the Holy Father?'

'Odran Yates, Your Eminence,' I said, standing up in order to kneel before him, but he dismissed this and told me to remain where I was.

'May I join you?'

I hesitated for only a moment. On any other occasion I would have been thrilled by such exalted company, but to be joined by anyone here, to be forced into a conversation which would deter from my preferred occupation, this was something that I did not want. I recovered quickly, however, and said of course he must sit, but I think he noticed my reluctance and the manner in which my eyes flickered towards the woman behind the counter; his own looked over and his smile faltered a little before he sat down. A moment later, she came over and placed a tall latte before him – perhaps he was a regular too and she knew his order – and she glanced at me, her eyes widening in a gesture that was a foreign language to me. Other boys, I thought, other boys would know what such a look meant.

'And how are you finding your responsibilities?' asked the cardinal, taking a sip from his cup. 'Does the Holy Father keep you busy?'

I shook my head. 'The duties are surprisingly light,' I said. 'I am the envy of the college for my proximity to His Holiness, but I'm not sure he even notices me most of the time.'

'And does that bother you?'

'He has many things on his mind, of course,' I said. 'I'm just the boy who brings him his milk late at night and wakes him in the morning.'

'But my dear Odran,' he replied, 'you are not a boy at all. You are a man. Why do you think of yourself in these terms?'

I considered it. It was true, I was twenty-three years old. I was in my final year of studies to become a priest. I had a position of some responsibility, even if it took no great intellect to fulfil it. Why was I unwilling to accept that my childhood was behind me?

'I feel sometimes,' I told him, 'that until my ordination I will remain a boy.'

'Perhaps I felt something similar myself when I was your age, all those hundreds of years ago.'

It was my turn to smile now. Although he was in his mid-sixties, he looked ten years younger and had a healthy, youthful complexion. I could scarcely think of anyone I had met in Rome with more vigour than he.

'Are you missing Ireland yet?' he asked and I shook my head.

'No,' I replied. 'I think about it, of course. Often. But I love Rome.'

'What do you love about it?'

'The buildings. The streets. The Vatican. The sense of history. The weather. The language, I adore. I have been reading what Forster says of Italy, do you know it?'

'Forster was an Englishman. He thought he could change a country simply by stepping into the heart of it. Italy will not be changed by Mr E. M. Forster and his flawed morality. The heroes of his novels come to Italy and profess to be enamoured of the people, but then when the natives behave as natives will, and not like characters out of a Galsworthy novel, the English turn their backs on them and pronounce them savages.'

'But doesn't he mock the visitors for their inability to recognize beauty when they see it?' I asked. 'Is that not one of Forster's themes? The appreciation of beauty from an intellectual standpoint, but our – or rather, the Englishman's – distrust of it in its native land?'

He sipped his latte, turning his head to look at the people passing. One caught his eye and waved and he waved back. '*Mio amico!*' he cried cheerfully. 'Cardinal Siri's secretary,' he said, turning back to me. 'You know Cardinal Siri?'

'Only by reputation,' I said. 'Is it true what they say about him? That he should have been Pope?'

He smiled. It had long been a subject of gossip that Cardinal Siri of Genoa had been elected Pope at the conclave of 1958 but had been persuaded at the last moment to step aside when threats were issued from Communist Russia. The white smoke had appeared, the balcony had been prepared, the doors flung open, but then the cardinals had mysteriously returned to the Sistine Chapel for a further two days, and when they finally reappeared it was with my companion's predecessor, the then Patriarch of Venice, Cardinal Roncalli – Pope John XXIII – at their head.

'Rome is constantly filled with rumours,' he told me, leaning forward. 'There is always gossip, always politics, always power-plays. It has been like this since the time of the Caesars and it will never change. The foolish man immerses himself in it, the wise man ignores it all. But you spoke of the appreciation of beauty, my young friend. You find other beautiful things in the city of Rome, perhaps?' He raised an eyebrow, glancing for only a moment in the direction of the kitchen, and I lowered my head. 'The coffee is very good here,' he continued, reaching across and placing a hand on my forearm. 'I can understand why you would spend so much time in this café.'

He sat back and pointed towards a building on the opposite side of the street, a yellow-bricked, six-storey structure overlooking the piazza. 'I have been staying here for two weeks, away from my beloved Venice,' he told me. 'Working on some documents for the Holy Father. He has seen fit to place his trust in me and I am humbled, but tomorrow, at last, I go home.' His face lit up in delight. 'Home!' he repeated. 'How I long to smell the canals, to sit in the Piazza San Marco, to cross the Bridge of Sighs once again! If I could stay in Venice for ever and never leave I would be a happy man.'

'I've never been there,' I said.

'Then you must come,' he said. 'If you can tear yourself away from the Café Bennizi, that is. You sit here every afternoon, Odran. I observe you from my window. You have fallen in love, I think?'

I felt my stomach twist in embarrassment. 'In love?' I asked.

'With the coffee here.'

'Yes,' I said.

He nodded slowly. 'It is not easy, this life we have chosen,' he said finally. 'There are temptations, of course. We would not be human if there were not temptations or if we did not sometimes allow ourselves to imagine the consequences of giving in to them. Whether our lives might be improved by succumbing. Or whether they might be destroyed.' He turned around as the woman I had fallen for cleared a table beside us. Her blouse had come loose from her skirt, revealing an arc of brown skin that electrified me. I locked the vision into my memory, knowing that I would savour it again and again as I relived the moment.

'And how are you today, my dear?' he asked, turning to her and smiling that glorious smile. She dropped to her knees and leaned forward to kiss his hand. I watched as those red lips blunted against his fingers, the tip of her tongue emerging as she stood again, and it was all I could do not to groan aloud.

'I am well, Eminence,' she said.

'You know my young friend, an Irish boy, Odran?'

'He is our regular customer,' she replied, addressing the Patriarch and not me.

'He cannot resist you,' he said. 'He is shameless in his regard for your coffee.'

She smiled and raised an eyebrow in mockery. 'We are grateful for all our customers,' she said. 'Especially you, Eminence.'

'Ah, but I leave tomorrow,' he told her. 'It is my last day in Rome.'

She looked genuinely crestfallen. 'But you will be back?'

'Always,' he said. 'I always return to Rome. But then I always find my way home again. And that is exactly as I like it.' He glanced at his watch. 'I should go,' he said. The woman walked away and returned to the counter as he stood, beckoning me to stay seated. 'If you ever find yourself in Venice, Odran,' he said, 'make sure to let me know. I enjoy the company of young people and there is much we could talk of, I am sure. You have a friend in me, should you want one.' He reached into his cassock and removed a set of rosary beads which he handed to me. 'Say a prayer for me occasionally, Odran. But perhaps you should think about sampling some other cafés,' he added. 'You are missing out on the best of Rome if you sit in the same place every afternoon.' He turned to leave, but stopped himself, turning back for a moment. 'Remember, my young friend, life is easy to chronicle, but bewildering to practise.' He winked at me. 'Forster.'

And then I started following her.

I felt embarrassed that my interest was so obvious and could not bring myself to sit at the Café Bennizi any longer, so I stopped coming and did something far riskier, far more stupid. My classes ended at five o'clock and I didn't need to be back at the Vatican until eight so I would stand halfway along the Ponte Vittorio Emanuele and watch as she left for the evening, sometimes stopping at a market on the way home to buy food, occasionally taking a seat at a café and relaxing for a half-hour, but more often than not making her way along the Lungotevere Tor di Nona, the Castel Sant'Angelo rising on her left, before turning right to slip into a small residential side-street, the Vicolo della Campana, stopping halfway along to put her key in the door and disappearing inside, at which time I felt safe emerging from the shadows. There I would stand, watching her building, waiting for a moment – not every day but some days – when she would appear in the upper window, and as she turned away her shirt might slip from her body so that for a moment, for only a few seconds, I would spy her bare back as she slipped away into the privacy of that privileged room.

I would not stay long – there were too many people passing through and I could not risk being caught – and if I saw her father walking home too, as I made my way back towards St Peter's Square, then I would cross the street and hope that he did not notice me. I would enter the Vatican by a private door, sign in with the Swiss Guards who were stationed there, and arrive in time to take the tray containing the Holy Father's milk and perhaps a slice of lemon cake, if he had requested it, into his private quarters as he sat in prayer, ignoring me as he always did. And then I would leave and return to my cot and pray too, for my mother, for Hannah, for the woman from the Café Bennizi. And I would try to sleep, and sometimes I would succeed and sometimes I would fail.

Escaping the heat of the city, the Pope was in residence at Castel Gandolfo in August when he died. He had been in ill health for some months and grown depressed when Aldo Moro, his friend from childhood, had been captured and ransomed by the Red Brigades, a crime which had provoked the unprecedented step of a papal intercession, Pope Paul writing directly to the kidnappers, pleading for mercy. But his appeals had fallen on deaf ears and Moro's body was discovered in a car on the Via Michelangelo Caetani in May, his body riddled with bullets, an assertion of the Brigate Rosse's growing fearlessness and the Pope's diminishing influence.

He faded visibly during those last days, and in my selfishness, my concern for the Holy Father diminished as my dismay at being stranded on the Alban Hills increased. Away from his private quarters I tortured myself with visions of who might be entering her building when I was not there to witness it, what man might be invited to her room, and may God forgive me, but when Pope Paul suffered a heart attack on a Sunday evening after Mass, my first thoughts were how quickly our travelling party might return to the capital. A shameful admission, but a truthful one.

Throughout the week leading up to the funeral, a spectacle of such drama and theatre as I had never seen before, I did not get to see her at all, so busy was I with the Masses being held, the rosaries being said night and day and the fact that the Camerlengo, Cardinal Villot, had asked me to assist with archiving and storing the late Pope's effects and helping with the restoration of the papal apartments for whoever might next be chosen by God to occupy them.

As the conclave approached, Rome was an electrifying place to be. One could scarcely move for groups of black-cassocked cardinals moving in groups through St Peter's Square or along the corridors of the Vatican itself, gathering in tight circles to discuss whether they should agree on a candidate. The heat was stifling and the gossips had it that the new Pope would be elected on the first count as these elderly men would not be able to suffer the intensity of the Sistine Chapel for any longer than that. There was talk of Cardinal Benelli from Florence, and Cardinal Lorscheider from Brazil as *Papabile*, and the suit of Cardinal Siri came to the fore once again. Media groups from around the world had been here since the Pope's death and they stood before their cameras and microphones, suggesting regnal names, comparing biographies, while the crowds gathered, packing St Peter's Square to capacity when the conclave actually began.

And when I think back to that August evening when the cardinals elected one of their number to serve as the 263rd Pope and the names written on scraps of paper were pulled from the pins and burned by the scrutineers, sending white smoke into the air above the basilica to the cheers of the faithful, I feel shame that I was not there to see it, for of course it was a moment of history and I was caught up in more secular affairs.

As the world waited for the new Pope to be introduced, I was making my way across the Ponte Umberto, in the opposing direction of the crowds rushing towards St Peter's; and when they stood together to receive his first blessing, I was taking up position in my usual place at the corner of the Vicolo della Campana for a glimpse of that bare back.

When she emerged on to her balcony wearing a light summer blouse and looked out towards the hills of Rome in the distance, I heard a great cry ascend and travel through the air as another balcony was occupied less than a mile from where I stood and Cardinal Luciani, the Patriarch of Venice – who had shown such friendliness to me upon my arrival in Rome, and kindness and humour when he suspected the depth of my attraction to this unnamed woman – stepped out into the overwhelming heat of a Roman summer's night, spreading his arms wide as the crowds cheered and smiling before delivering the first benediction of a new papal reign.

Chapter Ten

1990

During the summer, when the classrooms were empty and the library abandoned, I sought a break from Dublin and thought of Tom Cardle, who by now was based in a parish in Wexford. I cared far less for the school after the exams were finished, when the corridors, usually so noisy with the competitive chatter of effervescent schoolboys, fell silent. The building had a haunted feeling to it during July and August and if I found myself alone in the staff-room, puzzling over the *Irish Times* crossword with my morning coffee, then there seemed to be something slightly pathetic about my solitude.

Curiously, those boys who spent term-time doing everything they could to escape the place now gathered in clumps on the playing fields; were they afraid to leave, I wondered. Did the high walls of the college offer a security they could not find elsewhere?

Tom and I had agreed upon my visit a couple of months earlier when he was stationed in Longford, in the diocese of Ardagh and Clonmacnoise, and I had bought a return ticket, which CIE in their ignorance had refused to refund when he had been moved, once again and with little notice, to the south. The poor man was being treated unfairly, I thought, for no sooner did he find his feet in a parish than he was on the move again.

I had not been in Wexford since the summer of 1964, a

quarter-century before, when my family arrived as five and left as three. In the intervening years I had deliberately avoided the place, so when Tom told me where his new parish was located, I wondered whether or not I should cancel the visit entirely, but decided that I should face whatever demons might be lying in store for me in that county.

I look back now at those years and think of all the phone calls I made to Tom in different counties of Ireland and wonder that I did not make more of it at the time. He started his career in Leitrim, but spent only a year there before being transferred to Galway. There he had stayed for three years before moving to Belturbet in County Cavan, then Longford and then Wexford. In subsequent years he would spend time in Tralee in County Kerry, in a small parish whose name I forget in Sligo, another two years in Roscommon and two more in Wicklow, before passing through a corner of Mayo while barely taking his shoes off on his way to Ringsend. Eleven parishes! It was unheard of for a priest to be transferred so often. No – almost unheard of. There were others, of course. I simply didn't know their names yet.

By now I was thirty-four years old. I had been ordained a priest in the basilica at St Peter's in a ceremony attended by my mother and sister, one of whom wept while the other remained stony-faced, uncomfortable in the face of so much splendour and recognizable wealth. By then we had a Polish Pope, an astonishing thing in itself after 450 years of Italian dominance, and I found an opportunity to introduce my family to him at a ceremony afterwards in the Vatican gardens. My mother might have passed for a member of the Islamic faith for she had covered her entire body and head with dark clothing, her face concealed behind a heavy veil, and she practically curtseyed when the Pope approached her, smiling and taking both her hands in his. Hannah, I recall, was wearing a pale-green shawl around her bare shoulders that slipped slightly as she stepped forward for the blessing and the Holy Father reached out immediately, an expression of near disgust on his face as he pulled it back into place. She gasped a little in surprise and he tapped her twice on her cheek in what might have been intended as an affectionate gesture, but it left a red mark on her face and she appeared to be disconcerted by it, telling me later that she had felt it almost as a slap, a rebuke against her impropriety, and it had taken all her self-control not to challenge him.

'That man,' she said the following afternoon, sipping a glass of red wine as we sat together outside Dal Bolognese in the Piazza del Popolo, 'hates women.'

I rarely spoke of Rome to anyone and almost never to my colleagues in Terenure. I preferred not to speak of my past life, of the things I had seen, the people I had met, the mistakes I had made, which were multitudinous. But I did feel like something of a man of the world for having seen them. I was glad that I had spent a year outside Ireland, while others, like Tom, had been confined to the twenty-six counties and had little chance of escape unless they joined the missions. But I was also something of an anomaly, for those students who had been selected to spend a year in Rome could usually expect speedy advancement in the ranks of the Church. And there was I, ten years a priest and hiding away in the library of a boys' private school on the Southside of Dublin.

My brother-in-law, Kristian, asked me about that once, for although he was not a religious man he had a peculiar interest in the politics and internal positioning of the Roman Catholic Church. 'Am I right in thinking that those who held that role,' he asked, referring to my responsibilities as a student in the papal apartments, 'were usually top of their class in the seminary?'

'Usually, yes.'

'And you were top of your class, Odran?'

'Near enough,' I admitted.

'I read of another man who held that role who became the Prelate of Hungary. And another who became Archbishop of São Paulo.'

'It's a far cry from picking up a tray with an empty cup on it,' I said, smiling at him.

'But what about you, Odran?' he asked. 'Are you not ambitious at all? Would you not like to be a bishop? Or a cardinal? Or even—'

'You know what the Bible says about ambition?' I said, cutting him off.

'What?'

'*"For what shall it profit a man to gain the whole world and forfeit his soul?"*'

He frowned. 'That's from a film,' he said.

'It's from the Bible, Kristian.'

'No, I heard it in *A Man For All Seasons*. It was on television last Saturday night. Paul Scofield said it.'

I shook my head. 'I'd say he was quoting it, to be fair,' I told him.

'Oh, right.'

'Anyway, I'm happy as I am.'

'But there's so much you can do if you have advancement,' he insisted. 'Why do you not want more from your life?'

He seemed perplexed by me, and I in turn was confused by this, for Kristian was not a man who himself sought worldly advancement. Anyway, I had made a decision when I left Rome that I would not be one of those priests who wrote papers and published books or – God forbid – tried to muscle my way on to the national airwaves or *The Late Late Show* with an opinion on everything, a voice for rent to the highest bidder. I would not spend my days clearing my throat in front of a microphone or preening before a camera. My name would remain Father Yates, not Father Odran. Even if I had not disgraced myself in Rome, disappointing those who had put their trust in me, I did not have any ambitions towards climbing any ladder. The truth was that if I had a vocation, which Mam had said that I had, then I wanted to explore it privately. I wanted to understand who I was and why I had been chosen for this life and what I could offer the world from within it. That did not seem to me to be a bad ambition in itself.

But, of course, I could not live by austerity and contemplation alone. I needed friends. I needed company. And once in a while I needed someone who would challenge all the ideas that had been entrusted to me over seven years of study. At times like that, I needed Tom Cardle.

Wherever he might be at the time.

He had a housekeeper in Wexford, a monster of a woman named Mrs Gilhoole whose husband, she told me within minutes of meeting me, had died during the first year of their marriage, some thirty-six years before.

'The cancer took him,' she told me, a hand to her throat as if she had difficulty with the words even after all these years. 'And him only a young man with everything before him. The cancer can be a terrible thing.'

'It can be,' I agreed. 'It is.'

'Did you ever lose anyone to the cancer, Father?' she asked me.

'No, thank God.'

'Are your mammy and daddy still alive, Father?'

'My mother is, yes,' I told her. 'My father died when I was just a boy.'

'Was it the cancer, Father?'

I stared at her; it was difficult not to laugh at her terrible obsession. 'No,' I told her. 'I said already. I've lost no one to that disease.'

'Do you mind if I ask how he died, Father?'

'He drowned,' I said, feeling a desperate urge to get away from her.

'There's a man lives two doors down from here and he drownded last winter,' she told me. She pronounced the word *drown-ded*. Two syllables. 'And my uncle on my mother's side, he drownded in Lough Neagh on his twenty-first birthday. And my late husband's sister's brother-in-law, he drownded out at Salthill.' She paused and shook her head; something told me that, like Peig Sayers, whom she vaguely resembled, she had an army of the dead marching behind her, wringing out their wet clothes, whose stories she would be only too happy to recount.

'It comes to us all,' I said, trying to sound cheerful. 'But sure we might as well enjoy life while we have it.'

She raised an eyebrow; she seemed unconvinced by my platitude. 'Have you known Father long?' she asked, nodding in the direction of the hallway, where Tom was engaged in a phone call; he had waved me through to the kitchen without so much as a hello. His face was redder and older than I remembered it and he had put on a little weight. His manner was one of pure irritation.

'Seventeen years now,' I told her. 'We met in the seminary at Clonliffe. We started on the same day.'

'I see,' she said, looking me up and down as she wiped her hands on her apron. She had rather a pronounced beard and it was difficult not to stare at it. It was also not easy to settle on her age. She could have passed for eighty, but was probably no more than sixty-five. 'Of course, we had Father Williams here for the last twenty-two years,' she told me. 'A lovely man. A saintly man. Did you ever know him, Father?'

'I didn't, no.'

'We were sorry to lose him.'

'Was it the cancer?'

'No, he was moved. And sure wasn't he already in his sixties, so what was the point of moving him anyway? He was very upset about it. They put him across to Waterford. Can you imagine living there, Father?'

'No, I've never been to Waterford,' I said.

'I have,' she said, leaning forward, her deep-brown eyes bursting into life. 'They're a very dour people there. A very dour people. And I wouldn't trust their meat.'

I opened my mouth to reply, but found that I had nothing whatsoever to say.

'Father Cardle is nothing like Father Williams,' she said, her eyes looking down at the carpet.

'You're not getting along?' I asked.

'I'm saying nothing,' she said. 'And sure who'd listen to me if I did speak? They're not gone on women being heard in the Bishop's palace.'

I frowned, uncertain what she was getting at, but the door opened then and Tom came in. 'Bloody Gardaí,' he said. 'They say there's nothing they can do about it unless they catch the villain in the act. How are you, Odran?' he added, turning to me and shaking my hand. 'Are you well? How was the trip down? Did Mrs Gilhoole give you a cup of tea?'

'I offered,' she said, not looking at him but getting back to baking her cake. 'He said no. I don't ask twice.'

I laughed and turned it into a cough as Tom opened his eyes wide in irritation and shook his head. 'Come along in here with me,' he said, leading me into his office.

'That woman will be the death of me,' he said, once we were alone. 'If she is a woman. I have no verifiable proof on that score. Did you see the beard on her? It's like living with the Billy Goats Gruff.'

I laughed again. 'What was it with the Gardaí, Tom?' I asked. 'Is there trouble?'

He pointed out of the window towards the street beyond. 'I have a car parked out there,' he told me. 'A grand little thing. I bought it when I was in Longford and drove it here when the move came. Two weeks ago, I went outside first thing, only to find that someone had scratched the paintwork. Ran a key all the way down the side of it, if you can believe such vandalism. It cost me six pounds to have it redone. Six pounds! I had to take it from the collection box on Sunday, because I don't have that kind of money to spare. And now, only this morning, didn't I go out to find that someone has put a brick through the windscreen. What kind of person does such a thing, Odran, can you tell me that? I have a fella on his way out here to fit a new one, but that's going to cost me another three pounds fifty. And the Gardaí say that they can do nothing about it.'

'It'll be kids,' I told him. 'Do you have a lot of young people on the streets here at night? They lose the run of themselves over the summer holidays.'

'We do not,' he said, as if I'd insulted the honour of Wexford. 'This isn't O'Connell Street in Dublin, you know, with your burger restaurants and your tracksuit shops and your penny arcades. The young people here have a little more about them than that.'

'Well, someone must have done it,' I said.

'Aye. And I tell you what, if I find out who it is I'll wring his bloody neck.'

I turned away and looked around his office. It was stale and tired with drab wallpaper and a desk that looked as if it might fall apart at any moment, but the bookshelves were filled with religious books, which surprised me a little.

'They belong to the last fella,' he said, seeing my expression. 'And the cheerful décor was his idea too. I'm having all the books sent over to Waterford next week. I want shot of them.'

'Would you not have a read of them yourself?'

'Are you joking me? They'd bore the hind-legs off a donkey.'

'And that one?' I asked, pointing at a paperback on his desk which, from what little I knew of Father Williams's taste, seemed out of place here.

'*The Commitments*?' asked Tom. 'No, that one's mine. Have you read it?' I shook my head. 'The language in it,' he said, laughing. 'It'd make a gypsy blush. It's a howl, though.'

'I've heard about it,' I said. 'Some of the lads in the school said something.'

'The best soul band in Ireland,' declared Tom loudly, stretching his arms wide as if he was introducing them onstage at the Olympia. 'And look it,' he said, going over to a side table and picking up another book. 'Here's another one by the same fella. About a dirty little slut up there in Dublin who gets herself pregnant.'

I felt a little unsettled by the sudden violence of his language and recalled what Hannah had said about the Polish Pope. Could such a thing be true of Tom Cardle, too?

'There are some filthy pieces out there all the same, aren't there?' he asked. 'You must see them all the time up there in Dublin, do you? Walking round with next to nothing on. Their bits on display. Giving everyone an eyeful. I'd say they drive the lads in that school of yours crazy, do they?'

'Sure there's always been wild ones and tame ones,' I said, wishing we could talk about something else. For once, I regretted being here and felt the weight of the days ahead on my shoulders. It had been four years since Tom and I had met face to face and here we were, already in a conversation like this. What connected us anyway, I wondered, other than a shared past? Six years as cell-mates, the same profession, a part of our youths intertwined. Did we even have anything in common? I thought of my rooms at the school, of the quiet order of the library. And yet here I was, listening to Tom and his vicious tongue.

'You're home anyway,' I said, anxious to change the subject.

'Home?'

'Back in Wexford, I mean.'

'Ah right, yes.'

'Your family must be glad of it anyway. Those nine brothers and sisters of yours.'

He shrugged. 'Sure I don't see them very often. Three are off in America, two in Australia and another in Canada. And the two nuns are locked away. There's only one still here. He has the farm, of course.'

'Holy God,' I said.

'Sure it's the emigration, Odran,' he said with a shrug. 'There's no work here any more. It's like famine times. And Haughey doesn't care about anyone but himself. He's feathering his nest, boy. Have you seen that island of his on the telly? Does nobody wonder how a man can afford to buy a whole island when we know what his salary is?'

'People don't like to say anything,' I replied. 'Even when it's happening right in front of your eyes.'

'That's true enough.'

'But your mam and dad,' I said. 'They must be pleased to have you nearby.'

He shook his head. 'Sure they're both dead, Odran, did you not know that?'

'What's that?' I asked, not sure I'd heard him right.

'My parents,' he said. 'They're gone three years now. Mam went after a stroke and himself took a heart attack a few months later.'

I stared at him. 'What are you telling me?' I asked, baffled.

'You heard me.'

'But why didn't you say something?' I asked him. 'Why didn't you let me know? I could have helped out.'

'Sure what could you have done?'

'Come to the funerals, for one thing.'

'Half of Wexford was at the funerals,' he told me. 'You don't want to get mixed up with that crowd.'

'But for pity's sake, Tom, I'm your best friend. You should have let me know.'

He looked down at the desktop and drummed his fingers on the leather. I felt a growing anger inside me – how could both his parents have died and he never have let me know? What did that say about our friendship? But I could think of no way to let my hurt out. I could hardly berate him when, after all, he was the grieving party. But I felt wounded, utterly wounded, as if seventeen years of acquaintance counted for nothing.

A long silence ensued, an uncomfortable one, and finally he glanced up at the wall clock and simultaneously the doorbell rang. 'I was just about to tell you,' he said, 'that I have a couple of parishioners to talk to. A mother and her wayward son, if you please. One of my altar boys. A grand little lad. He's proving a bit of a handful at home though, so she brings him here every week for a chat with me. I'm trying to set him straight.'

'Every week?' I asked, trying to sound interested but still hurt by the revelation about the senior Cardles. 'Does that not take up a lot of your time?'

'I don't mind,' he said. 'The poor boy likes talking to me and I think I'm getting through to him. Will you meet me down at Larkin's in the village later? We'll say about six o'clock. Ah, don't look at me like that, I won't take you out on the lash. Sure we'll just have one or two and a catch-up.'

A tap on the door and Mrs Gilhoole stepped in, looking from one of us to the other, a decidedly apprehensive expression on her face. 'It's Mrs Kilduff,' she said. 'And her Brian.'

'Come in, come in,' said Tom, beckoning the pair of them inside, a woman of about forty, nervous and excited to be invited into the priest's parlour, and a small, thin little lad of about eight or nine, who looked at us both through troubled eyes; I wondered what problems this child had seen in his short life that would require a priest's help. He looked shattered, poor fellow.

'I'll leave you to it, Tom,' I said, stepping out into the hallway.

'Six o'clock,' he repeated. 'Larkin's in the village. And you go on now too, Mrs Kilduff, and leave Brian and me to our chat. Give us an hour or so, there's a good woman.'

'Would you not stay, Father?' asked Mrs Gilhoole, as Brian's mother left the house and the door to Tom's study closed behind us. 'Maybe two heads would be better than one?'

'Ah no, it wouldn't be right,' I said.

And then, to my astonishment, she rapped on Tom's door and without waiting for a word from within, flung it open and marched inside.

'Mrs Gilhoole!' said Tom, who was seated at his desk facing the boy, who was sitting in the chair that I had recently vacated. 'What do you think you're doing?'

'Father here was saying that he might like to sit in and see how parish work is conducted,' she said, nodding back at me. 'Weren't you, Father?'

'I was not,' I protested. 'I said no such a thing.'

'Perhaps I misunderstood you,' she said, not an ounce of shame in her voice for her blatant lie. 'But sure it would be a nice change for you, wouldn't it, Father? Go on in there now and tell Brian all about yourself.'

'Mrs Gilhoole, this is outrageous,' began Tom, but I cut him off, reaching forward to close the door with the housekeeper on my side of it.

'Sorry about that, Tom,' I said as I left. 'I'll see you at six, like you said.' Out in the corridor again I turned to Mrs Gilhoole, wondering whether she'd lost control of her senses altogether.

'Poor wee Brian can get scared easily,' she said quickly, before

I could even utter a word of remonstrance. 'I thought he would welcome someone else in the room.'

'Why would he be scared?' I asked. 'Sure what has he to be scared of?'

She hesitated, biting her lip. 'Little boys can take terrible frights,' she said. 'And the collar can be an intimidating weapon.'

'Well look, if he's scared of Tom, then he'd only be twice as scared of the pair of us together.'

'Would he have reason to be, Father?' she asked, a question that took me aback.

'I don't understand what you mean,' I said.

'Ah, you do now,' she said, her lip curling in distaste as she turned away. 'Don't be giving me that old manure. I'll put your bags in your room anyway,' she added. 'You take yourself off to wherever you're going. Sure aren't you all the best of pals anyway.'

With two hours to kill, I found myself walking towards the sea without making any conscious decision to do so. It was a sunny day, sunny enough that I had an idea to take my shoes off and walk barefoot along the sand, and indeed I did so, looking to my right, where I might reach Rosslare Harbour if I walked for twenty miles, but choosing left instead, in the direction of Wexford town, but before that the coastline near Blackwater and the stretch of sand known as Curracloe beach, where twenty-six years before my father had decided to say goodbye to this world.

I had never felt any desire before to revisit this part of the world, a place branded with bitter memories for me. I blamed the county for having a beach, I blamed the beach for taking my brother, I blamed my brother for taking my place, and I blamed myself for not accompanying my father when first asked. Christ, I might have fought him off when he tried to drown me – I was nine years old, after all, five years older than little Cathal, and a strong swimmer with it – and perhaps I would have even persuaded my father to follow me back to shore when he saw my pugilistic arm movements splitting the waves. What else did I blame this place for? Everything. A certain wound that existed deep inside my sister's soul that could never be healed. Its conversion of my mother from harmless housewife to fervent proselytizing believer, intent on making a priest of her only remaining son. Wexford. Bloody Wexford. What an irony that my best friend came from the place. And so yes, I had avoided it all these years, but I was here now, and with time on my hands I felt the importance of walking the beach once again and reclaiming this place from the sarcophagus in which I had placed it.

That summer lived forever in my mind; I could never forget it, but I could never think of it either. And yet it was branded into my memory – almost every moment of that holiday was – when whole years between then and now were almost completely forgotten. I could recall how happy Hannah and I had been every morning when we leaped over the dunes with our buckets and spades, little Cathal following after us, shouting to us to wait for him, but sure why would we wait for a little sprat like him when the whole beach lay open before us and every moment that we weren't there was a moment wasted? We might have won an Olympic medal, the pair of us, we ran that fast. And the look on Mam's face when the Garda appeared in the driveway. And, oh Lord, the train journey back to Dublin, a widow and two fatherless children, and how despite it all, Hannah and I had still been excited by the train, for it was only our second time.

What else? What else . . . what else . . . what else . . .?

A few miles down the road from our chalet was a railway crossing and I might wander down there of a morning, fascinated by the old man who seemed to live in the box by the side of the road, occasionally pressing a button that connected to a series of levers which would lower the railings when a train was due and then repeating the operation in reverse when the train had passed. He was as old as the hills, that man, but seemed impressed by my interest. But when I asked whether I could press that magical button myself he said that it was more than his job was worth, and that if anyone saw me that'd be it, he'd be sent for his chips.

'Sure I won't do any harm,' I told him. 'I've seen you do it. I know what to do.'

'In my job, you have to think of all the people who trust you,' he said. 'Who put their lives in your hands. Just imagine if any of them got hurt on account of your negligence. Or mine. Would you want that on your conscience? Knowing you were responsible for so much pain?'

I didn't see the sense of it at the time and told him so, and finally he said that I could come back on the day that the war in Europe came to an end and he'd let me have a go of it then, because that's what the old man who worked the levers when he was a boy had said to him sixty years before. When I reported this back to my father he had just laughed and shaken his head. 'Sure the war in Europe ended in 1945, son,' he told me. 'But stand still there now, for there'll surely be another one along before too long.'

I wondered now whether that railway box was still there; there was no reason it wouldn't be. The old man would be long dead, of course. And while there had been nothing to match the carnage of the Second World War, there had been revolutions in Hungary and Romania, a civil war in Greece, the Soviets had driven their tanks into Prague, and the Troubles in our own place showed no sign of coming to an end.

What else? What else . . . what else . . . what else . . . ?

Away ahead of me was a clean stretch of sand and I walked close to the water's edge, allowing the waves to rush over my bare feet as they danced in and out like a young one engaged in a hop jig. A group of teenagers in bathing suits were throwing a frisbee around, boys and girls together, and I kept my eyes off them, dreading the frisbee coming in my direction, for I would surely make a fool of myself if I stretched an arm up to catch it. A big gorgeous dog, a golden retriever belonging to one of them, was racing around and having great sport, waiting his chance, for whenever one of the kids did not reach far enough, or another took pity on the hound, the frisbee would sail above our heads into the Atlantic Ocean and off he'd charge into the sea to retrieve it; no matter who had thrown or missed it, the dog always returned it to the same boy, who heaped praise upon his head, and I supposed that this was his master, a fine-looking lad with a smile on his face that suggested he'd never known a day's trouble in his life.

Did he come from another planet, I wondered, to be so carefree?

A few couples were stretched out on the sand, desperate for a bit of colour in that rare thing we call a sunny Irish summer's day. A woman sat rubbing lotion on herself while wearing a pair of Jackie Onassis-style sunglasses and the type of wide-brimmed hat you always saw Princess Margaret wearing when they poured pictures of her into the tabloids to sneer at her vulgarity.

A man was engaged in some sort of yoga-like activity and making a holy show of himself.

I could sense that some of the beachcombers, old and young, were looking at me out of curiosity.

'Would you not take your collar off, Father, and loosen up a bit?' cried one woman, but she meant it kindly, there was not an ounce of malice in her tone, and I raised a hand to acknowledge her as I kept on my way.

And then I saw them up ahead. Another family, the last on the beach, it seemed, for above where they had placed themselves the sun was not shining with as much enthusiasm. Two parents, three little children, the boy and the girl digging a moat around a sandcastle while the infant tried to help but was pushed back time and again, an unkindness that led to tears. The mother and father did their best to restore order as the last of the sandwiches were put away, the empty Tayto bags replaced in the basket, the cans of 7-Up crushed and thrown into a plastic bag so they would not seep whatever drops remained into the cushioned lining of the hamper. And I watched as the father in the group stood up and spun around, a full three-sixty as they say, and kissed his wife on the head and pulled the two eldest children to him, hugging them tightly before taking the youngest fella by the hand, declaring that he was going to teach this boy to swim or what good was being down here at all, and I felt a surge of fright and ran towards them, calling to the man to stop, to come back, to let go of that child's hand and send him back to his family. And they all turned, all five of them, to hear me roar, staring at me as if I was little more than a joke, and in fact a moment later they all started laughing, laughing like maniacs as they pointed at me, but then the closer I got the more their smiles faded, and with them their legs and arms and heads and bodies until they disappeared altogether, for of course they hadn't been there at all. They hadn't been there in twenty-six years and it was too late to go calling for any of them now.

I took the path above the beach back towards the village and as I made my way towards Larkin's I saw a general trade store – beach balls, buckets and spades, toys in the window, packets of tea, biscuits, every sort of thing you might want – and the sign above it offered the unusual name of Londigran's, and I remembered a boy at the seminary all those years ago by the name of Daniel Londigran, only he had been from Dun Laoghaire so it could not have been his family who owned it. Still, it recalled him to me and I wondered what had ever become of him. I knew many of the priests around the parishes of Ireland, particularly those of my age group, but I had never heard his name since the extraordinary business that had seen him moved out of Clonliffe in the middle of our third year and relocated to St Finbarr's College in Cork, a geographical switch that had never happened in living memory.

Daniel Londigran made an allegation which was considered so deceitful and morally reprehensible that the Canon said he could not stand to look at him and that if he would not leave aside his vocation, then he was to be sent to the other side of the country, for he had no place in his seminary. His cell-mate was a lad called O'Hagan, who had been put on a train to Dundalk for a week as his mother was getting herself ready to die in a hospital bed. While he was gone, young Londigran claimed that while he'd been asleep in his bed one night – alone in the room, of course – a fella had come in wearing a black woolly hat pulled down over his face, climbed on top of him and put a hand across his mouth to stop him from crying out. He said that it was too dark to see who it was and he couldn't even tell whether it was a boy or a priest, for by that time some of the boys were grown men and some of the priests were slight enough. An altercation had ensued, according to Londigran; whoever the intruder was had pulled at the boy's pyjamas and tried to relieve him of them, but Londigran, who was no slouch, was standing for none of that nonsense and delivered a mighty blow to the intruder's shoulder which sent him running from the room and disappearing down a corridor.

By the time Londigran was out again, whoever it was was long gone. The next day, the boy put in a complaint and the Canon said that nothing like that had ever happened at Clonliffe College and never would, that this boy Londigran was a deceitful sort and probably a sex maniac and for him to stay would only have been a corrupting influence on the other boys. He had to go, that was the long and the short of it. He had to go to Cork. I, for one, felt sorry about it, for Londigran was a decent fellow who I had always got along well with and he played a strong game of backgammon, which interested me at the time, but he was also devoted to his studies and was a fierce advocate for the speaking of Latin; the poor boy was distraught that Vatican II had put the pipes on that in the Church and had even written a letter to Pope Paul asking whether it might be reinstated. His parents came across from Dun Laoghaire to protest the Canon's decision and I don't think the poor man had ever seen anything like it – his authority questioned! He gave them all short shrift and sent them on their way with a flea in their ears. And that was the end of that. I might have written to Londigran when he got to Cork, had I the strength of character, but I was afraid that one of the priests might intercept my letter and report me to the Canon and I had no desire to be branded a sex maniac too and put on the next 14 bus back to Churchtown, and so I did nothing and that was the end of that.

But that was Londigran. Londigran from Dún Laoghaire. And here again was a Londigran's shop in Wexford. I wondered whether Tom ever passed by, and if he did, what thoughts went through his mind.

The guest bedroom in the parochial house was situated at the front of the house, a small box-room with barely enough space for a single bed, a narrow wardrobe and a statue of the Sacred Heart on the wall. There was a photograph of the Polish Pope over my bed, his hands clasped in prayer, gilt-framed, looking like butter wouldn't melt. Tom's room was at the back of the house, while Mrs Gilhoole had the largest one of all, with an en-suite attached, and she told me before I went up to bed that her room was inviolable.

Inviolable!

I don't know what she took me for.

I brought *The Commitments* up to bed with me, hoping that it might send me to sleep, but of course it did the opposite, it kept me awake. I suppose that was the intention. Finally though, Joey 'The Lips' planted a kiss on Imelda Quirke and I could keep my eyes open no longer and turned the page down to mark my place before switching off the bedside lamp, cursing the fact that Tom had made me drink four pints of Guinness and two whiskeys, for the whole mixture was playing like Fossett's Circus in my stomach and I dreaded to think the head that would be on me in the morning. I closed my eyes, yawned, reached for sleep.

Before it could come, I heard a noise in the street below. Something difficult to define. Was it a cat, perhaps? No, not right for a cat. But there it was again. It was a most peculiar sound and I climbed out of bed, parting the curtain just a little to see who or what was out there. At first I could see nothing, but then I made him out. A man. No, a boy. A young boy. What was a young boy doing out on the street at this time of night? Where were his parents? And was he in his pyjamas? He was indeed. A pair of red pyjama bottoms and a black top with white sleeves. I leaned forward, almost pressing my face to the glass. It was Brian Kilduff. The boy who had come to see Tom earlier. What was he at? He leaned down. He took something from his pocket. Was it a Stanley knife? It was. I could make out the yellow moulding in the moonlight. The boy had a Stanley knife in his hands and was unleashing the blade. He was making his way around Tom's car, slicing each tyre, one after the other, and I watched the vehicle sink to the ground, one corner at a time, until the whole thing was on the level again, at which point the boy moved away, apparently satisfied with his vandalism, and looked up towards the presbytery with a blank expression on his face.

I stepped back quickly, pulling the net curtain in front of me so that he could not see me, and when I took the courage to look out again, there he was, running back down the street towards his own house in his bare feet, his damage done. I got back into bed and didn't know what to think.

But there's the lie. Because I did know what to think. Only I could not bring myself to think it.

Just as I could remember the day that poor Londigran was sent back down to Cork, and going to bed that night, looking over as Tom took his shirt off and seeing the great blossoming bruise on his shoulder, the purple on the outside, the green in the centre, the white skin surrounding it. And me lying there, saying not a thing.

And the guilt now, as I think of it.

The guilt. The guilt, the guilt, the guilt.

It is so strong that at times I can understand what my poor father felt when he woke up in his depression and decided that this was the day that he would go down to Curracloe beach, that this was the day he would say goodbye to his loved ones, that this was the day he would push one of us under the water until the fight was gone out of the child and he could set off in the direction of Calais, with no hope of arriving alive.

It is so strong that there have been moments in recent years when I have wondered whether I should make my own way down there to Curracloe beach and let that be the end of the matter.

Chapter Eleven

2007

Hannah was surprisingly cheerful on the day she moved into the Chartwell Home, a specialist facility for patients with developing dementia. She was enjoying one of her more lucid periods at the time, but one of the curious aspects of the disease was how it could occasionally allow the victim a few hours' respite, like a benevolent employer, leaving the patient more like her old self again. But then, just when you might be having a sensible conversation together, just when it seemed as if the monster had disappeared, the clouds would gather and she would stare into your face as if you were an intruder in her home – '*Who are you?*' she would scream, hands clutching at the side of her chair. '*What are you doing here? Get out!*' – and it might be weeks or even months before clarity was returned to her.

Was it me she was screaming at in those moments, I often wondered, or the disease?

It had started in 2001, only a year after Kristian's death, when she began having difficulty remembering names and faces, but it didn't progress quickly at this point. But then, sometime towards Christmas of 2003, she took a downhill turn and began making mistakes at work which led to disciplinary proceedings – her immediate supervisor showed scant consideration for her years of service and seemed determined to find a way to have her removed – and ultimately she made a shocking error that left the bank tens of thousands of euros out of pocket, and not only was she fired on the spot, but there was talk of a prosecution against her. It was Jonas who insisted then that there was something wrong and we took her to a specialist unit at St Vincent's, where, over the course of a few months, a team of doctors conducted cognitive testing, telling her to fill out a series of questionnaires which seemed to be full of daft and often repetitive questions, along with memory trials and language games that left her irritable. She said that they made her feel like a five-year-old again. They took blood samples, checked her calcium levels, investigated her diet for vitamin deficiencies, performed scans on her brain. And finally, when the diagnosis was made, the slow crawl towards losing her for ever began. She was stoical enough, it has to be said; at the time she seemed more concerned with clearing her name at the bank and putting Mrs Byrne in her place than anything else, although it's possible that she relied on this pyrrhic victory to cover up for her fears.

She managed to stay at home for another few years after that, with a bit of help from the Health Service Executive and the money that Jonas had earned from his book royalties, so we hired a home-help to look after her, a young French nurse who demonstrated extraordinary patience and kindness. Aidan helped out too, of course, but his money always went directly into his brother's account and when he came to Dublin to visit his mother I never heard anything about it until after he was gone back home again.

'Did he not give you a call?' Jonas would ask me, all innocent, and I would shake my head.

'He did not.'

'He said he would.'

'Well, he didn't.'

'I don't know, so.'

And to be honest, I'd given up feeling troubled by this. If Aidan wanted to behave like that towards me when I had never done a bit of harm to him in his life then that was his own business. I had bigger things to worry about.

But now, however, things had gone too far. The French nurse, God love her, endured an incident of violence that left her with a fractured wrist, and between us all we agreed that the time had come for Hannah to leave Grange Road altogether and move into a specialist facility where they could look after her and give her the care she needed.

She knew exactly what was going on; she even agreed to it and signed the necessary paperwork, for over those couple of weeks she had a series of surprisingly good days. She didn't force me or either of her sons to seek any kind of authority over her. She was only a young woman still, forty-nine years of age, and it seemed a cruel fate that would rob her of her mind and her reason when she could potentially live for another forty years, although this was a prognosis that the doctors assured us was unlikely for a woman with her condition. I could not contemplate her potential death, however; I had been robbed of enough things in my life without losing my beloved sister too.

Until then, Jonas was still living in his mother's house, despite the changes that had happened in his life. Success had come early to him – he was only twenty-one when *Spiegeltent* was published and became a surprise bestseller – and he was in demand for literary festivals around the world. He wanted to take advantage of the opportunities that were out there for him, but it was difficult when his mother was ill at home. He'd spent three months away from Dublin during the summer before his final year at Trinity, travelling to Australia, where he found work as a barman in the Rocks, but this was his only experience of life outside Ireland and I knew that he wanted to travel more, to see the world and let his various publishers pay for it. But he didn't push the move, by any means. If anything, it upset him greatly, but he and I both knew that it was for the best, and if a bonus was that he could fully embrace the new life that his talents had brought his way, well then I didn't think that that was something Hannah would begrudge him.

'I'm going to have my own room, amn't I, Odran?' Hannah asked me as we drove, the three of us, towards the nursing home.

'You are, of course,' I told her. 'Sure you've seen it already, do you not remember?'

'I do, I do,' she said, looking out of the window as we drove past Terenure College, where a swell of purple and black was making its way down a rugby pitch, the boys sweeping forward like waves along a beach as the tide came in, their upper lips jutting out over their teeth-guards like wolves baring their fangs. It had been more than a year since Archbishop Cordington had moved me from there and I missed it something awful. 'It's the one with the lilac wallpaper, isn't it?' she asked. 'And the chair in the corner with the scuff on the right leg.'

'That's your room at home, Mam,' said Jonas, turning around in the passenger seat. 'Your and Dad's old room.'

'But sure that's what I'm talking about,' she said, frowning.

'No, you were asking about your room at the Chartwell. It's painted light green and has a television hanging on one of the walls. Do you not remember you worried that it would fall down and break?'

She shook her head as if she could make no sense of what he was telling her.

'Odran, do you remember when we used to go into the pictures?' she asked after a long silence as we drove through town, past where the old Adelphi cinema used to be on Abbey Street. So many of the cinemas of our teenage years were gone now. The Adelphi, the Carlton at the top of O'Connell Street, the Screen on the Bridge, which was a terrible filthy place at the best of times. You couldn't move for the squelch of dried Coke and the crunch of dropped popcorn on the floor. Even the new Lighthouse cinema, where they showed the foreign films, was gone.

'I do,' I said. As a young priest in Dublin in the early 1980s, we used to have a standing appointment for a Wednesday-night picture and a bite to eat in Captain America's afterwards. 'They were great nights.'

'We would go for a meal, Jonas,' she said, sitting forward in the seat and tapping him on the shoulder as I drove. 'Even though we'd be full from all the popcorn and the Fanta at the picture. We saw everything in those days, didn't we, Odran?'

'We saw a fair bit of it anyway, yes.'

'What was the one with the monkey in it?'

'The monkey?' I asked.

'Ah, you know it,' she said. 'The monkey. And himself. Clint Eastwood.'

'*Any Which Way You Can*,' said I.

'*Every Which Way But Loose*,' said Jonas, correcting me.

'Similar titles,' I said.

'Simian titles,' said Hannah, and for a moment I wondered whether we were doing the right thing at all bringing her up to the Chartwell when she could make a joke as bad as that.

'Do you remember *On Golden Pond*?' I asked her.

'I do,' she said. 'Katharine Hepburn, wasn't it? Shaking away like she'd just got off a merry-go-round. And Henry Fonda. He died shortly before that film was made, didn't he?'

'If he died before it was made, sure he wouldn't have been in it.'

'After then. He died after.'

'He did,' I said, casting my mind back. 'Didn't he win an Oscar but he couldn't show up because he was so sick?'

'What was his daughter's name again?' asked Hannah.

'Jane,' I said. 'Jane Fonda.'

'No,' she said, shaking her head and frowning. 'Kristian, Henry Fonda's daughter. Do you remember her name? She did all the exercises. She loved to keep fit.'

'Yeah, that's Jane Fonda, Mam,' said Jonas, as we turned on to Parnell Square for Dorset Street. 'And I'm Jonas, not Kristian.'

'No, not her,' insisted Hannah. 'I know who Jane Fonda is and she had nothing to do with Henry Fonda. Wait now, it'll come back to me in a minute.'

We drove on in silence for a while.

'Will I be allowed out again?' asked Hannah after a while. 'Or do I have to stay?'

'It's not a prison, Mam,' said Jonas. 'It's a nursing home. They'll take care of you. But I'll be able to take you out for a day-trip now and again. And Odran might, too.'

'I will, of course,' I said.

'And where will we go?' she asked. 'It won't be anywhere dangerous, will it?'

'We could go for a walk along Dun Laoghaire pier,' I suggested.

'And over to Teddy's for an ice-cream,' she said, clapping her hands together in delight. 'The best ice-creams in Dublin.'

'They are,' said Jonas and I in unison.

'And you with your discount there,' she added. 'We'll be able to get them cheaper.'

I looked back at her in the rearview mirror. 'My discount?' I asked.

'On account of working there,' she replied. 'They have to give you a discount, don't they? We could have a 99. They still do 99s, don't they?'

'Sure they'd never stop doing a 99,' I said; there was no point getting into the issue of whether or not I worked or had ever worked as an ice-cream salesman. 'And a bit of strawberry sauce poured over the top.'

'No, I never cared for that,' said Hannah. 'Just the flake. That's enough for me. We'll go, just the three of us.'

'Great,' said Jonas.

'Not you,' she snapped furiously. 'You're not allowed to come. Odran, tell him he can't come. It's just to be the three of us.'

Should I leave it or should I ask, I wondered. Was it easier left alone? 'The three of us?' I said. 'The three of us here, do you mean?'

'You and me, Odran. And little Cathal, of course. He'll go mad if he finds out that we've gone for ice-creams and not brought him along.'

I breathed in deeply and blinked away the sudden rush of tears that were threatening to make a show of me.

'Are you all right?' asked Jonas quietly, turning to look at me, and I nodded but said nothing.

We were all silent for a few minutes after that, and finally I felt that I should speak again. I couldn't leave things on that note.

'We could take a spin up to Howth Head too,' I suggested. 'On a fine day, that would be great fun, wouldn't it?'

'Do you remember the time you got lost up on Howth Head?' she asked, tapping Jonas on the shoulder.

'No, that was Aidan,' said Jonas.

'Who?'

'Aidan,' I said, raising my voice, but I don't know why, there was nothing wrong with her hearing, after all. I was speaking to her like the Brits speak to the foreigners on the continent, pronouncing their words slowly, very, very slowly, syllable by syllable, as if it's the volume and speed that's the problem.

'Who's Aidan?' she asked.

'Aidan!' I repeated, as if that would make things any clearer.

She thought about it for a moment. 'I don't know any Aidan.'

'You do, of course,' I said. 'He's your eldest.'

'Ah, poor Aidan,' she said quietly. 'He'll never forgive me, will he?'

'Forgive you for what?' I asked.

'Aidan loves you, Mam,' said Jonas, turning around to her. 'He loves you. You know that.'

'He'll never forgive me. But sure he'd been drinking, hadn't he? He couldn't have driven home with drink on him.'

'When did Aidan try to drive with drink on him?' I asked.

'Not Aidan,' said Jonas quietly. 'She doesn't mean him.'

'Who then?'

Jonas shook his head.

'Who?'

'Leave it, Odran.'

'I was up Howth Head many's the time,' said Hannah. 'Do you remember when Jonas went missing, the day he was out collecting the blackberries?'

'I do,' I said. 'I was there that day.'

'You weren't, don't be telling lies. He was collecting blackberries, that's how it started. We were all there for a picnic, Mam and Dad, and Aidan of course – this is long before you were born, Odran.' She thought about it and I said nothing. I hated hearing her rambling like this, especially when a portion of the story was based in reality; it was simply the details and the characters that she was getting wrong. 'And I gave Jonas a margarine box to collect the blackberries in, one of those big old square ones, do you remember them? Yellow plastic. So off he goes and the next thing you know, hasn't he gone missing, and we're all up looking for him and calling out his name. And then we found the margarine box at the side of the cliff and I thought I was going to lose my reason, thinking that he'd gone over the side. I was hysterical. But then he came back, Lazarus returned from the dead. He'd only wandered off somewhere and lost track of the time. The margarine box must have belonged to someone else. I was never so frightened in all my life.'

I smiled. Some of the story was true anyway.

'Until now,' she added after a moment.

'You're not frightened, Hannah,' I said, more of a statement, to make her believe this, than a question. 'You're not, are you? Sure it'll be grand. They'll take good care of you.'

'Most of those nurses steal,' she said, pursing her lips. 'And will there be black ones there, do you think?'

'Ah now,' I said.

'We'll be in to see you all the time,' said Jonas, as we drew closer to the Chartwell. 'You'll be sick of the sight of us. And anything you need, you only have to ask and we'll get it for you.'

'You say that now,' she said, turned away. 'Let's see where things stand in six months' time.' She looked at her nails, holding her hands out flat before her. 'When I was a girl, shortly after I was married, they used to ask me whether I was related to W. B. Yeats,' she said. 'I used to tell them that our names were spelled differently. Were you ever in the Abbey, Odran?'

'I was,' I said. 'Many's the time. Sure I was there with you, do you not remember it?'

'No,' she said, shaking her head. 'No, I was never there. I wouldn't have been let. They put Daddy off the stage on account of his bad manners.'

'This turn,' said Jonas, pointing at the building coming up on the left.

'I know.'

I pulled into the car park and turned off the engine and sat there for a moment with closed eyes. It was hard on me, this move, but I could tell that it was even harder on my nephew. His life was taking off, he was a young man the world was taking notice of, but he was worried about leaving his mother in this place, whether it would ultimately damage him in some way, as if he felt that he was committing an act of treachery upon a person who had never treated him with anything other than kindness. He didn't want to abandon her, didn't want to be seen to be abandoning her either, but what else could he do?

'Is this it?' she asked from the back seat.

'Are you sure about this, Mam?' he asked, turning around, tears in his eyes.

'I am, son,' she said. 'Sure I can't be sitting in the front room going doolally, can I? We all know this is for the best.'

He nodded. I thought this was the cruellest part of it. The degree of her coherence when the disease was taking a breather. It was as if nothing was wrong at all. But it would change, of course. In an instant. In a heartbeat.

We got out of the car and Hannah looked into her purse. 'I want to keep a hold of my money,' she said. 'Will they have the *Herald* in here or will I have to go out to get one?'

'They're sure to have it,' I said. 'If they don't, we can place a standing order.'

'I can't live without my *Herald* of an evening.'

'Will you take this bag, Odran?'

'I will.'

A middle-aged woman, Mrs Winter, emerged from the front door of the hospital; we had met before. She seemed capable and efficient, the no-nonsense sort. Emma Thompson would play her in the film. 'Hello, Hannah,' she said in a friendly voice, reaching out and taking both my sister's hands in hers. 'We're so glad to see you.'

Hannah nodded; she looked a little frightened. She leaned forward and whispered in the woman's ear, '*Who are those two men?*', pointing at Jonas and me. Appearing through the door a moment later was a much younger nurse – Maggie was her name; she'd shown us around twice already and told Hannah what the routine would be and I was glad to see that my sister recognized her, for her face lit up.

'There's the girl I like,' she said, marching over to her and giving her a hug as if she was her long-lost daughter. 'You're a fine young one,' she said. 'Are you married at all?'

The nurse laughed. 'Chance'd be a fine thing,' she said.

'Do you have a fella?'

'I had one,' said Nurse Maggie. 'I threw him away.'

'You did right. They're more trouble than they're worth. This one's going begging if you want him.' She nodded in Jonas's direction, who rolled his eyes but smiled. Nurse Maggie looked him up and down; she had a filthy look in her eye that made me laugh but made Jonas blush scarlet. Maybe some of the adolescent was still in there somewhere, after all.

'Can I have him on approval?' she asked.

'What's that mean?' I asked.

'Ah Kristian, you remember,' said Hannah, turning to me. 'Like the old stamps. You bought them on approval. You held on to them for a while and if you liked them, you bought them and stuck them in your book, and if you didn't, you sent them back again and didn't have to pay.'

'Shall we get you inside, Hannah?' asked Mrs Winter, who did not seem to like the direction this conversation was taking. 'It's getting a bit chilly out here.'

'All right,' said Hannah in a resigned tone.

'Will you be here tonight, Maggie?' I asked. 'To look after her?'

'Not all night, no,' she replied. 'I'm on days all this week and next. Nine to five.'

'That was another one that we saw,' I said immediately. 'Who was in that?'

'Lily Tomlin,' said Mrs Winter.

'Dolly Parton,' said Jonas.

'Jane Fonda!' cried Hannah, clapping her hands in delight. 'Henry's daughter!'

*

In Waterstone's bookshop at the end of Dawson Street, I ran into one of my old pupils, Conor MacAleevy. He'd been going into fifth year when I last laid eyes on him and was studying for his Leaving Certificate now, but working weekends to make a bit of pocket money for a summer abroad when the exams were over. I'd dropped in to have a browse and found myself examining the E. M. Forsters for old time's sake. I'd read them all before, of course, but here they were with shiny new covers. I picked up *A Room with a View*, remembering the Café Bennizi in the Piazza Pasquale Paoli, where I had sat for so many afternoons pretending to read this same book while the woman behind the counter brought espressos out to her customers. I closed my eyes when I remembered how she had humiliated me in the end. And then, to counter this, I thought of my old friend, the Patriarch of Venice, and wondered whether there might be a book in the shop about his life, or had he not lasted long enough as Pope to warrant his story being told?

I put the Forster back where I found it and made my way past the fiction shelves, pausing at the Rs, where all of Jonas's books were gathered together. *Spiegeltent*, of course. About ten copies of it. And *Callomania*, his second, a novel about a man who believed himself to be possessed of extraordinary physical beauty but was capable of showing nothing but anger and violence towards the world. A pile of hardbacks on the table. I picked up a copy of each – I had them both already, of course, but I often bought more to give to friends – before heading up the central staircase in search of the biography section. I made my way along the shelves, but couldn't find what I was looking for; I was not to be deterred though, so approached the counter, where a teenager was tapping something into a computer.

'Father Yates,' he said, looking up, a slightly startled expression on his face, the type you get when you meet someone completely out of context.

'Conor MacAleevy,' I said. 'Is it yourself?'

'It is.'

'What are you doing here?'

'I work here. Part-time,' he added. 'Saturdays and Sundays.'

'Fair play to you.'

'How are you, Father?'

'I'm all right, I suppose. I don't imagine you want to hear about a recurring pain I've been getting in my knee?' He looked at me blankly. 'It was a joke, Conor. A joke.'

'Ah right,' he said. 'Are they for you?' he asked, looking down at the two novels that I was carrying with my nephew's name branded across the top.

'They are,' I said. 'Have you read them?'

'I have,' he said.

'Did you like them?'

'I thought they were a bit shite, to be honest.'

'Ah right,' I said.

'Pseudo-intellectual crap. He comes in here all the time and he thinks he's the man, you know. The stupid hair on him too.'

'Well sure I thought I'd give him a go anyway. On account of him being one of ours.'

'How do you mean?'

'Irish.'

'He only plays that card, Father. He's Norwegian really.'

'Did he not grow up here?' I asked innocently. 'Did I not hear something about that?'

'I think he spent a summer here when he was a boy. His father was Irish. He only pretends to be Irish because, let's face it, how many famous Norwegian writers can you name?'

'None,' I said.

'Well then.'

I nodded and looked down at the books. 'I heard they were great,' I said. 'I'm going to take them anyway.'

'Whatever.'

I couldn't help but laugh. They did a great job training the staff here, it had to be said. The manager ought to be proud of himself, whoever he was. 'Anyway, Conor,' I said a moment later, 'you wouldn't happen to have a book on Pope John Paul I, would you?'

'Pope John Paul II, you mean?' he asked and I stared at the young pup, correcting me like that.

'No,' I said. 'I mean Pope John Paul I.'

'*Was* there a Pope John Paul I?' he asked and it was hard not to laugh. Could he possibly be that stupid?

'Conor,' I said patiently, 'think about it for a moment. Do you think there could have been a Pope John Paul II if there hadn't been a Pope John Paul I? Would that make any sense at all?'

'You make a valid point, Father,' he said, grinning.

'I know I do. I suppose it's not worth my while asking you if you have anything then?'

'We could take a look, if you like,' he said and we took a wander down the shelves together, but could find nothing. I resolved to leave well alone and look it up myself on the internet. Someone must have written something about the poor man, surely? He'd been the Pope, for pity's sake. Even if it was for only thirty-three days.

'So how are things back in Terenure, Conor?' I asked. 'How are all the lads?'

'Ah, we need you back, Father,' he said cheerfully and something in his tone told me that he meant it. 'The fella we have teaching us now is only brutal. And the library's in a state. Is there any chance of a triumphant return?'

'It's only been a year,' I said. 'Could things have fallen apart that quickly?'

'You have no idea, Father,' he said dramatically, whistling through his teeth. 'No idea.'

'I'd love to come back,' I said. 'I'm supposed to come back. I was promised. Only I'm covering a parish for a friend who's away at the moment. The Archbishop said it wouldn't be for long.' As the words emerged from my mouth it occurred to me how true this was; he *had* said it wouldn't be for long. And yet there had been no talk of me going back. Perhaps it was time I called on him.

'Well it'll be too late next year,' said Conor. 'I'll already be in university.'

'But sure who knows,' I replied, 'there might be other lads still in the school after you leave it.'

He considered this and nodded. He looked at me as if I was a simpleton. 'Of course there will be, Father,' he said and now I did laugh. Was he as daft as he seemed or was this play-acting of some sort? I'd always taken him for a bright lad.

'Well I'll just take these two,' I said, handing Jonas's novels across with a twenty-euro note, and he rang them up.

'Ah, Father,' said Conor a moment later as he put the books in a bag. 'Did you hear about Will Forman?'

'Who?'

'Will Forman. You remember him, Father. Tall lad, real straight black hair. Was always getting his phone taken off him in class.'

'Oh yes,' I said, nodding. 'He used to sit in the seat behind you in English, didn't he? What about him, is he all right?'

'Ah he's grand, I suppose. But he only went and joined the Taliban.'

I stared at him in surprise. 'Come again?' I said, certain that I must have misheard him.

'The Taliban. You know the Taliban?'

'I do,' I said. 'I see them on the telly. Osama Bin Laden's lot.'

'Yeah. Well Will was always going on about how George W. Bush and Tony Blair were war criminals and how the whole 9/11 thing was a big con-job and how the US government had organized the whole thing from day one so they could find an excuse to go in and get the oil. I mean he was a total *plank,* the way he carried on about it. Anyway one day he gets into a big fight with Mr Jonson, the history teacher, about it. You remember him, right?'

'I do.'

'So they get into this big drama about imperial oppression and all that bullshit and Will stands up in the middle of the class, picks up his bag and turns round to the rest of us and says, *"That's it, lads, I've had enough of this crap. I'm off to join the Taliban."'*

I stared at Conor. It was all that I could do not to start laughing. 'And did he do it?'

'The funny thing is that he did. He bought a ticket to Iran or Iraq or wherever it is—'

'Afghanistan?' I suggested.

'That's the one. He bought a cheap ticket on the internet, stopped shaving and off he goes. His oul' one is having kittens over the whole thing. And his dad's down at the Department of Whatever every day trying to get Bertie Ahern to do something about it. They've gone ballistic about it, the pair of them. There's even a sponsored walk going on next Sunday to raise money for it.'

'To raise money for what?' I asked, mystified by this. 'For the Taliban?'

'No,' he said. 'Not *for* the Taliban.'

'Then for what? Where's the money to go?'

He thought about it. 'Now that you ask, I couldn't tell you,' he said. 'Maybe his oul' one and his oul' fella are going out there to Afghanistan too, to bring him back. I'd say those flights don't come cheap. You'd probably have to change at Heathrow or Frankfurt.'

'Might he not just be staying at a friend's house, do you think?' I asked. 'Might he be playing a trick of some sort? He was always a bit on the daft side, if I recall.'

'No, Father,' he practically roared, raising his voice so high that the other customers turned to look at him. 'I'm telling you, he's gone and joined the Taliban. Niall Smith's cousin saw him on the news. He said he was in the middle of a group of men burning effigies of Dick Cheney in the middle of . . . I don't know. Some city. Kandahar, maybe? Is that a place?'

'It is,' I said.

'Well then,' he said, nodding as if he had just proven his point. 'What do you think of that?'

There was little I could think of it. The school had gone to hell. The library was in disarray. Will Forman was in Afghanistan fighting for the Taliban. This couldn't go on any longer. I had to get out of parish work and back to my school. I went home and picked up the phone to call the Episcopal Palace. And that's when I found out the truth.

I found it surprisingly difficult to secure an appointment. Fifteen months earlier, when Archbishop Cordington had summoned me to see him, he had phoned – or rather, one of his secretaries had phoned – at nine o'clock on a Tuesday morning and I had been sitting before him, declining whiskeys, by three o'clock that same afternoon. Now, when the meeting was being arranged at my request, I ended up phoning on four separate occasions, and each time I was told that someone would get back to me, but this mysterious someone never did. On the fifth occasion, I may have sounded a little angry and so they finally acquiesced and offered me thirty minutes with His Grace two and a half weeks later. It was a long time to wait, but the summer holidays were almost upon us and as long as I could be reinstalled in Terenure by September, I didn't mind if a little more time went by.

'Odran,' said the Archbishop when I finally entered his office and knelt before him, pressing my lips against the golden seal of his office. How heavy it seemed on his finger, I thought. And how proud he was to wear it. 'This is a great surprise. There's nothing wrong, is there?'

'No, Your Grace.'

'Your health is good?'

'Yes, and yours?'

'I can't complain. Sit down, sit down. But listen, I don't have long, I'm afraid. I have Cardinal Squires calling me at some point this afternoon and I need to get my thoughts in order before I speak to him. That man can sniff out uncertainty like a basset hound on the trail of a fox.'

I sat in the same chair that I had occupied at our last encounter and he eased himself down opposite me. He had grown even more corpulent in the intervening time, a Friar Tuck for the Dublin diocese.

'How are you getting on out there anyway at . . .' He thought about it. 'Where was it that we sent you again?' I told him and he nodded. 'Ah yes, of course. Nice little parish. I'd say you're loving it there, are you?'

'Well,' I said, laughing a little, 'as parishes go, I suppose it's as good as any. *Loving it* might be over-stating the case a little though. To be honest, I wondered how much longer I might have to stay there.'

'How do you mean?'

'You remember, Your Grace, that you said it was just to cover for a while when Tom Cardle was away. But that was more than a year ago now. I haven't been able to get hold of him either. He's often gone missing in action, so to speak, over the years, but ever since I moved out to his parish it's as if he's vanished off the face of the earth. Have you spoken to him yourself?'

Archbishop Cordington's face bore no expression. 'Father

Cardle is grand,' he said. 'You don't need to worry about him. We have him somewhere nice.'

'What's that?'

'You heard me.'

'Where do you have him?'

'Does it matter?'

'Yes,' I said. 'Yes, it does. Is he away on the missions?'

'No.'

'Well he's not at any of the Irish parishes because I'd have heard of it if he was. I'm worried about him, Your Grace. You know we go back a long way, don't you? All the way to our seminary days?'

'I know all about your past friendship, thank you, Father Yates,' he said. 'I don't need reminding.'

It seemed as if I had said or done something to displease him, but I couldn't think what. Was it so unusual for a man to ask after his friend when he hadn't heard from him in over a year?

'I only ask,' I said, trying my best to sound reasonable, 'because if he's coming back soon then perhaps I could return to Terenure in September, for the start of the new academic year. I'd like to, if it was at all possible. I think I—'

'Odran, that's not going to be possible,' he said, bringing his left hand down firmly on the arm of his chair in a depressingly definitive gesture.

'It's not?'

'No.'

I hesitated. 'Do you mind if I ask why not?'

'I don't mind in the slightest,' he said, smiling but saying nothing further.

'Your Grace,' I began, but he held up a hand to silence me.

'Odran, we need you where we have you. Father Cardle will not be going back to parish work anytime soon.'

'Ah now,' I said, 'do you not think that's a little unfair? The poor man has been moved around from Billy to Jack since his ordination. If he's spent more than two or three years in any one parish, I'd be surprised. Would it not be better for him, for his parishioners, if he was allowed to put down roots?'

'He'll be putting down roots at Mountjoy prison if the Gardaí have their way,' he replied.

I felt my stomach lunge. So here it was at last. The moment that I had always imagined might come one day but in my silence and complicity had hidden at the very back of my mind. 'The Gardaí?' I asked quietly. 'Do you mean that the Gardaí have an interest in Tom?'

He stared at me and raised an eyebrow. 'Are you going to pretend that that's a surprise to you?'

I looked away. I could not meet his eye. Had there been a mirror in front of me, I would not have been able to meet my own.

'Look, Odran,' he said, sitting forward now. 'They're all out to get us, you know that, don't you? You read the papers. There's a witch-hunt going on out there and it's only just begun. It'll get worse over the next couple of years if Cardinal Squires and the Vatican don't get a hold on things, not better. We need John Charles McQuaid back in this city, I tell you that. He'd put manners on these pups.'

'What is Tom accused of?' I asked, ignoring this.

'What do you think he's accused of?' said the Archbishop, looking around, his face growing scarlet with indignation. 'And those journalists and the television presenters, the media as a whole, they want to tear us down. Bloody Pat Kenny, bloody Vincent Browne, bloody Fintan O'Toole, the whole shower. It's like that old joke that when a man marries his mistress, he creates a vacancy. If the media can get rid of our voices, then they can take our place. It's a power grab by RTÉ, nothing more. And by the politicians too, of course. They've cosied up to us for years and we stood by them when they were getting their jollies, sitting in parked cars in the Phoenix Park with their trousers around their ankles while the rent-boys sucked them off, but now they see the way the tide is turning and they're running scared.'

'Your Grace,' I said, but he was in full mettle now, practically hanging off the chair and spitting at me as he spoke.

'It started with herself in the Áras,' he said. 'You know that, don't you? Mary Robinson. It was with her that the rot set in. We have Charlie Haughey to thank for her. If he had stood by Brian Lenihan then he might have got in, but no, he looked after number one as usual. He should have put his foot down, not let her anywhere near the place. Her with her women's rights and her abortion rights and her divorce rights. She had a loud mouth on her, that bloody West Brit bitch, and if you ask me her husband should have found a way to silence her a long time before. *Mná na hÉireann* indeed. I'll give you bloody *Mná na hÉireann*.'

'Your Grace,' I said, raising my voice in a way I never had to him before. I didn't want to hear about Mary Robinson. I didn't want to listen to his bile and his hatred and his misogyny. I wanted to hear about Tom Cardle, I wanted to hear about my friend. 'Stop for a minute, would you, and tell me about Tom.'

'It's a lot of rubbish,' he said, sitting back and throwing his hands in the air. 'Some little lad saying things, making up stories. Wants to get his face in the papers, that's all.'

'What's he been accused of?'

'I don't need to spell it out for you, Odran, do I? For God's sake, you're an intelligent man.'

'He's been accused of interfering with a boy, is it?'

The Archbishop offered a bitter laugh. 'That and more,' he said.

'And what does he say about it?'

'He is, as they say in the films, in a state of denial. He says he did nothing wrong. He says that he would never do anything to hurt a child.'

'And is it just the one boy making a complaint?'

He shook his head. 'It'd be a lot easier if it was,' he said. 'We'd be able to do something about it if it was just one.'

'How many?'

'Nineteen.'

I took a hold of the side of the chair; I was unsteady. I could say nothing for a moment.

'Nineteen who have come forward, you mean?' I said finally in a quiet voice that I barely recognized.

He stared at me as if I was the enemy. 'Now what could you mean by that, Odran?'

'What does Tom say about it all?' I asked, ignoring his question.

'He says it is a conspiracy against him.'

'And is it?'

'Of course it's bloody not. Sure don't I have a file on him as long as my arm. Isn't that why the poor man has been moved from parish to parish over the last twenty-five years? We moved him in order to keep the little children safe. You can see that, can't you? That's our first responsibility. To keep the little children safe.'

I stared at him, wondering whether he could hear the absurdity of his words. 'Safe?' I asked. 'And in what way were they kept safe exactly?'

'Look, there's been allegations in the past, Odran,' he said, calmer now. 'I'll admit that. Quite a few of them, in fact. In different parishes. And whenever things got a bit hairy, we acted immediately, we took Tom away from wherever he was situated at the time and far from temptation. Oh, we were ruthless about it, Odran. He never got to stay more than a few weeks after an allegation came to light. A month at the most. The problem is that he gets too close to them. He wants to be their friend.'

'And so you just move him somewhere else?' I asked. 'Where he can do it again?'

'Don't you be looking at me like that, Odran,' he snapped, leaning forward and pointing a finger at me. 'Remember your place, do you hear me?'

'And the parents?' I asked. 'They were happy with that solution?'

He sat back and shrugged. 'They always were in the past,' he said. 'Usually the bishop would have a word with them. Once or twice, the cardinal has got involved. I know of one case where a phone call had to be made.'

'A phone call?' I asked. 'To the parents, do you mean? From who?'

He raised an eyebrow. 'Do you need me to tell you?'

'From who?' I insisted.

'Use your imagination. This thing goes right to the top, Odran. And sometimes when things go all the way to the top, then the man at the top has to intercede.'

'Jesus Christ,' I said, sitting back, a hand to my forehead in astonishment.

'Not him, no. The next rung down.'

'Do you think this is funny, Jim?'

He sat back and shook his head. 'I've told you to remember your place, Odran, and I meant it.'

'But these parents—'

'These parents have always been happy enough to see Tom moved. But now there's a couple who won't do what they're told. They've pressed charges. The Gardaí know they're on to something. They've found other lads who want in on the action. They're going after us, Odran, can't you see it? They're going after all of us. They'll tear us all down if they get the chance.

And where will the country be then? We have to think about the country, Odran. About Ireland. About the future. About the children.'

'The children,' I said.

'The thing is that this is going to get a lot worse before it gets any better,' he said. 'And poor old Tom Cardle is going to be next in the firing line, I'm afraid. It's going to break in the papers any day now, so there's no point me even telling you to keep quiet about it. The DPP got in touch and they feel they have enough to pursue a conviction, so the papers will feel free to write what they like once that gets out and a court date is set, to blacken a good man's name. That's what this phone call with the cardinal is all about. We have to figure out a plan. We have to find a way around it all. But in the meantime . . .' He stood up and beckoned me to my feet. 'Come on, up. In the meantime, we have to protect the status quo. All right, Odran? And that means you staying exactly where you are, it means leaving whoever's looking after the lads in Terenure exactly where he is, and it means doing everything we can to get Tom Cardle through this situation and out the other side without a stain on his character.'

I couldn't help myself. I laughed. 'But how would that even be possible?' I asked.

'It will be possible because the archdiocese will spend whatever it needs to spend in order to defend him. We will not allow the Church to be brought down by some attention-seeking child. It simply will not be allowed to happen.'

'But Your Grace?' I asked, feeling a light-headed sensation come over me as I made my way to the door and turned back to look at him. 'Did he do it?'

The Archbishop frowned, as if he didn't understand exactly what I meant. 'Did who do what?' he asked.

'Tom,' I said. 'Is he guilty?'

He spread his arms wide and smiled at me. 'Which of us,

Father Yates, are without a stain on our soul? *Let he who is without sin cast the first stone,* do you remember that? You remember what you were taught in the seminary? *We are all playthings for the Devil.* But we must fight to keep our wicked impulses at bay. And we will fight, do you hear me? We will fight and we will win. We'll bring these pups to heel if it takes every penny that we have. And Tom Cardle will have his name cleared and he'll go back to his parish, or perhaps a different one, and then Odran, do you know what will happen to you?'

I shook my head. I felt I was under a death sentence of some sort.

'You, my dear Odran,' he said, leaning forward on his desk, both hands before him, a big brute of a man like Orson Welles playing Cardinal Wolsey, 'you can go back to your precious school and teach those little bastards to respect the Church.'

Chapter Twelve

1994

Of all the places that my mother might have chosen to die, standing by the altar of the Good Shepherd in Churchtown, with a can of Pledge in one hand and a duster in the other, would probably have been close to the top of the list.

She started volunteering there in 1965, a year after the events in Wexford, arranging the flowers on a Saturday night in preparation for Sunday morning's Masses, hoovering the carpets twice weekly, laundering and ironing the altar covers or the priests' vestments and scrubbing down the sacristy counters when the room was empty. She wasn't alone in these endeavours, of course. There was a group of women, perhaps ten of them, who volunteered in a similar way and they enforced strict rules of seniority. One might be allowed to wash the parish priest's soutane, but another might only be allowed the curate's. My mother never complained; she was only thirty-eight years old when she joined their collective and most of the ladies were a good fifteen years older than her. She knew that she only had to bide her time and one by one she would see them off. She wasn't wrong either; by the day she died, she was firmly in charge.

There were men who volunteered as well, of course, but God

forbid that any of them should get stuck with the menial work. No, the men read the lessons on a Sunday morning when there was a decent-sized congregation present to testify to their saintliness. Or they became ministers of the Eucharist, standing at the edges of the altar with expressions of piety on their faces as they offered the body of Christ to those members of the flock who had failed to arrive early enough to sit by the centre aisles, where the priest himself gave communion. The men helped to write the parish newsletter, but the women delivered it; the men organized the church social evenings, but the women cleaned up when they were over; the men encouraged the children to take part in family Masses, but the women had to look after them when they did. This was not particular to my mother's day or my mother's church; I have known men and women like this all my life and there are some things, rotten and discordant to the eye, that will never change.

Mam had not been well for some time, spending a week in hospital the previous summer with high blood pressure and then falling on the ice in January when she was making her way along the Braemor Road for the post office at The Triangle, badly spraining her ankle. She wasn't an old woman, only sixty-seven, and I felt a strong sense of injustice that she was taken before her time, but then our family, it seems, was destined to be taken young.

I heard about her death on a Saturday morning while I was celebrating ten o'clock Mass in the church at Terenure College. We usually had a good turn-out at this time, at least sixty people of all ages would show up, but they were an impatient group, hoping to get in and out by half past at the latest in order to get on with their day. I glanced up during the Eucharistic prayer to see my brother-in-law, Kristian, entering through the rear door and taking a seat in the back row, and I hesitated with my words, trying to rationalize his presence, for in all the years that I had known him, I had never seen him set foot inside a church outside of his wedding day and the christenings of his two sons. Something must be wrong. Hannah might have had an accident; but no, if that was the case then he would be with her and someone else would have come to get me. Perhaps Mam had taken another fall and my sister was by her bedside in the hospital. I whizzed through the rest of the service and the faithful were back out on the street by twenty past the hour, delighted with themselves and with me, and I beckoned Kristian to follow me as I made my way back towards the sacristy.

'Will you sit down, Kristian?' I asked, when he followed me in.

'No, Odran, I think I will stand.'

'I suppose something has happened, has it? It's not often I see you here.'

'I have a bit of bad news,' he said, looking around at the unfamiliar objects, perhaps wondering what I did with all these ciboria, chalices and communion cups.

'Go on.'

'It's your mother,' he told me. 'She's had a bit of a turn.'

'Is she all right?'

'Not really, no,' he replied. 'She has decided to die, I'm afraid.'

'Ah here,' I said, sitting down, feeling the room begin to spin a little. 'Are you sure?'

'I'm sorry, Odran.'

'How did it happen?'

He told me and I nodded, trying to take it all in, but failing. A stroke was what they were saying. I had seen her only a few days before, when she asked me to meet her in town for a coffee to celebrate my birthday. We had gone to Bewley's Café on Grafton Street for old time's sake, but had to move seats as there was a young fella and a young one sitting at the table next to ours who couldn't keep their hands off each other long enough to eat their cream slices.

'Have they no shame?' she asked, leading me to a table at the rear of the room.

'Ah sure they're young,' I said, not wanting to discuss it particularly.

'I was young myself once,' she replied. 'I didn't carry on like a whore.'

I had noticed a bitterness enter her conversation and her language over the last few years. She'd grown angry with the world and it didn't suit her. She had always been a placid enough person – except when it came to matters of religion, of course – but since her late fifties she had started to view the world askew, as if it was a source of constant annoyance to her.

'Are you well anyway?' she asked me.

'I am.'

'Are you eating?'

'I am, of course. Sure I'd die if I didn't.'

'You look terrible thin.'

I raised an eyebrow for I knew full well that I could stand to get a bit more exercise. I spent too much time sitting in a classroom or behind the desk in the school library. I was thirty-nine and only a few days before had asked Jack Hooper, our permanently ill-tempered physical education teacher, whether he might not give me some instructions in how to use the gym equipment. He seemed irritated by the question, telling me that the weights and machines were for the use of the rugby team only.

'Well sure the rugby team can't use them all the time, can they?' I asked.

'Would you know how to use them though, Father?' he asked, looking annoyed by my audacity. 'You might break them or do yourself an injury.'

'That's why I'm asking for your help,' I told him, smiling. 'So you can show me. It's not a problem, is it?'

It turned out that it was. He wouldn't let me anywhere near them.

'How are things at the school?' she asked.

'Busy as always.'

'I was over with your sister last night. She has those two boys spoiled. Jonas is a quiet little fellow, all the same,' she said, sipping her coffee and pulling a face as if it tasted of sewage. 'Never has his head out of a book. But Aidan's a scream. So full of life. You'd never stop laughing when he's around.'

I smiled. It was true. At that time, Aidan was the life and soul of any gathering with his impressions and his jokes and the way he'd belt out a song at a party without even being asked. He moved his hips like Dickie Rock and stretched one arm out, the fingers waving in the air like Elvis. He was gas.

'He'll end up on the stage, that one,' said Mam.

'He might,' I agreed.

'He will, I promise you. I never saw a child so full of joy as him. Or with such a need to be on display.' She put her cup down and looked around as if she was afraid of being overheard. 'Did you hear about Father Stewart?' she asked, lowering her voice.

'I did,' I said, for it was the talk of the parishes.

'Has he been in touch with you at all?'

'Why would he be?' I asked. 'Sure I barely know the man.'

'You were at the seminary together.'

'He was two years behind me, Mam.'

She leaned forward, hoping for a bit of gossip. 'But is it true what they're saying?' she asked and I shrugged, for although I knew it was, I didn't much feel like discussing it. For Father Stewart had turned in his collar, resigned his office and run off to the Canary Islands with a woman he'd met at the Eurovision Song Contest in Zagreb. She'd been representing Czechoslovakia and came in sixteenth. I saw her on the telly myself. She had a decent enough voice on her. I thought she could have done better. In the contest, I mean.

'Did you ever hear the like of it?' she asked.

'I'm sure he struggled with his decision,' I said.

'I doubt it,' she said, shaking her head. 'He was always eyeing up the young ones. I didn't trust him. He had a glint in his eye that spoke of unwholesome appetites. I'm glad he's gone. If you ever did something like that, I don't think I'd ever get over the shame of it. His poor mother must be beside herself.'

I said nothing. I tried to imagine what would have happened if I had written to my mother from Rome and told her that I would not be coming back, that I was no longer living in the Vatican, nor even at the Pontifical Irish College, but was staying in an apartment on the Vicolo della Campana with a woman who worked as a waitress in a café.

'How are the neighbours?' I asked.

'Oh we're finished on Father Stewart, are we?' she asked me.

'I have nothing to say about him, Mam,' I said. 'I told you, I barely knew him and I don't know where he is now.'

'Well,' she said, unsatisfied, 'Mrs Rathley has the arthritis something awful. She's always asking after you, of course. She was always a great fan of yours. And Mrs Dunne across the road is in the garden all day and night. Those roses are all she has now, ever since himself ran off with his fancy piece. And you heard that those English people moved away?'

I looked up. *Those English people* was how she always referred to the Summers family. She'd never bothered to learn their names, or if she had she'd never felt obliged to use them.

'They have?' I asked.

'Sure they were never going to stay. They bought a house in Spain, if you can believe it. Said they were retiring there for the weather. More money than sense, if you ask me. I couldn't live in Spain, could you? The son became an estate agent, I heard. I wasn't surprised. He was always a shifty sort. He had a look in his eye I didn't trust. And the daughter, well you remember the daughter?' She fixed me with a hostile stare; the anger had not diminished in her, not even after twenty years.

'Katherine,' I said.

'Yes, something like that,' she said. 'She does the weather now on the ITV.'

'She doesn't!' I said, fierce entertained by this notion.

'Not the real ITV,' she said quickly. 'They wouldn't have her. No, one of the regional channels. ITV Anglia or ITV Jersey, I think. Sure no one would be watching her on them, would they, but she'll be lapping up the attention all the same. She was always desperate for it, as I recall. Do you ever hear from her at all, Father?'

Did I mention that my mother always called me *Father*? I had asked her time and again not to, but she refused.

'Sure why would I ever hear from her?' I said, irritated by the way she poked and prodded at me.

'Well weren't you the best of pals once?'

'Hardly. And if we were, it was so long ago that I'm sure she'd have forgotten about me by now.' I tried to imagine what Katherine Summers would look like these days. I pictured her carrying a little more weight, her glamour a little faded, but with the lollipop still hanging out of her mouth. I imagined she was married, with children and had a home of her own. I tried to see myself in such a scenario – with her or with someone else – and found it was impossible.

'Odran,' said Kristian, snapping me out of my daydream. 'Did you hear what I said?'

'What's that?' I asked, looking up. Back in the sacristy. Back in the real world.

'I said it was very sudden. She just collapsed in the church and by the time the ambulance got there she was already gone. There's that at least. She didn't suffer.'

'Yes,' I said, uncertain how much of a relief that was. We had not always been close, Mam and I, and there were parts of our relationship that I did not like to explore, but I could not imagine a world without her in it. And I was an orphan now, too, a word that seemed incongruous to me, a Dickensian notion out of date in the twentieth century. Could a man be an orphan at thirty-nine, I wondered. I supposed that he could.

'Where is she now?' I asked.

'They took her to St Vincent's.'

'Did someone give her the last rites?'

He hesitated. 'I don't know,' he said.

'And Hannah?'

'She's there with her. She's waiting on us.'

I nodded. 'And the boys?'

'I left them with a neighbour,' he said. 'They can stay there for the rest of the day. Until we get things sorted.'

'Right,' I said. 'I suppose we better get over there so.'

I finished changing and we went outside; he'd parked his car in the semi-circle outside the school reception and I saw the boys from the rugby team making their way on to the pitches for their Saturday-morning training session as if nothing had happened, as if the world hadn't changed entirely.

'Did she say anything?' I asked as we drove towards the hospital.

'How do you mean?'

'Any last words,' I replied. 'Did she say anything before she went?'

He hesitated for a moment. 'I don't know,' he said.

'Did you not hear?'

'There wasn't anyone there,' he told me.

'No one there? Do you mean that no one was there when she collapsed?'

Kristian hesitated as he watched the traffic. He was always a very careful driver, both hands on the wheel at all times in the ten-to-two formation. Both eyes on the road. A Norwegian thing, perhaps. Irish drivers would be practically eating their lunches and watching the telly in the car. 'Not as far as I know,' he said.

I thought about this. 'And how long was she there before she was found?' I asked.

'A few hours, maybe,' he said. 'One of the other women came in and discovered her lying on the floor. She called the ambulance.'

I took this in and tried to register it: the picture of my poor mother lying stretched out in front of the altar of the Good Shepherd Church, the life seeping out of her, her eyes slowly closing, her world growing dark, her breathing slowing down, her panic rising or a wonderful serenity descending. We would all experience such a moment in time.

'Then how,' I asked finally, my voice rising slightly, higher than it had any need to be in order to be heard in the car, 'how on earth do you know that she didn't suffer?'

For months afterwards I would wake in the morning having forgotten that Mam was gone. I would wonder whether I should call her that day, whether there might be anything she needed, whether we were due a chat or whether I could put it off for a few days more. And then I would remember and it was a kick to the stomach every time, and occasionally I would put my head in my hands and groan and feel a loneliness unlike any that I had ever known before. Had I spent as much time with her as I should have done? It must be a terrible thing to know that you have been a bad parent, but worse to know that you have been an ungrateful child. These were not thoughts I could allow to play on my mind for too long; they were dangerous for a man like me.

*

Tom Cardle celebrated my mother's funeral Mass with me. He was stationed in Tralee at the time, having recently been moved from his last parish in Wexford, but he drove up and I laid out a sleeping bag on the sofa in my room at the school and offered it to him for the night. It would be like old times, I told him. We could imagine we were just boys in the seminary again but without the Grand Silence to contend with. We could talk all night if we wanted.

He was late arriving, but came to see Hannah and me in the house just before we left for the church to ask us about our mother and our memories of her, in search of things that he might say in his homily. He seemed concerned about doing this right; he showed great compassion towards us both.

I had never seen him in such spiritual mode before and felt an urge to laugh when he placed his hands on Hannah's shoulders and looked at her with concern on his face. They had known each other a little over the years, probably hearing each other's name more often than they had met, and although Hannah had never been particularly religious, she thought well of Tom, perhaps because he was my best friend and she loved me. She took the boys to Mass on a Sunday, of course, but I suspected that was only because all the neighbours did so and it would have been more of a statement not to. She would have needed to feel a depth of opposition to the Church to go against it and she didn't feel that way; she was apathetic at best. Aidan had made his First Communion and would soon be confirmed; Jonas was halfway there.

The service itself was functional. Tom tried his best and I said a few words too, but it was not a demonstrative affair, although Aidan and Jonas, who had been close to their grandmother, showed some outward signs of emotion. Hannah looked a little shell-shocked and only when Tom mentioned little Cathal from the altar did she glance up and put a hand to her mouth, almost in horror of the situation unfolding before her.

The coffin frightened me; I could barely stand to look at it.

The burial left me fierce upset.

Afterwards, we all went back to Hannah's house where a spread had been laid on. There was a fair crew gathered. Most of the women who had volunteered in the church with Mam were fighting for supremacy in the kitchen as to who would get the right to boil the kettle, to wet the tea, to serve the two fathers in the living room. Their husbands sat in the front room watching a football match on the television. One of them lit a cigar when his team scored and his wife ran inside at the smell of it and asked him did he not have any respect for the dead, wasn't poor Mrs Yates only just getting herself comfortable in her grave and there he was lighting that filthy thing as if it was the middle of Christmas. The unfortunate man gave her a look that suggested he would have liked to put the cigar out in her eye, but said nothing in front of company, merely walking quietly to the kitchen sink and rinsing the end in water before wrapping the cigar in kitchen paper and returning it to his inside pocket.

'I'm sorry, Father,' his wife said to me, but I simply shrugged and said it didn't matter. He could do what he liked as far as I was concerned. It wasn't my house, it was Hannah and Kristian's. If they didn't mind, why should I?

As the evening wore on, the feeling of respectful misery gave way to light-heartedness, as these things tend to do. Kristian had a couple of crates of lager in a fridge out the back and the men, myself and Tom included, cracked these open while the women poured glasses of wine or sherry and told themselves that Mam would have been delighted with the send-off, even if Quinnsworth's ham was nowhere near as good as Superquinn's and they couldn't imagine what Hannah had been thinking opting for the processed coleslaw instead of making it fresh herself.

'What will we do with the house?' I asked my sister, uncertain whether or not it was too soon to make plans of this sort, but she didn't seem to mind.

'Sell it, I suppose,' she said. 'The price of property these days. And a good solid house like that in Churchtown. You realize how much it's worth, don't you?'

'I don't,' I replied. I never paid any attention to such things. I read in *The Irish Times* of how prices were rising and the sums that apartments alone could go for these days, let alone semi-detached houses in a good area, were shocking, but I never paid any attention. I had no interest. She named a figure and I put my glass down and stared at her as if she was mad.

'Are you having me on?' I said.

'And that would be on a bad day,' piped up Kristian. 'Realistically, you could be looking at twenty per cent more if there are multiple offers. Although there'll be estate agent fees, death duties, taxes and what not. But still, you're looking at a fair windfall. Sorry,' he added immediately, having the good grace to look embarrassed by how grasping he sounded. I didn't mind; he meant no harm. Kristian didn't give a damn for money.

'I'd never have thought it,' I said.

'The sooner we put it on the market the better,' said Hannah. 'There's no point letting it go downhill and there'll be vandals if the word gets out that the place is empty.'

'How would we go about doing that?'

'I can take care of it, if you like,' said Kristian. 'If you'd rather do it yourself, of course, then that's fine too.'

I thought about it. 'If you were willing, Kristian,' I said, 'then that would suit me down to the ground. I don't know the first thing about things like that.'

'Right so,' said Kristian. 'Leave it with me for now and I'll get back to you.'

'Fifty-fifty split?' asked Hannah and I thought it could only be the drink egging us on like this for surely it was a terribly inappropriate conversation for a funeral.

'Sure what would I do with money like that?' I asked. 'I'd have no need for it.'

She looked at me, an expression crossing her face that suggested she had wondered whether this might be the case and hoped it might, although she did not want to rob me of anything. She had a family life, of course, a mortgage. Two boys to look after. Schools to plan for. Universities one day in the future. Yearly trips for four of them back and forth to Lillehammer. I had none of those things. I was alone in the world.

'You might find a need,' said Hannah. 'Once it was in your account.'

'There's five of us, isn't there?' I said. 'You and Kristian, Aidan and Jonas and me. I'll take a fifth. That's all I'll need. I might find a use for it when I'm older.'

'A quarter,' said Kristian. 'I don't need anything.'

'We'll leave it for today,' said Hannah as Aidan hovered hopefully in the doorway with his guitar. There was a captive audience in the next room and he wanted to show off.

'Today's not the day for that, Aidan,' said Kristian, shaking his head.

'Sure maybe it'd cheer us all up,' I said and he nodded and in we all went.

Aidan sat down and started to play a song. 'Sealed With A Kiss'. It was hard not to laugh as this little eight-year-old lad pledged to send her all his love every day in a letter, his eyes closed, so consumed was he by his passion for this nameless creature. He had a fine voice on him for a boy his age and I could see that he was revelling in the attention that he was getting, while Jonas simply sat in a corner with his Bobby Brewster, probably hoping that no one would call on him to do a turn next. When he finished, Aidan told us all that he'd been learning tap dancing in school and did we want to see it? We said we did and he ran upstairs to get his wooden board and came back down again, clack-clack-clacking away as fast as he could like Fred Astaire without the top hat and tails. He was a gas little fella, there was no doubt about it.

'Have you been doing the dancing for long?' Tom Cardle asked him when I found them in the kitchen together a little later.

'Only a few months,' said Aidan. 'But my teacher says I could go all the way.'

'All the way?' asked Tom. 'Where's that then? The Olympia?'

Aidan took a step back and opened his arms wide like a junior P. T. Barnum. 'The West End!' he said. 'Broadway! The sky's the limit!'

I had a memory of my father saying something similar many years before and felt a deep sadness inside me, but Tom shook his head, thoroughly amused. 'This is a fine one, isn't he?' he asked me. 'He's after telling me about all the television programme he watches. He says he wants to be on it himself some day.'

'Do you not get goggle-eyed with all that telly?' I asked him. 'I'm surprised your mam allows it.'

'She says I can watch one programme every night and whatever I want on the weekend.'

'It's a fine life you have,' said Tom. 'I had no such luxuries when I was your age.'

'Did you not have a telly?'

'We did not,' he replied.

'Why not?'

'Sure we couldn't afford one. And my dad didn't like the look of them anyway. He said they'd probably explode and burn the house down.' Aidan sniggered. 'You may laugh, young man,' continued Tom, 'but you wouldn't have been laughing if my father was here. He was a terrible man for the stick.'

'What's that?' asked Aidan.

'Ah come on, Tom,' I said. 'Sure he's only a child.'

'Sorry,' replied Tom, turning away. 'All I'm saying, Aidan, is that you're lucky that you live here and now and not there and then.' He looked back at my nephew and smiled. 'You're a fine little fella though, all the same, aren't you? The big happy head on you.'

It was my turn to smile now; it pleased me that Tom liked Aidan. It made me feel proud to be the uncle of a boy that everyone so clearly adored.

'Uncle Odie,' said Aidan, turning to me now. 'Do you want to come upstairs and see my Star Wars figures?'

'Sure you showed them to me earlier,' I said, for I'd only been in the door when he'd dragged me up to the room that, to his great pride, was his alone as Jonas slept in the box-room next door. 'Do you not remember?'

'Oh yes,' he said, frowning, before turning to Tom. 'What about you, Father Tom?' he asked. 'Would you like to see them?'

'Ah come on now, Aidan,' said Hannah. 'Sure Father Tom has no interest—'

'Do you mean the film?' asked Tom. 'The old film? Are the boys still interested in *Star Wars*? That must be fifteen years old by now.'

'Of course we are,' insisted Aidan. '*Star Wars* is the best film ever made.'

'Did you never see *Willy Wonka and the Chocolate Factory*?' asked Tom. 'I always liked that one. Your man in the big hat and the little lads with the orange faces.'

'I have Darth Vader and Boba Fett and Luke Skywalker and the Death Star hanging off my ceiling,' continued Aidan, ignoring the question as he counted these off on his fingers. 'And loads of droids and a C-3PO with a wonky arm, but he still talks and—'

'Ah here, this sounds like it needs to be seen to be believed,' said Tom. 'I'll take a look if you'll show me.'

Aidan clapped his hands together in delight and off the two of them went upstairs as Hannah came into the kitchen with some empty glasses from the living-room.

'Are you all right, Odran?' she asked me.

'I am. And you?'

'Ah sure.' She turned the hot water on in the sink and put a few plates inside. 'That's most of them gone now anyway,' she said. 'The women leave when the sandwiches are finished. The men go when they're told.'

'Life goes on,' I said.

'It does. It was good of Father Tom to say the Mass with you, wasn't it? I was worried about you doing it alone.'

'Sure we go back a long way.'

'Is he staying with you tonight?'

'He is,' I said. 'I have a sleeping bag on the sofa for him. He's got the car outside.'

'A sleeping bag?' asked Hannah, turning around just as Tom and Aidan reappeared before us, having gone up and down the stairs in only a minute or two. Aidan was still chattering away at the top of his voice about the Force and what it meant to be a member of the Galactic Federation and how he didn't know how the actors in the film could bear to be in a scene with Darth Vader, even if it was only David Prowse under the suit, because there was nothing and no one in the world as scary as the Dark Lord.

'I'd wet my pants if I saw him in real life,' said Aidan. 'I'D WET MY FREAKIN' PANTS!' he roared in delighted excitement.

'Aidan!' cried Hannah in horror as Tom and I burst out laughing.

'What?' he asked, holding out the palms of his hands to display his innocence. 'I would! It's the truth!'

'I don't care if it's the truth. You don't say things like that in front of your uncle and Father Tom.'

Aidan shrugged, looking up at Tom then and grinning as Tom smiled back down, patting his head.

'Is it right what Odran's after telling me?' asked Hannah. 'That you're sleeping in a bag on his sofa tonight?'

'I am,' said Tom. 'Sure I've slept on worse. The beds in the cemetery were practically made of concrete.'

'The cemetery?'

'The seminary,' he said, correcting himself. 'There's one for the head-doctors now.'

'Would you not stay here?' asked Hannah and Tom looked across at her, hesitating for only a moment.

'Here?' he asked. 'In your house?'

'Sure we have lots of room. Jonas can sleep on a cot in our room and you can have the box bedroom, the one next to Aidan here. It'd be a lot more comfortable.'

Tom thought about it, frowning a little. 'I don't know,' he said after a moment, a shadow passing across his face. 'I'm happy enough with the sleeping bag.'

'You might be, but I'm not,' insisted Hannah. 'And you've had a few drinks, remember. You can't drive with drink on you.'

'She's right about that,' I said. 'I can get a taxi home, it's not a problem.'

'Come on, what do you say, Father?' she insisted. 'Will you not take the box bedroom? It'd be my way of thanking you for all you've done today.'

He looked down at Aidan, who was looking up at him hopefully; perhaps he wanted to show him more of his collections. 'All right so,' he said finally. 'If you're sure it's no trouble. It might be a bit easier on my back, I suppose.'

'It's no trouble at all. We'd be delighted to have you. Just don't let this one keep you up all night with his stories,' she added, nodding at her son. 'He can talk for Ireland, this one.'

I left about an hour later, when the darkness began to fall, saying goodbye to Tom and promising to give him a call later in the week. Jonas was already upstairs in his parents' bedroom asleep and Kristian came to the door with me, asking whether I was sure that I wanted him to look after the details on the house sale because he didn't want to force his way in – it belonged to Hannah and me, after all – but I said no, it was fine, and that anything he could do that would take the worry off my mind would be a great help.

And then before I could turn away, Aidan came running out of the living room like Speedy Gonzales and threw himself into my arms so hard that he nearly knocked me over.

'Goodbye Uncle Odie,' he roared. '*Adios amigo!*'

'*Adios amigo!*' I replied, laughing as I turned away, and when I reached the door of my car I looked back and there he was, standing in the doorway next to Tom, who had a hand on his shoulder, my nephew waving so hard that I thought his arm might fall off, the grin on his face threatening to split his face in two.

And that was the last I ever saw of Aidan. Of *that* Aidan. The next time I was in their house, a week or two later, he was a different lad altogether.

Chapter Thirteen

1978

Cardinal Albino Luciani, Patriarch of Venice for the last nine years, was elected Pope on the twenty-sixth of August and the friendliness which had existed between us on our previous meetings diminished immediately as he grew accustomed to his new responsibilities. I assumed that I would have more of a personal connection to him than I had enjoyed with Pope Paul, but this was vanity on my part for I was only a humble seminarian, tasked to wait on him twice a day. I was still the tea-boy, nothing more, and his mind was focused on more pressing matters than my conflicted vocation.

At first, of course, there was great excitement. It had been fifteen years since a new Pope had lived in these apartments and while the Curia seemed uncertain how to control a man who was already showing more informality than his predecessors, the world appeared to be charmed by him. At the Irish College there was a sense that real change might happen in the Church. Vatican II and its reverberations had dominated the papacies of both John XXIII and Paul VI; it was time to build on the decisions which had been made and who better to do so than a healthy, relatively youthful man of cheerful disposition? At sixty-five he was young for a Pope. He could reign for twenty years, perhaps longer. A golden age was about to begin, we told ourselves.

The cardinals remained in Rome for another week, long enough to witness the investiture, which Pope John Paul, as he had now become, chose over the pomp of a coronation, and some stayed even longer to intercede with him on their various plans and ambitions for their dioceses. He received them courteously, but by night, when he prepared for bed, I could see that he was exhausted, so numerous were the meetings he was forced to take, the documents he had to read and the daily routines that a man in his position, with his peculiar and unique relationship to God, was obliged to endure. Unlike his four immediate predecessors, he had not worked as a Vatican diplomat or within the Curia and I could sense the distrust among the old guard, who blamed the college of cardinals for electing someone they considered to be an outsider. Outsiders brought change, and change was feared; change had to be stopped in its tracks.

'It's incredible,' he muttered to himself one evening as he sat at his desk, piles of papers spread out before him, each one cramped with figures and printed on the thick vellum paper of the Istituto per le Opere di Religione – the Vatican Bank. He was dressed in a warm red and silver robe and when he took his glasses off I could see the heavy bags forming beneath his eyes; they had not been there a couple of months earlier when we had sat together at the Café Bennizi, talking of E. M. Forster. He tapped away now at a calculator as if he was an accountant in a small business and not the head of a billion Catholics worldwide. I turned down the blanket on his bed and brought his tea over to him. He sat back and sighed, shaking his head. 'These will have to wait until the morning,' he said. 'I will lose my mind if I stare at them any longer.'

I said nothing. It was not my place to speak unless he asked me a question.

'Rome is a peculiar place, is it not, Odran?' he said after a moment. 'One thinks of it as the heartbeat of Catholicism, a place of contemplation and spirituality, but no, it is a bank.' He tapped his fingers on the desk before him, his face filled with frustration. 'I began my life as a priest, I became vicar-general to the Bishop of Belluno, then Bishop of Vittorio Veneto before becoming Patriarch of Venice. And now' – he shook his head as if he could scarcely believe it himself – 'I am destined to end my days as a banker.'

'You are the Pope,' I told him.

'I am a banker,' he said, laughing at the absurdity of it all. 'The head of an extraordinary establishment which has corruption and dishonesty pouring through its veins. And how am I to solve it? At heart, I am still just a priest.' He sat quietly for a moment before thrusting out his right arm and propelling half the paperwork off the desk angrily. I bent down to gather up the documents as he sat, covering his face with his left hand.

'Do you think of your home often?' he asked me quietly as I placed the pages on the corner of the table, averting my eyes from their content.

'Sometimes, Holy Father,' I said.

'Where is it you're from again?'

'Ireland,' I told him.

'Yes, I know. But where?'

'Dublin.'

'Ah yes.' He thought about it. 'James Joyce,' he said. 'The Abbey Theatre. O'Casey and Brendan Behan.'

I nodded. 'My father knew Seán O'Casey,' I told him.

'Oh yes?'

'Briefly. He acted in one of his plays.'

'Have you read *Ulysses*, Odran?' he asked me.

'No, Holy Father.'

'No, neither have I. Should I, do you think?'

I thought about it. 'It's very long,' I said. 'I'm not sure I'd have the energy for it myself.'

He laughed. 'And Mr Haughey,' he said. 'What do you think of him?'

'I wouldn't trust him as far as I could throw him, Holy Father.'

'Should I tell him you said that, the next time he calls? You know he's phoned three times already and I've only been here a week.'

'I'd rather you didn't, Holy Father,' I said. 'He'd have me shot. Metaphorically speaking, of course.'

He smiled. He seemed amused by me and I thought that if I could take his mind off the papers before him, then he might sleep better that night and perhaps that was part of my job: to ensure that he was not agitated before bedtime.

'Of course,' he said quietly after a long pause, 'we have a problem with Ireland.'

'A problem, Holy Father?'

He nodded and massaged the bridge of his nose with thumb and forefinger. 'Yes, Odran.'

'May I ask what kind of problem?'

He shook his head. 'One that my predecessor chose to ignore. One that I intend to tackle. I have read some things that . . .' He paused and sighed. 'Things that make me wonder what kind of men are running the Church there. It is one of a hundred things that I must concern myself with, but I will attack it soon, I promise you that. And by God, I will put an end to it. In the meantime' – he waved his hands over his papers – 'there are these accounts to be sorted out.'

'Did you ever visit Ireland, Holy Father? Before your elevation, I mean?'

'No,' he replied. 'Perhaps some day. I would like to see Clonmacnoise and Glendalough. And the town where *The Quiet Man* was filmed. Where is that?'

'In the west, Holy Father,' I told him. 'Somewhere near Ashford Castle.'

'Did you ever see that film, Odran?'

'I did, Holy Father.'

'Seán Thornton and the Squire Danagher. And the little fellow on the horse, what was his name?'

'Was it Barry Fitzgerald?' I asked.

'Yes, but in the film.'

'I can't remember, Holy Father.'

'I've seen that film a dozen times. You could make a strong case for it being the greatest film ever made. If I ever go to Ireland, I will make certain that I visit that town.'

'Sure Maureen O'Hara would show you around herself,' I said, smiling. 'She lives in Dublin, I think.'

He slapped a hand to his heart and gave a sigh, bursting out laughing. 'I don't know that I could stand it,' he said. 'Mary Kate Danagher? I wouldn't know what to say to her. I would be like a tongue-tied schoolboy.'

Lord, I wanted to sit down on the seat right next to him, phone down for a couple of Italian beers and talk into the night. I loved this man.

'And what of your family?' he asked me then. 'You must miss them, being so far from home. Do you think of them?'

'Every day, Holy Father.'

'You have a large family?'

'Just my mother and sister. Both in Dublin.'

He nodded as he considered this. 'Your father is dead then?'

'Fourteen years now,' I told him.

'How did he die?'

'He drowned. On Curracloe beach in Wexford.'

He raised an eyebrow in surprise. 'Was he not a strong swimmer?'

I shook my head and told him the truthful story of the

summer of 1964 from start to finish. He listened without interruption.

'We cannot understand why the world turns as it does,' he said finally with an exhausted sigh. 'Perhaps if I could see more clearly, if I was a wiser man, then I would prove more capable in this position.'

'Do you miss Venice?' I asked and now that great smile of his filled the room, as wide as it had been when I had invoked the name of the goddess O'Hara.

'Ah, Venice!' he said. '*La Dominante! La Serenissima!* If only the Vatican could be relocated three hundred miles north, then I think I might have more strength for the task ahead. If the view from my bedroom window was across the Piazza San Marco and not the Piazza San Pedro. If it was not the Tiber I smelled or the shouts of the tourists that I heard all day long, but the cries of the gondoliers as they made their way along the canals.'

He shook his head sorrowfully and looked down at his papers once again and I took this as my cue to leave. I wished him a good night's sleep and he waved me away, returning to his paperwork.

'Odran, before you go,' he said, 'leave a note for my secretary that I want to see Signor Marcinkus in the morning.'

'Signor Marcinkus?' I asked; the name was unfamiliar to me.

'The head of the Vatican Bank,' he said. 'And say that I will need at least an hour with him. There are many . . .' He looked down and shook his head. 'It doesn't matter,' he said. 'Just make sure that he comes to see me. And Odran?'

'Yes, Holy Father?'

'Michaeleen Óg,' he said, smiling. 'That's who Barry Fitzgerald played. Michaeleen Óg Flynn.'

And then he broke into a quiet song:

'There was a wild Colonial Boy,
Jack Duggan was his name.
He was born and raised in Ireland,
In a place called Castlemaine.
He was his father's only son,
His mother's pride and joy,
And dearly did his parents love
The wild colonial boy.'

My obsession with the woman from the Café Bennizi came to a head towards the end of September. I no longer sat in my usual seat every afternoon with its narrow view of the dome of St Peter's, watching as she cleared tables and served espressos. I no longer had to endure the contemptuous stares of her father, who, I know, would have confronted me long ago were it not for the clerical garb that I wore. However, I still spent most evenings following her home, keeping at a safe distance so she would not see me, waiting in the darkness of the Vicolo della Campana in case she came out on to the balcony again or removed her dress with her back to the window, as she had done once before.

I do not know what I wanted from her exactly; it was not the obvious thing. Had there been an opportunity to pursue a romance with her, I don't believe that I would have taken it. I was still as determined to be a priest as I had ever been; I was not looking for a way out or an excuse to leave, even at this late stage. No, it was simply a desperate desire to be around her, to look at her, to have her near me. I felt more alive when I was in her presence. She was so beautiful. The pangs of desire were in themselves like an addiction, one that I had not experienced before. And yet it did not make me look at other women in a yearning way; she did not awaken a dormant sexuality inside me. It was her, just her. Years later, when Jonas wrote *Spiegeltent,* I would recognize those same qualities in the feelings that the young narrator felt towards the musician in Sydney's Hyde Park. The sensation that for the world to exist with such an object of beauty in it, and for that object to be unattainable, was the very sweetest kind of pain imaginable.

At nights, I did not go back to my room and touch myself as I indulged in fantastical scenarios involving the two of us. I never dreamed about her, not a single time. But awake, alive, alert, I thought of her constantly, wanted to know where she was and what she was doing. Had I known her phone number, I might have called to hear her voice, then hung up, like an awkward teenager, when she answered. Had it been thirty years later, and a less civilized world, I might have attached myself to her digital presence to follow her life, her friendships, her relationships and activities through random sentences and spontaneously taken photographs. I suppose today I would be called a stalker and it is true that I lived up to this word, following her from her café in the Piazza Pasquale Paoli, along the bridges and streets of Rome, towards her balcony.

And then, on the third-to-last night of September, I made an error of judgement that still, more than three decades later, has the power to wake me in the night with the horror of it all.

I had been held up in the Irish College later than usual that afternoon – a debate in our moral theology seminar had gone on tediously long – so rather than making my usual journey to the café and then following her home along the banks of the Tiber, I walked directly to the Vicolo della Campana and took up my usual spot, hiding in the shadows. Understand that I was so accustomed to living like this by now that I no longer questioned my behaviour; it was irrational and dangerous, of course, but it had become an addiction. She was a television programme, this woman. She was living her life for my pleasure before my eyes and even if I could not speak to her, I could watch and I could imagine. I felt a sense of ownership over her.

She was already at home when I arrived. The lights were on in her rooms and I could hear her as she moved around. Typically, she would stay in on these mid-week evenings; her father would come home later and they would eat together, at which time I would have to leave to return to my duties in the Vatican. Tonight, however, she surprised me by exiting the building shortly after I arrived, and as she left, I wondered should I follow her – was she meeting a man? If so, who was he? And what would they do together? – but instead I found myself crossing the road and opening the unlocked door that led on to the street, stepping inside the cool foyer and looking around.

I had never been here before and I felt a surge of adrenalin, such as a burglar must feel when after watching a home for a long time he finally breaks in. There was a small garden in the centre of the atrium with a fountain at its centre, a statue of a naked boy balanced atop, and I turned towards the wide stone staircase that led to each apartment before making my way up, keeping a clear idea in my head of where I was in relation to the street, so that I might know which was hers when I reached it. Happily, her door was built into an alcove so no one entering the lobby below could look up and see me, question what I was doing there. I put my hand, then my cheek, to the wood, listening for sounds from within, but all was quiet. What was I doing here? I didn't know. I turned, almost laughing at my own madness, and then, on an impulse, I lifted the mat outside the door, wondering whether she might keep a spare key there, but no. I tried behind the hanging light outside, but there was nothing there either.

Leave, I told myself. *Leave, Odran.* I turned, determined to make my way back down the stairs and out on to the street once again, when I noticed a heavy plant pot along the corridor, containing an oversized boxwood that looked badly in need of watering. I stared at it, swallowing nervously – I *knew!* – then walked towards it, spun it to the side and there it was, a single key, a spare key, hidden underneath. I lifted it, held it to the light; it was rusty and dirty from too long beneath the pot, the metal tattooed with soil, water and mildew, but when I inserted it into the lock of her apartment, it turned easily, the door swung open and I stepped inside.

My heart beat fast inside my chest as I looked around. I could scarcely believe that I was here, that I had behaved in such an irrational manner, but put any concerns to the back of my mind. I felt more alive at that moment than I ever had in my twenty-three years of life. Than I have ever felt since. To my right was a small kitchen and I saw that she had left an oversized saucepan of water boiling on a low heat. Should I turn it off, I wondered. But no, it was only water, it would evaporate and the pot would burn, but no harm could come to her apartment. I moved further down the corridor, passing a living room on my left and then a bathroom before reaching the bedroom, which was surprisingly large and led to the balcony where I had seen her so many times over these last few months. I stepped inside cautiously; her day clothes were strewn on the bed and the lockers on both sides held an array of items: half-drunk glasses of water, paperback novels, lipstick, an overflowing ashtray and a man's comb.

The bedroom was enormous; it was as if two rooms had been converted into one by the removal of a central wall. An oak wardrobe stood flat against the wall facing the bed – an antique, perhaps handed down through generations of her family – and I opened it, running my hands down the fine silk of a trilogy of nightgowns hanging within, their femininity overwhelming me as I pulled one towards me and pressed it to my face, closing my eyes and inhaling deeply; the lingering scent, so alien to me, was dizzying. It felt like being introduced to a stranger but feeling that somehow you had always known them, that their existence was hidden deep within your soul, a secret even to you. I closed my eyes and thought that I could happily smother myself inside her clothes.

Of course this was a sensory experience unlike any I had ever known. And I was engaged in an act of criminality that was as exciting to me as it was novel; perhaps that's why I failed to hear her key in the door or her footsteps in the corridor beyond, the sweep of her shoes as she kicked them off against the wooden floor beneath her bare feet, the sound the eggs made – the eggs that she had just bought in the market at the end of the road – as she set them in a basket on the kitchen table. Or why I did not hear her walking down the corridor towards me? It was only as she gasped and I turned around to see her standing in the doorway that I realized how stupid I had been, the risks that I had taken. I stared at her, the blood draining from my face, and she stared right back, showing no fear, her eyes aflame with anger. The memory of how she roared at her father at the Café Bennizi flashed through my mind.

'How did you get in here?' she asked.

'I'm sorry,' I said, the words catching in my throat. I threw her nightdress back inside the wardrobe and stepped towards her; she did not rear back in fright but marched towards me furiously, causing me to retreat instead.

'How did you get in here?' she repeated, raising her voice then releasing a wave of Italian invective that I did not understand.

'The key,' I said. 'The spare key. I guessed where it was.'

'What is it you want?'

'Nothing,' I said, shaking my head. 'I don't want anything. I promise. I don't mean to hurt you.'

She smiled, a look of contempt in her eyes, and shook her head. 'You think *I*'m the one in danger?' she asked me.

'I'll leave.'

'I know you,' said the woman, pointing a finger at me. 'You sat every day for so long, watching me.'

'It was stupid of me—'

'And you follow me,' she added.

'I shouldn't be here,' I said, trying to brush past her, but she pushed me back hard against the wall. The force of the blow winded me for a moment.

'Do you think I don't see you when I'm walking home?' she asked, sneering at me. 'And then at night . . .' She nodded towards the balcony. 'Do you think I do not know that you are down there?'

I looked down at the ground, mortified by my actions; I couldn't look her in the eye. 'You knew?' I said.

'Of course I knew,' she said. 'You don't even have the sense to hide yourself well.'

'Why did you never say anything?'

'Because I was laughing at you.'

I stared at her. 'Laughing?'

'Of course. There's something so amusing about you, don't you think? Something pathetic. A grown man – a virgin I expect, yes? – standing on a street corner like a prostitute, staring up at a woman he can't even talk to. I found it funny. We lay in bed, Alfredo and I, laughing at you.'

'Alfredo?'

'We work together. You know him. He laughs at you too.'

Not her father then; her lover.

'Did you think I would be interested in you?' she asked. 'A peeping Tom who likes to spy on me?'

'I'm sorry,' I said, desperate to leave but somehow unable to simply run past her and make my way out the door. 'I'll go. I'll stop.'

'What is it you want?' she asked, stepping closer to me so that I could smell coffee on her breath.

'I don't want anything.'

'Of course you do. Everyone does. Say it.'

'I don't want anything,' I repeated. 'I'm sorry.'

She was wearing a light summer dress, barely more than a thin skin above her own. 'Is this it?' she asked, her face close to mine now. 'Is this what you want? You think I would give this to a boy like you?' she asked.

I felt the room start to grow dark around me as she came closer, her fingers on my face.

Are you a dirty boy, Odran, are you?

There he was; he was standing next to me now, his foul breath in my ear, his arm around my shoulder, pulling me to him, his hands tugging at my pants, reaching inside. I pressed my hands against my ears. He was there. He was all over me.

I'd say you are. I'd say you get up to all sorts in this room, do you, Odran? Late at night. When you think no one can hear you. Are you a dirty boy, Odran, are you? You can tell me, come on.

The door opened and Alfredo walked in, his eyes opening wide as he stared at us, and I stumbled past him, down the corridor, out the door, tripping and almost falling down the stairs, before throwing myself into the street beyond and running as quickly as I could away from the Vicolo and the scene of my degradation.

It was what I suppose could be called a long dark night of the soul. Eight o'clock came and went, the very latest that I was supposed to be back at the Vatican, but I barely noticed the time. It could have been midday, it could have been midnight for all the difference it made to me. I wandered over bridges, in and out of streets, circled piazzas like an inebriate without thought for where I was going. I might have been in any city for all the awareness I had of my environment. And yet I remember the churches, for somehow they called out to me as I passed them, beckoning me home. I walked as far south as San Crisogono before turning back in the direction of the Franciscans' home at

Santi Apostoli; I passed the basilica of Santa Maria in Via, where they say that an image of the Virgin was discovered in the water, walked across the Piazza della Rotonda, where tourists congregated every day to enter the Pantheon, before resting with my head in my hands outside the Doric columns of Santa Maria della Pace near the Piazza Navona. I felt my spirits dip as low as they had ever been outside Sant'Agnese in Agone, then rise to unexpected levels of euphoria at San Salvatore in Lauro, before falling again, slipping again, diving again as I passed back across the Ponte Sant'Angelo and saw the dome of St Peter's basilica rise accusingly before me.

Two opposing thoughts ran through my mind as I walked around Rome that night:

You don't have to do this.

You can do this.

Had I really discovered my vocation for myself, I asked myself. Had I ever woken with a sense of it or was it merely my mother who had forced it upon me? Christ above, but a terrible change had come over that woman the week my father and brother died and God in His wisdom had sent a vocation towards the south-east coast of Ireland – not to me, a nine-year-old child with no more sense than a thimble, but to her, a middle-aged woman, grieving, reaching for a lifebelt as her loved ones sank beneath the surface. And when she passed it my way and said, *Here son, this is for you, it's a gift from God,* I picked it up without a thought and said, *Grand, so.*

A group of young Italian boys were gathered together near the Lungotevere Vaticano on the banks of the Tiber, balancing against the seats of their parked Vespas, all shorts and thin brown legs, sunglasses perched in their slicked-back hair like characters out of a Fellini film, handsome and vital as they laughed and joked with each other. They were younger than me, these boys, but only a little. In their late teens, perhaps, the world opening up before them. How many of them had been kissed tonight, I asked myself. Were they impressing each other with stories of young girls, their virginities taken? And there was I, in my black suit, my tie and my hat. My starched white collar. My fingers still stinking of her essence.

Twenty-three years old. A boy. A man. What was I? Even I didn't know.

'Padre,' they cried, stretching their arms out before me as if they were appealing to a referee to award a penalty to a felled hero. I approached them warily. I remembered what it was like to be an anxious boy, passing playing fields and hoping that a miskicked football would not make its way in my direction, and I raised a hand to signal a greeting without slowing my stride. 'This one needs absolution,' they called, pointing to a good-looking boy, perhaps the youngest of their group, who was rushing around from one to the next, trying to silence them. 'He needs to say a confession! You must hear the sins he has committed tonight!'

They meant me no harm, I knew that, but I was afraid of them all the same. I thought that if they teased me or surrounded me in any way then I would lash out, I would fight them one and all as I had not fought the woman from the Café Bennizi or her lover.

'What is it you want?' she had asked me and I had no answer to that question, for in my innocence, I didn't know.

That night, that endless night, I wandered through parts of Rome that I had never seen before, a city of run-down hotels, of squalid apartment buildings with laundry hanging on wires above the streets. Prostitutes appeared from time to time, curious as to whether a young priest was looking to release the tension of his calling, for I had not even removed my collar over the course of these hours. I waved them away, one by one. I had no desires in this direction. I simply wanted to walk. This was my night, the night when I would know whether the path I had chosen was right or wrong.

Ten o'clock, eleven o'clock. The bells at midnight. Church after church after church. One o'clock, two o'clock, three, four. Pope John Paul would be in the deepest of sleeps by now, his night-time tea stone cold outside his door.

Where were my school friends tonight, I wondered. The ones I knew before I entered the seminary. The boys I had studied alongside in De La Salle Prep on the Churchtown Road, with whom I had walked across to O'Reilly's for sweets at lunchtime and with whom I had strolled past the Bottle Tower as we made our way down to the Dundrum crossroads for our buses home. Working in their monotonous jobs in Dublin, no doubt. Paying their mortgages. Taking their wives out for a meal in the city centre on a Saturday night or doing a line with some girl they had met at a rugby match in Donnybrook. Or maybe they were only now leaving a nightclub on Lesson Street, recounting how they had scored the winning try in the Leinster Schools' Cup six years before, persuading their conquests back to their place or hers, laughing at how great it was to be young, to be doing what men and women did together when they were alone, and then forgetting her name the following morning. Did I want to be one of those men? Was that what I wanted? What was it that I was missing out on?

There were homeless people in Rome, too. Lying in sleeping bags in the Flaminio or outside the Tiburtina – as I would one day invite Tom Cardle to sleep in a bag in my room at Terenure College and he would decline – their heads poking out from their cocoons, woollen caps pulled low, past their ears, to keep the night cold away, their bodies hardly visible to the naked eye. A set of eyes, a mouth, little more. Signs printed in large black capital letters on cardboard ripped from boxes. *Aiutatemi!* Help me. Please help me.

The sun was beginning to rise. My eyes felt sore and my legs had grown tired. I had wandered around the city all night. What time was it now, almost six? It was a new day. How could I have walked so long? And yet I had. I was entering St Peter's Square and tried not to think of what Monsignor Sorley would say when he learned that I had not been at my post the night before. Would the Pope tell anyone? Would he even have noticed, considering how intensively he was studying his paperwork every night, how often and how late Signor Marcinkus from the Vatican Bank arrived in the papal suite, how loud the arguments behind closed doors were becoming. I had sat quietly while Marcinkus had dragged Cardinal Villot, who as well as being Camerlengo also acted as head of the Apostolic Camera, into dark corners after his meetings with the Holy Father and barked like a dog about how he could not get into the specifics of such complex transactions with a man whose idea of sophistication was to reference Pinocchio in his homilies. *This needs to stop,* he had snarled one night, gripping Cardinal Villot by the arm. *If it doesn't stop, I won't be responsible for what happens next. You have no idea what these people are capable of.* Could I lie to the Monsignor, who had shown me nothing but kindness since my arrival in Rome? Tell him that I had been ill? Or should I tell the truth, taking him for my Father Confessor? My time here was almost at an end, after all. The Italians were already choosing who should take my place in January.

The Swiss Guards were standing in place beneath the arch and although of course they recognized me, I showed them my pass and they separated to let me through. I had come home. I was at the Vatican once again, back in time to bring the Pope his breakfast, and I would ask his forgiveness for not attending to my post and hope that he would not reveal my indiscretion to anyone.

I met one of the nuns on the back stairs that led to the papal suite, curled up on a small sofa before an alcove window that overlooked the eastern side of St Peter's Square, a place that I had never seen anyone sit before, let alone a nun. Nuns did not sit, that was the truth of it; they were in constant motion, they went places, they had duties to fulfil. I recognized her and was surprised to realize that she was rocking back and forth, weeping.

'Sister Teresa,' I said, approaching her, kneeling down. 'Are you all right? What has happened?'

She looked up at me and I noticed for the first time how pretty she was. Such clear skin and deep brown eyes. She shook her head and pointed in the direction of the staircase, up towards the large chamber whose door led first to the small ante-chamber that housed my cot and then to the Pope's private bedroom.

I stepped past her and bolted up the steps into the parlour, where a small gathering of distraught nuns were huddled together, and in the corner of the room I spied Cardinal Siri and Cardinal Villot deep in conversation. Their faces were pale and all heads turned to me as I stepped inside. I wondered what I must look like after eight or nine hours of walking the streets, my hair askew, my face red, my eyes drawn.

Cardinal Siri turned to me with a disbelieving expression on his face and marched over, guiding me by the elbow towards the corner of the room.

'Your Eminence,' I asked in Italian, 'what has happened? What is wrong?'

'The Holy Father,' he told me. 'He is dead.'

I stared at him and resisted the urge to laugh. 'Of course he is,' I told him. 'He died more than a month ago. Why are you saying this?'

He shook his head. 'I do not refer to our late Holy Father, but our current one. I mean our most recent one.' He rolled his eyes, confusing even himself by his words. 'His Holiness, Pope John Paul. He is dead.'

I had no response for a moment. The idea was absurd. 'When?' I asked.

'In the night.'

'But how?'

'You don't need to concern yourself with that.'

'But it cannot be.'

'And yet it is. He was all right when you took him his tea last night?'

I thought about it, uncertain what to say. 'He told me that he wanted to be alone,' I said. 'I took it away.'

We both looked over towards the side table where Sister Vincenza had left the tray for me before retiring for the night. It was still there, of course, the silver pot full and stewed, the small plate of biscuits. Cardinal Siri noticed nothing unusual about it, but I did: there were always three biscuits left for the Pope and he never ate any of them; on this plate, however, there were only two, with some crumbs scattered beside them as if someone had picked up the third biscuit as they left the apartment but snapped it in two over the plate before eating it. No one who worked in this place would ever have done such a thing; it had to have been a stranger. But what would a stranger have been doing here?

'I left it there,' I added.

'And he was well?'

'He was tired,' I said, compounding my lie, wondering why I was getting locked into such deceit when the truth would surely emerge. 'He went to bed early.'

'Where were you this morning?' he asked. 'Sister Vincenza told me that you were not here to collect the breakfast tray.'

'I slept late,' I explained. 'I don't know why.'

'You weren't in your cot.'

'I was in the bathroom,' I said. He narrowed his eyes and I knew that he could tell I was lying.

'She brought the tray into the Holy Father,' he told me. 'She didn't know what to do, of course. She didn't want his breakfast to grow cold. She knocked, told him that it was ready, asked whether she might enter. He didn't answer, so she knocked again. Called out to him. In the end, she had no choice but to go in. That is when she found him. He died, Odran.' He leaned forward, so close that our faces were almost touching. 'He died of natural causes, do you understand me? When you are asked – and you will be asked – this is what you will say. He died of natural causes. Or you will answer to me.'

The new Pope, the Polish Pope, relieved me of my duties almost immediately after his election. I was tainted by the events of September 28th and although I was told at the time that my removal was no reflection on the work that I had done over my nine months in Rome, I didn't believe this for a moment. There was no more talk of Vatican banks in my hearing, and certainly no discussion of the problems in Ireland the Pope had mentioned, and when I would think of these, years later, I would realize that they had been locked away as too dangerous to consider.

Monsignor Sorley interviewed me at length in the feral days between the death of Pope John Paul and the October conclave about why I had not been at my post on that fateful night, and in the end, I told the truth – I told him everything that I had felt and done during my time in Rome, from my afternoons at the Café Bennizi to my conversations with Cardinal Luciani, who saw where my interests lay; from my crazed walks from the Piazza Pasquale Paoli to the Vicolo della Campana, up to and including my decision to break into her apartment – and although he was angry with me, he took me at my word and backed me up with the Vatican police, who were suspicious but could not afford to make it known that something unlawful may have happened in the Apostolic Palace that night. I held my tongue when it came to the issue of the biscuits; no one else had noticed and I could see nothing to be gained by expressing something that might sound ridiculous to their ears. The Pope had died of a heart attack, that was what was said, and whether it was true or whether it was not, that became the official story.

The Polish Pope spoke to me even less than Pope Paul VI had, seeming nervous whenever I was in his presence, and I imagined that he knew the tale of my wanderings on the night his predecessor died and thus considered me an untrustworthy presence. Perhaps he was right; I had proved myself to be an unreliable soul. But then, in time, he would prove himself to be my equal in this regard.

It was Monsignor Sorley who told me that I was no longer required at the Vatican. The Polish Pope had decided that the Italian should start two months early and so I was pushed aside, given a few hours to gather up any personal possessions and sent back to the Pontifical Irish College to complete my studies.

Between then and now, I have set foot in the Vatican only once. On the day of my ordination, four months later, when my mother and sister would be greeted by the Pope, in a meeting that would leave Hannah to utter those four words about Pope John Paul II that I have never forgotten, for they had a ring of truth about them that even I, as the years went on, could not deny.

That man hates women.

Chapter Fourteen

2008

It was a mistake to wear my clerical clothes to the first day of Tom Cardle's trial; I should have chosen something nondescript that wouldn't draw attention to my position within the Church. I kept a pair of corduroy trousers somewhere in my wardrobe, after all, and some shirts and jumpers. I rarely wore them, but they were there. I might have looked like anyone else and the day would not have proved so difficult. But then I had been dressing in my black suit and white collar every day for more than thirty years so it had become something like a second skin to me. I simply didn't give the matter a second thought.

However, even as I boarded the bus that morning into the city centre and made my way north along the quays towards the Four Courts, I was uncertain whether or not I should attend. After all, I could read about it the following morning in the newspapers. I could watch the coverage of the trial on the television news or hear about it on the radio. Cases such as these had been going on for a few years now and the media was obsessed with them; every prosecution only added to a growing anger in the country and a sense that the men being brought to court represented only the tip of the iceberg. They were the ones who'd been caught, that was all. But we were all under suspicion. None of us were to be trusted.

Tom's arrest had left me feeling shattered. He had often vanished out of my life for long periods at a time, neither replying to letters nor answering phone calls, but to disappear for more than a year as he had done since the summer of 2006, hidden away by Archbishop Cordington in a monastery like some medieval king's discarded wife, suggested only one thing. When I first heard where he'd been sent, it was in a phone call from my old friend Maurice Macwell, who had been parish priest in a thriving Mayo parish for a decade or more. I hadn't heard from him since his former cell-mate Snuff Winters had died and he had refused to attend the funeral, for reasons he wouldn't specify. To me, at least.

'You've heard, I suppose?' he said when I lifted the phone that day, not a word of introduction.

'Who's this?' I asked, although I knew well from the voice.

'It's me.'

'Who's *me*?'

'Maurice.'

'Maurice Macwell? How are you anyway? How's life in the West?'

'Wet. And in Dublin?'

'Cold.'

'Grand so. Anyway, you've heard the news?'

'What news would this be?'

'About your old pal?'

'Which old pal?'

'Tom Cardle.'

I felt a chill run through me. 'What about him?' I asked.

'Arrested. Kiddie-fiddling.'

'I know.'

'And what do you think?'

'What am I supposed to think?'

'It's all been very cloak and dagger. They first interviewed him six months ago and they've been building a case ever since. He's in hiding. Cordington will have the full story. Has he not talked to you about it, no?'

'He has.'

'What did he say?'

'That they have him somewhere safe.'

Maurice seemed to be taking great delight in the news, and in sharing it with me. I remembered reading an interview once with the writer John Banville, who said that if he got a bad review in the paper for one of his books, then he could rely on one of his friends to phone him up and let him know. That was exactly how this felt.

When the court dates were finally set, I spoke to my parish priest, Father Burton, and asked for a few days off, explaining where I would be, and he seemed reluctant to let me go, which surprised me for he was a relatively young man, only thirty-seven, and I would have thought that he would be less stifled by the old ways that were crumbling around us. I hoped he might show a bit more compassion.

'Are you sure about this?' he asked, sitting back in his chair and making a temple of his hands under his chin in the way that he did whenever he wanted to appear intelligent. 'Does it not seem a little unwise to get involved?'

'He's an old friend,' I said.

'You're aware of what he's accused of?'

'Of course I am,' I sighed. 'I know all about it.'

'So why do you want to go?'

I had asked myself this question many times over the previous few days and come up with no satisfactory answer. Only I felt that I should be there, that I wanted to see him with my own eyes, to discover whether, by looking closely at him, I would see something that I had missed all these years. Something terrible.

'The thing is, Father Odran,' said Father Burton – I hated this affectation; call me Odran or call me Father Yates. The whole *Father Odran* thing was the stuff of American television dramas – 'it's important that you think about the parish.'

'Sure what harm can it do the parish?' I asked. 'I'll only be gone for a few days, a week or two at most if it even goes on that long. And I'll still be here to celebrate Mass in the mornings.'

'I meant in terms of the publicity,' he said. 'You don't want to get your name dragged into all this, do you? It could reflect badly on us.'

'When you say *us*, Father Burton, who are you referring to exactly? You and me?'

'The Church.'

'The Church has bigger things to worry about than whether or not I sit in a courtroom for a few hours every day.'

'The man is accused of multiple crimes against children,' he insisted. 'Over twenty-five years, for pity's sake. And look around you, Father Odran. How many thousands of children do we serve in this parish? If you're seen to be supporting him too closely—'

'I'm not supporting him, as such,' I said weakly.

'Well, what are you doing then?'

'I'm just . . . attending. That's all.'

He shook his head. 'You said it yourself. You're old friends. Whatever you may tell me here, it will *look* like you're supporting him, and in the world that we live in, it's what a thing looks like that matters the most.' He frowned and leaned forward, an idea occurring to him. 'Wait a minute,' he said. 'Do you think he's not guilty? Is that it?'

I felt the words dry up in my mouth. I hadn't anticipated him asking me such a question. 'Isn't that what the courts are there to find out?' I asked.

'But you, what do you think?'

'I think I'm going to take a few days off, Father Burton. That's what I think.' I didn't add what I wanted to say: *And if you don't like it, you can fuck off with yourself.*

It was a question that, once asked, was difficult to dislodge. Did I think he was guilty? I had known Tom Cardle since 1973. Thirty-five years of friendship. And if, during that time, I felt that I had never really got to the heart of the man, then it wasn't for the want of trying. Yes, I knew that he had struggled to fit into the seminary, that he hadn't come to the priesthood of his own volition, but did that make him a monster in the way that the papers portrayed him? The photographers with their telescopic lenses must have taken hundreds of shots of him as he arrived back in Dublin and was brought to the holding cells in anticipation of the trial, but they always chose to publish the ones that made him look the most predatory, the most fiendish. Did *that* make him guilty? The pictures I saw in the paper did not look like the man I knew.

And yet, and yet . . . there were so many contradictions in my head. So many suspicions. Events over the years, things I had noticed and ignored that sat uneasily with me. Did I have blame of my own to carry here? I pushed ideas like these far to the back of my mind. I could not think about such things. Not yet.

Ahead of me, a scrum of photographers and television reporters were standing outside the Four Courts watching the protestors, maybe a dozen of them walking silently outside the courts in a circle, holding placards, condemning Tom, denouncing the Church. Their signs made for difficult reading, as did the hollowed-out expressions on these poor men's faces. How had it come to this, I wondered. Who was to blame for all this suffering?

I stopped and listened for a moment as a TV3 camera crew interviewed one of them.

'Six years,' the man was saying, a nice, respectable-looking fella in an ill-fitting suit with a neat haircut and tears in his eyes. A woman who had the look of him – his sister, I thought – was standing by his side, holding his hand, a steely defiance on her face. 'From the age of nine until the age of fifteen. I gave him a dig when I turned sixteen and that was the end of it.'

The reporter asked him a question and he nodded. 'I had no choice,' he said. 'I've spent all my life not talking about it. My job now is to spend the rest of my life making up for that mistake.'

There was a roar of questions from the press and I don't know how he selected which to answer, but when he spoke they all fell quiet again, scratching away on their notepads. 'I don't know if they all knew,' he told them. 'But I believe that most of them did. The men in charge did, that's for sure. There was a culture of conspiracy. The bishops, the cardinals, the Pope himself. It's not just one man on trial here today, it's the whole bloody lot of them. If you ask me, they should be taken out of their houses and their palaces, dragged out into the street by their hair if necessary, and made to stand trial one by one in the full public gaze. And if John Paul II was alive today then someone with courage should take him to the International Court of Human Rights and make him pay for what he did. People say he should be made a saint.' He was growing emotional now, his voice rising in anger. 'A saint?' he cried in despair before spitting on the ground in his fury. 'That's what I say to that. Because if there's such a place as Hell, you can rest assured that white skull-cap of his is being scorched off his head even as we speak. That man knew everything and did nothing. *Nothing*, that Polish prick. And Benedict's no better. He's in it up to his neck. They all are. Protect themselves, protect the money, that's what it's all about. Scumbags. Human life doesn't get any lower than that pair of criminals.'

The man's sister tugged at his arm and tried to pull him away as the reporters asked more questions. 'Of course I'm fucking angry!' he cried. 'Why wouldn't I be angry? Wouldn't you be angry? Listen, you hear everyone in this country talking about how wrong it all was, how the priests need to be held accountable for their actions – not just the ones who committed the crimes, but the ones who stood by and did nothing – and still you drive by a church on a Sunday morning and the poxy little sheep are lining up to climb into the pews, dragging their children along for communion or confirmation Masses, even though they don't believe a word of what they hear or live their lives in the way that their contaminated religion tells them to. The people are as bad, do you hear me? But the priests are still in control of ninety per cent of the schools. Do you think that if there was any other sector of society which has displayed such a predilection towards paedophilia we would let them within a mile of a school, let alone let them run the places? I mean what kind of country do we have here at all? We need to get rid of them, do you hear me? Put them out of every school. Keep them away from our children. Perversion is bred in their bones. We should stop at nothing to expel every last one of them from Ireland, like St Patrick got rid of the snakes.'

I walked on. I could listen to no more. The anger in the man's voice. The hatred. And why shouldn't he be angry, I asked myself. Why shouldn't he feel this fury? Sure hadn't his life been ruined on him by men in black suits with white collars. Men like me.

As I approached the steps of the courthouse the photographers turned to look at me, raising their cameras in case I was someone of significance.

'Who are you?' asked one and I didn't answer.

'Are you a friend of Cardle's?' said another immediately.

'Driving offence,' I said, unable to look the man in the eye. 'I haven't paid my parking fines. I'll be lucky if they don't take the licence off me.'

'He's nobody,' said the photographer, turning away, and his colleagues examined their cameras, flicking back and forth through their digital images, no longer interested in me. How easily they all believed a simple lie.

*

The courtroom was full when I entered, but I managed to find a seat at the back. I had never been inside a court before and found the atmosphere oppressive and intimidating, the oak of the benches, the sense that tens of thousands of people had passed through here over the course of a century: defendants, both guilty and innocent, victims, the families of both. A group of six women, all in their early sixties, were seated in the row in front of me and I assumed that they were mothers of some of the victims, determined to see justice done.

An announcement from the clerk of the court marked the arrival of the judge, who took her seat in the black cloak and white wig that signalled her authority. More black outfits; who first decided that this was the pigment of power? Was black not supposed to signify the absence of colour, a thorough emptiness? Of course the shades in my profession changed as one advanced through the ranks, from black to scarlet to white; darkness, blood and a cleansing at the very top.

A group of barristers were huddled together at the front of the court, most of them chatting away or laughing like old friends, but they took their seats when the judge sat down and the jury were brought in. I looked at their faces one by one, a cross-section of society if ever I saw one. Retired men looking pleased to have their opinions valued once again, young women in business suits putting their BlackBerries away, a few serious-looking thirty-something lads with carefully sculpted facial hair.

And then, emerging from somewhere beneath the courtroom, appeared Tom Cardle himself, stepping cautiously into the dock and looking around with a frightened expression on his face, as if he did not know how his life had brought him to this place, what cruel fate had led him from a troubled farm in Wexford to the Four Courts in Dublin. He seemed surprised by the number of spectators, whose voices hushed a little as they got their first look at him. The six women in front of me took advantage of the quiet and stood up as one to begin shouting:

'Good luck, Father!'

'We're all behind you, Father!'

'Don't let them break you, Father, with their filthy lies!'

I sat back, my mouth falling open in astonishment, as the entire room turned to look at them and the judge ordered that they be removed immediately. The bailiffs stepped forward and the women pulled crucifixes from their bags and for a moment I thought they were going to hit the uniformed Gardaí with them, but no, they simply waved them in the air as they were dragged roaring from the room, breaking into a round of Hail Marys as they went. What could inspire such devotion, I wondered. Would they stand behind him even if he was guilty? Did they even care?

The women's removal left a few seats empty in front of me and I moved forward, glad of the extra space, for no one else was to be let in once proceedings had begun. I had Tom in my sights now, he was no more than thirty feet away from me, and I noticed how he kept scratching his face, a nervous affliction, and throwing sideways glances at the jury one by one, as if he was trying to get the measure of them. He'd lost weight since I'd last seen him; the tendency towards corpulence that he'd developed as he approached middle age was gone now and an unhealthy gauntness could be seen across his features.

A series of remarks were made between the judge and the barristers – legal mumbo-jumbo, I could make no sense of it – and then there was a long period when nothing much happened and a Garda tapped Tom on the shoulder and told him to sit down. No sooner had he sat than the judge began to address the court and Tom was lifted brutally off his chair, the Garda's hand clasping him tightly around the upper arm, and I could see that he took a certain pleasure in the violence of the action. It crossed my mind then that Tom had chosen not to wear his priest's clothing today but appeared as a layman and I wondered about the thought process that had gone into this decision. Did he – or his lawyers – think that the jury would automatically think badly of him if he was clad in clerical garb? There had been so many of these men in the papers over the last couple of years, did they think that he would be conforming to a stereotype, the pervert priest in the dock? Or did he simply not feel like a priest any more? I might have asked him, had I the opportunity.

A moment later, the charges were read out. The DPP had decided that the evidence of only five boys was worthy of the prosecution, and although they were not in the courtroom, their evidence would be taken over the days that followed; one by one their stories emerged in the newspapers and they made for upsetting reading.

The youngest had been seven at the time, the oldest fourteen. The seven-year-old had lived next door to Tom in 1980 in his Galway parish. His father had died the year before and Tom, who was himself only twenty-four at the time, had been asked by the boy's mother to show an interest in him, for the poor lad wasn't coping well at all. And this was the manner in which Tom had shown his interest.

A ten-year-old boy had served as an altar boy in Longford in 1987 and been abused two or three mornings a week in the sacristy before Mass. The fourteen-year-old lived in Sligo in 1995 and had been taken to the beach by Tom every Wednesday afternoon, where Tom undressed him for a swim in the sea and then took him back into the dunes afterwards. A younger boy in Wicklow in 2002 had been taken for drives out to Brittas Bay, where similar behaviour had taken place. And there was a lad from Roscommon whose story was so upsetting that it was hard to believe that any human being could put another through such cruelty.

These were only the handful of boys whose stories had been

considered capable of securing a conviction, and as I read them I thought, what about Belturbet? And Wexford? What about Tralee and Mayo and Ringsend? These were other parishes where Tom had been based over the years. Were we expected to believe that he had not committed his crimes there, but been relocated by the Church anyway? And were we to think that he'd only had his eyes on one child in Galway, Longford, Sligo, Wicklow and Roscommon? Here were five; where were the nineteen that Archbishop Cordington had spoken of? And if nineteen had come forward, how many had not? Another twenty? Fifty? Hundred?

The judge asked Tom whether he pled guilty or not guilty and he looked around, as if uncertain whether the question was really being directed towards him or not. He offered a half-smile, perhaps out of fear more than anything else, and shook his head. There was a contemptuous murmuring in the courtroom. Was he taking none of this seriously? The judge repeated the question and looked up.

'Not guilty,' Tom said. 'Sure I'd never lay a finger on a child. It's a terrible thing to do.'

And his voice cracked at the end of it and I knew immediately that I had made a mistake in coming here and that I could listen to no more. My legs felt weak, my stomach sick, and I dragged myself to my feet, practically falling over myself as I rushed towards the door. I looked back for a moment and Tom had turned and was staring in my direction. He caught my eye and there was something there that said, *Odran, Odran, will you not save me from this? Odran, please.*

Odran, why didn't you save me from it long ago, when you might have been able?

I could not stay. I emerged into the Round Hall.

Despite the number of people lingering under the circular dome, making their way in and out of the other three courtrooms where different cases were being heard, I felt that I could breathe out here; I was not yet ready to make my way through the reporters and photographers who were still gathered outside on Inns Quay, but, mercifully, were not allowed through the open doors. I made my way to one of the benches by the side and sat down next to a woman on her own, bending over a little with my head in my hands. What kind of life was this, I wondered. To what sort of an organization had I dedicated my life? And even as I searched for blame, I knew that a darkness was stirring inside me concerning my own complicity, for I had seen things and I had suspected things and I had turned away and done nothing.

A hand touched my arm and I almost jumped off the seat in fright, but it was just the woman seated next to me. She had a tired expression and not a hint of a smile on her face. I thought she was going to say something like *Are you all right, Father?* but instead she just stared at me and I knew that I recognized her from somewhere, only I could not say where. Was she the mother of one of the Terenure lads, perhaps? No, that wasn't it.

'You're Father Yates, aren't you?' she asked me finally, her voice low and quiet.

'That's right,' I said. 'Do I know you?'

'You do,' she said. 'Do you not remember me?'

I shook my head. 'I do and I don't,' I said. 'You look familiar, but I can't place you.'

'Kathleen Kilduff,' she said and I closed my eyes. I thought I might be sick.

'Mrs Kilduff,' I said meekly. *Forgive me.*

'We met in Wexford. In 1990. You were down visiting your pal. I was the fool who was delivering her son into his hands every week for an hour.'

I nodded. What could I say to justify myself?

'Of course,' I said. 'I remember you now.'

'And you remember Brian too, don't you?'

'I do,' I said. 'I remember Brian.'

'Did you feel good about yourself, reporting him like you did? You know the Gardaí scared him half to death when they interviewed him about the damage he'd done to that monster's car?'

'I'm sorry,' I said. 'I didn't know what to do at the time. I thought there was something wrong with the boy. I thought that if Tom knew then maybe he could help him.'

'Oh, he helped him all right,' she said, laughing bitterly. 'Sure didn't he go to the Gardaí and tell them that if they just cautioned the boy then he'd see to it that he never did anything like that again. And then he persuaded me to send Brian into him Mondays, Wednesdays and Fridays, three days a week for an hour every time, and of course I did what I was told. Brian,' she added. 'My little lad. Who never did a bit of harm to anyone in his life. He wanted to be a vet, did you know that? He had a little dog that he just adored.'

I stared down at the floor. When I told that story earlier, when I told you about 1990, did I mention that I had reported what I had seen to Tom the next morning, who had called the Gardaí in? And that I had told *them* what I had seen, identifying the boy in his own house later that same day? Perhaps I didn't. If I didn't, I should have. Anyway, here it is out in the open now. We are none of us innocent.

'Mrs Kilduff,' I said, uncertain what I was going to say next, but she interrupted me anyway.

'Don't say my name,' she hissed. 'And get off this bench right now, do you hear me? I don't want you sitting anywhere near me. You disgust me.'

I nodded and stood up, turning to walk away, but before I could, I thought I should at least say something to try to atone for what I had done. 'I hope Brian is doing all right,' I said. 'I hope he's found a way to cope with whatever happened to him.'

She stared at me as if I was insulting her on purpose. 'Are you trying to hurt me?' she asked. 'Is that what you're doing? Are you deliberately trying to be cruel?'

'No,' I said quickly, failing to understand. 'I only meant—'

'Sure Brian is dead these last fifteen years,' she told me. 'He hanged himself in his bedroom. I went up one day after school to fetch him down for his dinner and there he was, his little legs dangling in the air, the poor dog staring up at him not knowing what to do. He killed himself. So tell me now, are you proud of yourself, Father? You and your pal in there? Are you proud of yourselves? Of all the things you and your pals have done? Do you even care?'

I did not go straight home but stopped instead at Roche's, a rather squalid-looking coffee shop on Ormond Quay, not far from the Four Courts. A regular gathering place for solicitors and barristers, I imagined, for space was set aside in a corner for those wheelie-bags more common in airports and railway terminals but which I had begun to notice members of the legal profession using to transport huge volumes of paperwork with them from office to courthouse whenever a case was reported on the *Six One News*.

I found an empty table, ordered a strong coffee and stared out of the window for a few moments, watching the people go by: the workers, the businessmen, the students on their way down to Trinity College. And I wondered what my young self would think if I could return thirty-five years to Clonliffe College in 1973 and tell him that the unhappy boy in the bed next to mine would one day be put on trial by the Republic of Ireland for the systematic abuse of young boys who had been entrusted into his pastoral care. That he would be accused of touching them, of molesting them, of penetrating them, of performing unspeakable acts upon them and forcing them to perform the same upon him in return. What was it that had twisted his mind to such things? Were they there from the start, implanted in his psyche while still in the womb, or did they come later? Was there a way to blame his father, who had surely damaged him in some way, and if there was, would that even be fair, for surely a man was responsible for his own actions, regardless of what had happened to him growing up. Bad things, awful things, could be visited upon you in your youth – I knew that as well as anyone – but it did not mean that you allowed yourself to act without conscience. Why did he have such a desperate need for flesh, and for young flesh at that, when the rest of us did not? Was it the fault of the priests who taught us? Was there a way to blame them? And what did any of it matter now anyway, for Tom Cardle was in the dock at last and could hurt no one any more. I could not envision his story reaching a happy conclusion.

I had not felt so lost since that night in Rome in 1978, the night when the woman from the Café Bennizi left me to wander the streets of the capital alone for hours while the Pope sat in his bedroom, awaiting his cup of tea, perhaps being visited by a menacing presence intent on causing him harm, perhaps simply being summoned home by a God whose creations had become a mystery for a simple man to comprehend.

In that moment, I did what I always did at moments of crisis or desperation in my life. I reached into my satchel and removed my Bible, a book that over the years had occasionally offered me answers but more often than not had left me with questions, but which had never failed to distract my mind and offer some comfort. I owned a few Bibles, of course, given to me over the years by friends or purchased on visits to places of pilgrimage as mementoes. But this Bible, the one I opened now, was the oldest one of all, given to me by my mother when I left her house for the seminary all those years ago, a handsome volume encased in black leather with a stamp on the inside cover stating that it had been bought in the Veritas Religious Bookstore on Lower Abbey Street for twenty-two pence in April 1972. It was well thumbed for it had travelled with me everywhere over the years, but it was a sturdy creature and not a page in it was loose. I didn't know what I was looking for, but I opened it randomly, hoping that a passage, a story or a parable would emerge and speak to me, guiding me back from my unhappiness to a place of understanding.

He was practically on top of me before I knew it. A man in his twenties, twenty-five or twenty-six at most. Tall, with a pair of piercing blue eyes that were astonishing to behold. Dressed in a suit but with the whisper of a tattoo – a thick, curlicued blackness – creeping out from beneath the left-hand side of his collar.

'What's that you're reading there?' he asked me.

I looked up in surprise. 'Come again?' I asked.

'That book,' he replied, pronouncing it to rhyme with *duke* instead of *took*. Where was his accent from, I wondered. A working-class area of Dublin. 'What is it? Give us a look at it.'

I turned it over so that he could see the cover and he sneered at me.

'You won't find any answers in there,' he said.

'I have in the past,' I said.

'Believe in magic, do you?'

I looked around, wondering whether anyone else was paying attention to us, but the other customers were all fully engrossed in their conversations and if anyone was listening, they probably wouldn't want to get involved anyway. 'Sure I'm just having a coffee,' I said quietly, turning away from him and looking out of the window again.

'Isn't it well for you?' he said bitterly.

'Good luck now,' I said.

'Don't you be wishing me good luck, you fuckin' pervert. I don't want your good luck, all right?'

I remained silent, feeling the tension begin to grow inside me, starting at the pit of my stomach and working its way up. The coffee cup was shaking a little in my hands and I tried to steady it, not wanting to show any fear or intimidation. But then I was a fifty-three-year-old man, unused to physical altercations, and had no idea how to get through such a thing. I thought the sensible plan here was to look out of the window, not rise to his bait, until he grew bored and left me alone.

'You're a priest,' he said.

'Well spotted,' I replied.

'Are you up there supporting your man?'

'Which man is that?'

'Your man up there in the Four Courts. The rapist. Are you up there to give him moral support, is it?'

I shook my head. 'I don't know any man in the Four Courts,' I said. 'Sure I'm just sitting here having a cup of coffee and minding my own business.'

He stood over me for another minute, starting to fume. For a moment I thought he was going to walk away, but no, he sat down opposite me instead.

'Ah here,' I said, looking over to the man working behind the counter, hoping that he would see what was going on in his café and step in to help. 'This isn't on. Will you not leave me alone?'

'Sure what am I doing to you?' he asked, opening his arms innocently. 'It's a free country, isn't it? A man's allowed to sit down. We're only chattin'.'

I looked into my cup. I was nearly finished anyway, but I was damned if I would give him the satisfaction of standing up and walking away.

'Now if I was a betting man,' he said, 'then I would say you came into Dublin to have a look at your man in the dock and say a prayer over him and try to frighten the jury into finding him not guilty.'

'Which man is that?' I asked again.

'Ah yeah, it's a big mystery to you, isn't it, you prick? You haven't a clue who I'm talking about. Give us a look at your Bible there.'

'I will not.'

'Give us a look at it, I said,' he growled, grabbing it off the table before I could stop him and starting to leaf through it.

'Give it back,' I said impotently. 'It doesn't belong to you.'

'Ah here, would you look at this,' he said, laughing as he turned to the inscription on the front page. *'To Odran, from Mammy*. Sure isn't that sweet? Your oul' one gave you this, did she? When was it, the day you got ordained?'

'Give it back here,' I insisted.

'I'll post it on. Give us your address, Father, and I'll send it back to you when next I'm in the GPO.'

'You'll give it back to me now, you pup,' I said. 'Come on now, that's enough of this.'

He held it out to me, and when I went to reach for it, he pulled it back like a child.

'Ah sorry, Father, I'm only messin',' he said, offering it to me again, but once more he pulled it back and laughed in my face.

'Can someone help me here?' I called, looking around, and for the first time, the solicitors and barristers and the man behind the counter looked in our direction. 'Please,' I beseeched them. 'This man here is bothering me.'

'Sure I'm doin' nothin',' he said, appealing to his audience, who had more sense than to intervene anyway.

'You want it back, do you, Father?' he asked me.

'I do, yes,' I said, not looking him in the eye. To do so would, I felt, provoke him even further.

'You want it back?'

'Yes!'

'Here, you can have it so.' And with that he pulled his right arm back, the hand tightly gripping the leather-bound Bible that my mother, poor woman, had probably spent one of the happiest hours of her life choosing for me in the Veritas Bookstore, and hit me a clatter with it across the side of my head, knocking me off my seat and opening a cut above my right eye as I fell to the floor, collapsing heavily in a pool of spilled tea and half-trod chips. He threw the Bible on top of me then as I heard chairs being pulled back all around me, useless people, for they were preparing not to help me but to defend themselves. I looked up, frightened and alone, and he spat at me, a great mouthful of phlegm that landed half on my cheek and half in my mouth, and I reached up to wipe it away and to spit the rest of it out and came back with a handful of blood from where my face had connected with the side of the table on the way down.

'*Fucking paedophile!*' he roared. Did I not live with that word every day of the week these days, one way or another? Hadn't the two words *paedophile* and *priest* become irrevocably attached to each other in some unholy way?

'Get out, you,' called the café owner to my assailant, but sure he was already halfway out the door; what good was the man's bravery now?

'Are you all right, Father?' said one of the barristers, a young woman, coming towards me now and helping me to my feet. I put a hand to my eye, which was throbbing painfully, and it came back stained with more blood. 'Has this something to do with that priest being tried up above?'

'I don't know any priest being tried up above!' I roared at the top of my voice, causing her to jump back, palms outstretched defensively as if I planned on assaulting her like the man had assaulted me. 'I don't know anything about it, do you hear me?'

I never went back to the courtroom, but I followed the trial daily in *The Irish Times*. There was a lot of evidence to be heard, and in the end it lasted almost three weeks. At first, it was front-page news; gradually it was demoted to pages four or five, where the domestic crimes were reported. And then, on the last week, there was a day when the jury retired to consider their verdict and it was back on the front page, albeit low down on the page, the journalists speculating about the outcome. I read each report carefully, even though it hurt me to do so. The things they said that he had done were wicked and I could not believe that Tom Cardle could have done any of it, and yet I believed that he had done all of it and more, if that makes any sense at all.

And then one morning I turned on Pat Kenny after ten o'clock morning Mass only to hear that the verdict had been returned. Guilty, of course. A unanimous decision. Apparently a cheer went up in the courtroom when the foreman announced it. Some of the victims were present, of course. They had all given their testimony, the country had listened to them at last, and they were allowed in to hear what the people said in response. Their families too, those parents and siblings who had suffered alongside their damaged loved ones. The shouts went up and, according to a reporter in *The Irish Times*, it recalled the crowds cheering in the Colosseum when the emperor twisted his hand, his thumb pointing downwards in the direction of hell.

Further to that, he reported that while the judge tried to silence the courtroom, Tom Cardle bent over a little in the dock and took his head in his hands, and I ask you now whether there is something wrong with me for I felt a sympathy towards him still, despite everything he had done, despite his viciousness and his cruelties and the misery he had brought into the world. For to think of him standing there alone, with a wasted life behind him and God only knew what horrors awaiting him in jail, made my heart ache, but this was not something that I could have explained to anyone for they would have looked at me with revulsion, as if I was complicit in his deeds, when I abhorred them entirely. But I hate to think of a man alone, no matter what he has done.

If I cannot see some good in all of us and hope that the pain we all share will come to an end, then what kind of priest am I anyway? What kind of man?

The crowds returned the following morning for the sentencing, and the ecstasy of the crowd gave way to catcalls and disbelief when the judge announced that Tom would serve only eight years for his crimes, that he would undergo therapy while residing at Arbor Hill prison, that he would be placed on the sex offenders list for the rest of his life and that he would be obliged to keep the Gardaí aware of his location on a weekly basis until the day that he died. Eight years! The spectators were incandescent with rage.

The media lapped it up, of course. The radio and television stations had their top people outside the courthouse, shoving their microphones in the victims' faces, hoping that their pain could be converted into sound bites for the lunchtime news. And they did speak, many of them, eloquently, passionately, but with a barely concealed wrath. Their sense of injustice was to the fore and they spoke with dignified contempt of the man who had turned their lives into an interminable darkness, who continued to make their lives hell, and one man – a very decent-looking fellow, surrounded by his family and loved ones, a beautiful wife whose arm was wrapped around his shoulders – could scarcely contain his tears as he said 'Eight years?' over and over. 'Eight years?' As if he couldn't believe what he'd heard in the courtroom. As if it made no sense to him that he could suffer so much and that his abuser could be punished so little.

'And sure he'll be out in four or five,' said another man, pushing his way to the front, and the people around him nodded and I sat forward in my chair, for who was it? Only the lad who had thumped me with my own Bible in the coffee shop on Ormond Quay. 'That's all he'll serve,' he shouted. 'For everything that bastard did to me and to these people here. Four fuckin' years? Do you hear me, RTÉ?' he asked, his deep-blue eyes staring directly out towards the viewers seated in their living rooms, and to their credit, the national airwaves did not censor a word of his speech when they repeated it endlessly over the coming days. 'Are you listening to me, People of Ireland? All of yous out there? Do you see what we're going through here? Four or five years is all he'll end up with, a man who has destroyed our lives. And then he'll be free, he'll wander among yous and he'll do it again unless you get them out, do you hear me? Get them all out! Pull down the churches! Tell them to pack their bags and get themselves off to the airports or the ferries, but we want to see the back of them. Are you listening, RTÉ? Are you listening, people of Ireland? We want a clean country from now on. Get them out! Get them out! Get them out!'

And the crowd picked up the chant and roared it down the streets, their voices carrying north across the trees to the President in the Áras and south towards the families walking their dogs in Marlay Park, east towards the workers emptying the shipping containers at Dublin port and all the way west to the Aran Islands, where the weather-beaten old men driving their horses and traps could carry the message to the furthest edges of the country and the tourists could carry it back to New York, Sydney, Cape Town and St Petersburg with them, telling the world that Ireland had finally had enough.

That was the simple message the newspapers carried the following morning when they showed nothing on their front pages but a confused and bewildered-looking Tom Cardle being bundled into a police van and a headline above that was persuasive in its simplicity.

GET THEM OUT!

Chapter Fifteen

2012

My black suit hung in my wardrobe and my white starched collar rested on my bedside table, ready for my return. I had not packed them for I would not need them. Where I was going, and considering who I was going to meet, to wear the symbols of my profession could prove a catastrophic error of judgement.

Waiting in the parochial house that morning for the taxi to arrive, I felt uncomfortable in the regular, everyday clothes that I'd chosen to wear. Glancing at myself in the mirror, I imagined various scenarios that strangers might consider when they first saw me: my wife had been dead for a year and I was risking the first solo holiday since our marriage thirty years before; my editor was sending me to a literary festival to interview a famous writer whose work had recently begun to appear in English; my firm was dispatching me to Europe for a week to oversee production at our underperforming plant in Munich. Any of these things might have been possible in a different life, had my choices been different.

I was fooling myself, of course. No one gave me a second glance at the airport; sure why would they when I looked just like everyone else?

At fifty-seven years of age, I could count on one hand the

number of trips that I'd made out of Ireland. Rome, of course, and Norway, for Hannah and Kristian's wedding many years before. America, once. And I had been to Paris for a weekend trip that my sister had given me on the occasion of my fortieth birthday, little thinking of the unintentional cruelty of sending a single, celibate man who had never known any form of intimacy to the city of love for three days and two nights. The fact that my birthday fell at the end of the second week of February made things even worse.

I had never been to Africa, Asia or Australia. Had never stood before the Sydney Opera House or the Winter Palace of the Russian Tsars. Instead, I had made my life in Ireland, and there was a part of me that wondered now whether that had been a terrible mistake, but then the list of mistakes I had made was so long that I could not bear the idea of it expanding even further.

But here I was out in Dublin Airport once again. I could remember standing here in 1978 clutching my ticket in my hand as I left for Rome, Mam and Hannah waving me off, pride on my mother's face, boredom on my sister's, as I marched from the ticket counter to the plane itself without any difficulty. Now it was like trying to enter China. Security checks galore, taking half my clothes off to be passed through an X-ray machine before being patted down by an overweight man with bad skin as he masticated loudly on chewing-gum. The threat of terrorism, everyone said. We were none of us to be trusted.

I was enough of a novice to enjoy the sensation of the plane rising into the air, taking time to look out of my window at the stretch of M50 beneath me, the way the city opened itself out towards the water and the twist of cliffs around Vico Road, where the big-shots lived. The woman beside me was reading a book by Bertie's daughter and wasn't to be disturbed for love nor money. The man next to her was watching a film on one of those portable machines and snorting through his nose every few minutes. I'd saved Jonas's new novel for the journey, but hadn't I forgotten it in my rush to leave the house that morning and I could picture it now, sitting on the table by the door. To make up for this, I had bought a copy of *The Irish Times* in the airport shop and of course it was full of talk about the radio interview that RTÉ had conducted the day before with Archbishop Cordington, who had moved me to Tom Cardle's parish six years before and who had been elevated to cardinal in the meantime, courtesy of the German Pope, for it was well known that the pair of them had been as thick as thieves for years.

The interview took place in response to a newspaper investigation which suggested that Cardinal Cordington had been fully aware of the crimes that had been going on in the Church for decades, that he had facilitated them in a way that made him as culpable as those priests who had committed these acts. In the past, no doubt acting on orders from Rome, he had refused to engage with any of these issues, but things had gone too far now; the Murphy Report had been deeply critical of him and more and more civil cases were being taken against the Church by victims of abuse. The point had come where he had little choice but to address the scandal and so he had agreed to do a live radio interview with Liam Scott.

No slouch, Scott started off with a few easy ones. He asked the cardinal to talk about himself, about his life, about what had led him to the priesthood in the first place.

'A calling,' he replied in a gentle, mellifluous voice. 'I felt it first when I was just a boy. There were no priests in our family. To be honest, my parents were not particularly religious, but for some reason I felt a vocation inside me and as I grew older I talked with a priest in our parish about it, a very nice man, and he gave me the benefit of his advice.'

'How did you feel about that vocation?'

'It frightened me,' said the cardinal. 'I wasn't sure if I could make the sacrifices or if I even had the mental resources for the life that it entailed.'

'Did you have any doubts about what you were giving up?' asked Scott.

'I did, of course.'

'But you went ahead anyway?'

'Did you ever feel, Liam, that the path you were walking along was one that had been laid out for you long ago? That you had no control over it? That's how I felt. Chosen. By God. And when I entered the seminary for the first time, I knew instinctively that I had come home.'

Listening to the interview, this, at least, had spoken to me, for I had felt something similar when I first arrived at Clonliffe College: that here was a place that had been waiting for me my entire life.

A few more platitudes were thrown out, the cardinal was put at his ease, and then things got harder. Scott started with the statistics. The number of child-abuse cases which had come before the courts in the last few years. The number still outstanding. The number of priests behind bars. The number who had been found not guilty through a lack of evidence, but over whose heads serious question marks remained. The number of victims. The number of suicides. The number of support groups. Numbers, numbers, numbers, and the man from RTÉ had them all at his fingertips and he rattled them off clinically, with no threat in his tone, content to sit back and let the statistics stand as challenge enough. When he got to the end and the cardinal had uttered not a word through it all there was a pause before he asked, 'Cardinal Cordington? How do you respond to all of this?'

It was a terrible thing, replied the cardinal, his tone filled with well-rehearsed remorse. A truly terrible thing. There was talk of barrels and rotten apples, of lessons being learned, mistakes from the past being rectified. Going forward, looking backwards, the usual guff. But then, misjudging the sense of the remark, he mentioned that for every priest who found his name in the papers, there were a hundred more who did not.

'It's like a plane crash,' he said, using a preposterous analogy. 'Whenever a plane goes down, everyone hears about it. It's on the news, it's on the television. Because so many tens of thousands of planes take off every day around the world and land safely, but a crash is so rare in the great scheme of things that every one is worth reporting. And so it is with these priests who have been accused: there are so few of them among the vast number of decent, honest priests that we hear every bad story.'

Scott picked up on this quickly, suggesting that this was an extraordinary comment to make, for generally speaking no one on board such a plane – captain and passengers alike – was responsible for what happened; it was usually a fault with the engine. The priests, he pointed out, knew exactly what they were doing. They had made their decisions, they had acted as they saw fit without care or consideration for the consequences on the lives of the children in their care. They were the authors of their own misfortunes and the cause of untold suffering for others. They were criminals; pilots of doomed jets were not.

'And one other thing,' said Scott, landing the killer punch. 'Even though we hear about every plane crash, it's not as if there are hundreds of other plane crashes going unreported around the world every day or being ignored due to lack of evidence.'

The cardinal stuttered in his reply; perhaps he realized that he had spoken badly. He dithered and Scott called him on it, asking him to respect the intelligence of the audience and give an honest answer. I heard a sharp intake of breath on the microphone; it had been a long time since anyone had spoken to him like this. Listening to the interview on the radio in the presbytery, I found myself rooting for Scott, urging him along, telling him not to let the cardinal off the hook. Let the truth come out, I thought. Let it all come out.

'Maybe we can come to some specific cases,' Scott said, moving on, and the case of Father Steven Sherrif was brought up. He had received ten years for abuses in a school that stretched back to the mid-1960s. Seventeen boys had come forward and told their stories. Four of them, with living parents, claimed that they had spoken to the principal of their school about what was going on and they had been threatened with expulsion.

'That would have been reported to my predecessor,' said Cardinal Cordington. 'Who is dead and gone now, may God have mercy on his soul. I can't be held responsible for what he did or failed to do.'

'But you were an auxiliary bishop in that diocese at the time, weren't you?' asked Scott.

'I was, yes.'

'So presumably, before it went to the cardinal, it came to you.'

'And I referred it to the authorities.'

'So you referred it to the Gardaí?' asked Scott.

A slight pause. Sure we all knew that's not what he'd meant. 'I referred it to the Church authorities,' he said quietly.

'But not the Gardaí?'

'No.'

'Why not?'

'It wasn't my place.'

'Hold on there,' said Scott. 'You become aware of a crime and you don't feel that it's your place to report it? If you looked out into our producers' booth now and saw one of my colleagues stealing money from someone else's bag, would you say nothing?'

'I would tell you,' said the cardinal, 'and let you deal with it.'

'And what if I said that it didn't matter?'

'Well then I'd assume that you understand your business here better than I do.'

'Why would these boys be threatened with expulsion when they had done nothing wrong?' asked Scott.

'You have to place these things in context,' said Cordington calmly. 'The case you're referring to took place decades ago—'

'The abuses continued until the 1990s,' said Scott.

'Yes, well I don't know the specifics of the timeline. But what you must remember is that this was an isolated case. And I had no reason to believe that any of those boys were telling the truth.'

'Or any reason to believe that they were lying?'

'Boys . . .' he began. 'They can be very . . .' Wisely, he chose not to continue with that thought.

'Cardinal Cordington, the Murphy Report shows that you were directly involved in eleven separate cases where allegations were made, isn't that right?'

'I haven't read the full report, Liam, but if you say that's so, then I'm sure you're right.'

'You haven't read it?'

'No.'

There was a slight pause. The presenter sounded astonished. 'Can I ask why not?'

'It's very long.'

'You're not serious.'

'I'm a busy man, Liam. You must understand that. Someone in my position has many calls on his time. Suffice to say that I have read many of the important passages and thought deeply about them.'

'You say that this was an isolated case, but that's not true, is it?'

'It is true. The priest in question had never been accused of anything before.'

There was a silence as Scott, along with the listening public, tried to make sense of this logic.

'And that makes it isolated?' asked the interviewer, baffled.

'Look, it wasn't right,' said the cardinal. 'Of course it wasn't right. We can all see that now. And I feel great regret about it. Great regret.'

The stupid man should have left well alone there, for at least there was something of an apology in his reply, but he'd been at this game too long to concede anything and he followed up by pointing out that they had been different times.

'What does that mean?' asked Scott. 'Are you saying that it was all right to leave children to suffer abuse in the 1950s? Or the sixties? Or the seventies?'

'Of course I'm not saying that. But we didn't know then what we know now,' insisted the cardinal and I could smell the perspiration through the airwaves. 'These men didn't know how to act when cases like this were brought to their attention.'

'So would you condemn your predecessor, the previous Primate of Ireland, for his lack of action?' asked Scott. 'Will you say out loud, here and now, that he was wrong?'

'Yes, he was wrong,' he replied after only a slight pause. 'And yes, I would criticize him for it. Condemn, however, is a very harsh word. I am not in the business of condemnation, even if you are.'

An ad break followed. Something about home insurance. And a place to get your windscreen repaired if a stone chipped up at it and caused a break.

'We'll move on to another case, if you don't mind,' Scott began when the show returned, pointing out that there were a lot of callers trying to get through, but that they were going to continue with their conversation first before letting the public have their say. 'The case of Tom Cardle.'

And here the cardinal made another mistake. '*Father* Tom Cardle,' he insisted.

Why do you not think before you speak? I wondered. *And how did you ever reach your elevated rank when it seems you do not have an iota of wisdom in your head?*

'It's been alleged,' continued Scott, 'and you know this because it's been widely reported, that you were aware of Cardle's abuse of young boys as far back as 1980. That you received a complaint from a parent in his second parish in Galway, when you were a bishop there, and colluded with the archdiocese of Ardagh and Clonmacnoise for him to be moved to Belturbet rather than investigate any further. Do you have anything to say about that?'

'Firstly, I was a very new bishop at the time,' said the cardinal. 'And the pressures of the job were immense. I had no proof whatsoever that Father Cardle was involved in anything like that. To my mind, he was a hard-working young priest who was doing a great job there in Galway. The parishioners loved him, so much so that when an opening came up in Cavan and it needed to be filled quickly, I recommended him purely on the basis of all the good things I had heard about him. The timing was coincidental, nothing more.'

'But had he not come to Galway after only a year in Leitrim?'

'He might have. I can't remember.'

'I can tell you that he had.'

'Well I'll take your word for it so.'

'Isn't a year a very short time for a priest to spend in his first parish?'

'It is, I suppose.'

'So why was he moved out of Leitrim?'

'I couldn't tell you,' said the cardinal. 'That had nothing to do with me.'

'The suggestion is that a complaint was made about him in

Galway,' continued Scott. 'And that's why he was moved to Belturbet.'

'No, that's nonsense.'

'So no one ever came to you with any allegation about Cardle during his and your time in Galway?'

'I can't remember, Liam,' said the cardinal. 'It's so long ago and I had responsibility for so many priests. I genuinely can't remember.'

'The fact is that over the course of twenty-five years, Cardle spent time in no fewer than eleven different parishes. And the Murphy Report makes it clear that at least one boy from every parish was found to have made a complaint against him. Multiple boys in some parishes, even if their cases did not ultimately make it to court. Parents reported threats being made against them if they continued with their allegations. They were told that they would be prevented from taking Holy Communion, that their children would not be allowed into the Catholic school and that they would face serious difficulties within their communities. Businesses would go under as no one would shop at a store that the priests spoke out against.'

'I don't know anything about that,' said the cardinal gruffly.

'Do you know what this reminds me of?' asked Scott, his voice even and calm. 'It reminds me of the Mafia. Of bullying, blackmailing and extortion. Reading about what the Church got up to is like watching the box-set of *The Sopranos*, do you realize that? A Martian coming down to earth and studying the Murphy Report would think that there was nothing that you and your pals would not do to protect the Church's interests. And it didn't matter who got hurt along the way.'

'I think that's a ridiculous allegation, Liam,' said the cardinal. 'And with respect, I think that you're trivializing something that is terribly serious.'

'But your officials were making these threats,' Scott insisted.

'So either they were acting under your orders, and the orders of the Church, in which case you are fully culpable and part of a criminal conspiracy, or they were acting without your approval, in which case you were merely negligent and have no business serving in any position of responsibility. Would that be a fair assessment?'

And once again, the cardinal decided to dig his grave a little deeper. 'Liam,' he said, 'if I was looking for fairness, do you think I'd be out here at RTÉ? Sure you're not exactly unbiased, are you?'

Quick as a flash, Scott was on him. Here was a man who'd cut his teeth on Charlie and Garret and sharpened them twenty years later on Bertie and Gerry Adams; he knew how to respond to this. The man should have been a barrister; the Church would have hired him in a heartbeat. 'Are you saying these allegations are something that RTÉ has made up?' he asked. 'That *The Irish Times* has made up? That the *Irish Independent* has made up? TV3? Today FM? Newstalk? The Irish media as a whole? Are you blaming us for this?'

'No, Liam, no,' said the cardinal, flustered now. 'You misunderstand me.'

'Did you and your fellow bishops move Tom Cardle from parish to parish because you knew that he was abusing boys?'

'Liam, if we knew that he was doing that, would we not have been right to move him? Should we have left him where he was?'

Ah here, I thought, shaking my head. Step away from the microphone, for pity's sake.

'You'd have been right to call in the Gardaí, is what you would have been right to do,' said Scott, raising his voice for the first time.

'Well of course, of course,' said the cardinal. 'And we did. In due course.'

'You did not,' snapped Scott. 'The Gardaí came to you.'

'Semantics.'

'Do you not sense the anger out there?' asked Scott, and for the first time it occurred to me that he had not finished any sentence in this interview with the phrase *Your Eminence*.

The cardinal paused. 'I do,' he said finally. 'Of course I do. I'm not stupid.'

'And do you understand why so much of that anger is directed towards you?'

'It's difficult for me to comprehend it,' he replied quietly, and there was honesty in his voice here at last. 'I've thought about it, Liam. Of course I have. I've genuinely thought about it. I'm not some sort of monster, even if that is how your friends in the media want to portray me. But I don't know. I can't understand why any man, let alone a priest, would do these things. And I don't know when the world changed so much. Nothing like this ever happened to me when I was a boy. Or to anyone I knew. The priests I knew as a child were very decent men.' He gave a sigh and I felt a certain sympathy for how lost he sounded. 'Sometimes, Liam, it's like I went to bed in one country and woke up in another.'

'People believe that you knew what was going on and that you covered it up.'

'Then people would be wrong.'

'If you had known about Tom Cardle, for example,' said Scott, trying a different tack, 'and then moved him to different parishes, would you agree that you would be an accomplice to his crimes?'

The cardinal thought about it. 'I can't answer that,' he said.

'Why not?'

'Because the question requires legal definitions that I'm not qualified to offer.'

'When you move a priest,' asked Scott, 'do you do all the paperwork yourself, or is it approved higher up the ladder?'

'Well, it's really down to me,' said the cardinal. 'But of course, as a bishop, I would send the papers to the Primate of Ireland to be signed, just as the bishops now send their papers to me. But that's more a matter of bureaucracy than anything else. He would simply sign off on whatever moves each archdiocese would suggest. There would be no reason not to.'

'And in turn those appointments would go to Rome?'

'They would, of course.'

Scott took a breath. 'So all these priests who were moved from parish to parish, all these crimes that were not reported to the Gardaí, the Pope would have known about them? He was in on the fix?'

'Ah now, Liam,' said the cardinal, 'show a little respect. The Pope is dead and can't answer for himself.'

'Would he have known? Would the crimes have been reported to him?'

'Who can say?'

'Would he have approved the moves?'

'I don't know.'

'Did he know what was going on?'

'I couldn't tell you.'

'If he did know, would it not be fair to say that he is tremendously guilty? That he was the brains of the operation, if you will. That he was, in effect, the criminal mastermind? The worst of them all?'

The cardinal took a deep breath. I took one myself. It was an extraordinary remark. One that I never thought I would hear over the national airwaves in Ireland. Not because I didn't think there was truth in it. But because I didn't think anyone out there in RTÉ had the guts to say it.

There was nowhere to go after that remark but to the phone lines and the half-hour that followed was predictable in its way. A caller would say how disgusted he or she felt at the Church, at the conspiracy of silence they had built up amongst themselves, at what a bunch of perverted criminals we all were; the next would condemn the media, saying that the radio stations and the newspapers were out to get the Church, to bring it down, because the media was full of hatred and what right had he to say these things to a decent man of God like Cardinal Cordington. A victim phoned in and challenged the cardinal, in a calm and rational manner, saying that fifteen years earlier he had sat in a room with him while his father begged the then-bishop to investigate what his son had told him and they'd been ignored. The cardinal said he had no recollection of the meeting but it certainly didn't sound like something he would do.

As the hour drew to a close and there was talk of the news coming up on the hour, Scott thanked the cardinal for being there, who said that he was always happy to speak to the people, a note of relief in his voice now that his trial – the only one he would ever receive – was over, but Scott found time for one last question.

'Do you feel any shame?' he asked. 'Do you feel even an ounce of shame when you realize what your Church has been responsible for? For the legacy of abuse, for the cover-ups, for the criminal behaviour, for the lives you have destroyed and the lives you have ended? Do you feel any shame for that?'

'I feel a great sense of the Holy Spirit, is what I feel,' replied the cardinal. 'And the certain knowledge that the Lord moves in mysterious ways.'

Ah goodnight, I thought, switching the radio off and getting on about my business. There'll be no recovery from that.

My plane landed at Gardermoen Airport, thirty miles outside Oslo, in the early afternoon. From my window seat I had looked down at the fjords and watched a single speed-boat cutting its way through the water, leaving an arrow of flume in its wake as it pointed me towards the city. I collected my suitcase and looked around for the sign directing me to the train station. Three decades earlier, when I had last been in Norway, I remembered a delegation of Ramsfjelds collecting me from the airport in a car that looked as if it had been around since the dawn of motoring and the great craic we had on the two-hour drive north to Lillehammer. Kristian had arrived with his uncle and two of his cousins, Einar and Svein.

I was still young then, of course, and there had been a part of me that had glanced at Svein as we drove north, trying to decipher something on his face, some knowledge of the world that was missing from my own. I envied him, a little.

Kristian's Uncle Olaf had brought two bottles of Vikingfjord vodka with him for the journey and by the time we reached Lillehammer they were both empty and we were none of us in complete control of ourselves. Hannah, who had been staying with her fiancé's family for a week before the wedding, took one look at us as we tumbled out of the car, giggling like idiots, and gave us no end of grief for the accident that might have happened on the roads. But still, we were there safely and in fine fettle.

Now, of course, I was travelling alone and found a quiet seat on the train, happy to sit back and watch the passing scenery, feeling a certain degree of calm that I knew would diminish the closer I got to my destination.

I was hypnotized by the sea that ran the entire journey on my left and the thick-forested hills across the water with their occasional villages nestled in the serenity. White-plastic-sealed oblongs of hay were stacked like ice-cream blocks left out to melt in the late-afternoon sun. Was it any wonder that Kristian had spent most of his adult life longing to return?

Halfway through my journey, at Tangen, the doors opened and the few other occupants of my carriage disembarked. A woman of about thirty boarded with her son, a blond-haired child who might have stepped straight out of an advertisement for the Norwegian tourist industry, and she sat about six seats down from me while the boy, who could not have been more than seven years old, sat next to her at first, then opposite her, then wandered down the carriage to sit next to me. The woman paid no attention – this was not Ireland, the people were not so filled with fear – but was listening to music on her iPod while flicking through a newspaper.

'*Hei*,' said the little boy, grinning at me.

'*Hei*,' I replied, standing up immediately and walking past his mother as I made my way to the doors at the end, then continued on to the very last carriage on the train, found another empty window-seat and sat down.

This is the way I do things now, of course. I do not put myself at risk.

I arrived at Lillehammer train station at half past four and left my luggage in a locker there before opening my map and re-reading the directions that I'd written down earlier in the week.

Was this sensible, I wondered. Or merely another mistake.

It was a long enough walk, perhaps thirty minutes or more, but I wanted to gather my thoughts as I made my way towards the hilltop houses above the Maihaugen Museum, where Einar and Svein had brought me all those years before to see the history and culture of Norway all gathered together in the open air: threshing barns, stave churches and young people dressed in nineteenth-century costume. I made my way along a twisting road with well-tended gardens, clusters of trees separating neighbour from neighbour, until finally, as I took one more turn to my left, I noticed a small brown King Charles spaniel truffling in the grass outside a gate, and as he turned to look at me I felt certain that this was the house.

I made my way down the driveway, the dog trotting happily at my heels as his head swung up to stare at me, and glanced at the car parked outside the front door; on the back seat was a car-seat for an infant and I felt a twinge inside me when I saw that.

I rang the doorbell and heard the sound of a second dog barking inside and then a voice, a woman's, calling out to him in words I could not understand before she opened it; her face changed slightly when she realized that she did not recognize me, that perhaps I was a salesman of some sort, or a Jehovah's Witness, or someone who was seeking her vote at a council election.

'*Hei?*' she asked, as the first dog slipped past her and disappeared down the hallway, returning almost immediately with a plastic rabbit in his mouth which he displayed proudly to me. The second dog, another King Charles, padded into the hallway and yawned.

'Hello,' I said.

She reverted to English immediately. 'Can I help you?'

'Is this Aidan Ramsfjeld's home?' I asked.

'It is, yes.'

'I wonder if I could speak with him.'

'He's not back yet. He should be here any minute. And you are . . . ?'

'I'm Odran,' I told her. 'Odran Yates. His uncle.'

Her smile faded a little and her mouth fell open for a moment in surprise. 'Oh,' she said. 'All right. Did he know that you were coming? He never said anything.'

'No,' I told her. 'Actually I didn't know myself until a few days ago. I thought I would just arrive and hope that he wouldn't be away on holiday.'

'On holiday?' she asked, laughing a little. 'We should be that lucky.' She stepped back and I entered the house, noticing a doctor's bag on a side table which could only have belonged to her.

'I'm sorry,' she said after a moment as we stared at each other, extending her hand. 'I should have introduced myself. I'm Marthe. Aidan's wife.'

'Odran.'

'Yes, you said. Would you like to come through?'

I followed her down the hallway into a large living room, carefully decorated with a rather good painting of a river-way on the walls. I recognized it, but wasn't sure why. Had I passed it on my train journey?

'Do you like it?' she asked me, seeing where I was looking. 'It's the Ponte Sisto in Rome. We went there on our honeymoon. I bought it to remind myself.'

'Yes, of course,' I said, the memories flooding back. I turned away from it to look around the rest of the room and staring back at me were two small children, a boy of about four and a little girl of about two.

'Children, this is Odran,' said Marthe. 'Your father's . . .' She hesitated. 'This is Odran,' she repeated. 'And these are Morten and Astrid.'

'Hello,' I said.

'*Hei*,' they cried in unison and I smiled at them; they were beautiful-looking children. 'What's that you're watching?'

The boy, Morten, uttered a long string of Norwegian words which he punctuated with hand movements, and when he was finished, he nodded thoughtfully and turned back to the television set.

'Ah grand,' I said. I turned back to Marthe and shrugged. 'I'm sorry to turn up unannounced,' I told her.

'I don't mind,' she said. 'Shall we have some tea?' I followed her into the kitchen, which was immaculate despite the fact that she was clearly in the middle of preparing the evening meal. 'Is everything all right?' she asked after a moment. 'Hannah hasn't taken a turn for the worse?'

'No, no, it's not that.'

'And Jonas?'

'He's fine, as far as I know. In Hong Kong, I believe.'

'Lucky him. Sit down, won't you?'

I sat and a few minutes later she placed a cup of tea before me. I sipped at it, unsure what to say.

'Well,' she said, sitting opposite me.

I looked at her and felt uncertain of what I was doing here. This was a nice house; a family lived here with a pair of beautiful, well-loved children and a couple of friendly dogs. Why was I bringing all this misery to her door?

'Maybe I should leave,' I said. 'I don't want to disturb you.'

'You're not disturbing me,' she said. 'Not in the least.'

'I had to come, you see.' Feeling the weight of all these years growing inside me. 'I have to speak to him. To explain.'

'To explain what?'

I looked directly at her. I shook my head; if I couldn't find the words for her, then how would I ever find them for him?

Her face changed and her smile fell. 'Oh,' she said, and at that moment I heard the sound of a key in the door and jumped to my feet, feeling a sense of fear, as if there was the possibility that I had stepped into a moment that I might not survive. Marthe turned, looked down the hall and whispered his name as he walked towards us.

'What a day!' he was saying. 'Einar was late with the invoices and when he finally finished them, he'd only gone and—'

He stopped when he saw me, a look of surprise on his face, and in a moment I felt the build-up of twenty years of lies and deceit, of trauma and cruelty, and recognized my hand in it, for had I not left that man alone with my nephew to do whatever he wanted with him?

And as the pain grew inside me, the tears came out of nowhere and I fell back to the chair, weeping as I had never wept before.

'I'm sorry,' I said, the words strangled in the emotion, not even a hello or a shake of the hand from me. 'I'm sorry . . . I didn't know . . . will you forgive me, Aidan, for I swear I didn't know . . .' And the rest of the words were garbled, for by now there were tears and spit and snot and I was crumpled over the table like a mess of a man while Marthe stared in amazement at the scene playing out before her, a hand to her mouth, and Aidan, that good man, better than all of them put together, put his bag down and came over to me, put his arm around my shoulder and pulled me to him and said, 'Stop crying, Uncle Odie. Stop crying. Stop crying or you'll set me off and I might never stop.'

We met two nights later in a bar in Oslo. I had stayed for only a short time at Aidan and Marthe's house, for after the emotion of that first half-hour passed, a strained atmosphere developed between us and he grew very quiet, staring at the floor as Marthe made small talk with me, and finally I suggested that perhaps I should leave.

'I took you by surprise,' I said. 'I should have let you know that I was coming. But maybe I could see you in a few days' time when you've had a chance to think about things?'

I watched his face, grown dark and lined now from outdoor work, as he considered this. He had a three-day stubble that looked as if it never grew longer nor was ever cut shorter. I could see Kristian in his eyes, Hannah in the way he turned to look at me when he thought that I was looking away. There was nothing of that boy entertainer about him now; he was a man through and through.

'How long will you be in Norway?' he asked finally.

'As long as I need to be,' I said. 'I've a hotel booked in Oslo for a few nights, but if you tell me to go home to Dublin, then that's what I'll do.'

He nodded, but his expression gave nothing away. I glanced at Marthe, but there was nothing in her face that suggested that she would intervene.

'Let me give you my details,' I said, writing down the address. 'Maybe you'll give me a call if you feel like talking.'

And without any more conversation on either of our parts, I left.

I spent the next day sightseeing, although my mind wasn't fully on it, watching the young people on their inter-railing holidays and wondering what it would be like to be twenty again – to be twenty *now*, in 2012, when everything was different – before pushing that idea to the back of my mind, for only misery lay inside those fantasies. In the late afternoon I visited the cathedral, lighting a candle before the wooden Madonna and Child, and when I got back to my hotel there was a message from Aidan, who said that he had to be in Oslo on business the following day and if it suited me, he could meet me for a drink at seven o'clock in a bar on the Aker Brygge Wharf. When I made my way there, I found him seated alone with a beer, reading the sports pages of the newspaper. He looked up as I approached and offered me a half-smile.

'I can't get used to seeing you in regular clothes,' he said. 'I've never known you without the habit.'

'The open collar doesn't suit me,' I said.

'Will you have a beer?'

'I will.'

He signalled for a fresh round and I welcomed the tall glasses when they arrived. I had a thirst on me and the drink would give us something to do while we settled ourselves.

'Marthe seems like a grand girl,' I said.

'Yes, she is.'

'She's a doctor, is that right?'

He nodded. 'A paediatrician. She has her own practice in Lillehammer.'

'She's not the woman you were living with in London all those years ago?'

'No, that didn't last. I only met Marthe when I came here.'

'And you?' I asked. 'What do you do?'

'I run a construction firm,' he told me. 'Or rather, I co-run it. My cousin Einar is in it with me.'

'I remember Einar,' I said. 'From when your mother and father got married.'

'No, that would have been his father. Einar's only in his twenties. Einar Junior.'

'Ah right. Einar, Svein, your father and I drove up together from the airport and drank vodka all the way. We got rightly hammered. How are they both?'

'Einar's fine,' he said. 'He lives near us. But Svein died a few years ago. Cancer.'

I felt an inexplicable burst of sadness for a boy I had only known for a few days thirty years ago. 'That's awful,' I said. 'He couldn't have been very old.'

'No, he wasn't. He was only in his early forties.'

'Did he ever marry?'

'Twice. Badly, both times.'

I sighed. 'And your children,' I said. 'Morten and Astrid.'

'What about them?'

'Nothing. It was nice to meet them, that's all.'

He nodded and took a long swallow from his pint before glancing up at a television screen in the corner of the bar that was showing a football match. He watched for a moment before frowning and looking back down at the table, running a fingernail along a groove at the side.

'I suppose I should have written,' I said finally. 'Maybe that would have been a better way to go about things.'

'I expected you months ago,' he replied, surprising me.

'You did?'

'Jonas told me that you asked for my address. I expected you that same week.'

'I wasn't sure if you'd welcome me,' I said. 'It's been years since we saw each other, after all. And so much has happened in the meantime.'

'To me, yes. I'd say your life hasn't changed at all, has it?'

I looked away. Was this a deliberate cruelty on his part? Or merely a statement with no hidden meaning? He was right though. With the exception of the fact that I was in parish work now and not in Terenure, my life had hardly altered since he was a child.

'I'm going to order another one,' I said, catching the waiter's eye, who pulled two more pints and brought them over.

'Steady on now,' said Aidan. 'We only just got here.'

'Don't worry, I've eaten. And tonight I feel like I need a few drinks.'

We clinked glasses.

'Sláinte,' I said.

'Skål,' he replied.

A silence descended on us then and for a time I thought we might never break it.

'Did you see the Grand Hotel?' he asked me eventually.

'On the square?' I asked. 'I did, yes.'

'The winner of the Nobel Peace Prize stays there every December for the ceremony,' he said. 'Marthe and I always come for the weekend and stay there too. It's where we met, you see. In the bar of that hotel. Mohamed ElBaradei from the International Atomic Energy Association won that year. It was the day after the ceremony and he was just relaxing, I suppose, having a drink, but Marthe asked me would I use her camera to take a picture of the two of them together and I did, and then I asked her to do the same for me, and ElBaradei was in such good form that he bought us both a drink and Marthe and I were so delighted that we just kept talking after he left. We've been together ever since.'

'And you go every year?'

He looked down at his fingers and started ticking off names and I imagined that this was a game that he and Marthe played together every December, the difficulty increasing every year as another name was added to the list. 'It was Yunus the following year,' he said. 'Then Al Gore, then a Finnish guy whose name I can never remember, then Barack Obama, but we weren't allowed into the hotel then because of all the security, then—'

'Aidan,' I said quietly, placing a hand down flat on the table and closing my eyes.

He stopped speaking and shook his head. 'There's no point getting into it,' he said.

'There is, of course. That's what I'm here for.'

'Did you know all along?' he asked, looking me directly in the eyes.

'You won't believe me if I tell you. You'll think I'm lying.'

'If you tell me, then I'll believe you.'

I shook my head. 'I didn't,' I said. 'As God is my witness, it never crossed my mind. It was only a couple of months ago when I understood what had happened. I was watching *The Late Late Show* and there was a woman on with her son, a lawyer who works with the victims of abuse. They were talking about his childhood and about the man who hurt him, the things that he'd done. It made for terrible listening, Aidan, terrible listening. But then your man, the host, turns to the mother and asks her did she never notice any changes in her son, was there never a point when she thought there might be something wrong? And she said that she had, but that she had put it down to his age. She said that he'd always been a happy-go-lucky sort of lad, one of those boys who lit up a room with his energy, that he'd been like that since he could first talk. And then one day, she said, he just changed. In the blink of an eye. He went from being full of beans to being full of anger. And I was sitting there watching her, Aidan, and I remember that I was drinking a mug of tea at the time because I dropped it, it was still nearly full and scalding hot, and I felt a surge inside me and the room began to spin and I thought that I was dying. Honestly, I thought I was having a heart attack or a stroke. I dragged myself off the seat and pulled at my collar but I couldn't loosen it. It was tied fast around my neck. And I could hear myself struggling for breath and when it didn't come I fell on to the sofa and I suppose I must have passed out for a few minutes, but then one of the other priests in the presbytery came running in and he whipped the collar off me and gave me some water. He wanted me to go to the doctor, but I said no, I'd be grand in a while, and I went to my room instead. And I sat there on the side of my bed and I thought of you, Aidan, I thought of how you had been as a little lad, with your singing and your tap-dancing and all the jokes you used to tell, and then I thought of how you changed, so suddenly, so unexpectedly, and I remembered that night, the night of my mother's funeral—'

'Stop. Please. Stop,' he said. I looked across at him. His eyes were closed and his face was pale. I took my handkerchief out, for I could feel the tears streaming down my face.

'It was then, wasn't it?' I asked.

'Yes,' he said.

'Was it just the once?'

'Yes.'

'Will you tell me about it?'

He shook his head. 'No.'

'I didn't know, Aidan,' I said, leaning forward. 'I swear on all that I hold sacred that I didn't know. If I had known that Tom was like that I never would have—'

'Please don't say his name,' said Aidan. 'I don't say his name.'

I felt my stomach convulse inside me, a disgust for everything that I had spent my life believing in. And hatred, pure hatred, for my oldest friend. 'I am overwhelmed by guilt and shame,' I told him finally and he looked across at me now, an expression of near-forgiveness on his face.

'You don't have to be,' he said. 'You didn't do anything.'

'I left him there alone with you.'

'You weren't to know what he would do.'

'But I was your uncle,' I said, feeling the weight of all that this poor boy had borne. 'I should have looked out for you. I should have protected you.'

He shrugged. 'Did you never guess?' he asked.

'No.'

He shook his head. 'Did you never guess?' he repeated.

'No.'

'I find that hard to believe. I'm not attacking you, Odran, but I have to be honest with you. I find that really hard to believe.'

'Do you think that if I'd guessed what he was like I would have left him alone with you?'

'You might have been afraid to challenge him.'

'This is why you've hated me for so long, isn't it?' I asked. 'Why you keep yourself so distant from me? You blame me for what happened.'

'No, I blame him,' he said. 'But yes, you brought him into our house. You left him alone with me. I understand that you feel guilt about that and that you can't be held responsible for another man's actions, but this has been a long road for me, a twenty-year road. The damage that man did to me in one night is damage that I will take to the grave with me. So it's not easy to forget your part in it.'

I nodded. I put both hands to my cheeks and slowly wiped them dry. 'I can't blame you for feeling that way,' I said. 'And you're right in what you say. I did bring him into your house.

And I did leave him alone with you. You were my nephew and I should never have let anything bad happen to you. I have nothing to say to you, Aidan, other than that I am sorry and that it is the greatest regret of my life. I'm sorry,' I repeated.

'Yeah,' he said. 'I know you are.'

A look passed between us then, a moment of tenderness, and I knew then that he did not want to be angry with me any longer, but that it would be impossible for him to bury the pain entirely or to forgive me completely. But there was hope for us, perhaps.

'Can I ask you a question?' I said after a moment.

'You can ask.'

'Why didn't you come back? Why didn't you testify in the trial?'

He shrugged. 'No one ever asked me.'

'But you must have read about it. You must have been aware that it was going on. Or were you? And if you were, why didn't you go to the Gardaí too?'

He considered this. 'I heard about it, yes,' he admitted. 'And perhaps I should have. It's difficult to explain. I've learned to deal with this in my own way. I've seen counsellors, on and off. They don't do much for me, to be honest. But there's Marthe, she helps. I've found my own way to move past it. Did I want to come back to Ireland and re-live it in a courtroom? No. Perhaps that was wrong of me, but no, I didn't. I knew there were enough people testifying to ensure that he would go to jail, but I also knew that I could not stand in a courtroom with that person. If I did, we wouldn't both leave it alive. I have a son, Odran. I have a daughter. I made a choice. On the days when the trial was taking place I was in Lillehammer with them. I took some time off. I spent my days with them, just the three of us. I took them out on a boat. I walked them around the Maihaugen until they complained about how tired they were. Marthe and I took them on a train journey to Stockholm and had the best four days of our lives. To go back to Dublin and immerse myself in that cauldron, or to be here with my family and to love and to be loved? There was no contest.'

I nodded. 'And you wouldn't come back now that it's all over?'

'To live, you mean?'

'Yes.'

He shook his head. 'I would never live in that country again,' he said. 'Ireland is rotten. Rotten to the core. I'm sorry, but you priests destroyed it.'

I had no response to this. Could I tell him that he was wrong? Was I even sure that he was?

'Jonas knows all about this, doesn't he?' I asked.

'Yes. I told him a long time ago.'

'But nothing happened to him that night?'

'No.'

'And what about your mother? Did you ever tell her?'

He shook his head. 'I never did. But I think she knew.'

'I think she did too,' I said, recalling something she had said on the day that Jonas and I had driven her to the Chartwell.

'Will you let me back in your life?' I asked him, afraid of the answer. And at that moment, the team on the television must have scored a winning goal for a great roar went up from the crowd. Aidan looked around and joined in the cheers.

'Aidan,' I said when he turned back. 'Will you let me back in your life?' I repeated.

He swallowed and took a deep breath before closing his eyes. I said nothing; I waited. It felt like an eternity. Finally he opened them and stopped a passing waitress.

'I'll have another beer,' he told her.

'And your friend?' she asked.

'Actually, he's my uncle,' he said. 'And yes, he'll have one too. And you might bring us a menu while you're at it. We're going to have dinner together.'

She nodded and I looked down at the table; it was a little while before I felt able to look up again.

'Tell me about your children,' I said finally. 'Tell me everything about them.'

And with that his face lit up and I saw again the boy that he had once been, the boy so full of life and joy and love. He was still in there somewhere, hidden behind the pain. And all it took to reveal himself again was the mention of that little boy and girl who were north in Lillehammer, probably curled up on the sofa as their mother read them a book and the dogs snorted in their sleep.

Chapter Sixteen

2013

I HEARD A RUMOUR that Father Mouki Ngezo was returning to Nigeria and made an appointment to see the Archbishop – the *new* Archbishop – to ask whether I might finally be allowed to return to Terenure College.

It was my first trip to the Episcopal Palace since his appointment and quite a few changes had been made in the intervening time. Gone were the symbols of old-world luxury, all replaced by a business-like modernity. The drinks cabinet had been taken away; in its place was a table that looked as if it belonged in a modern art gallery, with a widescreen computer monitor on top. Father Lomas, who used to sit in the outside office waiting on Archbishop Cordington hand and foot, had vanished altogether. Now there were two desks on either side of the room, complete with a communications system that wouldn't have looked out of place in NASA. At one sat a young man in a suit with a shaved head and stubble who introduced himself as the Archbishop's personal assistant. At the other was a woman who might have stepped right off a catwalk; the diocese's new media adviser, I was told.

'What happened to Father Lomas?' I asked her.

'James has been reassigned,' she told me. 'We're trying to mobilize our resources more productively.'

'Right so,' I said.

I was told to wait in a chair that didn't seem to be a chair at all and she forced a cappuccino on me. As I waited, she took part in occasional calls through an earpiece while waving her hands in the air as if she was conducting an orchestra.

'Are you on Twitter?' she asked me.

'Am I what?'

'Are you on Twitter?' she repeated. 'I can't find your name. Or are you using a different one?'

'I'm not, no,' I told her, trying not to laugh. 'Sure what would I have to be twittering about? No one's interested in what I ate for breakfast.'

'It's a common misconception that that's what Twitter is for,' she replied, rolling her eyes.

'My nephew told me to make a Facebook page, but I never got around to it.'

'Well why would you?' she asked. 'It's not 2010.'

Fortunately for me, one of the lights on her desk flashed on before she could quiz me any further and she nodded towards the door. 'He's ready for you,' she said. 'Ten minutes, all right? I need him for Today FM at half past.'

I said nothing; sure I wasn't the man's secretary. This would take as long as it took.

'Father Yates,' said the Archbishop when I entered, shaking my hand and pointing to a chair on the left-hand side of his desk, its back to the room but positioned so whoever was sitting there was at a right-angle to him. I'd seen this somewhere before but couldn't think where. It seemed awkward somehow. 'Good of you to make the time to come to see me.'

We exchanged a few pleasantries but, aware that herself would be in to evict me in eight and a half minutes' time, I cut to the chase and told him why I was there. I wanted to go home, I said. I wanted to go back to my school.

'I think you're exactly where we need you,' he replied, shaking his head and smiling at me in a way that suggested he couldn't think why I was asking such a thing. 'From all accounts you're doing a great job in that parish. Father Burton speaks very highly of you. Why would you want to go back to that school anyway? All those kids? They'd wear you out, I'd say. I had to attend an event at Blackrock not so long ago and I thought I'd pass out with the stink of all those lads. Do they never wash, no? Teenagers, I suppose.'

'Attendance at Sunday Mass is down,' I told him, prepared to condemn myself if it meant that I could get what I wanted. 'The collection plates are half empty. We have no altar boys any more, although of course that was a decision that was taken from this office.'

'It's safer without,' he said quietly.

'All told, Your Grace, I don't think I've done an exemplary job.'

'You can't be blamed for most of that,' he said. 'We live in difficult times, do we not? Very difficult times. This last decade has been an awful one for the Church. But it's up to men like you and I to rebuild things. Going forward,' he added with a smile.

The Oval Office. That's where I'd seen chairs placed like this. The president put his visitors at this ridiculous angle. I suppose it reminded them where the real power lay.

'When Cardinal Cordington first asked me to take over the parish,' I said, 'he promised that it would only be a temporary thing.'

'Promised, did he?' he asked, looking at me with a peeved expression, as if my level of disrespect was not something that he would be willing to tolerate for too long.

'Yes,' I replied, staring right back at him. 'He promised.'

'Well, sometimes we cannot stick to our promises.'

'Sure don't I know that well enough. Vows are broken left,

right and centre, as far as I can see. Only the thing is that I've been out there for six years now and I've had enough of it. Father Ngezo is going back to Nigeria, or so I've heard anyway, which means there's an opening for a chaplain at the school and I'd like to take it.' I tried a more conciliatory tone. 'Look, Your Grace, I'm not getting any younger. I'm nearly sixty. I want to live out my days there. It suits me, do you see? I put a lot of work into that library. And I always got on well with the lads.'

'I'm sorry, Father Yates,' he said – none of this *Odran* or *Father Odran* nonsense for him – 'only I have a very able young man in mind to take over from Father Ngezo when he leaves. I've promised that he can start in the autumn and he's looking forward to it. He's good friends with Colin Farrell, the actor, apparently. They went to school together. We might be able to get him in to give a talk to the boys.'

'Well, as you said yourself, Your Grace, sometimes we cannot stick to our promises.'

The smile remained fixed but he shook his head. 'Not going to happen,' he said. 'Deal with it.'

I tried not to laugh. How old was he anyway? Forty? Forty-five? *Deal with it?*

'Perhaps you're right,' I said.

'I am right.'

'After all, it's not as if Cardinal Cordington asked me to take on Tom Cardle's old parish so he could move him to a safe house, is it?'

'What's that?' he asked.

'I'm only saying,' I said. 'All this talk about a criminal investigation into the cardinal is a terrible thing. It wouldn't have happened in John Charles McQuaid's time, I can tell you that. Of course, the DPP have said that they don't have enough evidence to press charges against him. And a good thing too. He says he didn't know anything about Tom's abuses and I for one believe him, don't you? Although now I come to think of it, the day I sat in this office, when he originally asked me to move, he did imply differently. He started to tell me something, but then thought better of it. He said it was delicate and not for public consumption. What do you suppose he was referring to?'

'You're treading on very dangerous ground here, Father Yates,' said the Archbishop quietly, glancing for a moment at a phone that was vibrating away on his desk before picking it up, sliding a finger across the casing and setting it down again.

'How so?' I asked. 'It's not as if something like that would ever get out, is it? Although he'd have a lot of explaining to do if it did, don't you think? This office would bear the brunt of most of it, I'd say. Not that I'd talk about it, of course. To a journalist. Or . . .' – and I paused for a moment to utter the three dreaded syllables that the Irish Church despised more than any other – 'to RTÉ.'

The truth was that I'd had enough. I'd submitted to them all my life – first to Father Haughton and my mother, then to the Archbishop of Dublin, then to Monsignor Sorley and the cardinals in Rome, who forced a silence on me in September 1978 when I should have spoken out, then to the Polish Pope, who dismissed me before my time and whose rules I obeyed for decades before I realized what kind of man he really was – and I was damned if I was going to submit any longer. And certainly not to a young pup like this who hadn't even been in the job a wet weekend. With his bloody iPhones and his iPads and his twittering nonsense. I'd had enough. Sure hadn't the whole country had enough?

'What age are you now, Father Yates?' he asked finally. 'Fifty-five?'

'Fifty-eight.'

'And when do you think you'll be retiring? Sixty?'

'Ah no, sure I'm very healthy. Let's say sixty-five. Like anyone else in Ireland.'

'Seven years then.'

'And in my case with no time off for good behaviour.'

'Is that supposed to be a joke?' he asked, glaring at me, and I looked away. There was no point pushing my luck.

'I was good at my job in that school,' I told him, trying to sound conciliatory now. 'I was happy there. And I was told that I could go back. I *want* to go back. Will you just let me go back, please? Would it really matter that much to you?'

He sighed, defeated, and threw his hands in the air. I thought of Henry II wishing that someone would rid him of this turbulent priest and thanked God that there wasn't an axe man waiting for me on the blocks. 'Whatever,' he said. 'You can go back for the new term in September if you're that insistent.'

Whatever? Did this man spend all his evenings watching American television shows or what? He was a middle-aged man speaking like a spoiled child.

But the long and the short of it was that I got to go home. To my old room, my old colleagues, my old library. The books were all over the place, of course. The categories completely confused. With the help of a couple of lads from the fourth year we got it whipped back into shape over the course of a few weeks, and I gave two younger lads who were whizz-kids on the computer the task of setting up a catalogue of everything that we had on the shelves. They were delighted with themselves and told me about Excel spreadsheets and databases and all sorts of things until I said, 'Lads, I don't have the slightest interest in anything you're telling me; just get it done and thanks very much.'

All my old students were long gone, of course. The boys who had been in the first year when I left were in Trinity now, or UCD, or further afield, fighting with the Taliban. There were new boys and they were surprised by an old man like me appearing among them, even if the rumour did go round that I'd spent twenty years here before taking a leave of absence. They didn't know that I was only across on the other side of the Liffey. I heard one lad saying that I'd been living with a woman in Glasthule and the relationship had fallen apart. Another lad said no, that I'd been a TD for the Green Party and had lost my seat at the election. A third said that I used to be married to Twink and a fourth that I hadn't been here as a priest at all, that I'd been a nun, and had undergone gender-reassignment surgery in the intervening years. They had a high opinion of me, I thought. I'd never done anything as exciting as that in my life. More's the pity.

When Hannah died just after Christmas, I stood at the altar of the Good Shepherd church while Jonas and Aidan, Marthe, Morten and Astrid sat in the front pew and I told stories about my sister and the life we'd shared together.

I told them how she had written to Robert Redford every week from the end of 1973, when she watched him kissing Barbra Streisand outside the Plaza Hotel in New York City at the end of *The Way We Were*, until late in 1974 when she decided that she wasn't going to waste her time on him any more. It had cost her a fortune in international stamps, I said, and where she got the money from I did not know, but not once did Robert Redford reply and wasn't that a great shame all the same? A little post-card would have made her day.

I told them how when we were children we had spent a week at Curracloe beach, our whole family together, and I, with the help of our younger brother Cathal, had buried her in the sand up to her armpits and she'd screamed and begged to be set free and Mam had clattered me across the back of my legs for my trouble and said that was how accidents happened.

I told them how when I was in Rome she would send me the occasional care package from Dublin, filled with things that I missed but couldn't get in Italy – Tayto crisps, Lucozade, Barry's

Tea, Curly Wurlies – and how much those packages meant to me, even though they must surely have cost even more than all the letters to Robert Redford.

I told them how she had brought two fine boys into the world and reared them well. There's one of them now, I said, pointing towards the front pew, running his own business in Norway, a loving husband and father. And there's the other one, I said, writing all those books and making a name for himself and sure didn't everyone love his novels, especially the young people, even if they were filled with effing and blinding and all sorts of mad sex, and the congregation roared with laughter as Jonas put his head in his hands, as embarrassed as a teenager again, the poor lad.

I told them how she had met her husband, Kristian, when he came into the Bank of Ireland on College Green every afternoon to exchange Norwegian kroner into Irish punts, and how one day he hadn't phoned her when he said he would and so she'd taken the bit between her teeth and phoned him herself, and didn't our mother unplug the socket from the wall after that for she said that no decent girl would call a boy on the telephone of her own volition. And how they'd married young and lost each other young and that was a tragedy but they were reunited now, at least I believed that they were, and they could spend eternity together, for no two people I had ever known had loved each other more.

And I told them about her struggle with her mind over the last ten years of her life and how unfair it had been and how at times like that they might have expected a man like me, with the beliefs I held, to say that it was all part of God's plan, but that I couldn't say that to them because I wasn't sure if it was true, and if it was then I didn't understand any of it, for she had fallen ill when she was still a young woman and the disease had taken her and there seemed to be no justice in any of that.

And later, when we were all gathered together in her house, it felt strange to me to be the last surviving member of my family – Dad was long gone, little Cathal had been taken for no good reason whatsoever, Mam had collapsed in the church and now Hannah was lost to me too – but I realized that I was not one, I was part of six, and I would have to work at maintaining that. And when I asked Aidan could I take Morten and Astrid to the pictures the next day he said I could and that if I didn't mind giving them their tea too that would be a great help as there was a lot of work to be done clearing out his mother's home. I resolved on the spot that I would make sure that I was a part of their lives from now on. Sure the flights back and forth to Norway weren't that expensive anyway and the train journey north offered beautiful scenery.

Before parting that night, Jonas said that we should have lunch together when he got back from his trip to America and I said that was fine. He pulled out his phone and I pulled out mine – I did indeed – and he said how's the twenty-sixth of next month, that'll give me time to recover from the jetlag, and I shook my head and said no, the twenty-sixth was no good for me, could we make it another day for I had an appointment in my diary for the twenty-sixth, and he said that was grand and we chose a different date and I knew that I would look forward to it enormously.

The morning of the twenty-sixth came and I wrestled with my conscience about what I was going to do. I could leave well alone and get on with my day; stay in the school and immerse myself in my work. Jonas's publisher had sent me two boxes of books for the library and they needed sorting and cataloguing. Why would I go through with this plan, after all? I could tell no one afterwards, of course, least of all my nephews, who would see it as a betrayal, but it was not as if I would ever want to talk about it. But my mind was made up and so off I went.

It felt as if the world and its mother had been gathered at the Four Courts five years before when Tom Cardle had been bundled into a police van and taken off to Mountjoy prison, but the media showed no sign of interest in his release. A new set of national obsessions – the recession, the bankers, the death of a woman for no good reason in a hospital that was supposed to take care of her – had taken over, and for the most part criminal cases involving priests were receiving less attention. It was just more of the same, that's what people thought; how could it be news any more?

I sat in my car, looking at that forbidding building across the road and imagining the horrors that went on behind its stone walls, and when the doors opened, a young man emerged, a rough-looking type in a bright white tracksuit, and a girl jumped out from behind a tree, leaped into his arms and the pair of them started to practically procreate in the middle of the street. I looked away and was glad of it when they hailed a taxi and drove off.

A few minutes later, the doors opened again and there he was. Had he passed me on the street, I'm not sure I would have recognized him. He was five years older than the last time I'd seen him – I had never once visited him in prison – but looked two or three times that amount. He'd grown terribly thin and his eyes were sunk into the back of his head. His hair, which had always been thick and black, was almost completely white. He walked with a limp, aided by a cane; I had heard on the grapevine that he had been badly assaulted one day in the prison yard and the legs kicked from under him and there was talk at one point that he might not walk again, but here he was now, hobbling across the road, looking left and right for traffic as I sat motionless, not raising my hand in greeting as I watched him.

He was an old man. A convicted paedophile. A sex offender.

The diocese had arranged a flat for him, an awful place off Gardiner Street, four floors up and with an elevator that had a permanent *out-of-order* sign attached to it, and I wondered how he'd manage to get up and down with the bad leg. He was to collect a pension and live quietly. He was to give no interviews. He was to keep up with the court's order in terms of making sure the Gardaí knew where he was at all times. He was to see his probation officer weekly. He was not to make contact with anyone in the hierarchy, but he could attend any church that he wanted and confession, of course, was a sacrament open to everyone should he choose to avail himself of it.

'Odran,' he said, opening the passenger door. 'You came for me.'

'I said I would.'

I had written to him a month earlier, when his release date was set, and said that I would be outside to drive him wherever he needed to go. I kept my note short and on point, as they say, and made no reference to the letters that he'd occasionally sent me during his incarceration, nor to the fact that I had ignored every single one of them. Not knowing how many people might be waiting outside the jail, I told him the make and model of my car and said I'd stay inside, keep the engine turned over, and he should look out for me. I felt like a bank robber, a criminal ready to flee the scene of the crime.

'It was good of you,' he said, sitting in the passenger seat and closing the door. He sighed and shut his eyes for a moment. He was free at last; I suppose he was taking that idea in. 'How are you keeping anyway?'

He turned to smile at me as if I had just arrived down to visit him after a long absence in one of his parishes. One of his many parishes.

'I'm grand,' I said. 'You?'

'Never better. Never better.' He hesitated for a moment. 'Glad to be back in the real world.'

'We'll go so.'

We drove along in silence, me wondering whether I should have left him to find his own way there and him thinking who knew what thoughts. At least he had the decency to stay quiet and not pretend that things were normal between us.

I pulled up outside his new flat and we made our way up the stairs, letting ourselves in with the key that had been given to me by the archdiocese the day before. It was awful. Small and damp, wallpaper peeling off the walls, noise coming from the flat next to his, music roaring down from above. I think I'd have preferred to jump out of the window than to stay here, and he caught the expression of horror on my face.

'Don't be worrying,' he said. 'It's better than what I'm used to.'

There was that, I suppose.

'I wasn't worrying,' I told him. 'I'd only worry if it was me who had to live here. It'll do for you, I imagine.'

He nodded and sat down on one of the two armchairs. 'You're angry with me, Odran,' he said quietly.

'I should go.'

'Don't,' he said. 'We've only just got here. Stay a few minutes.'

'Only a few,' I said, sitting down. 'The traffic will build up.'

'You're angry with me,' he repeated after a lengthy pause. I almost laughed at the understatement.

'I don't understand you, Tom,' I replied. 'That's the truth of it.'

'Sure I don't understand myself. I've spent the last five years trying to.'

'And did you come to any conclusions?'

He shrugged. 'My father had a lot to do with it.'

'Your father?' I said, a quick, bitter laugh escaping my lips. 'Your old dad and his tractor?'

'Don't judge me too quickly,' he said. 'You don't know what he was like.'

'It had nothing to do with him. It was all you.'

He nodded and looked out of the window for a moment; it was a rotten sight, but at least it was a view. He had had none for years.

'Have it your way,' he said.

'Well sure you had it your way long enough. I suppose it's someone else's turn now.'

He turned to look at me, fixing me with a stare, and I saw there was little fear in his eyes, just exhaustion. I had no idea what he had gone through in jail and I didn't want to know, but I suspected that there were times when he had been forced to defend himself physically, times when he would have had the upper hand, more times when he wouldn't.

'Is there something you want to say to me, Odran?' he asked. 'Because I appreciate the lift over here, but if you only want to have a go at me—'

'Did you never think it was wrong?' I asked. 'The things that you were doing?'

He considered this, but shook his head. 'I don't think I ever thought about it in that way,' he said. 'Concepts of right and wrong, they didn't come into it much.'

'And the children, you never thought of how much you were hurting them?'

'Sure wasn't I little more than a child myself?' he asked.

'At the start, maybe. By the end, not at all.'

'But once I'd started, you see, there was no getting away from it. I should never have been a priest, that's the truth of it. Christ almighty, I don't even believe in God. I don't think I ever did.'

'No one forced you to be a priest.'

'That's not true,' he snapped. 'I was absolutely forced into it. I lived in fear of my father, who insisted that this was the life for me. You were forced into it yourself. Don't pretend that you weren't.'

'You could have left.'

'I couldn't.'

'You ran off once.'

'And he brought me back on the tractor, remember?'

'You could have refused.'

'I couldn't. You didn't see what happened on the days in between.'

'You were seventeen,' I insisted. 'You could have taken the ferry to England. Started a new life.'

'Odran, you may never believe anything that I tell you again, but believe this: you have no idea what you're talking about. None. You don't have the first concept of what my childhood was like. Of all the things that happened to me in the years before I arrived at Clonliffe. None.'

'And I don't want to know,' I told him. 'Nothing that happened to you back then makes anything that you did acceptable. It doesn't justify anything. Can't you see that?'

He sighed and looked away, staring out towards the city-centre apartment buildings and office blocks. What was going on inside that confused head of his? I had no idea.

'Not to mention what you've done to the rest of us,' I said quietly. 'You and all the men like you. Did you never think what it would mean to those of us who tried our best? Those of us who had a calling?'

He laughed at me. 'You think you had a calling, Odran?'

'Yes, I do.'

'You only think that because your mammy told you that you did.'

'You're wrong,' I said. 'She may have put the idea there, but the fact is, she was right. I did have a calling. This is what I was meant to do.'

He shook his head, saying nothing as if he was listening to the rantings of an imbecile.

'I should have reported you long ago,' I said.

'You should have what?'

'Back in Clonliffe,' I replied, all self-righteous now. 'I saw you. When you took your shirt off. The big bruises on your shoulder.'

He frowned, as if he had no idea what I was talking about. 'You've lost me, Odran,' he said.

'Daniel Londigran,' I said. 'The night O'Hagan was sent off to see his dying mother. It was you that leaped on him. He tried to fight you off. He was expelled on account of it.'

He stared at me for a moment, the wheels turning, before letting his mouth fall open in surprise and allowing a laugh to escape his mouth. 'Danny Londigran?' he said. 'Are you joking me?'

'I am not.'

'You haven't a clue, Odran. Do you realize that? You haven't a fucking clue.'

'I know that you tried to assault him and he got the better of you. He gave you a dig and you ran away in fright.'

He laughed again and shook his head. 'Danny Londigran,' he said calmly, 'was no more suited to be a priest than I was. He had a regular supply of pornographic magazines slipped into him by a cousin of his that the pair of us used to look at together and eventually it went further. It was women we were looking at, Odran, you realize that, don't you? But we used to touch each other in our frustration. One night, when his cell-mate was away, Father Livane came in when we were talking and trying everything we could to console each other for the dilemma we'd found ourselves in. Sure, Danny didn't want to be there any more than I did. Father Livane comes in, the lights are off, Danny in his fright gives me an almighty puck and off I charge. And of course he had to turn in a story to explain it all. You think

I attacked him?' He laughed bitterly. 'Are you joking? I did nothing to him that he wasn't doing to me.'

I looked away; I was uncertain of my response. 'And I'm to believe that, am I?' I asked eventually.

'You can believe anything you like for all the difference it makes to me. Do you think it matters now?'

'You've ruined it, can't you see that?' I said, raising my voice in frustration. 'There's none of us will ever be trusted again.'

'Maybe that's for the best,' said Tom. 'Don't you think this country would be better off if the Catholic Church just got the hell out of it?'

'No,' I said. 'No, I don't. And how can you say that, after everything—'

'Those people ruined my life,' he said, his voice deep and angry. 'They ruined it, Odran, can't you understand that? They took a poor, innocent seventeen-year-old boy who knew nothing of the world and locked him away in a prison for seven years. They told me that everything that made me human was shameful and dirty. They taught me to hate my body and to feel that I was a sinner if I looked at a woman's legs while she walked along the road in front of me. They threatened to expel me from Clonliffe if I so much as talked to a girl when we were out at UCD and my father threatened to kill me if they ever did. And don't think he wouldn't have, because I'm telling you now, he would have come into my room on my first night home and put a pitchfork through my head if I'd said that the priests wouldn't have me back. They twisted me and distorted me, they made sure that I had no release for any of the natural desires that a human being has, and then they didn't give a damn if I didn't know how to live a decent life.'

'They did nothing to you that they didn't do to me,' I said, leaning forward angrily. 'Nothing that they didn't do to hundreds of other boys. And we didn't end up doing what you did. Is it such a terrible thing to be a good priest, Tom? Would that not have been enough for you? It was for me.'

He laughed and shook his head. 'A good priest?' he asked. 'Is that what you think you are? But sure Odran, you're hardly a priest at all.'

I stared at him, baffled.

'Odran,' he continued, his voice calm now, as if he was explaining a complex idea to a child, 'you were ordained more than thirty years ago and you never spent a single day in a parish until Jim Cordington put you in my place after I had to leave.'

'That's not true.'

'It is true. Of course it's true. You locked yourself away in that school of yours for twenty-five years, teaching English and shelving your library books, and never did a single thing that a good priest, as you put it, is supposed to do. You hid away from the world. You're still hiding away from it. If you'd wanted to be a teacher, why didn't you just go out and get your H.Dip and *be* a teacher? If you'd wanted to be a librarian, why didn't you go and get a degree in Library Sciences and work out there on Kildare Street? You call yourself a priest, do you? You're not a priest. You never were.'

I stared down at the floor. 'I've taken care of thousands of boys in that school,' I said quietly. 'I've been a good friend to them. A good chaplain.'

'Really?' he laughed. 'Tell me this then. Over the course of an average year, how many teenage boys have come to you with some emotional problem that they thought you could help them with? Five? Three? One? None? I'd say it was none, was it? And if they did, I'd say you'd be running off down the corridor to make sure the Brontë sisters were still being kept together.'

I stood up, walked over to the window and stared out across Dublin. From where I was standing, it was a filthy city. The Liffey ran black, the streets were a shambles, the buildings were falling down. Roadworks were everywhere and the cars were beeping and honking at each other as they tried to make their way along. Somewhere down there, young men were passing money to each other and going back to bedsits to tie tubes around their arms and fill their veins with the only thing that could give them some release from the misery of the place. Old women were turning down their gas heaters, for they couldn't afford to keep warm and pay the property tax and at least if they froze to death then they wouldn't be sent to prison for non-payment. Teenage boys were standing on the quays late at night, looking out for some lost soul who might throw them twenty euros to kneel down before them with their pants around their ankles. The pubs were full of young men and women, graduating from universities, filled with fear as to what in God's name they would do with their lives now that there wasn't a job to be found in the country; where were they to go? Canada? Australia? England? The famine ships were being brought back and they knew they had to board them and leave their families behind. Men were retiring from their jobs after forty years and having to scrimp and save because their pension funds had been wiped out by a bunch of Fianna Fáil crooks who everyone would vote for again in a couple of years' time anyway. And over there, at the airport, a group of men from Europe were flying in to tell us that we hadn't the sense to govern ourselves any more and so they were going to do it for us. And for all of us, for all of these people, this was what Ireland had become: a country of drug addicts, losers, criminals, paedophiles and incompetents. What was it Aidan had said to me that night in the Oslo bar? *I would never live in that country again. Ireland is rotten. Rotten to the core.*

Aidan.

I turned around and looked at Tom, who, having defined my life for me, seemed pleased to have gained the upper hand.

'But Aidan,' I said, feeling the tears spring up behind my eyes again, for I would never be able to forgive myself, let alone him, for what had happened there. 'Why Aidan? Why my nephew, Tom? We were friends, you and I. How could you have done it?'

He had the good grace to turn away then, unable to look at me.

'Answer me,' I insisted. 'I have a right to know. I don't understand how you could have—'

'Sure you're as much to blame there as I am,' he said.

'I am? How?'

'I told you that I was happy to go back to the school with you that night. You should have insisted.'

'I wasn't to know that you were going to go into his room when he was asleep, was I? I wasn't to know what you were going to do to him.'

He cocked his head a little to the side and offered me something approaching a smile. 'Weren't you, Odran?' he asked quietly. 'Are you telling me that you never suspected?'

'Of course I didn't,' I shouted. 'If I'd have known then I never would have—'

'You know it's just the two of us here,' he said. 'You can lie to yourself if you like, but there's not much to be gained from it. Trust me, that's a lesson that I've learned well over these last few years.'

I stared at him. 'Tom,' I said, my face growing red with anger, 'you can't imagine that I knew anything about this. About what you were like. About—'

'You were down there that week in Wexford,' he told me. 'When the Kilduff boy vandalized my car. Sure you were the one who turned him in to the Gardaí.'

'I thought he was just acting up, like kids do,' I said. 'I didn't know where his anger came from.'

He raised an eyebrow. 'Really, Odran?'

'Yes, really!'

'And all those times that I was being moved from parish to parish, you never wondered even for a moment why that might be?'

'Look, there were rumours that priests who were being moved regularly were up to all sorts, I knew that much, but I never thought that you—'

'You see, I think you knew everything, Odran,' he said quietly. 'And I think you never wanted to confront me about it because that was a conversation that was beyond your abilities to have. I think you were complicit in the whole thing. Sure all you're good for is putting the Dickens books before the Hemingway books and keeping the Virginia Woolfs for the end. I think you knew it all.'

'I didn't,' I said and I could hear how half-hearted the words sounded even to my ears.

'And I think that on the night of your mother's funeral you knew well that it wasn't sensible to leave me there with your nephew, but you did it anyway. Because it was easier to do that than to cause a scene.'

'That's not true,' I whispered.

'I think you're just like everyone else, even though you've played the holier-than-thou your whole life. You knew it, you kept it secret and this whole conspiracy that everyone talks about, the one that goes to the top of the Church, well it goes to the bottom of it too, to the nobodies like you, to the fella that never even had a parish of his own and hides away from the world, afraid to be spotted. You can blame me all you like, Odran, and you'd be right to, because I've done some terrible things in my life. But do you ever think of taking a look at yourself? At your own actions? At the Grand Silence that you've maintained from the very first day?' He shook his head and stood up, reached for his cane and turned his back on me as he went towards the cavity in the wall that led to the tiny kitchen.

'Go on, Odran,' he said. 'Go on out of here now and leave me to unpack. There's nothing left for us to say to each other.'

I remained where I was for a few moments, unable to move, but then focused my eyes on the door and walked towards it. I could feel my collar tightening against my throat and felt an urge to rip it off and throw it away.

'We won't be seeing each other again, I imagine?' he asked, turning back to look at me as I opened the door to the outside world, and I shook my head.

'No,' I said. 'I won't be back.'

'Right so,' he replied, turning away as if we did not have forty years of history between us. 'I'll wish you well so.'

'I'll pray for you, Tom. Despite it all.'

He laughed and turned away from me. 'Pray for yourself,' he said. 'You need it more than I do.'

I looked around the flat one last time. 'This is an awful place,' I said, unable to comprehend what could have led the boy that he once was to somewhere like this. He would stay here, I imagined, for the rest of his life. He would be found here, some day, dead.

'It is,' he agreed. 'But I'll survive.'

'Will you be lonely?'

'I will, of course,' he said, smiling at me. 'But then I have a history of loneliness, Odran. Don't you?'

There are no boarders in my school; did I say that before? Years ago, there were. Up until the early 1980s, I think. They closed down that part of the building a year or two before I arrived, when parents fell out of the habit of sending their boys away for the week and everyone had a car anyway.

Because of that, and because of the size of the building, it can be a fierce lonely place at night. Every sound echoes through the corridors, every breeze rattles a doorframe or shakes a window.

If you had a mind that turned towards ghost stories, then this would be a place to unsettle you.

Anxious in my thoughts, I took a notion to take a late-night drive over to the grotto in Inchicore, the same grotto that I had been visiting for so many years and where I had once seen a priest and his mother crying together in pain at the realization of what he had done and who he had hurt and how he would one day have to pay for his crimes.

It was dark when I arrived, as dark as it had been that night, but deserted, a half-moon offering enough brightness for me to find my way towards the statues.

At first, I kneeled and tried to pray, but I could find no prayers. And then, without intending to, I found myself lying on the ground, face down, the cold of the earth against my cheek, just like that man who was tortured by his own actions. I closed my eyes and realized that I could stay at my school no longer. Despite how long I had wanted to return, it was time to move on, to find another life, either inside or outside the Church. I could hide behind those school walls no longer.

I thought of that moment almost forty years ago, in Wexford, when I had desperately wanted to operate the barriers at the railway crossing. *In my job, you have to think of all the people who trust you,* the railway keeper had said to me. *Just imagine if any of them got hurt on account of your negligence. Or mine. Would you want that on your conscience? Knowing you were responsible for so much pain?*

But once, in his anger, Aidan had asked me whether I thought I had wasted my life and I had told him no. No, I had not. But I had been wrong. And Tom Cardle had been right. For I had known everything, right from the start, and never acted on any of it. I had blocked it from my mind, time and again, refused to recognize what was staring me in the face. I had said nothing when I should have spoken out, convincing myself that I was a man of higher character. I had been complicit in all their crimes and people had suffered because of me. I had wasted my life. I had wasted every moment of my life. And the final irony was that it had taken a convicted paedophile to show me that in my silence, I was just as guilty as the rest of them.

Acknowledgements

Early readers of the manuscript offered valuable advice. For that, many thanks to Con Connolly, Claire Kilroy and Thomas Morris.

I'm indebted for their constant support and encouragement to my agents, Simon Trewin, Eric Simonoff and all at William Morris Endeavor, as well as my editor Bill Scott-Kerr, whose skills and insight helped the book immeasurably. Thanks also to Larry Finlay, Patsy Irwin and all at Transworld.

In my research, I gained a valuable insight into the life of a priest from several members of the clergy in Dublin who wish to remain anonymous, but I'm grateful for their openness and their willingness to discuss frankly the cover-up of child sexual abuse in Ireland over the years. Thanks, too, to those in Rome, Oslo and Lillehammer who provided assistance during my research trips there.

And above all, much love to the most important people in my life: my parents, Seán and Helen Boyne, my sisters, Carol and Sinéad, Rory, Jamie and Katie, and my husband Con.

It's impossible to estimate the number of children who suffered in Ireland at the hands of the Catholic Church, nor is it easy to guess the number of dedicated and honest priests who have seen their lives and vocations tarnished by the actions of their colleagues.

This novel is dedicated to all these victims; may they have happier times ahead.

John Boyne was born in Ireland in 1971. He is the author of nine novels for adults and four for younger readers, including the international bestsellers *The Boy in the Striped Pajamas*, which has sold more than six million copies worldwide, *The Absolutist* and, most recently, *Stay Where You Are and Then Leave*. His novels are published in over forty-five languages. He is married and lives in Dublin.

www.johnboyne.com
@john_boyne